I0758471

The KNOTTY GIRLS Club

The KNOTTY GIRLS Club

SAINT VISTA PACK REGIMES, BOOK ONE

by

GINNA MORAN

SUNNY PALMS PRESS

Copyright © 2022 by Ginna Moran

All Rights Reserved.

All rights reserved under International and Pan-American Copyright Conventions, including the right of reproduction in whole or in part in any form or by any electronic or mechanical means including information storage and retrieval systems, without written permission, except in the case of brief quotations embodied in critical articles and reviews.

ISBN 978-1-951314-72-9 (soft cover)
ISBN 978-1-951314-73-6 (hardcover)

This is a work of fiction. All of the characters, organizations, and events portrayed in this novel are either products of the author's imagination or are used fictitiously.

Cover design by Silver Starlight Designs
Cover images copyright Depositphotos

For Inquiries Contact:

Sunny Palms Press
9663 Santa Monica Blvd Suite 1158
Beverly Hills, CA 90210, USA
www.sunnypalmspress.com
www.GinnaMoran.com

To Ashley,

Thank you for cheering me on. You're the best!

Chapter 1

Kinsey

Vixen Lounge

The neon sign of the Vixen Lounge buzzes as it flickers on and off outside of the dimly lit, smoky club I've spent every night at for the last two years. I can smell the scents of sex and desire permeating the air as a couple strolls the block.

The man hugs an arm around his girlfriend, touching every surface they pass on purpose. The power move by the betas, leaving their scent trail behind, will fuck with the rich assholes frequenting the Vixen Lounge, looking for a drink, a good time, and if they're lucky, a nice piece of ass.

But not mine. I'm not on the menu. Tonight, I'm only a server and considered both undesirable and unworthy.

I wouldn't have it any other way, though. Alphas who come around here like the benefits of claiming an omega without actually caring for them. They are the elite and wealthiest of Saint Vista, Calico Proper, Mountain View, and Pacific Crest, the territories that make up the southern region of California. Self-proclaimed royalty, authoritative heads, and politicians—the men and women in power who have established the rules for generations. Omegas must have a pack if we want anything from life. Without an alpha, we have no rights.

It's why I'm here, far from where I grew up, and why I pop suppressant pills daily. My life depends on it. It's how I pass as a beta. I'll never have power, but at least I'll never be without anything either.

A car horn blares, startling me from my thoughts. I slip my hand into my pocket and shake my pill bottle, listening to the single blue capsule rattle. Fuck. I swear Gillian better show up like she promised. She's already skipped out on me twice this week, even knowing that my world depends on these fucking pills. I'm not a drug addict, but without the suppressants, my hormones will go out of whack, and alphas will be able to scent that I'm impersonating a beta. My anxiety stems from the thought of losing everything. Of course, I'm not even sure I'd know if I were one. The only addict I can reference is Madame Tamsin, who eats a collection of rainbow pills as if they are candy. I've seen her in withdrawal, and fuck, I'd think I'd know if I was. She's better chasing her fix. I prefer her that way. She's far nicer when she's flying on a high than when she is dead sober. I can't exactly blame her, considering this is her life as an alpha. Her power only comes from training omegas to entertain those who are truly in power. She is the owner of the Vixen Lounge and in charge of her Gorgeous Girls, as she calls them—the ones she knows will get her somewhere other than this shithole of a city. Because that's what everyone really wants. To escape the Gutter District, where the lowest of the low reside, while those of wealth and power stroll in and out, treating us as toys and possessions, laughing as we beg for just another dollar, another dime, and sometimes, just a little bit of attention.

Not me, though. The last thing I want is attention. I would prefer to stay under the radar and continue serving those and being unnoticed. Bland and plain, undesired. A packless beta who is so average that I deserve nothing more than what I work to earn.

That is if Gillian would hurry up. She's already fifteen minutes late, and my shift is about to start. If that happens, I won't be able to step out for another eight hours. You don't need breaks when you work for Madame Tamsin. With breaks, comes less pay. If I made any less than I do, I couldn't even afford to live in the damn closet apartment I already struggle to maintain.

A small whistle cuts through the air, and I twist on my heels and spot Gillian peeking from around the corner of the old black-painted brick building. Why doesn't she come to the front? She most likely owes someone money. That's probably why she's been avoiding me up until now.

I peek at the entrance to the club, catching sight of Madame Tamsin collecting dirty money from a fat man in a suit. I can smell his body odor from here, and it repulses me more than anyone else in the club. That's what the pills help with. They suppress my very nature, keeping my head clear and my body fragrance bland and uninteresting, so I can continue life as one who awakened into a beta upon my maturity.

I don't like to think about the day my true nature manifested, marking me as an omega and one responsible for bowing down to those who rule and those who decide who is worthy and who is not. From the moment the small heart-shaped birthmark appeared on my right hip, and my eyes turned more vibrant green in color, I knew that I would be forced to follow in my mother's path. If only she were there to see things through as my father and pack leader had intended. If only I wasn't left in my uncle's care after she and my father died in a fire he caused during a gang war in the east side of Fall Harbor, the area north of Pacific Crest and out of the Southern Pack Regimes of California. My uncle did the worst thing imaginable, not turning me into the system and instead doing what many other alphas do by holding tight to the omegas born to the family to use later as leverage.

In the territory of Fall Harbor, many don't manifest into omegas, the perfect vessel for breeding and helping certain Pack Regimes keep their power and purity. Because omegas are the only ones who can procreate with alphas and handle their knots, being marked and claimed in a way that ensures they are theirs forever.

"Sorry, I'm late, Kinsey. I had a late dinner with Mr. Donahue. You know how that goes. He refuses to give me what I want at a discount unless I suck his cock, and he took fucking forever to blow his load." Gillian crinkles her nose and laughs, her soft voice trickling through the air. "Do you have the cash? It's going to be two-fifty."

Ice trickles down my back. Did she say what I think she did? The last time I paid, it was only one-fifty. She's just added on an extra hundred, and that's two weeks of groceries for me. It also could be the electricity and water. Fuck.

"An extra hundred? You know I can't afford that shit." I shake my pill bottle, trying my best not to panic. Maybe it was a mistake. Maybe she doesn't really mean two hundred and fifty dollars.

Gillian tightens her jaw and gives me a once-over, her lighthearted smile vanishing. It's in this moment that I know she didn't say it as a mistake. She really is trying to get another hundred dollars out of me. She knows I'm desperate. It's either suck it up and go without to get these hormone suppressants or risk having someone find out that I'm not who I portray myself to be. I'll lose my job. My apartment. If I don't have these damn pills, I might as well just walk to the corner of Sixth and D Street, waiting for some asshole from the local Pack Regime to pick me up to make a couple extra bucks at auction to someone like Madame Tamsin.

"If you can't give me the entire amount, I can give you half a bottle for one-fifty." Gillian shifts on her feet, clicking her heels on the sidewalk. "You have five seconds before I leave. I can't be seen here. Madame Tamsin is accusing me of selling her shit narcs. She's out for my fucking tits right now."

I knew something was wrong when she was late and when she avoided me. And now this? What am I going to do? I have to have these pills. Gillian is the only one who can get them for me.

My eyes water and I blink, pushing away the sudden desperation trying to steal my senses. I wonder if I could take Gillian in a fight. I know how to throw a punch, but she looks twice as strong as I do, her muscles rippling with her movements, showing off the fact that she's here out of pity because she doesn't have to help omegas. She just likes the extra cash and working for Mr. Donahue, who treats her like his alpha for shits and giggles, his kink acting as one of the unworthy who suddenly finds someone to save him. If only I could be Gillian. She was one of the few lucky females that manifested as an alpha in a strong pack alongside some of the best alphas of the Pack Regimes.

And she uses it to her advantage. Can I blame her? Fuck no. I'd probably do the same bullshit if our positions were switched, but I wouldn't just throw it on someone like this. I would warn them so they could be prepared for next time. I could've done something extra for Madame Tamsin. Occasionally, there is some horny fucker who wants a beta like everyone believes me to be. I would suck it up if I had to, as long as it meant that I got what I needed.

"Kinsey? Take it or leave it. I can't wait for you to decide." Gillian bounces on her feet, clicking her heels again anxiously, stealing glances at the corner of the building as if she expects Madame Tamsin to come charging out.

It wouldn't be the first time. She is especially territorial with who loiters outside of the Vixen Lounge because she's afraid that one of the gangs or some asshole will scoop up one of her poor, defenseless Gorgeous Girls. She can smell another alpha from a mile away, and I'm pretty sure that Gillian took one of the suppressant pills just to get here unnoticed.

Because I can barely smell her. Not like I could smell the couple that passed by and the greasy, bulbous, bulging belly man who was waving hundreds the second he entered the club.

I dig into my other pocket and pull out the wad of crinkled bills and hold it out to her. She counts it, knowing that I'm short, and she pops the cap of the bottle she clutches and dumps them without waiting for me to get my own bottle ready. The blue pills scatter across the sidewalk, and she turns on her heels and rushes away, running as if she's about to be chased by Madame Tamsin.

Fear tightens my chest, and I groan and fall to my knees, scooping up the blue pills as quickly as I can. The fucking bitch. I need to figure out something else with another dealer and fast. I've heard rumors whispered among some of the other servers about one of the gangs having an injection available to take over the pills, but it is twice as much. I just...

A tear trickles onto my cheek, and I pluck the remaining pills from the sidewalk, trying not to cry. I spot a handful dissolving in the gross water streaming down the gutter, washing into a grate at the corner.

Fuck. My. Life.

I don't even have half a month now. I have ten days, and I don't get paid for twelve more. So that leaves me one day without. Maybe I can call in sick. Maybe I can—

"Kinsey, what are you doing? You're late." Madame Tamsin's voice shocks me in the heart, and I nearly drop the pill bottle.

I whip my attention to the Vixen Lounge's owner and quickly get to my feet and tuck my pills into my apron. I say a silent prayer to the universe that she didn't see anything. If she did, she doesn't call me out on it. It's the only thing that gets me to stride forward and dust my hands on my jacket.

"I'm so sorry, Madame. The strap on my heel came undone without me knowing, and I fell." My voice shakes with the words, and I keep my gaze trained on the ground, knowing better than to meet her eyes. No one can look at Madame Tamsin without permission, and I would never risk it.

"I'm going to have to deduct an hour's worth of pay for this. We have visitors who are waiting for you. You know how Mr. Doyle doesn't like anyone else serving him." Madame Tamsin latches her fingers to my elbow, rubbing her thumb over my sleeve, purposefully leaving her scent on me. She wants to ensure all her guests know that's all they are to her. Guests. She is the true alpha of the Vixen Lounge, and even though I'm not one of her Gorgeous Girls, I'm still hers.

I should feel bad about it. I should hate it, and maybe a part of me does, but this is life for me. One day at a time. One pill. And hopefully, one day, I can just escape.

Who am I kidding? No one leaves the Gutter District unless they are either bought, kidnapped, or killed. I'm stuck here, relying on the generosity of others because I can't even rely on myself. Without a pack, I'm just another nameless, powerless person. At least I have my freedom. No one cares about a beta—we're the ones who just fill space, bringing only workers and servers to the Pack Regimes. With the suppressant pills, I leave no desirable scent, can skip any chance of going into heat and dying to breed, and my only purpose is to serve the community. I wouldn't have it any other way.

"Good evening, Ms. Kinsey. It's a full house tonight. Watch yourself. They smell a bit rowdy." Mr. Holt offers me a waning smile, his eyes not lighting up. He's in the same position as I am, except he was born a true beta. He's asked me out a couple times, but I learned early on that I have to keep my distance from everyone. The pills can only do so much, and if I get too worked up, someone might notice. If that happens, it's over. I'm a lawbreaker, after all. The crime of pretending to be a beta will end with me behind bars or worse. The Pack Regime doesn't take kindly to omegas trying to be anything more than what they deserve. An unbonded omega serves no purpose to society. We are only as good as our pack and what we can offer—children, families, and pleasure. The leaders love and hate us. They control us when no one else does.

I push my thoughts away. If I continue to dwell on my circumstances, I'll think about the trauma that led me to the Vixen Lounge. It'll ruin my entire night, and I have enough stress to battle.

"Mr. Doyle is waiting in section three," he adds, holding out his hand. "Hurry up and serve him, so Anita can take him in back."

"That bad?" I don't have to ask specifically, because I can smell Mr. Doyle's scent from here, and it leaves me on edge.

"Worse." Mr. Holt tightens his jaw and wiggles his fingers, waiting for me to hand him my belongings.

I shrug out of my jacket and hand it to Mr. Holt. I force my mouth to smile as music fills the air. The collection of scents assaults me in a hot wave of lust, annoyance, and something I can't decipher. I glance around, trying to avoid eye contact with a couple of alphas and their beta packmates, those whose packs take care of them and give them a purpose. I can't stop the jealousy coursing through me. If I don't get myself in control, I'll need to douse myself in perfume to be safe.

"Kinsey, sweetheart. You're late. Where have you been?" Mr. Doyle doesn't even let me get to the bar before he sets his sight on me. The husky man rubs his hands together and smacks his lips. "I need my usual and make it double. Madame Tamsin is letting me have a moment of Anita's time, and you know how much that darling loves what I have to offer." He strides toward me, flaring his nostrils. I'm glad Madame Tamsin touched me now. He bares his teeth, growling lowly under his breath. Her scent sets almost every man off in a bad way because they crave the power she has here. Swinging out his arm, he smacks my ass, making me jump. "Be quick. Time is money." His friendly demeanor vanishes, and I straighten my shoulders and ignore the looks of a couple other patrons watching our interaction. I can't let them get to me. They will fuck with me if I do, because I'm unwanted. They will never let me forget it.

"Sure thing, Mr. Doyle," I say, gritting my teeth. "Anything for a fucking bastard asshole." I regret my words immediately because the song changes, and I hear my voice echo through the air.

"What did you say, bitch?" he snaps, jerking out his arm to latch onto my shirt.

I freeze, my eyes widening. A shadow materializes at the edge of my vision, and my heart crashes in my chest. It's another alpha, and he smells like vetiver and wood, the fragrance of his dominance overwhelming me.

"Back off, Doyle. You don't fucking have power here." The smooth, throaty voice snatches my attention, and I meet the stunning blue eyes of a dark-haired man I've never seen in the Vixen Lounge. I don't recognize his scent either.

Mr. Doyle drags me closer. "Mind your business, Wilder."

Another figure towers behind Mr. Doyle, blocking him. I cower at the sight of another handsome alpha with sapphire blue eyes and hair so dark it could be black. His presence alone freezes my insides as if his existence can drain the drugs from my system, turning me into the powerless omega I truly am. His deep blue eyes lock onto mine, his features similar to his packmate's. His hair hangs on his forehead, and he cracks his neck, whipping it from his vision. I shift on my heels, my body begging me to run. To flee and get out of harm's way.

"Show some respect. It's Prince Wilder, asshole, and this is our business. The lady is trying to do her job, and you need to show her some respect," the blue-eyed, attractive alpha says, caging me between him and Mr. Doyle. His sharp jaw accents his high cheekbones and full lips, his handsome features drawing me in.

"Fuck off." Mr. Doyle swings his arm, punching the man over my shoulder.

I spin out from between them and yelp, catching my heel on the edge of the dance floor. I twist my ankle and lose my balance. The midnight-haired alpha lunges for Mr. Doyle, but he stumbles out of his reach and into my path. I can't avoid him, my voice cutting through the air as I scream. My terror gets the best of me, and my body slackens. Mr. Doyle snatches my apron, trying to use me as a shield, but it tears and breaks free, sending me sprawling on my ass.

I can't move fast enough as my pill bottle smacks against the wooden dance floor, and the blue suppressant pills scatter everywhere.

Oh fuck.

Oh shit.

I grab as many as I can and jump to my feet. Turning toward the kitchen, I spot a clear path and break into a sprint. I'll leave out the back. I have to. I was so concerned about not getting my pills and being caught by Madame Tamsin that I failed to take the one I needed to tonight. And now I know why Mr. Doyle and the new alphas grew aggressive and hostile. They sense me as an omega. They just don't know it yet.

If I don't leave now, someone will call the Pack Regime leader of the Gutter District. My life will be over.

A strong hand locks onto my hair and rips me off my feet. It's too late. I fucked up, and there's no hiding it now. "Kinsey, what is all of this?" Madame Tamsin's eyes flash with the colorful lights above the stage. Two security guards break up the fight behind her, escorting the unfamiliar alphas out while guiding Mr. Doyle toward the VIP lounge. "I don't understand."

I can't get my words to work. I can't find the will to fight against her as her dominance fucks with my head, her fragrance weakening my resistance.

I close my eyes and shut down, wishing that the world would just swallow me whole.

"Go to my office. Now. If you try to leave this club, you will regret it." Madame Tamsin shoves her hand into my back, pushing me. "You better hope Anita can settle Mr. Doyle down."

The potent scent of her anger wafts through the air, overpowering the collection of foul fragrances radiating from the males frequenting her club.

"I can explain," I say, finally managing to get my mouth to work. "Please, you—"

Madame Tamsin smacks me across the face, leaving my cheek stinging. Tears well in my eyes, and I recoil, shrinking down against her rage.

"Don't say another word and do as I say. Go to my office." She growls the words and points her finger, not even caring that everyone stares at us. "Now!"

I drop my gaze to the floor and do as she commands.

My life is truly over. I can't hide my true nature any longer, and without having any connections to a pack or any of the leaders in power, I'll be at Madame Tamsin's mercy.

But she doesn't have any.

She is absolutely merciless.

Chapter 2

Kinsey

Omega Order

I stare at the letter opener sparkling on Madame Tamsin's desk. The hilt glimmers with jewels, screaming of the luxury she craves to surround herself in. With the ornate hardware on her desk, elaborate light fixtures, plush rugs, and swanky artwork, I can easily forget the trash piling the streets outside. The Vixen Lounge truly captures the world Madame Tamsin desires to live in.

I glide my finger over the cool steel of the letter opener, imagining picking it up to use as a weapon. I know I couldn't outmatch Madame Tamsin in a fight, but using the small blade intended for paper would give me at least a couple of seconds to run. Where would I go? I have no idea. Anywhere has to be better than staying here and finding out what Madame Tamsin could possibly do to me.

"Kinsey!" Madame Tamsin startles me, standing in the doorway. The tight fabric of her dress accentuates her vivacious curves, the hourglass silhouette of her body undeniably attractive. "Get your filthy fingers off my belongings."

I knew better than to even consider fighting her. She could decide to take my hand for leaving even a molecule of my scent behind on her stuff. No one touches things that don't belong to them without permission. It doesn't only include her precious Gorgeous Girls that I can hear laughing from their dressing rooms. I train my eyes downward and fold my arms over my chest. Taking a step away, I back against the wall and slouch my shoulders, trying to make myself smaller. If I don't look like I'm a threat, Madame Tamsin will settle down. She always does. I know how to handle alphas, especially ones like her. Obedience keeps her calm. Loyalty ensures her nicety. If only one of these things could save me now. Unfortunately, keeping secrets and lying could ignite her hostility. And I've done both.

I consider dropping to my knees and begging her for mercy, but that would be taking things too far. I will not admit to doing something wrong. She will need more proof than the handful of blue pills. I won't give it to her willingly. She can accuse me and call the authorities, letting them deal with it. If she does so, it'll give me a moment to think. There are bars on the window to my right, but I can probably squeeze through the small one over the toilet in her office bathroom.

"I should call the Pack Regime of the Gutter District and turn you in. Those pills are against the law, and turning you in would guarantee a reward." Madame Tamsin strolls in and closes the door behind her. Her warm scent trickles toward me, her anger morphing into something different. It's not the tang of musk I smell on the men who frequent the club, but it does have a hint of desire. Just not for me. I know what her desire smells like, and it's bitter like coffee and just as dark.

This doesn't send my heart racing in the same way. Yeah, I am scared, but she gives me no reason to panic yet.

I lick my lips, trying to moisten my mouth, so my voice doesn't crack. "What do you want?" I could try to explain my situation to her, but it's obvious that she doesn't give a fuck. She sees an opportunity in me, and what she plans to do will determine what I do next.

Madame Tamsin clicks her tongue and wags her finger at me, her grimace spreading into a wicked smile. I've seen this expression a dozen times. She knows exactly how to play the situation to her benefit, and regardless of what she decides, she'll come out on top. I'm an omega hiding as a beta, after all. Without a pack or a mate bond, I'm nothing. I'm at the mercy of the Pack Regimes of Saint Vista, and there have been many rumors about what they do to people like me.

I shudder even thinking about it.

"My dear, sweet Kinsey. You know me too well, don't you?" Her hazel eyes drink me in, starting from my mouth and working her way down my body. The warm amber fragrance grows stronger, twisting around me and sending goosebumps over my skin. My reaction isn't caused by her pheromones, because the suppressant pills help balance me out, but by the fear instincts that grip me, refusing to let me go, setting me off. I see a predator before me, and my very nature as an unbonded omega wants me to escape. Those who don't want me, desire to destroy me, and my very soul recognizes it.

I curl my fingers and dig my nails into my palms. I wish I could rush out of here. Her dominance freezes me in place like a scared animal. "I've been with you every day for two years, Madame Tamsin. It would be a problem if I didn't know you. Now please, tell me what you want. You said that you should turn me in, not that you would. You know I don't have any money." Because she doesn't even pay me much. I get most of my income from tips, but that's just how it is. I've always been considered weak in her eyes. I've had nothing to offer except my ability to serve and not in the way that alphas crave.

Until now.

She recognizes me for who I am, and there's no way I'll be able to talk my way out of this and persuade her otherwise. She's a pill popper, and I'm sure she knows exactly what the pretty blue pills do. They are one of a kind, a drug that can put me in prison or worse for a long ass time. I'm committing fraud and hiding my true order. But the risk was worth it. Because even prison would be better than me accepting my fate as an omega.

"Watch your tongue, or I will ensure you never use it again. You do not speak to me as if we're equals. You can't demand answers." Madame Tamsin rushes me and shoves her hand to my throat, pushing me against the wall. Her desire shifts and the potent smell of gasoline ignites the scent of her anger, turning my muscles more malleable, my body relaxing, because she can use her power against me. She's not my alpha, but she's strong and determined. I'm at her mercy. It pisses me off how just her presence can do that to me.

I let my hair fall into my face, remaining silent.

She doesn't say anything for a long moment, studying my face as I refuse to look at her. My heart thrashes wildly, and I blink my eyes, trying my best not to let the tears slip free.

"Good girl," she says, her small comment enough to ease the tightness in my chest. "I knew you were smarter than you looked. And you're right. I said I should call the authorities, but you know me better than that. I don't want them anywhere near my business, but I also don't want to risk the status of the Vixen Lounge. You know that many of the Pack Regime leaders visit. If they knew I was harboring an unbonded unregistered omega, I would be the one at fault. You know it costs me thousands of dollars to house my current Gorgeous Girls, and they all have been acquired legally through their packs. So, to skirt around the law, I'm going to give you two choices." Madame Tamsin touches my chin, pinching my skin between her fingers as she forces me to meet her gaze. "I have an opportunity that will benefit us both. You can either accept my offer and be one of my traveling Gorgeous Girls, appreciating my generosity and minding your manners as one of my personal entertainers, or you can find out what it's like to be the omega of the Devil Lands. Your pussy is worth a decent price to those alphas."

My stomach twists and I press my tongue to the roof of my mouth, praying that I don't get sick. The Devil Lands is the nickname of the community just outside the Gutter District, controlled by alphas who were denied positions of power within the Pack Regimes. I'd rather her just turn me into the authorities than have her sell me like a piece of property to a gang that is known to breed and kill omegas, ensuring they don't bond.

"Please, Madame Tamsin. I'll do anything for your generosity." I flutter my eyelashes, trying to keep my heart from exploding.

"I know you will. You don't have a choice. Thank your good fortune that you caught me in a pleasant mood." Madame Tamsin releases pressure from my throat. She lowers me to my feet, parting her plum-colored lips with a smile. I shouldn't be so scared of a grin. But it triggers something dark and terrifying in me.

I don't respond to her, breaking my stare, doing my best not to set off her dominance.

"You know, I take care of my Gorgeous Girls. But you're not quite good enough for that. I have a better idea and something more suited to fit both of our needs. Some gentlemen prefer not to come to the Vixen Lounge. They're a bit more...needy. But they treat my Knotty Girls quite well as long as they behave. Like I said, you would be one of my traveling entertainers." Madame Tamsin strokes her palm over my cheek, scenting me.

The Knotty Girls? Traveling? I've never heard Madam Tamsin mention any of these things before. But why would she? I've always stayed out of her way and got my work done. I don't ever speak to any of her entertainers either. Only the bouncers and the bartenders. The clients.

"What do you think? Can you handle being one of my Knotty Girls? You would have to audition for my special clients, but if you're chosen, you'll have the opportunity to see the true luxury of the state, stay in beautiful places, meet some of the wealthiest and most powerful alphas of the Pack Regime. You will stay for weeks at a time and then return to me until you've been requested again. I think it would be very fitting for someone like you. Because I know you must have many secrets. Maybe we can talk about them sometime. I'm sure your life is very interesting," Madame Tamsin continues, filling the silence because she knows that I won't say much more. She has won. She has already used her power to make me into someone who complies.

I lick my lips and bob my head slightly, responding to her without moving much. It's been a while since I've acted like this. It hasn't been this way since my uncle was my caretaker after my parents had died.

Fuck. He would've told me this was the life I deserved. It's the life he had wanted for me, after all.

Madame Tamsin smiles wider, flashing her perfectly straight, white teeth. I don't know if I've ever seen her smile in such a way. And the fact that I'm the reason why awakens something inside me.

I hate it. Despise it. I shouldn't want to make her happy. I shouldn't want to make her proud.

All I should desire is to grab the letter opener and shove it into her stomach.

"You will start tomorrow, my Knotty Girl. I'll have Mr. Holt escort you to your apartment to pack your bags. You'll be staying with me until tomorrow. We can get you situated and send my client everything he needs to decide. You better hope he picks you." Madame Tamsin releases me and takes a step back, bringing her hands to her nose to sniff.

"Yes, Madame. Thank you for your kindness. I won't let you down." The words come automatically, and I just give in to the darkness clutching my soul. I need to focus on guarding myself. I need to prepare myself for the worst.

Because I know something awful will come. Unbonded omegas without a pack tend to be used and discarded.

I just hope I can survive. Unfortunately, a huge part of me hopes I don't.

My fingers tremble as I jiggle the lock on my apartment door. Mr. Holt stands behind me in silence, and I can feel his sad, sympathetic gaze boring into my mahogany-brown hair. The moment I exited Madame Tamsin's office, she escorted me to him and told him the plan, Mr. Holt's whole demeanor changed. He went from seeing me as his equal and his coworker to putting me beneath him. But his bland, soap scent permeates the air with his pity. I'd usually ignore the smells, but now that my secret is out, I can't. It's like my mind won't let me. The suppressant pills continue to run their course from my system. I have one left. I feel it in my pocket, and I clutch onto it like a lifeline. I'll take it the moment I have a chance to escape. I might have agreed to Madame Tamsin's terms and the opportunity she gave me, but it doesn't mean I have to do it forever. I can escape again. I can take this last pill and find more. I can leave the city and get a job elsewhere. I'll figure it out. I've done it before. I have to now. My future and freedom depend on it.

"Let me help you," Mr. Holt says, reaching for the doorknob because I just can't get it to work.

He wiggles the lock and swings open the door to my studio apartment, not even the size of Madame Tamsin's office. My mattress rests on the floor with only a blanket and no sheets. Tears burn my eyes as I drink in the place I called home for the last two years. I can't believe this is over.

"Hurry. Madame Tamsin said we have to be back in ten. Only take what you absolutely need. You will be provided with everything else. I suggest sticking to anything of importance. Sentimental." Mr. Holt keeps his voice low and stands in the doorway without entering my place. He does it out of respect, because I didn't give him permission to follow me in. I appreciate it. It was the one place that was mine, and no one has ever been in it.

"Thank you," I say, trying my best not to lash out at him. He's doing this because he was told.

Cutting my nails into my palms, I stroll across my closet-size apartment and grab a duffel bag from on top of my small dresser. I unzip it and snatch all of the clothes I own and shove them in. I know he's probably muttering to himself over my choice of sentimental, but I picked these. I bought them with my first week of tips. They are sentimental to me.

I head to my nightstand and open the drawer, pulling out a small photo album that I managed to save all these years. I tuck it into my pocket instead of putting it in the bag, wanting to keep it close. I pick up a pearl necklace that belonged to my mother and a chain with my parents' wedding bands. And that's all I own. I've never wasted money on frivolous things. It only went to food, rent, and drugs. Pathetic, I know. But I don't regret it. Material things mean nothing to me anymore, because I know how quickly they can vanish.

I know how quickly my life can change. If only I had been more prepared. I shouldn't have been so surprised tonight. It's not the first time. I just had hoped things would be different.

They never are.

I sling the duffel bag over my shoulder and clutch it for dear life, strutting to Mr. Holt. I don't look back at my apartment. It's better if I don't dwell on it. It was just a roof over my head and somewhere to sleep at night. Nothing else.

At least, telling myself that helps ease the heartache burning my chest.

I swallow hard, keeping my chin up. It might be the last time I can do so without consequence. "I'm ready."

Mr. Holt nods his head and closes the door locking it up. He tucks my key into his pocket, and I wonder what will become of this place. Will I ever get to return? I have no idea.

I hope not.

I hope that I can find somewhere new and put the last two years behind me. Maybe my entire life behind me.

A phone chimes from Mr. Holt's pocket, and he pulls it out and looks at the screen. He tightens his jaw and sighs. "There's been a change of plans. Madame Tamsin's client would like to meet you tonight. There won't be an audition. If he likes you, he'll let you stay. Madame Tamsin said that you better hope he does. She's not keen on having to retrieve you."

What? Already? I thought I would have the night to prepare myself. I thought I could better plan things.

This is happening too quickly.

Something inside me steals away my good senses, and I flick my gaze from the hallway to Mr. Holt.

Swinging my bag, I clock him over the head with it and break into a sprint. Mr. Holt yells my name, my sudden actions distracting him enough to give me a chance to beat him to the stairwell that will lead from the building. I know both of us will face punishment, but I don't even care. It's my life or his, and I choose mine.

I dash down the stairs, jumping the last four, and slam my shoulder into the exit door. Cool air engulfs me, and I search the area, making sure no one lingers around. There aren't many alphas in this part of the Gutter District. I can't blame them either. Why would they want to hang out here unless they were into some shady shit?

"Kinsey! Stop! Don't do this to me!" Mr. Holt shouts, rushing from my apartment building.

Ignoring him, I pick up my pace, my heart racing and my body screaming at me to hurry the fuck up. No one will stop a chase like this, and it's up to me to find someone willing to give me a ride or somewhere I can hide until I can manage to get on a bus. All I need to do is get out of Madam Tamsin's domain. She has several establishments in this part of the city, but she won't go into the next neighborhood and risk getting questioned by another alpha.

Run. Run, and don't stop. It's what the sweet neighbor of my uncle said to me when I chose to leave him because of his idea of my place in life, considering that I was the only thing left for him to use. My mother was gone, and the pack that was supposed to bond with me got caught in the crossfire of my uncle's business.

My heels click on the sidewalk, and I keep flicking my gaze from the concrete to the world in front of me. I'm so afraid of breaking my ankle, but I refuse to slow down. Just another block. If I can reach the alley next to the Townsend Market, I can cut across to the next street and take cover in the old diner that doesn't allow male betas inside. That will give me enough time to get away.

A shadow pops out from one of the closed businesses, and I can't dodge out of the way fast enough before a heavy body crashes into me. I scream and cling to the man as he takes the brunt of our fall with me on top of him. His arms lock tightly around me, and I gasp for breath, recognizing Mr. Clive's familiar cologne. He is one of the Gorgeous Girls' security guards and Madame Tamsin's brother.

"Tammy thought you were going to pull this shit, sweetheart, and you proved her right." Mr. Clive holds me with one arm as he pushes himself up and carries me to my feet. "I don't understand why you just couldn't mind your manners. You know how volatile she gets when someone tries to fuck with her business. Now we're going to have to do this the hard way."

"Please—" I gasp as Mr. Clive jabs a syringe into my arm, surprising me.

My stomach twists and my eyes roll to the back of my head. Fog clouds my vision.

I try to fight. To scream. But I can't resist the intoxicating sedation.

The world turns black.

Chapter 3

Kinsey

Kidnapped

The world jostles me awake, and I clutch my throbbing head and stare at the crowded room around me. No, not a room. I smell the familiar scent of gasoline and leather. The world shakes again, and the sensation of moving helps me recognize that I'm in a vehicle. Maybe one of the utility vans Madame Tamsin uses to transport supplies.

I stare at the roof, trying to get my head to stop spinning, but it doesn't work. I feel like hell. The last time I felt like this was after unintentionally drinking too much alcohol. I was young and unaware that just because I couldn't taste the tequila didn't mean it wasn't there. If only that was the case. The memory snaps me to the present. I was drugged. Fucking drugged. I should've expected something so awful, knowing Madame Tamsin.

A whistle echoes through the air, cutting over the recognizable hum of an engine. Every passing second helps clear my foggy mind. "Hey, Kinsey. You're awake just in time. Come sit up front, sweetheart. I want you to take a good look around and see how generous Tammy is. The city here is beautiful." Mr. Clive smacks the headrest of the front seat, and I blink my eyes and meet his gaze in the rearview mirror. "Don't be shy. You know I won't touch you. Tammy would kick my ass, though I'm sure the Platinum Shores Pack will insist you bathe immediately. Get the stench of the Gutter District off you."

The Platinum Shores Pack? I run every client I've ever met through my mind and try to visualize who he refers to. I've only really known most clients by their formal names because no one likes to divulge where they're from. They don't ever leave receipts behind either. The Vixen Lounge isn't a place you want to get caught at. Not if you're someone of power. There are too many businessmen and politicians who could tarnish their spotless reputations.

"No one wants that lingering. The reminder will make them aggressive, so you better behave during your stay. Give them what they want," he continues, bouncing in his seat as if he imagines being on the Platinum Shores Pack.

"What they want?" I swallow with the words, the lump in my throat refusing to go down.

"You know, some entertainment. Offer to let them watch or help you clean off. Take advantage of the attention and use that sweet ass of yours to get what you want in return. It's not often you'll get the perk of a pack without all the other shit. The more compliant you are, the better. Make things fun for them. Get them all riled up by showing off that you're an unbonded omega. Maybe they'll ask to keep you." He chuckles and smacks his hands against the steering wheel. "Shit. I still can't believe you passed as a beta in front of Tammy for so long. It was truly fucked up, pretending. Pissed her the hell off. You should've just come in and announced your order. She would've taken you in and protected you. You're attractive enough to be a Gorgeous Girl, but now she doesn't even want to look at you. Such a shame."

"Such bullshit," I mutter under my breath.

"But maybe things will change, and she'll get over it. Now, come up here, sweetheart. I mean it. This view is astounding. You don't want to miss it." Again, Mr. Clive smacks the head-rest.

I remain silent in protest, refusing to get up and move. I don't care to see where we are. It's not like I can get out of the van. I'm sure only Mr. Clive's door opens from the inside. Instead, I search around the cargo space for something, anything, I can use to help me in this situation. Bungee cords tether crates in place, ensuring nothing slides around. I can't see what's in the dark containers, but some of them smell like the Gorgeous Girls. Probably some panties, bras, or socks for some horny fucker to include in his spank bank.

I remember after my order manifested, my uncle had stolen a lot of my clothing to sell. It was one of the reasons my parents and him fought. If another pack outside of the ones they arranged for me became too obsessed with my scent, it would cause problems. You have to be careful with alphas, especially when omegas near their heats. They don't share outside of their packs, and when they begin their rut, they'll fight whoever they think might try to intervene with the one they want to bond with. And some packs have more than ten alphas. They each have an area to control in their territories, and they usually stay out of each other's ways except for during their omega's heat.

It has always been like this. Alphas who ban together are stronger than alphas who kill anyone they consider a threat to their power.

"Come on, sweetheart. You don't want me to have to drag you from the van. It won't make a good impression. It's better for you if you just comply. I've heard that the Platinum Shores alphas have no problem breaking an omega. You don't want that to happen, now do you? I care about you, Kinsey, and so does Tammy. It's why you're here and not elsewhere. You know we're not going to get caught harboring a criminal."

He's full of shit, and we both know it. Madame Tamsin is just taking advantage of the situation. She'll use me and abuse me and make as much money as she can until someone either discovers what I am outside of the shady clients that frequent her businesses or I die.

If only the latter didn't sound so tempting. Because I have nothing left.

I squeeze my eyes shut, suppressing the dark thoughts. I know better than to believe them. I've gotten through them before, and that's how I managed to pass as a beta for so long. I know that I can escape. I know that I can do whatever it takes. I'm living proof of that already.

"Kinsey, sweetheart. This is the last time I ask you nicely to come up here. You don't want to miss this incredible view. Have you ever seen the ocean? Saint Vista looks incredible from here. You can see several territories." Mr. Clive continues to fill the silence as if it makes any of this better. I refuse to acknowledge him and curl on my side, shifting myself out of his view and using some of the containers to block the world out. If he wants me in the front beside him, he's going to have to pull the vehicle over and put me there, which I know he won't.

After another couple of minutes of small talk, he gives up and turns on the radio, listening to rock music that vibrates the speaker near my back. He purposely turns up the volume, probably trying to get me to move, but all I do is cover my ears. At least it drowns out my racing thoughts. I'd rather focus on the pounding in my head instead of the fear clutching me. I need to get myself in control. Panicking won't do me any good. If anything, it'll make me more vulnerable. The suppressant pills will only do so much now that so much time has passed since I've last taken one. My wild emotions could rub off on the alphas of Platinum Shores, and some don't take kindly to people who reject their nature without giving them a chance, especially because I'm supposed to be one of Madame Tamsin's girls.

Digging my fingernails into my palms, I focus on the pinch of my skin, using it as a distraction. The smooth road turns bumpy, and I allow myself to bounce around instead of bracing against the floor. Whatever takes my mind off my impending doom.

"We're coming up to the border. Last chance to see the ocean before we head into the city, Kinsey. The bioluminescence waters look fucking magical. You might never see something like this again. Don't be a stubborn bitch!" Mr. Clive yells over the music, annoyed by the fact that I don't acknowledge his existence. He should be used to it, but this might be one of the few times he's alone around an omega. The Gorgeous Girls aren't allowed to talk to anyone apart from Madame Tamsin and the client they have been tasked to entertain. They never even talk to me.

"I can't believe you are—" Mr. Clive jerks the wheel and hollers, yelling a string of swearwords.

I roll from one side of the van to the other, hitting my back against the crates. I wince in pain as a corner jabs into me. I'm sure the container will leave a bruise. Forcing myself to sit up, I reposition my body into the small space. If I get any more bruises, the pack of Platinum Shores might deem me ugly and reject me, choosing to send me back to Madame Tamsin. If that happens...I have no idea. Nothing good could come of it. She said so herself.

"Fuck? What the fuck are they doing?" Mr. Clive growls and jerks the wheel, sending me bouncing. "Goddamn it."

The van skids to a stop, the brakes squealing. Mr. Clive cusses as he fumbles with the glove compartment, trying to find something. He yanks out a gun, sending papers scattering. I hunker down at the sight. Why does he need a weapon? What's happening? Twisting in his seat, Mr. Clive accidentally hits the gun to the headrest, and it knocks from his fingers, thumping against the metal floor by the passenger's seat.

"Fuck!" he shouts, trying to reach for it.

I duck down in panic, hearing voices demanding Mr. Clive to keep his hands up. Glass shatters, the crack deafening. I startle and curl in on myself, the sudden attack freaking me out more than the thought of heading to a strange pack to entertain them. I don't even get a chance to move or try to escape before a loud gunshot pops through the air. My hearing vanishes as my ears ring, and I reach around, looking for anything I can use to protect myself. But the containers are closed, and I can't get my body to get its act together to move from my hiding spot.

"We have five minutes, brother. Get the fucking tracker off now!" The deep, snarly voice strikes me in the heart as I listen to a man call out to someone.

The scent of vetiver, sage, and something sweeter like whipped cream wafts through the air, sending goosebumps prickling over my skin. Something familiar lingers in the fragrance, but I can't place it. It's no doubt an alpha man and maybe he'd been to the Vixen Lounge. Regardless of who he is, I'm nearly certain he just murdered Mr. Clive.

I need to get out of here. I need to do something. Except my body won't allow it. Another door slams and a softer voice trickles over the music, but I can't hear or smell whoever joins the alpha—his scent far more potent.

I lean forward and peek between the seats, catching sight of two men stealing Madame Tamsin's van. Neither of them looks into the cargo area, quickly getting settled and tapping things into their phones. I'm nearly certain neither of them realizes I'm back here. If they did, they'd call me out.

Fuck me.

I glance toward the back of the van, wondering if I could break the lock and open the door. If I'm quiet enough, they might not notice. They're too busy mumbling to each other over the music.

Shit. Shit. Shit. I need to try.

The man behind the wheel stomps the throttle, and I smack into the containers. I lost my one chance to try. There is no way I'll be able to escape from a moving van without hurting myself or worse. Biting my bottom lip, I silence my cry and try my best to stay quiet. I pray to the universe that my fear doesn't alert them of my presence. I'm sure my scent grows by the second, triggered by the alpha engulfing me with his dominance, more so than even Madame Tamsin. He must be the leader of a fierce pack, one not afraid of the consequences of stealing from another alpha.

I inhale shallow breaths, trying my best not to let the alpha's alluring scent linger on my palate for too long. The suppressant pills wear off faster if an alpha is affecting me, but I just don't know how much faster. Hopefully not enough for me to mess with the man because an alpha's sense of smell is sensitive. At least, I think he's the only one here. The other man doesn't set me off like the driver. He might be a beta, but he doesn't act like any of the ones I've met. He is obviously a member of this alpha's pack and considered important.

The van bumps and jostles over the uneven road as we pick up speed. The guys keep their voices low, and I can't eavesdrop on what they talk about. Without windows in the cargo area, my sight proves useless. The unknown of everything does nothing to help me think straight. If I could summon an ounce of bravery, I could peek out again, but the cowardly side of me doesn't want to risk looking through the windshield.

I fist my hands, counting each of my breaths as I hang tight and clutch onto my duffle bag. I wish I had brought something to use as a weapon. I don't think Mr. Clive even checked my belongings. It would've been easy enough.

An eternity passes, though I know it was probably only an hour because the emcee on the radio calls out the time. We're still in Saint Vista, but I know we're far from the Gutter District and wherever the Platinum Shores Pack resides. The compass on the dashboard had said north when Mr. Clive was driving, so I think we were headed toward Calico Proper. Now? I have no idea. Not that it matters. I'm screwed regardless. They'll kill me on sight, especially if they think I'm a beta for Madame Tamsin. I can tell this wasn't a random attack. There is nothing descript about any of her utility vans to encourage someone to just steal one. It's not one of her fancy sports cars.

Remaining quiet feels utterly torturous now. I'm antsy and bored, and my body just wants me to shut down, the exhaustion is real, especially as the night wears on me. It takes everything in me not to fall asleep, and it doesn't help that the sedative makes me groggy. I want to kill Mr. Clive for that. Madame Tamsin too.

"It's all clear, Enzo. Head around back to the garages, and Arsenio will help you unload there. Be careful. Some of those weapons are explosives." The voice sounds through some sort of radio, and I tense in fear. What is he talking about? What weapons? I knew that Madame Tamsin ran some shady shit, but I had no idea she was that deep into the illegal activities of the Gutter District. I bet she was never going to turn me into the authorities. There's no way she would want to draw that kind of attention to herself.

These guys? They obviously know something. Maybe they were even casing the Vixen Lounge, and that's why the alpha smells so familiar.

The van comes to a halt, and I smack my shoulder on the crate next to me, unable to keep the whimper from escaping my mouth. I cover my lips with my hand and squeeze my eye shut, wishing the world would just swallow me whole.

No such luck.

Absolute silence falls through the van, and I prepare for the worst. The two men in the front heard me. There's no doubt about it, and now they're listening, trying to figure out what it was.

And then I hear the intake of a breath.

Shit.

The van door slams and I startle, clutching onto my bag and preparing to use it as a shield. I hate being trapped in this place. I can't even move if I wanted to. There's only one way out, and there are two dangerous men in the way. Men that don't mind killing for what they want. The sound of the gunshot replays in my mind, and I tremble with panic.

"Fucking hell. There's a girl back here." The soft voice grumbles with the words, and I can't stop myself from peeking at the familiar man with startling deep blue eyes shining against his suntanned complexion. He's from the Vixen Lounge. He fought with Mr. Doyle. "She's either a stowaway or a captive. Did you have any idea that the Dark Alley Pack was transporting anyone?" The man keeps his eyes locked on me, though he doesn't speak to me directly. "She's a beta."

"Just take care of her. We don't need this kind of problem." The unfamiliar voice strikes me in the heart.

For the first time, I regret someone thinking I'm a beta. Because no one wants a packless beta. At least with being an omega, they could see me as some use.

I hold my hands up. "Wait! I'm not a beta. Please, you have to believe me. I'm not a beta. Don't hurt me!"

The man drops his hand from his jacket and cocks his head, flaring his nostrils as he inhales a deep breath. I remain frozen, praying that he can pick up my scent, despite the suppressant pills. Jerking his hand out, he grabs onto my wrist, wrenching me forward as if I weigh nothing at all. I screech and allow him to drag me, trying my best not to fight. If I fight, I'll set him off. No alpha likes to be challenged, especially by someone they consider beneath them.

"Wilder, get your ass over here. I need you to tell me if she's lying. The bitch of Dark Alley's scent is all over her, and I can't get a good idea." The man sets me down far gentler than I expect, setting me on my feet only to spin me around and hold me in place.

My eyes widen as I spot another familiar man from the Vixen Lounge. He was the one who initiated the fight and punched Mr. Doyle for me. He protected me. He was also one of the reasons I got caught with the pills.

He raises his eyebrows and gives me a once-over, drinking me in from my green eyes to my dirty heels, my shoes nearly unusable now. Something awakens inside me, and I catch a hint of his woody vetiver scent with a hint of mint, his lust as prominent as the ripple of a shudder coursing through his body, declaring that he senses what I am. That he might even recognize me.

"Please," I say, my voice just a whisper. I can barely stand still, the delicious scent emanating from him turning me on more than it should. And he's far more attractive now that I realize he was the one to protect me. If only such an act mattered now. This man bulges with muscles in all the right places, his biceps probably as big as my thighs, and his sharp jaw and neck corded with veins, showing me how strong he is. I bet beneath his button-up dress shirt hides rock-hard abs and a body fit for an alpha, one that looks ready to devour me.

I wouldn't mind either.

What the fuck am I even thinking?

"She's definitely an omega. Probably taking suppressants." His eyes search mine for a moment longer, recognition settling in. "I think she was a server."

Stepping closer, he grabs my cheeks and rubs his thumbs across my skin, tilting my head slightly to inhale a deep breath, his soft lips tickling the nape of my throat. A deep rumble escapes from him, and he jerks back, staring behind me at the man holding me in place.

"She could be useful. Take her inside, Enzo. We need to unload the van first. That's our priority." He releases me and rubs his hands over his cheeks. "We can find out information from her later."

"You got it, brother," Enzo says, quickly flipping me around and lifting me off my feet. He hangs me over his shoulder without a second thought, and I smack him in the back, startled by his actions.

He growls at me and adjusts me in his arms, but he doesn't retaliate. "Careful, baby. Next time I'll spank that ass of yours for doing that. There is no need to fight. We won't hurt you. Relax."

I've heard that line a million times, and it's not true.

But what can I do right now? I'm trapped.

At least I'm alive.

For how long? I guess I'll find out.

A whistle sounds through the air, and I spot a pair of boots stride past Enzo. "Looks like you caught a plaything, brother. You can put her in my room. I don't mind."

I try not to react, my eyes burning with tears.

Enzo spins and whacks the guy on the back of the head. "Shut the fuck up. You're going to scare her. She wasn't working with Madame Tamsin. I think the bitch woman was transporting her to the Platinum Shores Pack. They must've had some sort of agreement for one of her slaves."

The other man growls in response and whispers an apology to me, surprising me. The last thing I expected was for this rough man to have a gentle side, and it helps settle my nerves.

I try my best to look around, but he strides too quickly, and all I can see is the sparkling concrete from outside shift into gleaming granite floors. Decorative wallpaper lines a hallway, and I bounce as he climbs a wide set of stairs that takes us to an elevator. This is unlike any house I've ever seen. The pristine cleanliness of it doesn't give me any clue of what kind of men they are. The only fragrances I can smell are warm musk and something growing in intensity. It's the alpha. I think he finally recognizes my scent as an omega, and it's getting to him. Because I can recognize his lust the same as I had with the man with the stunning blue eyes. Wilder.

I remain quiet, tipping my head up, trying to sneak quick peeks around, but it's hard on my neck. I glimpse a decorative table with big bouquets of white flowers and metal artwork twisted on the wall.

Enzo slows at the end of the grand hallway, and I wiggle, wishing he would set me down. As if he can read my mind, he flips me and plops me in front of him, giving me a view of the double doors leading into a grand suite four times the size of my apartment. A massive king-size bed sits in the middle against the back wall with four posts and a heavy, intricately carved headboard. A gray rug softens the gleam of the dark hardwood floors, and a glass case displays…more sex toys than I've ever seen in my life. I inhale a deep breath, trying to catch the scent of another omega, but there is nothing here. Only his pure, unaltered fragrance of vetiver and mint.

"The bathroom is through that door. Take a shower and get cleaned up. I can't stand the bitch's smell on you. I'll leave you something to wear on my bed. Try not to touch anything while I'm gone." Enzo nudges me forward, getting me to stroll into the room. His room. That fucking giant display case belongs to him, and I can't stop myself from wanting to see what kind of kinky ass this man is.

"Did you hear me, baby? Shower. Now." Enzo flicks his fingers toward the open door to a dark bathroom. "I won't be long."

Without waiting for me to respond, he slams the door behind me. I remain frozen in place, listening to his footsteps vanish. I spin around and lock my fingers around the doorknob, flinging it open.

"What the fuck?" I mutter, staring at the tall bookcase blocking the door. He couldn't lock me in, so he trapped me. The bastard.

"Shower!" Enzo calls, his voice booming from the hallway.

I startle and slam the door shut. He was testing me, and I failed.

I need to get my shit together and mind my manners. This isn't my home, and I'm not a guest here.

Squaring my shoulders, I force my feet to move. I'll do what he says for now. I need to wait this out. I need to strategize. They can't see my escape coming.

It's the only way I'll get out of this.

I just hope it's not too late.

This pack already proved they're dangerous, and I'm pretty sure they'll eat me alive.

Chapter 4

Enzo

Princes of Gilded Sands

"Does she have an ID? Anything we can search the database for?" Arsenio scrubs the back of his neck, watching as Wilder and Desmond unload the crates of bribe money, top-notch arsenal, and a couple of hard drives with classified information about the other leaders of the area's Pack Regime.

We knew that Tamsin was coercing and bribing several alphas in Saint Vista, and now we have what we need to interfere with the power move the Platinum Shores Pack currently tries to make, buying their way to the edge of our city.

"All she had was a duffle bag of clothes, some photos, and wedding rings. Maybe she was kidnapped and being trafficked." Desmond tosses the bag to Arsenio, only to return to the back of the van to help Wilder slide the last container from the van.

"Give that here. I told her I'd be back, and she's scared." I snatch the bag from my brother and tuck it under my arm without going through it.

"She fucking should be. We need to find out where she's from so we can get her out of here. You know she can't stay." Wilder growls with his words, flicking his gaze toward the east side of the palace where I took the supposed omega. I couldn't decipher her scent from Tamsin's, and I know my brothers don't fully believe who she says she is.

I can smell a damn omega from a mile away, especially a claimed one, so this whole fucked up situation messes with my head. She knows too much already, and while we all know she can't stay here, we can't exactly just let her leave either.

Fucking fuck. We should've checked the van, but we needed to get the tracker out and leave the area before Tamsin knew we took her shit.

"You both need to chill out. No one saw, and if she was being sold into a household, she might not say anything. We just need to talk to her. I feel bad. You saw how frightened she was. It didn't help that Wilder suggested we kill her. Like what the fuck man? The other guy deserved it. Can't just go around killing people without a good reason, asshole." Desmond huffs and rocks on his heels, shoving his hands into his pockets. He's always been more thoughtful, easy-going, and our good sense. He's the only beta out of us siblings, and the only one not up to take our father's throne.

"You know we have to do whatever is necessary. There are several packs who want what we have, and we need to protect ourselves. Dad is growing weak, and you know that the shit with Holly caused huge fucking problems." Arsenio speaks up for Wilder, reminding us for the millionth time about what we're up against. Because Holly was betrothed to an alpha away from the kingdom, we ensured she wouldn't bond. It left a lot of animosity and the Valley Point Pack still wants compensation.

"Killing this girl isn't necessary. Now, get the shit we need, so we can go on a run. There is supposed to be another drop in a couple of hours. We need to be ready." Desmond looks at me. "Go back and find out who she is. And goddamn it, don't scare her. Don't touch her. Don't let her touch you. We can't have that shit distracting us. If it turns out to be a problem, call me, and I will handle it." Because as a beta, Desmond isn't as consumed by our birthright orders. He might not be as powerful as us, but he knows his shit, and we'd be lost without him.

I nod my head and crack my knuckles. "I got it handled. I already know what we're up against."

I fist bump Desmond and smack both Wilder and Arsenio on the backs of their heads, making them lunge at me. Laughing, I dodge out of the way and jog back to the grand foyer of our palace. It's far smaller than what we grew up in with our dad and leader, the king of Gilded Sands and our territory in Saint Vista, but I don't mind. It's far better and easier to protect everything we have this way. We don't need as much staff either, which is important because of what we do and what we have done. We had to fire mostly everyone after Holly begged us to help her. She had no interest in the pack my father had chosen for her, using her to help establish an allegiance with Valley Point.

Climbing the grand staircase to the second story, I head toward my private elevator leading to my wing of the palace. Each of my brothers has a wing, built as separate units with our own living spaces and kitchens. We have a central living area that we share, which is also where our small staff resides. It's not often that we go there, preferring our space. It also helps not having to constantly worry about whether or not one of our employees will betray us. Because it happens more often than not with many packs. It's far too easy to use valuable information to get ahead. Everyone is a bit shady. It doesn't help that the Pack Regime leaders are so damn dirty and crooked. We can't even trust the police force to treat our territories equally.

So we have become the authority ourselves.

I hesitate outside the double doors to my living quarters, trying to listen for the girl. I really can't wait to know her name, because it'll be easier to consider her more than just our accidental captive.

Cracking open the door, I sweep my gaze across my sitting area and toward the bathroom. The shower runs, and I thank the universe that she actually obeyed me. I head toward my wardrobe and pick out a long shirt for her. I'll have to find something more fitting, but I don't want her putting on the dress she was wearing again. I'm going to throw that shit away altogether. I don't want it in my room or my palace. Just the stench of Tamsin gets under my skin. It ignites anger inside me, and I don't want to accidentally get carried away and scare her even more.

I listen as the water shuts off. I know I should just leave the shirt on the bed and exit the room. I should wait a couple of minutes outside and then knock to be invited in. But something wild keeps me in place. I'm afraid to miss the very first breath of her clean, unaltered scent. The second she puts on the shirt, it might change. We purposefully use a scented laundry soap to keep things more subtle for each other. Because regardless of being brothers, we can still get under each other's skin. But our awareness keeps our pack strong. Despite my father believing only one of us should take the throne, we know that we'll do it together, and we will be unstoppable. Powerful.

My heart thunders, my whole body rippling, my muscles cording in anticipation. The door to the bathroom swings inward, and the girl steps out, clutching a towel around her petite yet supple body. My dick hardens the second I lay eyes on her, the way she ties her towel enhancing her cleavage. It doesn't help that she grabbed one of the smaller towels I use for the gym, and it barely covers her ass. Luckily, she doesn't move or else I know I would sneak a glimpse, wondering if she shaves her pussy or goes natural like I prefer.

"Oh, you're back." Her voice shakes, and her pretty green eyes dart to the bed where the long shirt lies and back to me. "I'm sorry. Let me just grab the shirt, and I will get dressed."

I cross my arms over my chest, digging my fingers into my ribcage to stop myself from strolling closer to her. There is something wrong in this moment that triggers me, numbing my mind. I can't think about anything except for her and how fragile and small she looks. I want to ensure she knows that she is safe here. I want her to be able to scent me, knowing that I'm not angry, nor am I annoyed with her presence. She should know how I find her so sexy and attractive, enough so that I already imagine her lying beneath me, biting her full bottom lip and spreading her legs to let me ravish her body in a way she'll desire.

My mouth remains tight, the words refusing to come. I know better than to say any of those things. She's not mine to handle with care. She is unwanted. A danger to us. I can't allow my emotions and very nature as an alpha to control me. She doesn't belong here.

"What are you going to do with me?" the girl asks, breaking the silence. She stands at the edge of the bed and lifts my shirt carefully, ensuring she doesn't touch my comforter. The gesture of respect strikes me right in the balls, and I flare my nostrils and shift on my feet.

"What's your name? I'm Enzo, by the way," I say, instead of answering her question, because honestly, I don't even fucking know. I scratch my fingers through my black hair, hoping I don't freak her out.

"Kinsey," she says softly, lowering her gaze to the floor.

Kinsey surprises me by dropping the towel and exposing her body while she dresses right in front of me. My jaw slackens, and I lock my dark blue eyes on her, wishing she would slow down before shrugging the shirt over her head. I've never seen someone so beautiful, so enticing, in my life.

And it's in this moment I realize why she bares her body to me. She knows that I will spot the small heart-shaped birthmark that appears with her order manifestation, proving that she is a true omega. Sometimes the mark appears on the back, on the wrist, behind the knee, but hers kisses her hip like a love bite, and all I can think about is grazing my fingers over it, kissing it, tracing it with my tongue, doing everything I can just to ensure myself that it's real.

"I don't have a formal last name because I'm packless, but I've been going by Kinsey Kane. It's what all my forged documents say. Not that it matters now." Kinsey scrunches her nose. "Please, don't hurt me. I'm not bothering anyone. If you let me go, I'll keep this to myself and move. I'll never go back to Madam Tamsin."

"That's why you were being transported, wasn't it? She caught you. How? I mean, how have you been passing as a beta?" I step closer, wanting to close the space so I can get a better breath of her fragrance. I know the shirt will taint her a bit, but this might be the only time I get it clean and fresh just for me. Because she will only be reacting toward my body and my words. If my brothers were here, we wouldn't be able to distinguish anything.

She sighs and combs her fingers through her tangled wet hair. "It's not important. All that matters is she caught me, and now I'm here. Please, tell me what you plan to do. I need to prepare myself. Grant me that one mercy."

Her comment surprises me, and I frown, unable to hide the displeasure from crossing my face. She sounds as if she's been in this type of situation before. Fucking hell. It must've been awful if telling her our plans would be kind and merciful of us. It's pretty shitty. It ignites a dozen more questions in my mind. Where did she come from? What happened to her pack? How did she even end up in Tamsin's care?

Something overcomes me, and I close the distance to her completely, bringing my palm to her cheek to caress her skin. She remains utterly still as I explore the softness of her face, combing my fingers into her damp hair to play with the mahogany tresses.

"We won't hurt you, Kinsey. You were never supposed to be here, but you can't leave just yet. We don't know exactly what to do, and we won't make the decision until we have our current shit together. But I assure you, you don't need to be afraid." I lean in with my words and inhale a soft breath of her delectable scent, my words stimulating relief through her, the arousing scent of honeysuckle mingling with citrus making my mouth water. She likes me. Knowing this satisfies me deeply. It does nothing for my aching cock, throbbing to know exactly what this omega can do to me.

It would be insane to suggest to my brothers that we keep her. I'm sure she is wanted for something, if not by a member of the Pack Regime then by Tamsin and one of her despicable clients. It would complicate things. We already have enough to worry about.

"How about I make you something to eat? You must be hungry." It only takes one look in her eyes to know that I'm right. Her stomach growls at my suggestion, solidifying exactly what I'm going to do with Kinsey next.

I don't give her a chance to respond and drop my hand from her hair only to lace my fingers with hers, tugging her along across my suite to where a small kitchenette hides behind a decorative wall, separating it from my living space.

She resists entering the kitchen, still nervous about being in my space. I drag her forward just a bit until she finally stops trying to stay out and joins me instead.

I look down at her, studying her shifting eyes, her bottom lip trembling. "What did I say, baby? You don't have to be afraid. I've invited you into my suite. If I didn't want you here, you would be in one of the guest rooms. Now, do you have any preference? Favorite foods?"

"You're lying to me. I'm here because you're afraid that I'll try to escape from a guest room." Kinsey tightens her jaw, her comment probably intended to be just for herself. Because she doesn't consider herself wanted. At first, she was right. I didn't want her near my things, but this was the most convenient place to keep her. My possessive side wanted her around me first instead of with Desmond, even though he offered.

"That too, but it's just easier." I know better than to invalidate her concerns. I've learned that from my little sister, and I promised her that I would never do it again. "Is there anything you don't like?" I decide it's best to change the subject, because I can tell that she wants answers, and if she asks me enough, I might give in. That'll only piss my brothers off.

Desmond would understand. Wilder and Arsenio? Fuck that shit. They will be pissed off enough as it is.

"Being treated like a prisoner," she responds, tugging her hand away from mine, leaving a cool spot against my palm.

I can't stop the smile from crossing my face. She might be timid and nervous, but I can tell she has some spitfire in her veins.

"I guess I'll just have to make something and find out for myself, won't I, baby?" I open the small fridge and pull out a steak from the butcher drawer. She watches me as I heat up the cast-iron skillet and plop the meat on, sending it's sizzling and smoking. Her nostrils flare as she takes a breath, and I know from just her emerald eyes widening that I made the right call.

I quickly prep a salad and steam some broccoli, trying my best to give her a little of everything. She watches as I slice up an apple and mix up a couple different berries, putting them into a bowl.

Her stomach rumbles again, and I glance at her, catching her staring at the two plates I prep as if she might just snatch one before I even have the chance to finish.

I pick up an apple slice and offer it to her. She stares at my hand for a second before leaning forward and snatching it with her teeth. My eyes widen, and I jerk my hand away, the gesture like a zap to my cock. It's like she's afraid to touch me with her hands, but man, I think that mouth of hers is going to get both of us in trouble.

Her desire grows, and I realize that she might have never been offered a meal like this before. If she was in hiding and passing as a beta, I can guarantee it.

They are just...betas without packs are basically the sheep of our society. They live, they sometimes will gravitate toward each other, but they don't hold power, and they're not exactly desired among alphas. Only an omega can take our knots and procreate with us.

"Why don't you go sit at the table over there, and I will bring everything out." I motion toward the small dinette just outside of the kitchen.

"I don't understand you." Kinsey places her hands on her hips. "Why are you being so nice? What do you want?"

I lift an eyebrow. "I want to stop freaking you out. Your fear does nothing for me. Not like it does for some other bastards."

She blinks a few times and relaxes her shoulders. "Oh." Shuffling away, she doesn't argue with my reasoning and follows my suggestion, taking it as a command. I quickly finish cooking the steak, cutting it into pieces small enough for her to easily chew, and I plate everything. Kinsey stares at her hands, resting them on the table. Her chipped nail polish sparkles under the overhead lighting, catching my attention, and she tucks her hands on her lap.

"Water? Wine? Something else?" I ask her, setting the plate in front of her.

She peeks up at me, her long lashes casting shadows on her reddening cheeks. "Water is fine." I don't know why I assumed she'd ask for something different. "And thank you. This smells amazing."

I grin and fork a piece of the steak, my desire to feed her at least the first bite overwhelming me. Parting her lips, she takes a bite, humming softly as she shuts her eyes, savoring the food. And damn it, does it stir warmth inside me. Her appreciation radiates as potent as her attraction to me, sweetening her scent with something gourmand. Maybe marshmallows. Caramel. Fuck, I want to taste her to be certain.

A bang on my door snags my attention away from Kinsey, and I swear under my breath. I bet one of my fucking brothers checked in on my room cams, curious as to what's going on.

I'm about to get my ass beat for this, and only Desmond might understand. Wilder and Arsenio won't. They're far too concerned with everything else that they won't take a moment to appreciate what—who was dropped into our possession.

"Enzo, we need to talk." Desmond's voice trickles through the door of my suite. "I have something I need to show you."

I turn my attention to Kinsey and shake my head. "I'll be back. Make yourself comfortable."

Kinsey bobs her head, taking another bite. I could watch and listen to her eat all day. Somehow, she makes the simple gesture incredibly sexy, and I find myself obsessing over her pouty mouth.

"Enzo," Desmond calls again, cracking open my suite door.

Anger at his intrusion rushes through me, and I spin away from the table and strut toward my brother. He darts his eyes past me to Kinsey. She won't look at him, not in my presence. A part of me finds content knowing so. As a beta, he would never get between me and an omega, whether or not she belongs to me, which she doesn't. She can't.

I shove him, knocking him back in the hallway. Growling, Desmond shoulders me, fighting back just as hard. I slam the door behind me and force him against the wall, scowling in his face.

"What the fuck is it?" I ask, heaving a breath. "She just settled down."

Desmond doesn't back down, surprising me. He's never one to challenge any of us. "I'm saving your ass, brother. What the hell do you think you're doing? You can't just start treating her as a guest. We know nothing about her. She could—"

"She's who she says she is. I saw her order mark. She's harmless and alone. I was only being nice. She was starving. You, out of everyone, shouldn't be pissed that I'm trying to make her comfortable." I release him and step back, glancing over my shoulder.

Desmond shakes out his hands and cracks his neck. "I'm not pissed. I'm concerned. We need to be careful. You shouldn't even be alone with her."

I tighten my jaw, trying not to react. He's absolutely right. I've made a huge fucking mistake, and I let Kinsey already get to me. I can't help it. She awakens something inside me I've never felt, and I can't explain it.

"I—I'm sorry. I just..." I let my voice fade, getting my head straight. It helps that I can breathe without Kinsey's intoxicating scent numbing the world around me. I sigh and scrub my hand to the back of my neck. "You should take her. If I go back in there, I'm not so sure I'll let her leave."

Desmond smacks me on the back, pushing past me when I'm not quick to move away from my door. I tighten my fists, remaining straight-backed, not letting him push me around. We glare at each other for another moment, but I still don't back down, and neither does he. Locking his fingers to the doorknob, he swings it open, giving me a view of my suite. Kinsey no longer sits at my table, and I flick my gaze around my room.

"Fuck me," I mutter, spotting her lying on the edge of my bed, curling in on herself. She was obviously exhausted and took my comment to heart. But damn. My bed?

Desmond shoves his hands into my chest, pushing me out of my room. I hit my back to the wall, groaning as the breath escapes me.

"Go help Arsenio and Wilder. I'll take over from here." Desmond meets my gaze. "Please, brother. Don't fight me. It might scare her. Just go get some air. I'll fix this."

It takes everything in me to nod my head in agreement. He knows me as well as I know myself. If I go anywhere near Kinsey in my bed, I might not leave. I might lose my fucking sanity, her very nature encouraging me to stake my claim, something unthinkable until we take over our kingdom when our father leaves the throne.

"We'll get it figured out, okay? Trust me." Desmond nudges me again.

I squeeze his shoulder. "I do, Des. You've never let me down."

If only I could say the same thing about myself.

Chapter 5

Desmond

Beta Order

I don't know what the fuck Enzo was thinking. I should've let Wilder and Arsenio see him with the omega, so they could set him straight. He's lucky I can't stand when the three of them fight. Their fucking scents test my ability to remain neutral. I sometimes wonder what it would be like if my manifestation hadn't failed me and deemed me unworthy of following in our father's footsteps. I'm our weakest link, and King Asshole would never let me forget it. I barely consider our pack leader as my father. Not like the others. But they don't know what it's like being born to follow and bow to them, especially when our pack rules over so many.

A soft breath draws my attention away from my thoughts, and I turn my gaze to the short, slender omega lying on the end of Enzo's bed. He's lucky she didn't climb in, or else he'd fucking owe me a lot more for having to change out all his bedding. The maids only come once a week, and it's usually us who strip down the beds and make them ourselves. We might be royalty, but we are all picky, and I know how much my brothers hate people touching their things.

I ruffle my fingers through my light golden-brown hair and stare at the omega, listening to her breathing, her mouth parting as she instinctively breathes in the scent of Enzo's bed. I shouldn't be so jealous, because I know it's not intentional, but a part of me wishes to see her do such a thing in my bed.

Damn. I'm letting my envy get to me.

I don't want to startle her, but I need to get her to wake up. Or maybe I can just move her. It's probably better that way. She looks so exhausted that I doubt she'll even get up. There's something comforting to an omega when an alpha takes care of them. She feels safe after a night of fear. I'm sure of it. I've learned how to pick up such scents. It helps that I was born to a powerful bloodline.

Moving closer, I decide to wrap Enzo's comforter around her, making it easier for me to lift her without shoving my hands under her body. It's better if I don't touch her anyway. I don't need to start a pissing match with my brothers. We all knew that one day we would most likely share an omega, but it definitely can't be this one. The woman we will spend our life with will be chosen by the king when we—I mean, one of my brothers— take the throne.

I don't even want to think about that. We need to get everything else together first to ensure a smooth transition. Because the king grows weak with his age and lacks strong alliances. We'll be able to challenge him soon enough, and he will relent, following our kingdom's traditions. No alpha dies on the throne. If he were to die, that would give another pack the opportunity to steal what belongs to us. And there's no way any of us would let that happen. They can fuck with their own territories. The Gilded Sands kingdom is ours.

I struggle with the omega in my arms, trying not to jostle her too much. I flick my gaze from the hallway to her, checking every so often to make sure she doesn't wake up. Of course, I'm sure she will scream or some shit if she thinks I'm kidnapping her from my brother's room. And now I'm starting to regret my decision. Fuck me. I was so concerned about getting her out of there to help him that my dumbass is about to scare this gorgeous woman even more.

If I can just get to my room and set her down, I can exit and knock to wake her up. She'll be disoriented, but at least she won't think her cute ass is getting kidnapped...again.

Fuck. Fuck. Fuck.

I stride as fast as I can to the west side of the palace, wishing for once there wasn't so much space between my living quarters and my brother's. But it helps keep us close without being obnoxiously overwhelming. All of the staff live in apartments in the center of the palace and the rest of our pack members live in casitas either on the north side of the property or within the walls of my father's fortress.

I enter the west wing and pass the massive library and study Arsenio favors. It's where he used to teach Holly more than my father allowed her tutors, sharing his knowledge with our little sister before things went down.

I prefer the entertainment room, where I can watch all the movies I please. It helps me avoid everyone and everywhere else. Wilder basically lives in the gym and outside on the sports field, loving to challenge some of the local kids who are allowed on our property. Because we're not dicks like some other royal packs, we like to immerse ourselves in our community, ensuring that our people remain loyal despite the ruthlessness of our father.

The omega groans, the softness of her voice tightening my chest. She's going to fucking wake up. I'm not being careful enough with her. I brave sprinting the rest of the way to my room. Flinging open my door, I toss her to my bed only to spin and run out.

Am I a coward? Maybe. If it were one of my brothers, they would probably just stand and watch her, waiting for her to calm down before they even speak. But that's not me.

"What the fuck?" The omega's voice rings out, her confusion rising her words in volume. "Enzo? Hello?"

I straighten my shoulders and crack the door open, peeking in. "Sorry, little omega. My brother had somewhere to be and asked me to relocate you. I didn't want to wake you up, but I didn't want to scare you either. I'm sorry." The words rush from my mouth as I try to get everything out, feeling the heat of her gaze bore into me.

"Don't call me that, please. My name is Kinsey." She sits up on her elbows and peers around.

I purse my lips, realizing she doesn't want to be known for her order. And I guess I get it. She somehow managed to hide it. Something must've happened to her at some point to make her despise her place in this world.

"But you are an omega," I say, leaning on my door frame. "Just because you were passing as a beta means nothing. I will respect your wish and call you Kinsey, though. I'm Desmond."

"You're a beta," Kinsey says, straightening her back and scooting to the edge of my bed, grasping the blankets, not bothering to be careful with her touch. "I'm surprised Enzo was okay with you bringing me here." I wasn't the only one to recognize Enzo's sudden shift. An omega would know when an alpha was interested, and this one might try to use it to her advantage.

"Why? You're no longer in the Gutter District, pretty girl. You're in our palace, and we have mutual respect for our pack members. My brother would never get pissed off at me for saving his ass. You're not even supposed to be here. Once my other brothers are done with their business, we're going to figure out what we need to do and get you there, okay? I'm sure you don't want to be here either. It was our mistake, and I apologize for not taking better care to make sure the van had no one else in it. Maybe you can help me out. Where are you from? Did the Dark Alley alpha kidnap you?" I stride closer, ensuring my door closes behind me. If I don't ask these questions now, I might not get her to open up again. She sees she can speak freely with me. It's probably the biggest benefit of not falling into the order of the alphas.

Kinsey bows her head, staring at my rug. She's silent for a minute, collecting her thoughts. I shuffle even closer and ease down on the bed beside her, hoping that my calmness helps diminish her worry. I need to be at her level and not towering over her. The last thing I want is for her to be intimidated by me. It's a shitty situation, but I will do my best to ensure shit doesn't escalate even more with my brothers.

"We won't send you back to her, so you don't need to be afraid. I just need information. It'll help us make a better plan. Are you originally from the Gutter District?" I rest my elbows on my knees, keeping my gaze trained on my royal blue and white patterned rug, though I watch her in my peripheral vision.

She laces her fingers together. "I'm not. I've only been living there for a couple of years."

I realize that the only way I'm going to get information out of Kinsey is if I ask the right questions. She's been trained to only respond with what is necessary.

"Where were you before that?" I shift on the bed, turning slightly to face her. I study the side of her beautiful face, her green eyes glancing at me for a split second. She lets her dark mahogany hair veil her face, cutting me off from getting a good look at her. "What about your pack? Were they unkind? Correct me if I'm wrong, but I'm going to assume that if you were hiding your order, then something happened. Was it with the ones chosen for you?" Because I know that situation all too well. It happened with my little sister Holly, and we're still dealing with the aftermath.

Kinsey rubs her lips together and fidgets, my questions obviously making her uncomfortable. But I need answers. I need to be able to come up with a plan to present to Wilder, because he will be the one to make the final decision. It's not often that he sways from agreeing with our brothers, but there's always a chance. Especially when it comes to our personal affairs.

"It's complicated. I never got the chance to get to know my chosen, and my pack is...dead. I'm alone. You know what happens to omegas under those circumstances." Kinsey turns her head and meets my eyes straight on, her green depths watering, but she doesn't cry. And I feel like shit for having to stir up a conversation that clearly hurts her. The scent of her sadness overwhelms me, the sour tang of lemon nearly burning my eyes. "So, I don't really have anywhere to go. As long as you don't send me back to the Gutter District, I'll figure shit out."

We both know that's untrue. If we were just to toss her out in another territory, her fate could be far worse.

"How? You have nothing of value." I regret the comment immediately, because she narrows her eyes at me.

"You went through my bag." She crinkles her nose and puckers her mouth with her annoyance. The scent of her sadness shifts to anger, and I'm hit with a spicy wave of cinnamon. I haven't smelled anything so powerful in a while, not even from my brothers, and it sends the hairs on my arms on end.

I refuse to break my stare, challenging her glare right back. She's feisty as fuck, and it's her strong will that probably helped her survive all this time. In fact, I know that it was. She isn't the docile omega many are, probably influenced by her birth pack just like Holly. We made sure she wasn't ever going to turn into just another omega to submit to alphas. We believe in bending the purpose of our orders, which is why my brothers treat me equally, too.

"Don't worry, Kinsey. We didn't touch too much. We just needed to see if you had an ID or anything we could use to figure out who you were." I clench my jaw and remain expressionless.

"I'm no one. So please, just let me leave. You don't even have to take me anywhere. I'll walk." Kinsey taps her bare feet on the floor, bouncing the bed beside me.

I furrow my brows at the thought of just letting her go. I shouldn't worry so much, but a part of me knows how unreasonable and dangerous granting such a request would be. "The nearest populated area in Gilded Sands is twenty miles from here. You can't just walk."

She groans. "Then give me a ride. Let me take the van. I don't care if it's now stolen. I'll get rid of it as soon as I reach the city."

"No." I'm not even going to humor her demands. She's too desperate to think straight. "I will discuss things with my brothers, and we'll come up with something safer for you, Kinsey. Why don't you make yourself comfortable here and get some rest? I can tell you're tired. I have extra linens and can strip the bed for you." Or me. My fucking thoughts.

"This place is huge. You don't have a guest room? I know that Enzo wanted me to stay in his room so he could watch me, but I'm obviously not going anywhere. Not like I could get far anyway. I don't want to intrude on your space." Kinsey looks around the room, her emotions settling and her scent fading. I'm definitely going to have to be the one to watch over her. I might be the only one capable of doing it. Enzo really set her off in all sorts of ways, and none of us needs that. They trigger each other.

"All of our guest rooms are in the center of the palace along with the staff's. We're not going to let word get out that we have you here. So, no. I'm sorry. You must stay here." I get to my feet and motion for Kinsey to do the same. I start to grab at the comforter that I took from Enzo's room to bring her here in, but she snatches it and holds it close, not letting me take it.

If this was any other circumstance, I would overpower her and steal it back, but she looks like she might lunge at me if I try now. This isn't good. I know she's doing it out of need, but this is going to drive Enzo crazy. Fucking pheromones. Fucking alphas. Fucking orders. I sometimes wonder how things would be if my brothers manifested as betas too. Though, the king would've probably slaughtered us all and made mom try again.

"I'll just take the couch." Kinsey doesn't give me a choice in the decision. She spins and heads toward my sitting area, curling up on the loveseat instead of the sectional. I know it's because she wants to take up as little of my space as possible, and I feel bad about it, but for being an omega, she seems stubborn as hell. That's only going to make things a bit more complicated. I know how much my brothers love that kind of thing.

"Fine. Just for the night. I will go get you some more appropriate clothing. My brothers aren't ready to give me your bag back. I'm sure I can find something around here in your size to make do until then. I need to step out for a bit anyway, so if you need me, just send a text to Enzo. His number is the first one in my phone contacts." I pull my cell from my pocket and hand it to her. "Please, don't leave the room. If one of my other brothers finds out, it won't be as easy to convince them to let you go. Do you understand?"

Kinsey gingerly holds the phone, staring at the lock screen and the picture I have of me and my brothers. "Yes. I understand."

I dip my chin in affirmation. "Thank you. The code is my name spelled out with the number keypad."

She bobs her head and turns over on the couch, giving me a view of her back.

I wish I knew what the best thing was to do with her. A part of me knows better than to even consider keeping her here, but there's a huge fucking part of me that doesn't want to sentence her to a shitty life or worse if we let her go. Her order will always catch up with her. I don't know how she did it until now, but it's obviously not the solution. Next time, it could be far worse for her. I know what the Pack Regime does to unbonded, packless omegas. They're useless to society without a pack, and there are many who would trade a lot for someone like her.

I shake my head, pushing the thoughts away. I need to put some space between us for a bit before she becomes too overwhelming. It's not even her order that gets to me. There's something about her, and I think it's because of Enzo. As a pack, we've always done everything together, and we always expected to claim an omega to be our wife because of the rarity of the order. I would be the last and most likely one to not procreate, considering I can't ensure such a thing without my body being able to knot. As a beta, I've come to accept that my cock is second-best. If I were on my own, I'd end up with another beta, and I'd never have to worry about my children being anything other than a beta. Two betas always spawn betas. Alphas and omegas? Their children can manifest into any order. Plus, I can't really satiate an omega's feral needs. But fuck it, I sure can try. I work harder than any of my brothers.

What am I even thinking? *Move, Desmond. Get your ass out now.*

I stride from my room with the thought and cut right to head toward the hidden access door that'll take me to what should be our panic room. It's the only place with halls that princes can use. They all connect to our suites, but there was no way I was going to enter through my wardrobe for Kinsey to see. It would absolutely be even worse than keeping her here. We already risk a lot with her presence. There's no need for her to get into the rest of our business.

I enter the study and close the door, only looking around for a moment before I open the storage closet and press my hand to the keypad, opening the door. Cool air engulfs me, the concrete stairwell leading down to one of the coldest places in the palace, especially when the temperatures rise in the summer, turning our territory into a desert wasteland. I take the stairs two at a time and jog in the direction of our former panic rooms. I know I shouldn't go there, but I really don't want any of the staff to know that I need some women's clothing. And Holly looks to be Kinsey's size.

I release a deep breath and hit my palm to the keypad, unlocking the door to the panic room. Only five people have access to our hidden sanctuary, but it's only Holly who stays within the impenetrable walls.

I knock my knuckles on the second door, the first one intended to keep everyone out, and the second one intended to give my little sister privacy.

She calls out, inviting me in. "You're early, Des. Did something happen?" Holly stretches her arms above her head, sitting up in her four-poster bed. The suite is just as big as ours, if not bigger, because if shit went down, a lot of us would be staying in here. "Did you get everything we need?" She's been antsy, knowing that we've been stealing all illegal contraband that's been transported within a two-hundred-mile radius of the palace. It's the only way we'll ever get shit the way we want.

"I need some clothes. Anything you don't like, because they won't be coming back. We'll pick you up anything you want to replace it." I tighten my jaw, bracing myself for her interrogation. She knows that I won't indulge her by giving her the information about the contraband, because I leave that up to Wilder.

She frowns and narrows her hazel eyes at me, the scent of her suspicion bitter like black coffee. It's one of the only things I can usually smell on her. "Why? What have you done?"

I bounce on my feet. "Come on, Holly. You know it's better if you don't know this kind of thing. Just let me have some of your clothes. I swear once Wilder gives me the word, I'll tell you everything. But please, she has nothing."

Holly tilts her head, staring at me. She challenges me because she knows that if she persists enough, I'll give in. At least, I would usually if it didn't involve a shitshow. The less she's aware of, the better. I know my baby sister all too well that if she even suspects we have another omega, one unbonded and packless, she'll get the wrong impression. She'll automatically start matching us and...fuck. I need to get out of here.

"Please, little sis. I have shit to do," I add, popping out my bottom lip to match hers.

"As soon as Wilder says? You promise?" she asks, batting her lashes. "I'll kick your ass, rearrange your room, and spray my favorite perfume all over your shit if you break it."

I chuckle, knowing she'll stay true to her word. "I'll help you do the same with Wilder."

"Arsenio and Enzo, too." Holly grins, the light in her eyes returning for the first time since we all agreed she would be hiding out in the panic room after shit went down.

"They're going to kick my ass," I mutter.

"Not if you keep your promise, big brother." Holly steps back and spins, flinging her pale blond hair in my face. "Now, come on. You can grab a few things yourself. I'm sure the last thing you want is me touching them."

I shake my head. "You're ridiculous."

"It's just to remind you that you're going to owe me. Massively." Holly plops back down on her bed. "Forever."

"No reminder necessary." I head to her wardrobe and select a few modest garments, ensuring pants and long-sleeves for Kinsey. "And thanks."

"Anything for my sweet brother. Just make sure the others know that they're still on my shitlist." Holly's smile fades. "Tell Wilder he can't avoid me forever."

"I'll do my best to get him to come by, okay?" I force my smile to remain, knowing that Wilder won't until he knows he has good news. "Just hang tight. We'll get it taken care of. I promise."

If only I knew for certain that I could keep my word.

Chapter 6

Kinsey

Dickhead

I tap my fingers on the small table, staring at the plate of cheese and fruit. I haven't seen Desmond since I fell asleep, but when I woke up, there were new clothes draped over the back of the dining table chair, a plate of grazing food, a glass of water, and a couple of necessities for the bathroom.

I wish I would've checked the time before passing out, because I don't know exactly how much time has passed. All I know is that it's almost dusk, according to Desmond's cell phone. I lift it from the table and stare at the screen for the twentieth time in the last hour. Do I need to text Enzo to ask for Desmond? No. Am I dying of boredom and just want some answers? Absolutely.

Sucking up my nerves, I type in the passcode and open the contacts.

Dickhead? Desmond has Enzo listed under dickhead? I guess I'll find out.

Me: Where are you?

I stare at the screen for seemingly forever, wondering if I might've messed up and maybe clicked the wrong number. Swiping my finger, I scroll through the contact list, annoyed by the lack of familiar names. I recall the other two brothers being named Wilder and Arsenio, which neither are listed either.

The phone buzzes in my hand, flashing *Dickhead* across the screen.

Dickhead: Miss me?

I close my eyes and shake my head. How do I even respond to that? I don't even know for certain who answers on the other side of the line.

Dickhead: You want Des?
Me: Yes.
Dickhead: Why?

I sigh, trying to stay calm. His texts leave me unsure. I can't tell if he's fucking with me or being flirtatious. It's not like I need to talk to Desmond, but I'm anxious and getting annoyed.

Me: Never mind. I know why you're listed as Dickhead.

Setting the phone down, I grab the plate of fruit and cheese, taking it with me back to the couch. I curl my legs under me, listening to the phone buzzing a dozen times on the table. Ignoring it, I pop a couple of cubes of the cheddar cheese into my mouth, savoring the taste. I forgot how good cheese was. It's been a while since I've had any since it was out of my budget.

It's in my best interest not to look around, but I can't stand just sitting here for another moment.

I set my empty plate next to me and get to my feet. Desmond has a huge TV in the sitting area, but I don't know how to use it or where the remote is. I stroll to his bookcase, my curiosity getting the best of me.

A couple of knickknacks and a few framed photos rest alongside books I've never heard of. Some look like fantasy and others historical. He might even have a romance or two, but they all look like they're on the shelf merely for decoration none of the book spines cracked or bent.

Seeing the collection ignites my nosiness, pushing me along, and I meander around the perimeter of his suite, taking my time to check out every inch of his living quarters. I look into his kitchen, smaller than Enzo's, and open each cupboard. He has a stockpile of nuts, dried fruit, crackers, and granola. Nothing sugary or sweet apart from a small container of chocolate-covered raisins. And I can't resist. I snatch the bag and open it, digging in. I pop a handful into my mouth and close my eyes, savoring the sweetness. I discover a cupboard of expensive-looking alcohol and another full of different kinds of tumblers and wine glasses. There's not much else in the kitchen except for a basket of fruit and bread.

I wonder if he might be vegetarian, because I don't see any meat like in Enzo's fridge. It looked like he had raided a fucking butcher shop.

The phone continues to buzz on the table, and I walk past it, only peeking to see twenty-two unread messages. It takes everything in me not to read them. If I give in to the temptation, I won't be able to resist responding. If I do, I doubt anyone will check on me in person.

While Desmond and Enzo might want to, I suspect the other guys will deem me okay because I can text and force them to ignore me for another day or two. They've made it obvious that they don't know what to do since they accidentally kidnapped me. I suspect there is a lot more going on because of it.

The phone lights up, buzzing with a phone call. Again, I resist even touching the device and turn in a circle, trying to decide what else I can search through. I spot the door to Desmond's wardrobe. Peering over my shoulder, I study his bedroom door, squinting as if I can see through it to check for

Desmond coming, and then turn back to the double racks of clothes I spot through the small crack.

Fuck it.

I know I definitely shouldn't go into his wardrobe and snoop around. There's a huge difference from riffling through the common areas like the kitchen and living area, but if I'm going to make my way through anyone's personal belongings and clothes, it's best to stick to a beta.

Desmond's less likely to scream at me for touching his things without permission. Maybe I'll find out something that can help me. Yeah, it's unlikely in a wardrobe, but since I've gotten this far...

A line of tuxedos and suit jackets hang neatly along one wall with pants beneath them. There's a shoe rack with all sorts of dress shoes, and a small display case of glittering jewelry, mostly watches and cufflinks. I can't really imagine Desmond wearing any of this, considering he was only wearing a shirt and jeans when I saw him, but I soon discover he keeps casual clothing in the drawers on the opposite side with the long mirror and accessories like ties, hats, and belts. I stroll the perimeter, touching the different fabrics, wondering what exactly they are. I've never felt fabric so soft.

"Kinsey?" a familiar voice calls through the air. "Fuck, where is she? I thought you said you didn't think she was going to try to leave? I knew you should've blocked the door."

I freeze in my spot, listening as Enzo talks to who I think might be Desmond, though I can't see him.

"Calm the hell down. She hasn't left." I was right. Of course, it would be Desmond. I'm nearly certain that the other two alphas might be avoiding me completely.

I can't really blame them. I don't exactly want to meet them face-to-face either, especially after one of them was about to command my death for being a beta just to get rid of me like they had done to Mr. Clive.

"Kinsey? What are you doing in my wardrobe? Didn't you see the clothing I left you?" Desmond stands in the doorway, his arms folded over his chest. I was too concerned about being quiet and controlling my breathing that I didn't even hear him cross the room.

"What does it look like she's doing? Touching all your shit for fun. You know, baby, it's not going to mess with Desmond. Though, the fact that you're still wearing my shirt might." Enzo stands beside Desmond and drapes his arm across his shoulders. "I guess it was pointless of you getting her something else. She looks good in my stuff anyway." Enzo traces my silhouette with his finger. "Wear whatever you like. I don't mind if you keep borrowing my clothes. Might as well come back to my suite, too."

I knew he was flirting with me before. My body warms at his suggestion, the smirk on his face testing me for a reaction.

His scent grows stronger, his desire clear with the way he drinks me in, and it takes everything in me not to smile back at him. I'd be crazy to do so. Just because he shows me attention means nothing. Someone like him wouldn't ever want someone like me for anything other than a good time. I'm sure his pack has someone lined up, and it won't and can't be me. I have nothing to offer besides my body. Omegas are chosen for alphas for more than that. Usually, territories and alliances with other packs are involved.

"She's thinking about it, brother," Enzo murmurs, speaking to Desmond as if I can't hear him.

It knocks some sense back into me. I look between the two of them, their casual banter stopping fear from rising inside me but also reminding me of who I am in this moment. "I have my own clothes if you guys can just give me my bag back already. I don't know why you don't. My clothes are of no use to you. The other things are purely sentimental, so all you're doing is proving you're dicks and power-hungry." I tighten my hands into fists, trying not to cower back in case my comment sets them off.

Enzo twists his lips and side glances Desmond. "Point taken. It wasn't my decision to keep your bag, but I'll make sure you get it from Wilder. Promise. He was just...looking into some things."

"Yeah, sure. That's it. I know alphas like you guys, and I bet he's just keeping my shit to be a perv. Sniffing my clothes to get off." I huff a breath, the thought angering me. I don't want them touching my belongings as much as they wouldn't want me touching theirs.

Desmond shakes his head, kneading his hand to the back of his neck. "I'll kick his ass if he proves you right, but really, Kinsey. We have nothing to suspect that it's anything like that. You didn't only have clothes."

"So he's keeping my pictures? You're not going to find any-thing. It's pointless. My family has been dead for a while." My chest clenches, and my voice cracks with the words. It's hard to say them out loud, especially to strangers. It makes it seem more real. I've been able to pretend none of it ever happened and that I was not caught in the middle of a feud between my dad and his brother.

"I'm so sorry, Kinsey. I'm sure he didn't know. I promise you'll have them by dinner. You need to join us to meet with my brothers anyway. We'll get everything sorted out and we'll hopefully have a solution to this situation." Desmond shrugs away from Enzo and enters the wardrobe, offering his hand out to me. Something softens on both of their faces, though Enzo remains silent, no longer looking at me. Is it guilt in his eyes? Maybe. I hope so. They should all feel like shit for this.

"I offered you a solution," I murmur, shifting in front of Desmond.

He clasps my hand gently, testing to see if I'll let him touch me. "I know. It's being considered. Until then, why don't you change and freshen up?"

I bob my head, shifting my gaze to Enzo. "Your other two brothers will kick his ass otherwise, right?"

Enzo finally meets my gaze again, his smile returning. "Why does it sound like you want to see how tough I am? Prove my strength?"

I shrug. "If it'll get me what I want. You can encourage them to let me leave. I just need a ride. You can take me anywhere at this point. I don't want to be a bother to you anymore, and

I know how to take care of myself. I've been doing it for two years now."

Something crosses both their faces—pity, maybe—but I ignore their reactions and slide past Enzo and back into the living area of Desmond's suite. Neither of them responds to my comment, and I stroll to the chair and take off the long T-shirt Enzo gave me, keeping my back to both men while I shrug into a much smaller long-sleeved T-shirt and a pair of yoga pants.

I can smell another omega immediately, and everything starts clicking into place. I hadn't realized there was another. No wonder they've been tense. That's why things seem so complicated to them. It is forbidden for a pack to have two omegas like this. But why not just tell me? Why even keep me here this long?

My mind screams to call them out, but now isn't the time to suggest such a thing with only these clothes as proof. It'll get me nowhere. I have nothing to gain for acknowledging that I know why they're isolating me like this.

I try not to react as I turn around, catching both of them staring at me as if I'm growing a second head.

"Damn, Kinsey. You gotta stop doing that." Enzo shifts his weight from foot to foot and rubs his palms over his cheeks. "Especially don't do that in front of my other brothers."

I frown, staring at him in silence for a moment. It's now that I realize my mistake. I just undressed in front of them without even much thought. I hadn't really considered that the act would bother them. It's because I've been living as a beta for two years. No one ever pays attention to us, and...fuck me.

My face flushes with heat, and I swallow and clench and relax my fingers. "I'm so sorry. I haven't even considered my nudity would make you uncomfortable."

Enzo's brows peak on his forehead. "Uncomfortable is the last word that I'd use to describe what I'm feeling."

He's right. Shit. The attraction I felt toward him before comes back in full force, and I find myself taking a step forward. Desmond shoves Enzo, getting between us and acting like a wall. But it does nothing for the wave of desire that crashes through me.

"I swear to God, brother. If you force me to be a cock-block, you won't be able to use your damn dick anytime soon. We don't have time for this. Control yourself." Desmond straightens his shoulders and silently threatens his brother with a fisted hand.

It only sets Enzo off, and I brace for him to swing his fist, but he finally takes a step back. His eyes meet mine from over Desmond's shoulder, and he licks his lips. He knows what his scent did to me, and he's not even sorry about it. He wants me to give him a reaction to go along with what he's done to me.

I refuse to give it.

I won't let this control me. I still have some will left in me. If I get my bag back, I can see if my last pill is in it. Because between them discovering me and now, I have no clue where it went, and I really fucking need it.

"Brothers!" The snap of the deep voice shocks fear inside me. "You were supposed to bring her to me immediately. What is taking you guys so fucking long? Why does it smell like your horny ass in here?"

I take a step back and cower next to the table. I don't even have to see the guy to know his place in the pack. Enzo might be an alpha, but whoever speaks right now is the leader. He is definitely what I would consider a mega alpha, and someone I really don't want to face.

"Wilder, chill. You're scaring her. She's just finishing getting ready." Enzo swivels to stare behind him.

A hulking form towers in the doorway of the suite before a man strides forward. He enters the room without asking, proving my suspicions. I was too scared before to really get a good look at this alpha, and he's at least six inches taller than his brothers. More muscular too. Handsome as hell with his startling blue eyes, now a lot colder than when he confronted Mr. Doyle in the club on my behalf. I bet he regrets it now. I can smell his rage from here. He's pissed, and I'm nearly certain it's just at my existence.

"What the fuck is she wearing?" The man, Wilder, crosses his arms over his chest, glaring at me. At least he doesn't demand the answer from me. I only know I wear another omega's clothing, and if it's someone he claims, then it would explain why he's so worked up.

I wish a sinkhole would open in the floor and swallow me. Desmond made a huge fucking mistake by bringing me the clothes of another omega, especially if she belongs to them. Or maybe Wilder has a complete claim on her, period, and seeing another woman in his omega's clothing will surely piss off any man. Because I'm taking something that doesn't belong to me, even though it wasn't me who decided this.

"It was either Enzo's shirt or this," Desmond says, puffing out his chest to make himself bigger. And damn. An act has never looked so sexy. He's challenging someone who is obviously his superior in his pack. I have never in my life seen a beta challenge so many alphas, even if they are his brothers. "Must I remind you that you still have her bag, you bastard? We tossed her dress because it smelled like the bitch. We needed to get rid of the evidence."

"Had you fucking taken a moment to check in with us, we could've told you that already. You've been far too concerned with the second heist to even consider it. Now back up. She is terrified, and we just managed to get her to relax." Enzo stands beside Desmond, joining the thick wall of muscle that separates me from Wilder. It's enough to get my heart to stop racing, but my chest remains tight.

Wilder scowls, his jaw tightening, sharpening his features. I shrink down even more, climbing under the table as if I'm a scared animal, but all I want to do is get out of his line of sight. He's as bad as Tamsin was when it comes to anger, and I can't stop myself from thinking about what this means. There's no way he's going to let me leave alive if he has a say. He sees me as a threat to his pack, even though I have nothing. I'm no one. He's far too suspicious to even realize it. I bet he would never believe me, even if I could show him the proof.

Wilder pokes his finger into Enzo's chest, refusing to back down. "You know we have fucking priorities for a reason, Enzo. Get your head straight before I—"

"Enough, brothers. This is getting out of hand. We're supposed to be a team. Now, listen. I have something to show you. Why don't you bring the omega and move this conversation somewhere more neutral? The staff brought dinner for us, and I had them set it up in the study." Another man appears in the hallway outside of the suite, but he doesn't enter. His muscles ripple as he stretches his neck, trying to search around to get a look at me. I remain tucked away, clutching onto a chair for dear life. There's no way I'm leaving my spot. Half of them look like they want to devour me as their next meal and the other two look like they want to devour me for fun.

Why did I think that?

Just the thought of their mouths on me adds to my mix of emotions, and I'm sure it's not going to help the situation any.

Silence falls in the room, and I shift, trying to peek out to see if they decided to leave, and I missed it because my pounding head made it impossible for me to hear their fleeting footsteps. I could use a damn miracle and mercy right now.

A leering face pops in front of me, startling me, and I scream and scramble back. Wilder latches his fingers to my ankles and drags me from beneath the table, letting me go when I'm no longer protected. Enzo shoves him, and Desmond quickly scoops me into his arms, spinning me away protectively.

Tears burn my eyes. I bury my face in the crook of Desmond's neck. My sheer terror sends my mind spinning, and I can't stop thinking about my family and my parents. I can't stop thinking about my uncle and how he let his rage get the best of him. How he nearly destroyed me. How he destroyed everything else in my life. I'm nearly certain that Wilder is about to do it all over again. But this time, I won't make it out alive. I'll never be able to recover.

And I know why he does it. I know there is an omega in this household, and he wouldn't ever do something to risk her life or heart. If only it didn't mean he'd have to destroy my life in the process.

"Arsenio, get him out of here. I will bring her, but not until he cools off." Desmond clutches onto me, stroking his big hand down the length of my back, trying to soothe my trembling body. I've never felt so weak as I do in this moment. It's as if the last two years never happened. It's as if I've forgotten how to take care of myself and how to be on my own. These men have gotten to me and cracked me open as if I'm glass and at their disposal to shatter, their carelessness ensuring I end up in a million pieces.

"Come on, Wilder. They're right. You're not thinking clearly, and like I said, I have something to show you. Let's look at it first." Arsenio remains even in tone, his ability not to react impressing me. "You two wait a couple of minutes. Just let us get some space between us. When we go to the study, keep her in the corner."

I don't watch as Arsenio leads Wilder out of Desmond's room. I sense Enzo's presence nearby, and a soft hand touches my shoulder. I refuse to look at him. I refuse to speak or to show my face. As long as I keep my head buried against Desmond, I can pretend none of this is happening. I can pretend that I'm not moments away from the end of my life.

"I'm so sorry, Kinsey. My brother is an asshole. He doesn't like strangers. He just needs a moment to see how unthreatening you are." Enzo leans in, his breath tickling my ear. "We won't let him hurt you."

I don't respond to him. I can't.

Desmond whispers for him to give us a bit of space and to head out. Surprisingly, Enzo listens to his brother, and Desmond waits another thirty seconds before adjusting me in his arms and carrying me from his suite.

I don't look around. I shut down, just thinking about the good moments of my life the best I can. It's all I can do to stop all of the bullshit from eating at me. Because I know there's a lot to come, and I'll have no control except for how I handle it. How I react. And even then, that's iffy.

"Don't worry, Kinsey. I already have a plan. I'll present it to my brothers, and we'll get you out of here and somewhere safe, so you never have to deal with him again." Desmond keeps his voice low, his whispering words helping to ease the panic refusing to release me.

"Thank you. I just want to get out of your way. I swear you don't have to worry about me. I'm no one to anyone." At least, not anymore. I was someone to my parents. They had picked me out a pack they felt was worthy as well. But I never did get the chance to know them. My uncle—

"Shut the door. Now." Wilder's voice cuts through my thoughts, the heat of his still lingering anger slicing through me.

I cling tighter onto Desmond, refusing to look.

Someone will have to pry me out of his arms at this point. My muscles clench, my body frozen. There is just something about Wilder's command that gets to me. He sounds even more aggressive than before. But why? What did Arsenio show him?

"Set her in the corner and look at this." Wilder growls with his words, smacking his hands on something—probably a desk. I know what the sound of palms slapping against wood sounds like from the many times Madame Tasmin lashed out at someone or something.

I clutch onto Desmond, releasing a soft whimper into his ear. I can't help it. "Please, no. Please."

He runs his hand over my back again. "What did I tell you, Kinsey?"

"We won't let that jackoff hurt you, baby," Enzo says, answering his question for me. "Just take a breath. He's always a moody son of a bitch."

"Stop coddling her and look. Now!" Wilder's voice startles me.

I release Desmond and can't snatch him tight enough before he sets me down in the corner of the study in front of a recliner.

"I'm right here, Kinsey. I'm not going anywhere. We'll get this all figured out and settled, okay?" Desmond whispers the words into my ear, rubbing my shoulder gently, the gesture barely managing to keep my heart from exploding from my chest.

But I'm nearly certain there will be no figuring any of this out. The way Wilder looks at me makes me nervous as hell.

I glance at the door, silently counting how many feet I have to run to get out of this room. There are fewer feet between me and the door than there are between me and his brothers, and I decide to risk it. Is it incredibly stupid? Absolutely. But I have nothing left to lose. I don't know where I'll go, but I have to figure it out and soon.

Desmond joins his brothers, and they hunch around a computer monitor sitting on the desk with a window behind it. If I make it out of this place now, I might still have enough light to get at least some distance between me and them.

I watch them in silence, waiting for the four of them to finally release me from their stares.

This is it.

It's now or never. I know I won't find the courage again.

I lunge from the chair and race across the room, counting on the fact that a desk blocks their way. Flinging the door open, I dart into the hall and head in the direction I think we came from.

I rush into the first room on the right, wanting to hide as they hopefully run past me, thinking that I would make a straight shot to where the elevator is. Searching around the room, I smell the scent of Wilder immediately. I've made a huge mistake. He's going to murder me for even stepping foot in his suite.

Footsteps thud outside the door, and I glance around, bolting toward a balcony door. It might be too far to jump from, but I know how to climb.

"Oh shit. Who the hell are you? I knew my brothers were up to something." The feminine voice steals my attention away from the window, and I jerk to look at a sinewy, lanky girl an inch or two taller than me who might be a couple of years younger than I am. Her pale blond hair cascades over her shoulders, reaching her waist. Standing with her hands on her hips, she stares at me with bright hazel eyes from Wilder's wardrobe. And she's not just any girl. I recognize her scent. It's all over me. She's an omega like I am.

It dawns on me that she said her brothers were up to something. These guys have a little sister.

Now nothing makes sense.

The door slams, and I freeze, the wave of intense vetiver and somethings smokier like paprika assaults me, stealing away my senses.

A heavy hand grabs my shoulder, yanking me back until I hit Wilder's hard, muscular chest. "What the fuck do you think you're doing?"

"Wilder, stop it. Put her down. You know better than to touch someone like that who doesn't belong to you. You've told me that a million times." The girl speaks from the wardrobe, her voice raising with her words.

Wilder freezes in his tracks, his hold tightening around me. "Holly, you're supposed to be in your room."

"You can't tell me what to do. You're not my alpha." She challenges her brother, taking a couple steps closer, her hazel eyes shining with more flecks of green than brown. "Now, put her down and explain yourself. I know that Dad—"

"Arsenio, take Kinsey. I need to have a word with Holly." Wilder spins and tosses me as if I weigh nothing at all at his other brother. "Don't let Desmond or Enzo get near her. Shit just changed. Meet me in the study. Do not take your hands off her. Do you understand? Everything counts on it."

Arsenio grunts his agreement and tosses me over his shoulder. I'm getting really tired of being treated like this, but what else am I going to do?

These alphas can overpower me so easily.

I'm going to have to think of something else. I'm going to have to really think about what it's going to take to get out of here and use my order to do so.

I have to. If I don't, I'll never get another chance at life. These guys will be my demise.

Chapter 7

Kinsey

Flirty Alphas

I can't believe this shit. I went from glowering at Arsenio standing like a statue in the study to being locked in the bathroom. He gave me some couch cushions to lay on, told me the counter could be used as a table, and the fucking toilet as a chair. Could be worse. They could've locked me in the closet and gave me a fucking bucket or some shit.

Even though Arsenio apologized profusely, and I almost believed him, it doesn't change the circumstances and why I'm here. They don't trust me to stay alone in one of their rooms and needed time to discuss things. Scream about these things and about me. I think I even heard glass breaking at one point.

But that was two nights ago. Maybe three. I can't remember anymore as I just sit in my spot without moving, staring at my untouched plate of steamed veggies, cold chicken, and a roll. I don't feel much like eating, and I'm certain the suppressant pills have completely left my system. I forgot what being around alphas unmedicated does to me. My body wants to flood me with hormones, reminding me of my order. Coping with the sudden rise of my emotions along with how the guys treat me like a prisoner... I'm about to break shit around here too. What am I even thinking? They're not just treating me like a prisoner. I am a prisoner. I need to remember that.

A strange buzz hums nearby, and I stare around the bathroom, trying to figure out where the noise comes from. Arsenio never left me a phone, but the buzzing definitely sounds like one. I scoot forward, lifting up some of the towels I've been using as a blanket. The hum stops, turning the silence even heavier. It drives me crazy, because I know I wasn't hearing things. Lifting up the plate, I look at the tray. I stab my fork into the veggies, stirring them around. Another buzz vibrates against my leg, and I study the metal carafe. I lift it up and glance into it. The fucking thing is empty, and a cell phone hides within it.

What the actual fuck? Did Desmond sneak me contraband? Someone did.

Sexy Beast: My brothers are dicks. I want to make it up to you.
Sexy Beast: What's your favorite dessert?

I stare at the text message on the lock screen of Desmond's phone. Sexy beast? Stupid Enzo. This shouldn't make me smile, but it does. I'm still pissed off, though. His brother locked me in a fucking bathroom, and he hasn't even come to bug me.

Me: Desmond? What's going on? It's been weeks. Save me. You're obviously the only one capable of handling me. I need you.

I bite my lip, clutching the phone in anticipation. There isn't a point in trying to yell at him through a text message, and deep down, I know he'd be here if it weren't for his brothers. I can't resist punishing him, though.

Sexy Beast: Baby, really? I can handle you better than any of my fuckhead brothers.

Me: Come on, Des. Don't play with me. I know it's you. You don't have to fake being Arsenio. I'm so over alphas right now. I need you. I'm lonely, and my mom always told me betas were best for comfort.

Sexy Beast: Seriously, Kinsey? It's Enzo. Why you gotta fuck with my head?

Me: Oh, Enzo. I had no idea. I'm sorry. The contact said Sexy Beast. I thought you were Dickhead.

Sexy Beast: Dickhead? That's Wilder. Plus, none of my brothers would ask you your favorite dessert or ensure it gets to you. Don't you think Sexy Beast is more fitting anyway? I mean, look at me.

A photo pops up on the screen with Enzo pulling up his shirt to reveal his abs. I glimpse the table he stands in front of, catching sight of a collection of mini desserts like cupcakes, fruit tarts, and chocolate truffles.

Me: You're blocking the real goods. Can I have a picture of the desserts?
Sexy Beast: …
Me: You asked me what kind of dessert I like.
Sexy Beast: Damn it, baby. Your teasing is going to get us both in trouble.

I can't stop the smile stretching across my face. I wish I could see his reaction. I know he's fishing for a compliment, but I refuse to give him one. Not now. I know that it's Wilder who commanded I get locked in this bathroom, but Enzo hasn't even come by. I shouldn't hold it against him, except I know better than to take his bait. I don't know what kind of game he's playing or if he's just messing with me because he's bored.

The phone buzzes and another picture pops on the screen with Enzo lying on the table with two cupcakes resting on his pecs. I flush and laugh, enjoying his teasing way too much. Setting the phone down, I decide not to respond. I can't. The emotions coursing through me feel too good, and I don't want any part of this madness. I just want out of this fucking room, and if he wants to know what kind of dessert I like, he can come here and talk to me face-to-face.

The phone buzzes again with another picture in the message.

Sexy Beast: What about this?

Enzo stands shirtless behind the table, the deep V of his hips drawing my attention to where the red velvet cake blocks the view of his naked body. Heat blossoms between my legs, and I squeeze my eyes shut and set the phone down, once again not responding.

Sexy Beast: Baby?

Why do I keep torturing myself by looking? It's as if something draws me in and restrains me. I shouldn't feel this attraction toward Enzo, but I do. And he feels it too, because I know he wouldn't call me anything other than Kinsey otherwise.

Sexy Beast: U OK?

This time, I slide the phone away and watch it smack against the cupboard beneath the counter. I turn over and lay back down on the makeshift bed, pulling the throw blanket and towels over me.

The phone buzzes again and again. My lack of response must be driving Enzo crazy. It drives me crazy too. I just...I can't deal with this. His flirting is getting to me in a good way. I know better than to allow him in.

Muffled voices sound from outside the bathroom, and I remain in my spot, pulling my knees to my chest. Something crashes. Glass shatters again. I tense, half-expecting the door to explode off its hinges.

"Get out!" We both know you can't be here," Arsenio hollers, his voice booming through the door.

"I don't fucking care!" A bang sounds on the door with Enzo's words.

A couple more thuds startle me. Curling in on myself, I train my eyes on the door, waiting for it to crash down with the fight between Arsenio and Enzo. My heart races, the anticipation as painful as the not knowing what to expect. Footsteps grow louder, and I quickly turn over, facing my back to the door.

Silence blankets over the commotion, and the door creaks open, the soft whoosh making me hold my breath.

I expect Enzo to come tiptoeing into the bathroom, but it's not him. I've already become accustomed to his scent and the fresh minty, woodsy fragrance. It's not Desmond or Wilder either. It's Arsenio. I guess he won the fight with his brother.

"Kinsey, it's me. I'm sorry for the commotion with my brother. I hope we didn't scare you. Things are a bit tense right now." The scent of apples wafts through the bathroom, Arsenio's fragrance captivating me. It's more intense than be-fore...or I'm more aware. He surprisingly doesn't act gruff and distant like I expected.

I open and close my mouth, trying to think of the millions of things I have to say, but I can't get my brain to function as his shadow casts over the wall, and I spot his reflection in the mirror, peering down at me.

Rolling over, I stare up at the handsome alpha, meeting his hazel eyes. His features mimic Wilder's the most, but he shares the same jawline as Enzo and straight smile as Desmond. He breaks eye contact, taking a moment to drink me in, his muscles flexing with my attention on him.

"Would you like to come out for a bit?" he asks, encouraging me to respond to him. "I'm sure you could use some exercise. I'm sorry this has taken so long. It was never my intent to keep you locked in here. My brothers and I have an agreement, and your presence…tests us." Arsenio's voice remains even, but his scent grows stronger as he bends down beside me. I don't move an inch, keeping my face toward the ceiling. Something clinks—the fork on my uneaten plate of food—and he moves it, setting it on the counter. "Was your meal unsatisfactory?" He's prying for information to see why I haven't eaten.

I don't respond again as I shut out the world around me. I'm far too proud to make this easy on him despite the palpable attraction emanating between us. I don't know what he was expecting coming in here acting kind, as if I'm not a prisoner, but I won't let him think it's okay because he's acting friendly.

"Enzo brought you some cupcakes. They're a bit messy, so you can eat them at the desk. Maybe we can talk for a bit. What do you say?" Arsenio leans down, darkening the world as he blocks out the light with his tall frame.

He crowds my space, completely oblivious to the fact that I don't want him anywhere near me. His scent fucks with my head as my order runs rampant, free from the suppressants holding it back. It's been too long since I've had to deal with being an omega, and I was warned by Gillian that once I stopped the pills, things would be super intense for a while until I allowed myself to go into heat again.

I lick my lips, inhaling a soft breath. "No, thank you. Just leave me alone or get the courage to do whatever you want to do. This is bullshit, keeping me in a fucking bathroom. I'd rather you turn me into the authorities. It would be better than this."

"Sorry, sugar. I can't do either. Now, let's get you up. You'll be happier. Promise." Arsenio surprises me by sliding his hands beneath my body and lifting me. Holding me under his arm like a ragdoll, he carries me from the bathroom. I screech and smack at his legs, realizing just how close I'm to his hardening body. I'm setting him off.

"What the actual fuck? You can't treat me like this." I squirm and thrash, forcing him to tighten his hold on me.

"And you can't just waste away in the bathroom. I understand that you are unhappy and frightened, but things are going to change." Arsenio sets me in the rolling chair at the desk. He slides the ceramic plate closer, putting the cupcakes right in my line of sight in front of my nose. "You aren't going to be treated like a prisoner any longer. We just...need you to promise not to try to escape. If you agree, then you can have all the cupcakes you want."

Damn him. He's not bribing me with cupcakes.

My stomach roars in anticipation, the sugary frosting smelling just as good as the marshmallow caramel scent wafting from him to me, his amusement over my reaction consuming me.

Shit. Who knew I would be so easy to sway? Fucking delicious cupcakes. I'm nearly certain there are the exact ones Enzo modeled for me, which doesn't help.

"Here, let me help you." Arsenio offers me a smile. "Sweets always cheer me up too." His offering sends butterflies fluttering inside me. I have to be careful, though. Arsenio might be responding to my pheromones and my sudden appreciation over the act of Enzo and nothing more. Now I feel a bit bad that I started ignoring Enzo. The poor dickhead.

Why I do? I know I shouldn't. This whole situation is complete bullshit, and no one is giving me answers. No one is telling me what's going to happen. Yet, they're acting kind. It's been so long since an alpha or pack has done that...I'm embarrassingly desperate. Pack and alpha issues, and all that crap.

I fold my arms over my chest and lean back in the chair. "No, thank you. I'm fine without your dessert bribery. I'm not that easy." My stomach screams, the rumble catching Arsenio's attention, calling out my lie. Stupid, treacherous stomach.

Arsenio growls in his throat, the noise sounding so incredibly sexy. It makes me hate him even more. Someone so attractive shouldn't be a monstrous kidnapper and a tolerable alpha in one. It fucks with my head.

"Don't be stubborn, sugar. If you want them, eat them. You deserve a dozen after everything. It might even sweeten you up a bit to me. I know you're angry and confused." Arsenio picks up one of the red velvet cupcakes and tugs at the wrapper. Pinching a piece off, he holds it to my lips.

I heave a couple of breaths and relent, opening my mouth and surprising him by chomping down on his fingers. He jerks away, spinning and tensing. I brace for him to shove me. Maybe even hit me. It's what Madame Tamsin would do. But he only growls again and tightens his fingers into fists.

I hum under my breath and lick the cream cheese frosting from my lips, satisfied by my quick thinking to fight back while getting what I want. Reaching for another cupcake, I attempt to pick it up only to have Arsenio take the plate away from me.

He narrows his eyes. "I don't think so, sugar. How about we try this again? I want to help you."

I glare right back at him, pursing my lips. He's crazy if he thinks he can just try to persuade me to be nice by taking away a cupcake. "It's your hand on the line. I don't know why you just won't let me feed myself."

Arsenio tears another piece of the cupcake off, gingerly offering it to me. "I'm trying to prove to you that I'm kind and won't hurt you. Let me show you that I'm not a bad guy. It's just...the situation is complicated. It's why I want to talk. I ran your photos through our recognition database and—"

I jerk forward and lock my hand around his wrist, stopping him from yanking away. I glide my tongue over his fingers as I draw the piece of cupcake into my mouth, sucking his fingers in a way that sets him off. I can smell the potent fragrance of his growing lust, like baking apples and rainfall, fresher and fruitier than any of his brothers.

I peek up at him, smacking my lips together. "And what? What did you find?"

Arsenio blinks a few times, whatever thought on his mind vanishing. His biceps bulge and flex, and he offers me another bite of the cupcake like it's the only thing he currently knows how to do. Pleasure courses through me. I never knew how easy an alpha could be shut down. I don't have that kind of experience as it's never worked before. Blood-related alphas don't act the same way. They can sense a related omega's pheromones, but it doesn't mess with them the way a potential mate's does.

It usually wouldn't mess with a bonded alpha either, but now I know we're both unbonded. I'm absolutely certain of that, because the scent of the other omega belongs to their sister. This might change things. They're going to have to. I don't like the way Wilder acts, and I desperately need Arsenio to challenge him like Enzo and Desmond. He might destroy me otherwise.

"And?" I repeat, letting him absently feed me another piece of the sugary cupcake.

Shaking his head, Arsenio clears his throat and steps back. His face flushes, his pretty hazel eyes look more green as they shift from me to the computer.

"I'm sorry. What was I saying?" Arsenio perches on the desk, scrubbing his palms over his freshly shaven cheeks. I can't see any similarities to Wilder apart from their noses and the shape of their oval eyes. He's more clean-cut and proper than Desmond and more tense than Enzo. Controlled. Aware.

There is nothing more that I want to do than fix that. I just don't know how far I can push him.

Or if I even should.

"You were just telling me how you and your brothers have agreed to drive me into the nearest town, give me a couple hundred bucks, and send me on my way." I dart my hand out and snatch another cupcake from the plate before he can react.

I shove it in my mouth and chew, probably looking like a wild animal or a scorned woman on a mission, but I can't help it. It tastes so fucking good. It helps with the ache in my stomach. I can resist eating bland chicken and veggies. But dessert? It's my undoing.

Arsenio gapes at me in shock, tilting his head, unsure how to respond or what to do with me. And he won't stop staring at my frosting-lined mouth.

I don't even care if I look a mess. Serves him right for trying to manipulate me.

"I was hoping your personality would match how sweet your scent is, but goddamn it, woman. You are so full of spice." Arsenio bows closer, capturing my gaze with his own. "I didn't think anyone liked sweets more than me. And seeing it on you like this?" Reaching up, he wipes his thumb over my bottom lip, scraping the red chocolate from my face to pop his thumb into his mouth to suck.

My nipples harden at his gesture, and I push back in the rolling chair, nearly falling. Arsenio catches the arm and drags me closer, trapping me between his long legs, so I can't move. He's tall enough that his hardening bulge is only inches away from my face. And holy hell. He's right about his enjoyment of sweets. He smells like apple pie, brown sugar, and caramel now, his fresh scent shifting to a mouthwatering gourmand with his blazing desire. I wonder if his skin tastes as sweet. I didn't really get a chance to find out when I bit him.

"There's a lot that you don't know about me." I refuse to break my stare, not wanting to give him the satisfaction of getting under my skin first. We're now at war with each other, our bodies yearning to be closer while our minds remain stubborn.

"Then tell me." Arsenio rests his big hand on my shoulder, spinning my dark hair around his fingers. "It'll help."

I ease the chair back enough to get to my feet, meeting his eyes more at his level, so he no longer looks down on me. Licking my lips, I taste the frosting of the cupcake. He watches my every move, and I hope it's enough to distract him. Because I don't want to tell him anything. He has his secrets, and I have mine. We don't need to share. He could just let me go.

"It's nothing. There's nothing really to tell. I don't have a pack or a family. I've been taking suppressant pills to pass as a beta. But then I was caught. Your brother was there, you know. He defended me. Did you know that? I know you guys were casing the Vixen Lounge." I lean even closer, stopping my mouth only inches away from his.

"What are you talking about?" Arsenio's eyes search mine, flicking back-and-forth, his pupils dilating as he once again looks at my mouth before easing toward me another inch.

"Ask him. It's his fucking fault. He should've just let Madame Tamsin's client be a dick to me, and I probably wouldn't have fallen and spilled the damn pills I had just bought. I would still have my life. I would still have my freedom. Now I'm fucking stuck in this enormous palace as a prisoner in this tiny ass bathroom with fucking assholes who refuse to even tell me why they won't let me go. If it's about your sister, you don't have to fucking worry about me. It's none of my business. I know you're hiding her, and I don't even care why. I'm sure she's facing some fucked up shit if she's anything like me." My emotions get the best of me, and I try to pull away from Arsenio, but the chair traps me.

His hand slides around my waist, steadying me, and he frowns. "Kinsey..."

"Please. I'll do anything. Just let me go." I clutch his face, getting closer into his personal space. I can use his own desire against him. I know he wants to kiss me. I know he's attracted to me. Maybe if I give him what he craves, he'll finally just let me have my way.

Crashing my mouth to his, I kiss him hard and passionately, gliding my tongue into his mouth as I twist my fingers into his dark blond hair, playing on his every need as an alpha.

Moaning, he falls for my charm and kisses me back, his ability to see clearly now fogged with everything fighting between us. I know I'm walking a dangerous line, and I don't even care. I have always done what I've had to ever since my uncle destroyed everything. He broke me. He broke me so he could try to put the pieces back together, but I managed to crawl away even at my weakest and rebuild myself. I was never going to let him hurt me again. And these guys can't hurt me either.

Breaking away from his mouth, I kiss down his jaw and glide my tongue over his neck, nipping his skin. I reach between us and unfasten his belt, slipping my hand into his pants to feel his cock flexing as I wrap my fingers around it and pull it free.

"Kinsey, what are you doing?" Arsenio asks, his voice deep and throaty with his desire. He doesn't stop me, though. He reaches out and caresses his fingers over my hard nipple through my shirt. "We shouldn't do this."

"Says who? I want to do this. Don't you? I think that's all that matters, right?" I explore the length of his hard-on, rubbing my fingers over his tip, feeling the slipperiness of his pre-cum on my fingers. His sweetness grows in intensity, and goosebumps prickle over my skin. A part of me screams to get myself together. He's the one holding me captive. He's more like Wilder than he's like Desmond or Enzo.

But he's here. He's the one in charge of me now, and I know he has more influence.

"You have no idea how badly I want this, sugar. I want to taste you and find out if you're just as you smell right now. Fucking delectable." Arsenio reaches for me, grabbing the waistband of my yoga pants to bring me even closer.

I kiss him again, trying to lose myself in the moment, shivering as his fingers tease into the front of my pants to touch between my legs. My whole body buzzes, and I gasp and break away as he slides a finger over my wetness but doesn't dip it inside me. He only brings it out and holds it to his lips, gliding his tongue over his finger, tasting me just as he said he wanted to.

His desire for me heats my own, and I realize how starving for companionship I've been, isolated and faking my way through life. Omegas aren't meant to be alone. We need the interaction. We need everything an alpha has to offer us and the closeness a pack can provide.

My heart hurts knowing that this is just a game. What am I even doing?

A tear splashes on my cheek, surprising the both of us. Arsenio stiffens and jerks away, his eyes widening as he drinks me in. I don't know what to do, so I push away from him and scramble back to the bathroom. He tries to chase after me, but I beat him and slam the door in his face. I lock it and return to my spot on the floor, pulling my knees up to my chest.

"Kinsey, I'm sorry. I let things get too far. Please, open the door. We really need to talk." Arsenio taps his fingers on the wood. "Please."

Ignore him and lie back down, closing my eyes.

I don't know what to do or what to think anymore. This is all so crazy.

"Kinsey, please," Arsenio says, not leaving like I expect him to.

"Leave me alone. We have nothing to talk about. I was using you to get you to let me leave, but it didn't work. So go away.

Don't bother coming back until you guys figure out what you're going to do. Just make it quick. This shit is torture. I've already been through enough." I turn my back on the door, waiting for Arsenio to respond.

He doesn't. I hear his footsteps grow quiet as he walks away.

I should like being alone. I should relax because he didn't put up a fight.

But now I just feel empty.

I feel the same way I had the day I ran.

I feel hopeless.

Chapter 8

Kinsey

Secrets

The door to the bathroom swings open, startling me. Wilder looms in the doorway, his arms crossed over his broad chest. He clenches his jaw, and a small dimple peeks out on his stubbly cheek. Staring at me in silence, he shifts on his feet. His muscles ripple and flex with his movements, and I notice a change in breathing. I think he might be trying to hold his breath.

"All right, you little brat. Get up and follow me. Don't do anything stupid. You remember what happened the last time. If you had just minded your business and let us work things out, you could've been out of here. Now, I can't fucking let you leave, and my brothers are going crazy." Wilder steps forward and points at me. "We don't have all day. I need to set some rules."

A part of me wants to be the brat he just called me, but fear sizzles across my skin at his looming presence, and I do as he asks and get to my feet. I can't test this man like I can the others. It's obvious he wants nothing to do with me, forcing himself to be in my presence because he knows his brothers desire to do it instead. He'd know. Their scents give them away, especially to Wilder, if he's acting as their leader.

"What do you mean you're not going to let me leave? You can't do that. If you have a problem with me, then just turn me into the local authorities." I twist my fingers together, my nerves quaking my voice. I should keep my mouth shut, but I just am so fucking tired of not getting answers.

Wilder grabs me by the elbow and forces me to stride beside him, my legs practically running to keep up with his quick movements. "We are the authorities and part of the Saint Vista Pack Regimes. I can keep you here, and I will. There's no fucking way I'm going to risk you saying something about Holly."

So it is about his sister. I knew something was up. But I have more important things to think about, like how the hell I'm going to overpower this man twice my size to run away. Even if he doesn't think I'll make it, I won't know unless I try again.

"We have too much on the line. I will not endanger my sister like that. Not with your history. I've learned all about you, Kinsey." Wilder struts from the study and down the hallway.

I try my best to look around, drinking in the decorations, hoping that it will help me recognize where we're going.

"My history? Sure, whatever. There's no possible way you have learned everything about me, asshole." I struggle against his strength, sliding my feet on the floor, not wanting to make it easy on him. Now that I'm no longer trapped in the bathroom, I find my will to fight.

"I've learned enough. I know about your family and your chosen pack. I know about the fire and the murder-suicides. I know that you went missing." Wilder swivels and snatches me, yanking me to him to lift me onto his shoulder, deciding that I'm not worth dragging.

I scream and smack my hands to his back, thrashing and bucking. He's a monster. All the stuff he says? He still has no fucking clue. The fire my parents died in was gang-related, tied to my uncle's shady business. And the murder-suicide? It was purely murder. My uncle staged things. "There's only one person that could possibly miss me and not for reasons you think. I would rather die before I go back. I'd rather die before you forced me to fucking stay here with you. Just let me go. I'll make your life a living hell otherwise."

Threatening him is probably the dumbest thing I could ever do, but I'm angry. I'm pissed the fuck off. I'm hurt and scared, and I have no idea how to even handle the situation. How he even found a link to my past, no matter how wrong the papers got it, is beyond me.

It's all just a cover-up.

Wilder yells, his voice loud and booming, and he swings his arm, punching his fist to the center of a framed painting, shattering the glass and ripping the canvas. The scent of his anger stabs into me in a violent wave, stealing my breath for a second.

I gasp and sob, my whole body losing its shit, making it impossible for me not to cry. I can't even think anymore. Whatever plan I had rushes out of my reach, leaving me drowning in the potent scent of Wilders volatile dominance. He triggers me so badly that I gag, my body wanting to revolt against me.

My heartbeat pounds in my ears and I shut down, no longer fighting. I can't. If I try, I know I'll die. And right now, the fear of death overwhelms me. I can't find the will to do anything. He's won.

"You son of a bastard, Wilder!" Big hands lock onto my waist, yanking me away from Wilder.

A figure blurs in my periphery, and something crashes into the wall. Glass shatters, and the quick thuds of fists hitting muscles sound in my ears. My eyes blur with my tears, and I can't get a clear view of anything unfolding before me. All I know is that I'm about to be in the middle of a fight for dominance. One of Wilder's brothers challenges him in my honor, and that'll surely only lead to my demise.

"You're a dead man, brother. I don't know what the fuck you think you're doing, but I have had enough of your attitude. You cannot treat Kinsey like this. You're acting as if she's some sort of threat when she's clearly not. You're so fucking far out of line with this bullshit. I won't stand for it." Enzo growls with the words, and Wilder shouts. The world spins as whoever holds me relocates me down the hallway. My whole body shudders with my uncontrollable sobbing, and a gentle hand rubs between my shoulder blades.

"You're not our leader. We're a team, and you'll recognize your place. If you can't, don't think I won't challenge you. Right now, you're acting like fucking Dad." Arsenio's sharp tone shocks energy through me. Whatever happened between us was enough to push him away from the bullheadedness of Wilder.

A part of me prays that he follows through with his threat. Another part of me wants to watch the man who scared me get the shit beat out of him. But the most dominant part of me wants to break down and never recover. I want the world to swallow me whole. I just want all of this shit to end. I don't know what I've done in my life to deserve such a fate, but I'm over it.

The noise of the fight diminishes, and Desmond enters into a room I haven't been in. It's feminine and smells like his sister, the scent enough to calm me down. There's just something about it that makes me feel safe, and it might be because she stood up for me without even knowing me. I wonder what's going on with these guys. They're obviously hiding her for some reason. If someone would just explain, then maybe things wouldn't be so tough.

"I'm so sorry, Kinsey. He was not to approach you like that. There is no excuse for his behavior, and he'll be held accountable and punished for it by my brothers. We're equal in our pack. This is unacceptable." Desmond sets me on the edge of a queen-sized bed, the blankets neatly made and fresh like laundry detergent. They've been recently changed, and the scent of his sister just happens to linger on other things. But the room is void of anything personal. There are no pictures or clothing. Nothing that declares someone lives here. It confuses the hell out of me.

I hiccup, my sobs subsiding, and Desmond sits beside me and drapes his arm over my shoulders. He continues to rub my arm, trying his best to smooth out the trembles seizing my body.

"Try to take a breath with me. In and out. Inhale...one, two, three. Now exhale...one, two, three. That's good. Do it again." Desmond leans forward and meets my gaze, inhaling and exhaling a breath alongside me until my chest loosens and my muscles relax.

I open and close my mouth, my voice hoarse. "Th-thanks," I say, stuttering, my words cracking. "Can I please have some water?"

Desmond bobs his head and abandons me, heading toward the bathroom. I hear him run the faucet and return with a small glass of the sink water. Instead of handing it to me, he slowly holds it to my lips, waiting for me to take a sip.

He waits until I swallow a couple of times before finally letting me hold it, and I gulp until it's empty and gasp for breath. Rubbing my knee, Desmond soothes me in an unexpected way. I lean into him, focusing on his breathing, using it to adjust my own.

A yell echoes outside the room, the fight continuing, drawing closer. I reach out and grip Desmon's hand. The door crashes open with a bang, hitting the wall. Yelping, I climb into Desmond's lap in fear, burying my head in the crook of his neck, silently begging him to protect me.

"Make it stop," I whisper, mostly to the universe.

"I got you, pretty girl. You're safe. Look around. I told you my brothers would handle it." Desmond leans away from me, trying to get me to ease away from his neck, my tears dampening his skin.

Someone thuds on the floor, and I recognize Wilder's groan. A thump muffles over my quick breathing. The air thickens with scents of the alphas, their presence demanding attention from me. My mind begs me to look, but my body wants none of it.

"Come on, Kinsey. Just a peek." Desmond taps his fingers to my back, encouraging me to listen to him.

I flutter my eyelashes, clearing my vision of tears.

"You better fucking apologize, Wilder. And mean it. You've already done enough damage. We were supposed to talk to her together." Arsenio's deep voice helps with my nerves, his scent of cinnamon apple reminding me of our closeness. He's pissed off, but not at me. The spice to his scent reflects his protectiveness.

I finally turn my head and peek at him hovering over Wilder on his knees. Enzo stands behind him, looking just as fierce and smelling like pepper and vetiver, his masculine fragrance pricking goosebumps over my skin. Damn it. I've never seen anything so hot. He doesn't even have to take off his shirt like in the flirty pictures he sent me to turn me on.

Wilder pushes up. "You guys are already acting like—"

Kicking out, Enzo knocks his boot into Wilder's back, forcing him to face plant in front of us. "This isn't about our behavior. It's about yours. Now, shut up and apologize, brother. Your insolence is embarrassing as fuck. You know your behavior was wrong, so alpha-up and accept it. Apologize, or we're going to be here all day."

Wilder punches his fist to the floor, the thud muffled by the decorative rug. "Goddamn it. I will remember this, you fuckers. I won't go easy on you next time."

Arsenio points at me. "Apologize to Kinsey now!" His yell rings so loudly that I'm certain everyone in this gigantic palace could hear. My eyes widen as I flick my attention to him. Wow. He's so fucking hot too. I could get used to this...

What am I thinking? I can't get used to it. This is almost over. I can feel it in my bones. This situation is far from permanent. I'm letting their pheromones get to my head. It's hard to be smart when I'm exhausted by everything—not physically but mentally.

Heaving a sigh, Wilder bows his head, refusing to look at me. His fingers dig into the carpet. Redness shades his neck, his ego now broken. The scent of his shame confuses me. I wish I could decipher if his shame comes from his actions or because his brothers bested him.

Silence fills the room as everyone stares at Wilder expectantly. I'd think this was the hardest thing he has ever had to do if I didn't know any better. I'm sure whatever happened with his sister led to his attitude now. I want to feel sorry for him in this moment, knowing what this does to his very nature as an alpha, but mostly, I want him to just get it over with and leave.

Shuddering, Wilder finally glances up, catching my gaze. The whites of his eyes redden with his emotions, turning the blue even more startling. He clears his throat, flaring his nostrils. "You have my sincerest apology, Kinsey. It's not your fault that you're here, and it's unfair of me to treat you as if it is. Will you please forgive me?"

I furrow my brows, pursing my lips. I'm surprised by his apology. I had expected a half-hearted sorry or for him to twist it in a way that would prove he's only sorry that he's in this position.

Staring at me in silence, Wilder waits for my response. "Please?"

My heart skips a beat at how sincere he sounds. I nearly believe it, but I know better. He just wants to manipulate his brothers to get them off his back. The second he's able to, he might smother me with a pillow or some shit. I don't trust him not to, especially because he was forced into apologizing instead of doing so because he realizes he's in the wrong.

"Thank you. I'll forgive you if you let me leave immediately. You admitted it was your fault that I'm here, and that I don't belong here. You obviously don't want me here, which is fine, so let's make things easy. Give me a ride to the city, and you'll never see or hear from me again. Your secret is safe." My voice comes out stronger than I thought possible. Is it a good thing? Not exactly.

It looks like I might have just barely missed the detonator on Wilder's asshole alpha switch. It takes Arsenio towering beside him to get him not to react with more than a scowl at my response. I don't care if my forgiveness comes with stipulations. His apology isn't exactly genuine either.

"Why don't you join us in the sitting area, sugar? We can discuss everything now that we're all together." Arsenio steps forward and offers his hand out to me, remaining even in tone. He manages to swallow his anger toward Wilder so much so that all I can smell is his apple and rain shower scent without the spice.

"Are you sure about that? Are we really going to have a discussion, or are you going to just tell me what happens to me now? Because it's unfair to me. I'm not yours to boss around and control. I also want nothing to do with Wilder. He's made his feelings clear." I bite out the words, my fear finally gone, only to be replaced by my annoyance.

"Consider yourself lucky, little brat." Wilder sneers, staring at me as if he would like nothing more than to wring my neck. "If the decision was mine—"

Enzo silences him by smacking him upside the head. He looks so incredibly sexy doing so. I nearly ask him to do it again. Who knew watching him humiliate the guy who freaked me the fuck out would be such a turn on?

Silence falls through the room, and I tilt my head up and catch Enzo staring at me with his eyebrow cocked. Arsenio and

Desmond also drink me in, and Wilder looks like he's about to have a coronary, the thick vein in his neck bunching and cording with his flexing.

Enzo leans closer to Arsenio, a flirtatious smirk softening his features. "She liked that," he whispers, but not so quietly that I can't hear. He wants me to know he knows.

Desmond whips his head back and forth and stands up, carrying me with him away from the bed. "I'm pretty fucking sure we all liked that, but it doesn't mean anything. Let's get this all out in the open, make some decisions—" Looking at me, Desmond meets my gaze. "That work for everyone. I'm over your guys' power-pissing match. We need to get things straightened out before shit catches up with us."

It takes everything in me not to argue, but I know better. If I continue to do so, I'll just prolong this misery, and I want to be left alone again. I want Wilder to storm off and sulk somewhere else. Mostly, I want answers. I will demand them. This has gone on long enough, my emotions constantly fluctuating as if they're on a rollercoaster with unexpected freefalls around every corner.

"You mean Wilder's pissing match. The rest of us are good." Enzo waits at the small sitting area, the loveseat and recliner not big enough to accommodate all of us.

"Enough. I mean it." Desmond glowers at each of his brothers. "We're moving past this. Now."

"Fucking finally," Wilder mutters.

Arsenio smacks him on the back of the head. "Blame yourself."

I exhale a long, soft breath, trying to relax even with the lingering annoyance between everyone.

"For fucking real." Holding his arms out, Enzo wiggles his fingers at me. "Come here, baby. You can sit with me. We have some catching up to do, and I brought something you might like."

Enzo reaches into his jacket pocket and pulls out a bag, shaking it at me. His smile widens as he tugs a chocolate chip cookie out and waves it. Is he serious? Carrying around cookies in his pocket as a snack for me? He makes it extremely hard to remember my place in this world as an unbonded omega. No man has ever been so thoughtful. It almost hurts me just thinking about it.

"You know, since you ignored me before and my brother had the pleasure of giving you the cupcakes that I spent forever watching the chef bake," Enzo adds. He takes a bite of the cookie and hums. "These took twice as long. So good."

Damn him.

"You can't bribe her, brother." Desmond sets me on my feet, motioning me to the loveseat. "We all agreed."

"Um, yes, he can." I hold out my hand to Enzo, my stomach screaming for the chance to taste his offering.

Tipping his head back, Enzo roars a laugh, picks me up by my waist, and spins me around to sit on his lap as he slouches in the recliner. He puts out the footrest, and I laugh, falling into his chest.

"Cookies, now," I demand, squirming to reach for the bag, setting off Enzo's body in the process. "Please. I'm so hungry."

"How could I resist that sweet, sassy mouth?" Enzo dangles the bag in front of me.

I expect him to feed me, but one look at his three brothers declares something like that won't happen. At least not here and now. Arsenio got away with it because we were alone. It's obvious things have changed a bit, and I'm about to find out by how much.

I avoid the silent stares of everyone, shoving one cookie after another into my mouth until it becomes nearly impossible to chew. Maybe this is me unintentionally trying to choke myself to evade the impending conversation. I know that they managed to find information about my past—even if it's out of context and misreported—but they have no reason to believe anything else otherwise. It was enough to set Wilder off. If a murder-suicide didn't, I'd probably be more concerned about it. I just...ugh. Bringing up my past opens wounds I've managed to bandage and ignore.

I slow down eating before I run out of my saving grace in the form of the best cookies I've ever had in my life. "Are you all just going to watch me eat? You wanted to talk, so talk." Am I rude? Who cares. They've kept me locked in a bathroom. All I did was get caught and landed in a situation out of my control.

Wilder straightens his back. "Let's start with who the fuck—"

Desmond smacks Wilder on the back of the head. "I'm sorry, Kinsey. I know this whole situation sucks, and all you want to do is leave...but we've all agreed it would be in everyone's best interest, including yours, if you stay. We can't exactly have you on our staff for obvious reasons—"

"Because you couldn't mind your business, you're now a part of ours. I'm sure you don't want to land in some breeder house or club like the bitch of Dark Alley intended, so we've decided to grant you mercy as long as you care for our little sister." Wilder spits out the words in a hurry like he can't stand his brother speaking over him.

What? I hear his words, but my brain refuses to process them. I minded my damn business. They've all declared none of this was my fault, yet Wilder still wants to put some of the blame on me.

My mouth twists in fury, my eyes capturing his. I can't control my emotions. He's such a dick. "Are you kidding me? Mercy? Mercy? Fuck you and your mercy, Wilder. Your little sister has obviously manifested as an omega. She doesn't need a caretaker. I know how things work. You can't expect me to believe you don't have some pack lined up for her." I wave my hand around, motioning at the room. "I don't know exactly who you all are, but you obviously have power and ties to the Pack Regime. You're strong enough to have the resources to screw up Madame Tamsin's business without a care. So don't give me this bullshit about you showing me mercy."

"Damn, sugar. Yell at my brother some more. His douche ass deserves it. Even he knows that." Arsenio leans forward, reaching over the small table, silently asking for me to touch his hand. I wonder if I should. It's the subtle things like a simple touch that can leave his fragrance on me. If I didn't know any better, I'd say he was jealous that I was currently sitting on Enzo's lap. Especially after I touched him how I did. How I let him touch me. How we kissed.

Ah fuck. I need to get that out of my head right now. I don't need to get all horny while I'm trying to stand up for myself.

"You be quiet, too. You're not innocent either, Arsenio. None of you can expect anything from me until you tell me what's going on. I want to know what the fuck is up with your sister. You're hiding her, aren't you? This used to be her room, but it's obvious she no longer stays here. What are you doing, Wilder? Keeping her in your closet as a prisoner?" The moment the words escape my mouth, fear courses through my veins. What if that's exactly what they're doing? What if they want to use her to gain power like my uncle had done with me?

Oh shit.

"Settle down, baby. Holly isn't a prisoner. She was only in Wilder's room because she wanted to piss him off. We have hidden corridors in the palace where we can travel unseen. It's part of our security measure, and until now, we have managed to keep Holly hidden since we faked her death some months ago. That's why we don't think it's a good idea if you leave. If anyone finds out, especially our father, that Holly is alive, a lot of shit will go down. We're protecting her. Our father doesn't care about her because of her order. He sees her as a means to barter for power. She deserves better." Enzo rests his chin on my shoulder, sliding his arms around my waist. I should move. I shouldn't be so comfortable with his body enveloping mine, but his words touch me so deeply. This is how a family should be. Now, I understand why they acted as they had for the most part. Except for Wilder. He's still a dick.

"Oh." I don't know what else to say.

"I know it's complicated, and you don't deserve to be put in this position, but what do you have to lose? You've been passing as a beta. You won't have to hide who you are here. We just need someone who can help Holly. And by helping Holly, you can help yourself. You can have this room and the protection of the Gilded Sands Pack." Desmond offers me a small smile, his eyes pleading with me to understand where they are coming from. And I do.

I purse my lips and bow my head, letting my hair veil my face. "Why? Why offer me this?"

"You were passing as a beta for...how long?" Wilder manages to keep his voice even for the first time since I've ever heard him talk. "Years?"

I slowly nod my head in confirmation. "Just over two."

"That's why. You can help us teach her how to pass. You obviously knew what you were doing. It won't be forever, but it's going to get harder for her. She's up for her second heat." Sitting up straighter, Wilder holds my gaze, trying to gauge my reaction. "You know what it's like."

He's right. I do. Many packs look forward to the time when omegas are fertile except for those unbonded omegas like me. Like Holly. There's a reason apart from suppressing my order that I took the pills. It's stopped my heats. Just thinking about it reminds me of the very first heat I had that ruined any excitement I could ever have for another one in my life. I don't even want to think about it. I'd never expected my uncle to be such a brutal man. The torture he put me through. What he put the men who were supposed to be my pack through…fucking disgusting. I shiver, pushing the thought away.

"It'll just be until we get everything we need to take the throne of Gilded Sands from our father and claim power as ours under the Pack Regimes," Arsenio adds. "After that, you won't have to worry. Neither will we."

"What do you say, baby? Help us out? Let us help you? I promise to ensure you always have dessert to eat. We can go shopping. This doesn't have to feel like the fucked up situation Wilder makes it." Enzo presses his lips to my ear. "You don't even have to talk to him. I'll keep him away from you."

I don't respond. My mind whirls with memories and with thoughts of everything that could go wrong here. These guys might seem kind, but what happens when they no longer need me? What happens if Madame Tamsin discovers who they are and comes after them? Or they just throw me to her?

"What do you say, Kinsey?" Enzo prods, shifting me.

The edges of my vision darken. What do I say? What do I do? I need to think. I know I don't really have a choice, but I'm not going to just agree and pretend that everything is fine. Too much can happen.

"Kinsey? Hey, look at me," Desmond says, materializing in front of me. He searches my eyes. "Someone get her a glass of water and a damp washcloth. She's losing color. Something's up. Her breathing is off too."

"I think she's having a panic attack." Arsenio hovers in front of me next, squishing next to his brother.

Enzo stands with me in his arms. "What do we do?"

Arsenio holds open his arms. "She's overwhelmed. You guys get out of here and give her some space. I will make sure she's okay."

My breathing quickens with my racing heart. I clench my fingers, digging my nails into the palms of my hands. Worry permeates through the air in a collection of scents that combat against my own.

The world spins, my head pounding.

I go limp in Arsenio's arms, pushing the world away.

I just want it to stop.

I just want to forget my past completely. I want to forget me.

Chapter 9

Arsenio

Handling Alphas 101

"It's been days. You need to figure out what to do. She's of no use if she doesn't get out of bed and refuses to talk to anyone." Wilder keeps his voice low as he stands in front of me outside of Kinsey's door. He's such a jackass. He doesn't understand that even if he is a heartless bastard without emotions beyond the scope of his anger and horniness, it doesn't mean that everyone else is the same.

"She is acclimating, Wilder. She'll be of no use if you constantly linger and hound at us. Holly is fine. We have time. How about you go do what you're best at and see if you can get your hands on some fucking suppressant pills?" I block his way, ensuring he doesn't try to bang on Kinsey's door. She made it clear that she doesn't want him anywhere near her, and I'll make sure that she at least gets that. He can be pissed off and annoyed by it, but it's his own damn fault. If he wants Kinsey to treat him like she does the rest of us, then he needs to figure out how to act right.

Wilder grumbles and spins on his heels, stomping away. And thank fucking God he decided to be smart and not test me. I don't like fighting with him, but he is making it difficult.

I huff a breath and adjust the collar on my shirt. Raising my hand, I knock on the door. "Kinsey, it's me. I wanted to see if you'd work out with me or something. It might help. Or we could go to the library. Go swimming. You name it. I want to give you a tour of the palace."

I listen as Kinsey crosses the room, the soft shuffle of her feet agonizingly slow. I can smell her scent, the sweetness of marshmallows exciting me in a way that I can't control. God, I need to stop thinking about our moment together and how wet she was. How much she desired me, and how incredible her touch was as she explored my body.

The door cracks open, and Kinsey greets me with a beautiful smile. It feels as if it's just for me. I wish she would do it more often, but this is the first one I've seen unprovoked by me trying to tease her or feed her.

"Are you sure it's okay for me to leave my room? Wilder sounded annoyed." Kinsey looks past me, peeking into the hallway. "I feel like he's waiting to corner me at any second."

I step back, letting her exit her room and into the hallway. "I sent him out. It'll be at least a couple of hours before he comes sniffing around."

"Good. He's driving me crazy." Kinsey ruffles her fingers through her dark hair, sending her scent wafting toward me.

Wilder says the same thing about Kinsey. So do Enzo and Desmond. They aren't as closed off to their senses and emotions as I am. I've been constantly working on it my entire life, knowing that I would be at an advantage if I learned to ignore everything that triggers me. I even sometimes dab a fragrance under my nose to help with the pheromones constantly battling against mine, especially with Kinsey here. Things have gotten more intense. It's what happens when an unbonded, unrelated omega enters our home. Anyone's home really.

Which is why I think getting the suppressant pills will help. We can do it for Holly, but if things keep growing more intense with Kinsey, maybe she will want them again.

I frown at the thought. I'd prefer she didn't try to suppress her order. She is incredible as she is, my attraction to her is strong but manageable. She shouldn't have to hide who she is with us. I'd understand if she wants to but...I shake the thought away.

"That makes all of us," I say, reaching out to graze my fingers across her shoulder. She's freshly showered and untainted by any of my brothers, and I just want to know what it's like for my scent to mingle with hers all over again.

But I must resist.

Kinsey laughs and whips her head back and forth, the musical sound of her voice stirring something wild inside me. "I can tell. I'm pretty sure Wilder's touching everything he can just so I don't forget he's lurking. He even touched you."

Goddamn it. I'm so used to him being around that I didn't realize why he was here, wanting to suddenly talk when he knew I was going to try to get Kinsey out of her room. I know exactly when he did it. He smacked my cheek, turning this into another damn pissing match for power and recognition, considering Kinsey won't give him the time he refuses to admit he wants.

Kinsey pulls at the hem of her shirt and stretches it up, wiping it across my face. "Here, I'll help you out."

My eyes break from hers, and I glimpse down at her exposed perky tits in the slightly sheer bra. Desire squeezes my balls, the sight of her being the sexiest thing I've ever seen. She's unintentionally—or maybe purposefully—scenting me. I want more. Need more. Her closeness does indescribable and unexpected things to me. I never expected to be so attracted to an omega, especially one not picked out for me. Relationships have never been a priority since it's forbidden under my father's reign to be anything except casual. Kinsey is different. I can't imagine anything purely casual. I'm far too invested in her. She's perfect.

Giggling, she catches me staring. Blush tints her cheeks, yet she doesn't cover up quickly. She sucks her bottom lip into her mouth, her desire growing stronger. I wonder if she considers our moment. If she wants to push me until I get on my knees for her.

"I can't smell him anymore. Just you. But let me make sure his scent doesn't return." Bringing her hand up next, she rubs her palm across my skin. Fuck, it was purposeful. The little tease. "Much better. You'll have to let me into his room to touch his shit as payback. I think that's what I want to do now. What do you think? Are you willing to risk it, because I am?"

I chuckle, already hearing Wilder swear to the sun and back. She truly does want to torture him, and usually, I'd be all over it, but she underestimates his intentions. He'd love it. He'd just never admit to it. "And give him that kind of satisfaction? Fuck no. I know he fights his attraction to you. You'd just be rewarding him for his dickish attitude. It's why he won't give you your belongings. It's the only thing he can get close to without getting punched in the nuts."

She rolls her eyes at me, puffing a breath. She doesn't see what we see. "Attracted to me? Hardly. All I ever sense is his anger and annoyance."

I caress my thumb to her cheek, drawing a line down her jaw and neck. She doesn't stop me, stepping closer to press her face more firmly to my hand, the act enough to excite me about her craving my touch.

"It's basically indistinguishable with him. He's a moody bastard." I dart my gaze down to her lips, thinking about how soft and sweet they felt against mine.

She shivers under my exploration of her neck, finally reaching up to stop me, linking our fingers together. "If he were really attracted to me, I'd know."

Wilder is a much better actor than any of us, but I know my brother. He'll be jerking off the moment he is alone, his face buried in whatever fucking thing Kinsey touches. And after his uncalled-for behavior, the last thing I need is for him to start thinking he has a chance with her. Omegas only go out of their way to leave their scent when they see potential. If Kinsey recognizes it, then she obviously has convinced herself otherwise. It's not her fault, though. He is a strong, loyal man.

"Whatever you say, sugar. Just be mindful around Wilder. He is far more...aggressive? It's hard to explain. He has lived his life with different expectations. He carries the stress of our kingdom on his back, because if we fail to properly take the throne, we'll have far worse problems. It's why we need to ensure Holly's safety in case." I don't want to get into more details and scare Kinsey, but our father believes Holly is dead. He was the only one who could arrange a bonding with another pack, and he chose wrong, which is why we did what we did. If we can't throw him out of power the right way, Holly needs to be able to escape. She needs to be able to make it on her own. She needs someone who can help her. Kinsey is that someone. It was as if fate put her in our path for a reason, and I'll spend forever thanking her for being our saving grace. Fate might destroy us otherwise. We can't turn our back on such a gift of a woman.

"If you don't want me to mess with Wilder's belongings, then I'd like to formally meet your sister." Kinsey swivels on her feet, peering around. "I think that's what I'd like to do with my time. I need to see if the task you guys want is actually possible. I got lucky passing as a beta. I knew how things worked. If you've sheltered Holly all her life, it's going to be a huge wake-up call to her."

"Oh." I swallow, trying not to react toward the truth of her words.

She's absolutely right about my sister. Holly has never strayed far from our father's royal fortress. When we manifested our orders, the king pushed us out, which is why we live separate from him in this palace on the edge of our kingdom. He didn't want to risk us realizing just how bad of a person he was. He tried to give Holly away without even telling us. She managed to run away from him, and that's when we decided what had to be done.

It was dangerous, but we had to make Holly's death look real. She has the scars to prove it. We did things I never expected we'd have to do, but it was the only way. We needed a body. We needed concrete evidence that Holly left this life. Finding someone to match her took searching every damn hospital and morgue in all of Saint Vista for a beta with bad luck.

I shudder at the memory, pushing it away. Wilder will never forgive himself for what he thought he had to do, begging the sick woman for help with her sacrifice. If Kinsey knew, she'd probably look at us all as monsters.

Or maybe not. Kinsey might be a monster too. I've seen the reports. I know what happened to her pack, and some suspect that she was the one responsible. The murder-suicide was all too convenient, considering everything would be left to her. That's the only way an omega keeps their pack rights.

"I mean, if that's okay," Kinsey says, rubbing her hand down my shoulder, gently touching my wrist and setting me off. She senses my disconnection, coaxing me to pull myself from my thoughts without calling me out. Her touch is so soft and light like a caress of the wind, and it stirs me from the darkness created by my past. "With both of you."

"I'd love for you to meet her. She's been waiting. She's used to having females around, but she's never met another omega. Our mother died shortly after her birth." I clear my throat, trying not to dig up that memory either. It's as if Kinsey yanks everything I've suppressed free, and it makes it harder and harder for me to focus.

"I'm so sorry," she murmurs, slowly lacing her other hand through mine, holding both of mine, surprising me. She's braver than the last time and more open with her teasing affection. The sudden tranquility coming with her sugary scent helps ease the tenseness of my muscles brought on by Wilder.

"It was a long time ago. Maybe we could talk about it some other time, and you can tell me more about yourself as well." I'm dying to know exactly how she ended up in her position, but I know better than to push her. She shuts down easily, and the last thing I want is for her to push me away.

Her eyes gloss over. "Yeah, sure. Some other time."

I offer her a smile and tug her toward the wardrobe instead of the hallway. It's best that we take our secret passageway, limiting the amount of time Kinsley moves through any shared domains that the staff go through. The betas will definitely catch the unfamiliar scent, so we must be careful.

Kinsey stares at me with her big green eyes and then flicks her gaze to the spot on the wall I tap to release the doorknob. I open it and motion for her to lead the way, the access door not wide enough for the both of us to enter together. Closing the door behind us, I pull her into my side and drape my arm across her shoulders. She sinks against me instead of putting space between us, and I can't stop my heart from racing. I know I shouldn't be so close to her. I know better than to want to pick her up and prop her against the wall to kiss her again, to feel her heat against mine and smell her lust, taste her the way I want, but I risk desiring it anyway. There's just something about Kinsey I can't ignore.

We walk in silence through the winding corridor, passing by the entrance to my room. I point it out to her, and she touches the door as if she wants to leave a trail to follow later. We make our way to the panic room, the heavy door only activated by one of our touches. I'll have to have Wilder reprogram it to include Kinsey.

"So, she's basically like a prisoner," Kinsey says, twisting her lips to the side as I open the first heavy door, revealing the one intended for Holly's privacy.

"No, Holly can go anywhere she pleases. As long as it's not anywhere the staff can see her." I knock on the door, listening for Holly.

She's a lot louder than the rest of us, always wanting to test us with her noise. Something smacks on the wood. Maybe a book. "You have a hand, Wilder. Use it! I'm not getting up when we both know you're going to come in anyway, you asshole."

I swing open the door, nudging Kinsey in front of me. "Damn, Holly. You're never going to let Wilder catch a break, are you?"

"Shit. Sorry, Arsenio. I thought you were the asshole. He said he was going to come by and finally face me instead of hiding like a scared baby." Holly stands up from her couch, a collection of books around her. Setting her eyes on Kinsey, she dashes toward us, not missing a beat. "I'm so happy you're not him, though. I've been dying for you to bring the omega by. It's Kinsey, right?" Holly turns her attention to Kinsey, breaking one of our society's rules by addressing her directly in the presence of an alpha. Stuff like this is what we need help with, working on her habits, so she understands the true extent of her order. She really has been sheltered. My brothers and I can only blame ourselves though. We thought that the king would choose someone worthy.

Kinsey turns her attention to me, waiting for me to speak first. It prods at me just a little that she feels like she has to.

"Yup, this is Kinsey. Kinsey, meet my little sister Holly." I release Kinsey, allowing her to greet Holly. I watch them in silence, wondering how they'll interact with each other.

Omegas aren't usually touchy-feely with other omegas, but Kinsey surprises me and kisses each of Holly's cheeks. It's such a familial thing to do and something that happens within a pack.

"It's so nice to meet you," Kinsey says, her voice light.

Holly freezes for a second, her stare flicking to mine. Blush crawls up her neck, and she smiles wider. Most people used to treat Holly as an untouchable. No one outside our pack would've dared get within arm's reach. She's been denied affection outside of our family. We all have, really, but for my sister, it's taken a toll.

"Arsenio, she's perfect. Beautiful and kind. I don't know why Wilder is a fucking psycho about this. It's not her fault you dumbasses kidnapped her. You should be thanking the fates." Holly glances at me from over Kinsey's shoulder. Pulling her closer, I watch the two of them hug as if they've known each other all their lives.

I ignore her comment about fate because I'm not sure how Kinsey truly feels about it. "You know he's just overprotective," I say, clicking the door closed behind me. I don't trust Wilder to cut his day early to search us out. If I can keep Kinsey out of sight, maybe he'll realize just how right Holly is. Fate gave us someone to help Holly, not hurt her.

"And in denial." Holly beams brighter. Locking her hands to Kinsey's, she tugs her deeper into her suite. "Totally his loss and your gain."

Kinsey giggles and slides onto the couch beside Holly. She quietly pats the spot beside her, asking me to join her. My heart picks up speed, her subtle desire for my closeness driving me wild. A part of me hopes Holly doesn't steal too much of our time, because I don't want to waste any more time with my brother away than I have to. None of us have told Kinsey yet, but we've decided to split the week into shifts to keep her company and watch out for her, and Wilder demanded one day.

"You say that like he ever had a chance. I mean, look at me." I grin with my words, sitting down next to Kinsey only to pull her onto my lap. I can't help it. I crave her closeness. I yearn to breathe in the scent of her neck. To kiss her throat. To show her attention in front of someone important to me.

Holly laughs and shakes her head. "Don't settle, Kinsey. Enzo hasn't stopped talking about you, either. Desmond too, but I know he might not be of interest to you because—"

"He's sweet." Kinsey shifts off my lap, squishing next to Holly. Leaning close to her, she whispers something in her ear.

Holly groans softly, her disappointment hitting me hard as if it is my own. She whispers something back, watching me as she does. I know they're allowed some privacy, and I should excuse myself, giving them time to get to know each other, but I've never been jealous of my sister before. I wish Kinsey would include me in the conversation. I'm infuriatingly desperate to know what she said about my brothers. Maybe about me.

My jealousy gets the best of me, and I wrap my arms around Kinsey, tugging her away. "Okay, okay. You two should save this conversation for later. I promised Kinsey she could fuck around in Wilder's room. Teach him a lesson." Petty? Maybe.

But my words brighten Kinsey's face, extinguishing the serious whispers she shares with Holly immediately.

"Fuck yeah! I'm helping!" Holly launches to her feet, yanking Kinsey with her.

I glower at the back of Holly's head, wishing she'd have gotten the hint. Or maybe she did and something Kinsey said to her makes her want to cock-block. Fucking hell. I hadn't realized until this moment how much I want Kinsey. I thought she was beautiful since the moment I laid eyes on her, but my sister stealing her attention from me drives me batshit crazy, which is stupid as shit. We agreed that Kinsey could help Holly. I just didn't realize it would be without me.

I rub the back of my neck, trying to remain expressionless. Kinsey laughs and smiles over her shoulder, winking at me like the sassy, sweet woman she is.

"I like her," she mouths, nodding her head toward my sister.

Rushing the few feet to Kinsey, I snatch her other hand, spinning her into me. I lift her off her feet and dodge past Holly, my long legs managing to get me to Wilder's room first. I dart inside, spinning Kinsey around only to throw her onto his bed.

She gasps, her eyes widening. "Arsenio! Fuck! He's going to lose his shit. I didn't want to make it obvious."

Holly sucks in a breath. "Oh, shit. He's going to kick your ass, brother."

"It'll be worth it." I stride to the end of the bed and jump beside Kinsey, pulling her on top of me. She squeals and pats her palms to my chest, her shock of my actions vanishing as desire sweetens her scent even more.

Our eyes lock, and she bites her bottom lip, drawing my attention to her mouth. I can't stand how lonely her pout looks without me. Bending up, I flip her onto her back and kiss her, exploring her soft mouth until she parts her lips, letting me slip my tongue over hers.

A pillow smacks into me hard enough to break our kiss.

"Ugh, stop. This wasn't what I had in mind when you said mess with Wilder. I wanted to annoy him, not turn him into a brother killer." Holly swings the pillow again, screeching as I yank it away from her.

Kinsey steals it from me, hugging it to her chest. "Serves him right...but yeah. Handling Alphas 101—don't test the dickhead ones." She scoots to the edge of the bed, tucks the pillow under her arm, and holds her other one out to me. "And give the cute, friendly ones extra attention."

"Got it," Holly says, bouncing on her feet. "Lock my door for the next day until Wilder cools off."

My cell phone beeps, drawing my attention away. Tugging it free, I see a text message from Wilder.

Bastard Brother: No luck. Get Kinsey to tell you who her dealer is.

I tighten my jaw, glancing from Kinsey to Holly.

Me: You fucking do it. Your shift is tomorrow.

Bastard Brother: Just do it. We don't have time to mess around.

Me: Fuck off. You better prepare to be nice, dickhead. It's the only way she'll help you. Also, sorry about your bed.

I shove my phone away and swipe my arm over the blanket, straightening it out. "Fuck, speaking of psychos. Wilder is on his way. Let's get out of here."

Holly screeches and motions for Kinsey to hurry. The two of them rush away, leaving me in Wilder's room. I peer around one more time and shut the door. I'm playing with fire, and I know it. Do I care? Fuck no. I want nothing more than for Kinsey to set my world ablaze.

Chapter 10

Wilder

Broody Alpha

I couldn't go near my room. I could smell the brat from down the hallway, her scent leading right to my room. I know she was in there. I'm already enough on edge. If I had gone inside, I'd have fucking lost it. And not because I'm angry. I'm really frustrated by the entire situation. It's as if I'm cursed.

I roll on my side, staring at the soft glow from outside the study. It's not much better than my room, but it's a shared space between my brothers and me. When my personal belongings are fucked with, I lose my shit.

Even though the couch cushions smell like Kinsey, it doesn't mess with my head as much. Not like a pair of her panties I stole from her duffel bag that still remains in my closet. I know I should give it back to her, but a part of me doesn't want to. I want her to accept the idea that she's not going anywhere now. If only it didn't mean a possible war. If King Winston finds out that I'm not only hiding the Gilded Sands omega in our palace but also that I technically stole from the Dark Alley Pack of the Gutter District, he might take my fucking balls.

Intervening in my sister's supposed bonding ceremony already cost us an ally. Do I give a shit? No. The bastards of Emerald Bay can fuck off. I would slaughter all of them before I ever allowed my sister into their care. They killed their last omega, something that is usually unheard of, but something is wrong with them. They don't have what it takes to be in the presence of someone as priceless as Holly.

Mom would have been devastated by our father's decision, and I would never let her down, even if she no longer blesses this world.

A tap sounds on the door, drawing my attention from my thoughts. I shift and look at my watch, seeing that dawn approaches, and I haven't even slept yet. Today's going to be hell. I know I shouldn't complain because I demanded to get at least a day of Kinsey's time to make sure my brothers don't bond with her completely, but also because I need answers they might not get. I'm the only one of us who has experience being around an unbonded omega, and I know how to handle myself. Cold, closed off, and smart about the whole fucking thing. Kinsey cannot and will not ever be someone we can consider as part of our futures. King Winston has yet to decide on someone for us to bond with. And that won't happen for a good while or at all, considering that we must take his throne and pretty quickly. He already grows weak, even if he's in denial.

"Hey, brother. Kinsey tends to wake up with the sun, so you better either get your ass up and get her breakfast or back off and don't bother taking any of her time. It's pointless anyway. She hates you." Enzo's voice muffles through the door. I thought Enzo was the one I needed to worry the most about, but I suspect Arsenio has already made some annoying moves. It was his scent with hers, after all.

I groan and swing my legs over the edge of the couch. "You have that wrong, but whatever makes you feel better, Enzo." I scrub my fingers through my dark chestnut hair and down my cheeks, trying to wake myself up. I'm exhausted but can't get my damn brain to quiet. Maybe Kinsey will ignore me enough that I can just pass out in the hallway outside her door.

Enzo pushes the door open to the study and raises an eyebrow at me. The cocky bastard. "Whatever you say. Make sure she gets something of everything. She'll eat nothing but sweets if you allow her to, and she needs some vegetables and protein. Offer her the fruit last. Maybe give her some extra carbs. I think she's been skipping on meals for who knows how long, probably because being a server for the bitch paid in pennies."

"I know how to fucking prepare a meal. I don't need your damn tips." I crack my knuckles and move past him, getting into his face while I do so. "Also, tell Arsenio that if he doesn't fix my damn room, I will fuck up his belongings."

"Damn. What did I miss? You gotta stop giving me shit to do. He's fucking being his suave self. He didn't say anything, but I could smell her lust all over him." Enzo flares his nostrils. "Drives me nuts."

He's not wrong. It wasn't just her lust on him either. I could smell her slick from a mile away. It's all over the damn cushions still, too. Maybe that's another reason why I couldn't sleep. My damn hard-on won't chill out. I hate how much I want what Arsenio already managed to get. But I'd be setting a terrible example. We can't do this. It would be unfair to all of us to even consider Kinsey as a prospect.

"Get used to it. I couldn't get anyone to deal me suppressants. They think I want to set them up with one of the Pack Regimes." I smack my brother on his cheek. "Maybe you can try, Enzo. Your reputation precedes you."

Enzo growls at me and slams his palm into my chest, smashing my back to the doorframe. Should I have left my scent on him? No. But I can't help it. I want Kinsey to know that we're a pack, and I'm our leader despite the three of us being manifested into the order of the alphas.

Enzo goes for my gut next, and I trip him and lunge over him, jogging toward the elevator that'll take me to the kitchen. We haven't stocked up Kinsey's fridge yet, and Enzo would probably clear it out anyway, because he uses food as a damn excuse to visit her.

Chef Bronson has a tray prepared when I enter the kitchen, knowing that I like to eat in my room, but I'm a shitty cook. I look over the meal and nod my head. "Do you have any muffins? Some fruit?" I never ask for anything like this, and the chef furrows his brows quizzically before strolling to the glass cabinet with several different pastries already made.

"You must be in a good mood, Prince Wilder. Why don't you try one of my chocolate croissants too?" The chef wraps the pastries in paper and sets them on the tray. He quickly adds cut-up fruit to a bowl and plops it on. "Anything else I can do for you, your majesty?"

I shake my head. "This will do. Thank you."

I don't wait for him to respond. Striding through the swinging door, I climb the stairs, feeling as if I need to burn some energy before I reach Kinsey. What is up with me? Everything is bound to catch up with me, but all I can think about is getting to her room before she opens her eyes. I know if I don't make it and have to knock, she might ignore me and not let me in. If I come bearing breakfast, she might at least hesitate before attacking. Though I wouldn't resist her if she chooses to use her mouth as a weapon.

I thrash my head, knocking the thoughts out of my mind. I need to keep my shit together. She really got to me, and she barely even did anything. Fucking Arsenio set me up. He's lucky he's currently hiding like the coward he is, knowing well enough that I'll prove my strength and knock him down a notch.

I stand in front of Holly's old room, glad that Kinsey stays here now. It helps get me in control, because it's easier to kill a boner with the lingering scent of my sister. If the others wouldn't resist the thought, I'd keep the two of them in a room together. That would really cement anything from happening.

But there's only so much I can do. I don't want to push away my brothers because of this, so I just need to be careful. Staying strong together ensures our plan will work.

I heave a breath and quietly knock my knuckles to the door. If she complains about me intruding, I'll just bring up surveillance from the hallway. We have cameras hiding everywhere outside of our personal spaces, though I'm pretty damn sure I might put one in my room to catch my brothers or Kinsey fucking with my things to throw in their faces. We're the only ones with access to the security feeds, so I could get away with it.

I sneak my way into the suite, trying to be as quiet as possible as I click the door closed. Damn. I don't know if Kinsey purposefully touched every damn surface in this room or what, but Holly's scent has vanished completely. It's only on the door.

My dick hardens as I spot Kinsey fast asleep in the middle of the queen bed. She rolled herself in the blankets, turning into a burrito that I just want to unwrap and devour. It's almost as good as ripping off her clothes, seeing her exposed and bare.

Goddamn it, Wilder. Get your mind in order. You can't think this way.

I growl with the thought and step forward, tightening my fingers on the tray. I should wake her. I mean, I really fucking need to wake her up, but there's something about the quiet comfort of her dreaming and not trying to bust my balls that gets to me in a good way. I imagine what it would be like to lay beside her, enveloping her in my arms, just feeling the heat of her body, the fragrance of her hair, listening to her soft breathing, and her heart beating.

And then I see it. She stole one of my favorite fucking pillows. It's not in her bed, but she tucked it in the corner of the room beneath the desk with what I'm nearly certain is one of Enzo's shirts. It was the one she was wearing on her first night here.

She's really going to make it hard on me.

I stride toward the corner of the suite, my eyes locked on my pillow, but I don't notice the decorative pillows she tossed on the floor beside the bed. I stumble, yelling out. I hold the tray of food for dear life, flipping and managing to keep it from spilling on the floor. I hit my back hard and growl.

Kinsey screams, her voice ringing through the air. "What the fuck! What the actual fuck! Why are you here?" She scrambles from her bed, showing off the fact that she only wears a T-shirt and panties, the lacy thong showing off her perfectly smooth ass. And now I can't stop looking. She is so damn sexy without even trying. Her bedhead makes me want to grab her hair and bend her over. I can imagine her pouty mouth bobbing over my cock. And her scent? God, I want to bury my face between her thighs and taste her sweet slick. My muscles ripple thinking about it. My cock throbs.

I don't even have a chance to prepare myself before she grabs one of the decorative pillows and smacks me in the face a couple of times.

"You asshole! You scared me. What the hell are you doing in my room?" She pauses and meets my gaze, standing over me. Her tits keep the shirt away from her stomach, showing off the underside of them, the perfect shape to bury my face between.

I grab the pillow from her and push up on one hand, shaking the tray with the other. "I brought you breakfast, brat. Instead of attacking me, why don't you take your damn food? I knocked. It's not my fault if you didn't hear it." I narrow my eyes at her, wishing she wouldn't step away, stealing the incredible view before me.

She taps me with her foot a lot more gently than I expect. "You're full of shit. Where are your brothers? You shouldn't be the one here."

I can't stop the wicked smile from crossing my face. The others were too damn chickenshit to tell her how we all agreed to split up her week. Maybe that'll give me an advantage, because I know I'm on her shit list, where I must remain. It's the only way to handle the situation. She needs to hate me, so she doesn't come on to me. My resistance is pulled tight and being tested constantly.

"They didn't tell you? Of course, they didn't. The fucking cowards. We've divided your week into shifts. They each took two days, and I have the remaining one. You have them so fucking wrapped around your finger that I need to make sure you remember your place here. You're in our care only because they're too nice to do what needs to be done." The words burn on my tongue, watching her eyes gloss over. I'm a fucking asshole. I know I'm an asshole, but a lot depends on my behavior.

She sets the tray of food down, grabs a pillow, and swings it again, clobbering me upside the head. I stumble in surprise, the force of her anger nearly knocking my head off. And damn, do I like her feistiness.

"Get out! Get out, or I will fucking kick you in your balls. You're not wanted here. You're an asshole, and I didn't agree to any of that. Now get out!" She points at the door, her face reddening.

This might be the most juvenile thing I have said in my adult life. For fucking Christ's sake. I'm a thirty-year-old man. I just don't know how to react to her hostility. I might deserve it, but it doesn't mean that I'm going to just take it.

I reach out and snatch her wrist, pulling her on top of me. I flip her over and restrain her arms over her head, straddling her body, pressing my knees tightly together to pin her legs in place.

I bow down and lock my gaze to hers. "Make me, brat. I was trying to be cordial. I brought you breakfast. I knocked, and you didn't answer, and I didn't want things to get cold. Now, if you agree to stop trying to murder me by pillow, I will let you up. But I'm not leaving. This is my day to watch you, and I'll ensure that you don't sneak off to my brothers. You've already gotten under their skin."

She doesn't make it easy and thrashes, wiggling and moving so much that she manages to break free and knee me right in the cock. I grunt and lose all my strength, flopping right on top of her. She gasps as my weight steals her breath, and I quickly flip back over with her on top of me. My face scrunches in pain, but all I can think about now is how I might've accidentally hurt her.

That was the last thing I wanted to do.

"Kinsey, I'm sorry. I didn't mean to crush you. Shit. Are you okay?" My muscles bunch and I trace my hand over her without touching her.

Something shifts in her expression, her anger softening as she tilts her head. The spice of her rage morphs into something incredibly sweet, reminding me of marshmallows and caramel, something delicious and addictive. My mouth waters as she doesn't move.

Is that lust? Absolutely. It radiates from her, her body warming against mine even more.

"I—I'm fine. You didn't hurt me. I'm tough." Snatching one of the discarded pillows from beside us, she picks it up and plows me in the face with it. Planting her palms down, she pushes her weight onto the pillow, smothering me. "But you're still fucking in trouble. How dare you come in here and try to boss me around."

I don't move, relaxing my muscles, losing myself to her body squirming as she finally releases me and slides away only to hit my hard cock with her back. I'm about to risk losing it, but I flex it, tapping it to her.

Her eyes widen, and she smacks her palms to my chest and gets off me, hopping to her feet. She retreats around the bed, using it like a wall between us, and she crosses her arms over her chest.

"You better watch that thing. Don't think I won't ensure that you can't procreate." Kinsey points at me again, her expression adorable and far from scary.

She's not mad either. She's all talk. Her scent and body language tell me otherwise. But I won't push her. Her closeness is a gift I need to earn. I won't do anything despite what her order declares. I want her mind on board. I—fuck me. This was a mistake.

"It'll be the only way I ever touch you on purpose," she adds, burning a look.

"I believe it, little brat. I have a feeling that you might try to neuter all of us in our sleep. It keeps me up at night." I press my hands into the floor and get to my feet, dusting myself off even though there's not a speck of dirt in this room.

"You got that right." She gingerly slides back on her bed and eyes the tray of food, the sound of her stomach rumbling drawing my attention. "Now, if you don't plan to leave, go sit over there. I want to enjoy my breakfast, and I can't do it with you hovering over me."

I tighten my jaw and hide my expression. Because there's nothing more that I want than to help her enjoy her breakfast by hand-feeding her and discovering exactly what she likes the most. I'll just have to watch her from a distance, I suppose. Not that it's a bad thing. It already takes everything in me not to drop to my knees and apologize for my behavior. But I'm a goner if I do. I don't want her to like me. I don't want to test my restraint even more.

It already kills me seeing that she has one of my pillows. It's like she wants to be my tormentor, but she also doesn't understand that I'm far from tortured. I crave to see what else she tries to take. To see what she does without thought. Because I don't even think she realizes what she does to every single one of us.

"Fine by me." I smirk at her and head to the sitting area, plopping down on the recliner. I sit back and rest my feet up, crossing my arms.

She glares at me, staring at her, and our gazes go to war, refusing to break away from each other. She absent-mindedly feels around to navigate the tray, picking up the chocolate croissant, and bringing it to her lips. She tears into it, biting and chewing like a rabid animal, and it gets to me in a good way. I like that she challenges me. I enjoy her testing everything I do. It makes me feel stronger. More powerful. I can't wait to…

I lose the battle and divert my gaze, rubbing my hands into my eyes, trying to clear my mind.

Kinsey laughs out loud, her voice ringing through the air. She knows she has won, and all it does is make me yearn to challenge her over and over again. Push her limits. See exactly what I can get away with.

She takes a bite of the cut-up orange next, letting the juice trickle down her chin. "Today is going to be so fucking fun. What are you getting me for lunch? What's on your agenda,

Wilder? You won't survive just sitting there all day. I know guys like you. You always have something you need to take care of."

I drop my hands and rest my elbows on my knees. "Actually, the only responsibility I have today is you. But if you want to help out, how about you let me know your dealer's name, and I can pass it along to my brothers. We would like to get our hands on some suppressant pills for Holly."

Her eyebrows shoot up in surprise. "What?"

"You know what will be coming soon. We want to be able to help Holly the best we can. She needs to be able to learn to be a beta. We can't expect her to stay hidden forever. She deserves some normalcy." If she were in any other pack, she wouldn't have to face such a life, but I don't trust the king. I'm certain he was responsible for my mother's death, despite what he claims. I was old enough. I saw how he treated her. They weren't in love, and she was just a trophy given to him by another territory. He destroyed them. He destroyed her. And I think he just wanted to destroy Holly because she reminded him of her. I won't let it happen.

Kinsey shakes her head, dropping her fork to her plate. "No. They will know I told you guys. They'll come after me."

I suppress my anger, closing my eyes. "Why do you think that? I'm sure they deal to a lot of people."

"Not omegas. They'll know. They'll also wonder who you're getting them for. It's a bad idea." Kinsey trembles in her spot, her fear ignited.

I groan. "Come on. You can't really think that—"

"I said no. I'm not giving up my source. If you want me to get suppressant pills for you, I can do that. But I'm not going to send you in to get them." Kinsey meets my eyes, daring me to argue.

But I don't have it in me. She is stubborn as fuck. That's one thing I know for certain about her.

"Fine. Hurry up and finish eating and then get dressed." I get to my feet. "I'll be back in twenty to get you."

"Seriously?" she asks, her eyes widening.

"Absolutely serious. Now hustle. We don't have all day, and I want to be back here before nightfall." I stride across the room and glance over my shoulder at her. "If you need anything, just holler. I'll hear you."

I abandon her, leaving her shocked in silence on the bed. Clicking her door closed, I lean against it and sigh, lowering myself to the floor.

What am I getting myself into?

What am I getting Kinsey into?

I'm afraid that I'm about to send both our lives straight to hell.

Chapter 11

Kinsey

Gutter District

I should be scared out of my mind, watching as the world blurs outside of the window. This is a far better view than I had in the back of the utility van belonging to Madame Tamsin, but it does nothing for my nerves. The sleek, silver sports car zooms down the main highway, leading toward the one place I never expected to see again.

Wilder is crazy if he thinks we aren't going to draw attention. He could've picked something less obvious, but I don't even think he has a car that would blend in with the rest of society. The two-seater probably cost more than the salary some betas make in their entire lives.

I feel weird sitting here, touching the seats, half-expecting Wilder to yell at me for holding on.

"I have some connections just outside the Gutter District. I want you to cover up. There's a hat and a scarf in the bag on the floor. It's not uncommon for us to hide our staff members to ensure their safety. We're always a target for someone or another, and not everyone lives at the palace." Wilder motions to my feet, where a bag takes up half of my foot room.

"This is a terrible idea." I know I've said it a dozen times, but Wilder's head is far too thick to even consider that he's wrong.

"I'll protect you, Kinsey. Now don't be a brat and do as I asked. It's important." Wilder reaches toward the floorboard this time, pulling up the bag himself to plop it on my lap.

"I'd believe you if you were one of your brothers. I'm pretty sure you would just shove me at some asshole to escape if things went down." I shift on the leather seat and fidget with my seatbelt.

"What kind of man do you think I am? If that were the case, you wouldn't even be here." Wilder stomps the throttle, sending the car lurching forward faster.

"I think you're a cocky bastard. You can't just accept that you aren't thinking straight." I pull the baseball hat from the duffel bag and put it on my head, trying not to inhale a deep breath. It smells just like him, the intoxicating cinnamon, vetiver, and something wild drenching me.

"Things are clearer. Now hurry up. There are sunglasses in there as well. Don't try anything stupid either. I can outrun you." Wilder glances at me in his peripheral vision, a smirk curling his lips. He loves messing with me and getting under my skin. He is probably aware that I struggle not to pull the hat from my head to bury my face in it.

Fucking alphas.

Fucking body of mine.

The only thing that keeps me from panicking is that if we do get ahold of suppressant pills, I can start taking them again. It would really help me out.

"You're going to owe me for this," I say, putting on the dark sunglasses a bit too big for my face. I can't wait to get some of my own belongings. Or at least the things I had in my bag. But it's like this bastard doesn't want me to have any part of my past as if it'll somehow bend me to his will in the future.

"Is it not enough for me to give you a life beyond your wildest dreams, brat-girl?" Wilder switches lanes, sending me sprawling toward the door.

I swing out and smack him in the arm. Laughing, his face lights up in amusement. He enjoys this way too much, his usually potent anger morphing into something softer, sweeter. A little bit of lust too. He likes when I touch him, but I know he'd never admit it. He thinks he can resist me, but I notice him secretly scenting things and leaving his mark. He touches my wrists and my cheeks often. And it's not in the same way he does to his brothers, trying to get to me. It's definitely more territorial, and being alone with him proves that Arsenio was right. I guess I've been lying to myself about knowing he fights his attraction to me all along.

I should use this against him and to my advantage. Push him. Test him. Tease him until he can't stand it and finally gives in. Then I can deny him and show him what it's like to mess with a woman who's been scorned. He'd deserve it.

Too bad I'm far too anxious about returning to the Gutter District. I suppress my urges and choose to ignore him and stare out the windshield, watching as the city grows and envelopes us, the clear border vanishing as we enter the territory I've lived in for the last two years. I hunker down in my seat, fear blossoming in my chest to curl around my heart and lungs, squeezing tightly. The dark tint of the windows should obscure us from the outside, making it impossible to identify me, but it doesn't stop the panic resonating inside me. While I have mediocre memories of the Gutter District, the last night I spent here really fucked with my head.

"Kinsey?" A warm hand touches my knee, rubbing smooth circles. "Kinsey? Hey, I'm here. You don't need to be afraid. I won't let anything happen to you. I swear on my life."

Wilder's voice hums softly, breathily. He's cautious as if the tone of his voice could send me over the edge. And it might. I had no idea how hard it would be to see the place that I called home. The place that was ripped out from under me all because of my omega order. It's as if I relive the trauma my uncle caused me all over again despite things being different. No one hurt me in the Gutter District per se, but Madame Tamsin destroyed my resolve. It might not be the same place, but the baggage I have left behind scatters across the dirty streets. It stirs memories I like to keep locked up.

"Hey, look at me real quick," Wilder says, reaching out to touch my chin. I hadn't realized that he pulled over into a parking spot in front of an old store with barred windows, a half-lit sign, and loitering warnings. There's no one around either. It's not unusual for neighborhoods in the Gutter District to lack life. Some places are just not worth being invested in, and obviously, this old strip mall is one of them.

I let Wilder turn my head, his fingers light yet attentive, coaxing me into moving when my body refuses to do so on its own. I meet his pale blue eyes, the beautiful depths shining with the sunlight coming in through the windshield. He smooths his thumbs over my cheeks, rubbing gently as he kneads my skin, working his way to my temples, before he combs his fingers through my hair, easing my head toward his. He closes the space, only leaving a millimeter of air between our mouths, but he doesn't kiss me. He rests his forehead to mine, blurring the world around us until it's only him I see. It helps take my focus off everything. When I look into his sky eyes, all I can think about is how much my existence has changed. He's a dick, but he brought me into his household. He relented to his brothers' desire to allow me to stay. He even went so far as to allow me near Holly. While I still don't know his sister well enough, it's obvious that she is one of the most important people in the world to him. It's why he acts as he does, and I understand. I truly do, and I hope that Holly realizes just how lucky she is. I wish my pack had been like this. My parents would still be alive. I'd...no. I refuse to think about what I've lost before it was even mine.

"Take a breath. I want you to listen to me." Wilder breathes slowly, inhaling and pausing and then exhaling. He waits for me to join him, and I manage to shut my mind off. It's easy to distract myself with his overpowering scent. He massages all the places necessary to let me into his world, marking me in a way that claims me as his even if I'm not. I don't know if it's intentional because of where we are or if it's because of the need he's been resisting. Regardless, it helps me relax. It settles my wild emotions, getting them in control.

"Good girl. You're safe with me. I understand it's hard to believe, but I will prove it. Trust is important to me, too. I know that you don't want to be here, and I get that you hate me, but I need you to know that I wasn't lying when I said I would protect you. You're my responsibility, and I will not let you down. Whatever fucked up shit you've been through doesn't matter. The only thing that matters is what we make of things now." His soft breath caresses my lips, drawing me even closer. How can I be so attracted to a man who purposely goes out of his way to be mean and cold? He might have his reasons, but there truly is no excuse. It's his fault that I am in his care to begin with.

Easing away, he clears my vision, allowing me to study his handsome features. He looks similar to Arsenio with the same eye shape and nose, but he has Enzo's full lips and eyes a bit lighter than Enzo's dark blue color. His rugged features mimic Desmond's, his jawline hidden by stubble.

"You keep saying you'll protect me, but if things came down to it, I know you would throw me to the streets. So don't lie about it. You need to be honest with me. It's okay. I understand that your life comes before mine, but I don't want you to fuck with my head. I've been fucked with enough." It's as if a couple of inches of air and space between us helps clear my mind.

Wilder frowns, his soft expression twisting. A new scent wafts from him, one I can't decipher, and then he closes the space again.

"My life is not worth more than yours. I realize I'm not easy to be around, but I wouldn't lie to you. I don't think you recognize how truly amazing you are. You need to understand something, though. This is dangerous. My brothers and I get zero say in the omega we're intended to bond with. It falls on our leader, my father. The idea kills me. No one but those involved should make that choice. If it were up to me... I'm drawn to you so much that it scares me. I know nothing about you apart from what I've found on record." Wilder tightens his fingers through my hair but doesn't pull. He remains ultra-close.

"What have you found exactly?" My throat burns with my question. I should deny everything, but my curiosity wants to know what was said.

Something darkens in his eyes, his scent shifting even warmer. "It doesn't matter."

"Why?" I hold my breath, my anticipation trembling through my body.

"It's hard to explain. I thought I would, but it's funny, Kinsey. I don't even care. I don't give a damn about your past or where you've come from. I don't need a history lesson. Because

I've seen you with my brothers. I've seen you with Holly. And now, I see how you are with me. You're guarded, but you feel what I feel. We need to figure this shit out. I want nothing more than to protect you so we can. Do you understand? I need—really fucking desperately need—for you to trust me."

Leaning forward, Wilder surprises me with a kiss that steals my breath away. I remain frozen in my seat, his lips molding to mine, and all I can think about is how good he tastes. How hot he feels. How his words resonate with a truth I can't deny.

But like he said, it doesn't matter.

It can't change anything.

Pulling away, I swipe my arm across my mouth, trying to get my wild heartbeats under control. "Don't do this to me, Wilder. I've had enough fucking disappointment in my life. Let's just get this over with so we can go home." I blink my eyes, praying that my tears don't spill.

Wilder slams his hands on the steering wheel and thrusts his door open.

He leaves me alone in the car. He disappears.

A tap on the window wakes me up, and I blink my eyes and stare at Wilder hovering on the sidewalk. I hadn't realized I nodded off, my fear and agitation exhausting me. I scrub my palms into my sleepy gaze, not moving or acknowledging him with more than a second glance. He opens the door without waiting for a response, and I'm sure he just didn't want to scare me.

"Come on, my little brat. We're going to swap vehicles. I have a location to meet up with your dealer. She's expecting you." Wilder offers me his hand, waiting for me to take it.

I don't right away, yawning and shaking the sleep from my mind.

Unlatching the seatbelt, I get to my feet on my own, stretching my arms over my head. Wilder's eyes rove down my body, focusing on the skin of my stomach peeking from the hem of my shirt.

Surprisingly, I had no idea boredom could entice one of the best naps of my life. It was as if the scent of Wilder helped ensure that I slept peacefully. But I'd never admit it to him. I'm so annoyed by his actions and unexpected kiss. What was he even thinking?

He said it himself that nothing could ever come between us. I'm not someone to entertain him until he's betrothed to another. It hurts too badly to think about. He can't just toss my emotions around. I want him to be an asshole all the time or never. I hate this in-between bullshit, not knowing what or who I'm going to get with him, constantly leaving me in a state of confusion.

I sigh and clasp Wilder's proffered hand, letting him pull me into his side. He rubs his fingers up and down my bicep, not even thinking twice about how close we are. I guess he wasn't lying about protecting me, because I'm pretty sure he would murder anyone who got within a foot of us. He doesn't show me anything, but I know he carries a weapon on him. A lot of alphas do. He and his brothers aren't afraid to use them either, especially because I know that they have enemies in the Gutter District. We're all aware that Madame Tamsin might be on the lookout to find out who murdered her brother and stole not only her goods but me.

But the Vixen Lounge is on the other side of town, and that's the only reason I'm not as frightened as I should be. I'm not near my apartment either, so no one should recognize me. I never left the two-block radius around my home or work. There was a grocery store and a couple other shops that I frequented, so I lived a mundane, uneventful beta life.

If only I could've predicted this was where I'd end up. I wonder what Gillian's going to ask. News travels fast around here, and she'll be suspicious that I've found a pack—a powerful one at that—on my own. Because even if she doesn't know or recognize Wilder as the son of a leader on one of the Pack Regimes, she'll recognize him as a strong alpha.

With the thought of Gillian, fear clenches my heart. What if she goes to Madam Tamsin with information about me? I know that she was running from her, and it's why she was charging extra to meet with me. She could buy her way out of whatever bullshit she was involved in.

Just the thought slows my steps. I'd be naïve not to think it. People do whatever it takes for power in the Gutter District, and I know Gillian and Madame Tamsin will always crave more.

"Keep up, Kinsey. We can't be late." Wilder tugs me with him, forcing me to keep his pace.

I yank back, trying to buy some time before facing Gillian. "Wilder, wait. I'm scared. I can't do this. What if this is a trap? Gillian was avoiding Madame Tamsin because of something to do with her addiction. I think she either owed her money, or Madame Tamsin wanted to take over for Gillian's boss. She knows who and what I am. We can't trust her. There has to be another way." The words tumble from my mouth as I drag my feet. The only reason I continue walking forward is because Wilder pulls me along as if I'm on a string like a balloon.

"I already thought about that possibility, Kinsey. Money can buy loyalty. So can fear. I made your dealers an offer they can't refuse that will also keep you safe." Wilder reels me closer until I hit his side, coaxing me along. He doesn't give me a chance to get myself together. I'm nearly certain if I resist him, I'm going to end up on his shoulder and be carried like a child throwing a tantrum.

"You can't truly believe that money buys trust. Madame Tamsin has a lot of power and resources." I suck my bottom lip between my teeth, biting it to stop my mouth from trembling.

"Well, the threat of destroying them completely does. Plus, I have offered them access to Gilded Sands. I'll ensure our authorities don't monitor their behavior as long as they don't commit serious offenses." Wilder pulls me down an alley, cutting between the buildings. At the end of the alley, I spot a beat-up pickup truck, the paint worn and rusted. A crack crawls across the windshield, and one of the worn tires misses a hubcap.

Wilder stops and shoves the key into the lock, opening the door to reveal a filthy, shredded leather bench seat. He motions for me to get in. "Please have a little faith in me, Kinsey. I know what I'm doing. I've dealt with people like Gillian and her boss before."

Arguing is pointless, so I just follow his command and slide in behind the wheel to scoot over. He sits beside me, pulling me into the middle to keep me ultra-close and within reach. He slams the door, startling me, and I practically bury my face into his side, forcing him to drape his arm across my shoulders. I hate that I feel so vulnerable, so weak, but being this close to him also makes me feel safe.

My trust issues scream at me to knock it off, but he's right. I have to have faith in him and hope he truly wants me around for his sister's sake.

Wilder maneuvers from the curb, the truck shaking me to my core. It feels as if the tires might fall off at any second, but it doesn't stop him from stomping the throttle and speeding down the street toward the meet-up point.

I hunker down, trying my best not to look out the window. I don't feel safe in this vehicle, even with Wilder clutching me. I wish we didn't come alone. I wish I could be sandwiched between one of his brothers too. His insistence on keeping this time for himself makes more sense since our kiss. I get it. He fights his attraction to me, but he also doesn't want to miss out because of it.

He's a piece of fucking work. I can't judge much because so am I.

"This should only take a couple of minutes. If you reach into my jacket, there's an envelope in the inside pocket. That's for Gillian. Also, there's a gun in the glove compartment that's not connected to us. I want you to take that as well. Have you ever shot one?" he asks.

I shake my head. "No, and I'm not starting now. You use it if you have to."

He groans under his breath. "Note to self, teach the brat some self-preservation skills and basics on weaponry."

I groan and wonder why he wants to put so much effort into me. I get that he doesn't want me to leave because of his sister, but what happens after? She's supposed to work toward rejoining society, and these pills are the first step.

I don't get a chance to really think more about it, because I spot a familiar woman standing outside the door to an old book shop. Gillian peers around, bouncing on her feet, looking as nervous as the last time I saw her.

"That's her. Over there." I point out the window.

"Fuck." Wilder growls under his breath. "Get down."

I whip my attention to where he stares. Gillian doesn't see the man crossing the street like we do. I open my mouth to scream, but Wilder stifles my voice, yanking me into him. Peeking from my spot, I cry softly at the sight of the man reaching into his jacket.

I startle and squeeze my eyes shut at the sound of a gunshot. Gillian screams, her yell ringing through the air, her pain palpable enough for me to feel as if it was my own.

Snapping my eyes open, I watch as the woman who has helped me for the last two years falls to the ground. She bleeds everywhere.

Chapter 12

Kinsey

Survive

Wilder swerves the truck, screeching to a halt at the curb. Reaching over me, he grabs a gun from the dashboard and hops out, leaving me in shock. I jump at the sound of more gunfire, watching as Wilder shoots the guy in the back, not letting him leave.

My brain finally kicks on, and I hop out of the truck and run to Gillian. She gasps, her body shuddering as she lies helplessly on the sidewalk. Blinking slowly, she stares at the sky, her eyes wide. I press my hands to the bloody spot on her abdomen, trying to stanch the bleeding, but it just keeps seeping between my fingers.

"Gillian, oh my God. Hold on. We're going to get you help." It hurts to say the words, because I know that there's no way we're going to call the authorities. A part of me hates that she suffers helplessly, without any hope. This isn't right. No one deserves to die like this. Not even the woman who turned my life upside down. In a way, she still saved me. I wouldn't have had the last two years of beta normalcy without her. "I'm here. I'm not going anywhere."

Tears escape my eyes, dripping down my cheeks in hot trails. I gasp a couple of breaths, attempting to hide my panic. Gillian opens and closes her mouth, unable to speak. Her eyes flick back and forth, looking over my face, and then she goes still. The light leaves her eyes, and she dies right before me without a word and without anyone who loved her. She should've been with her pack. I know she got herself into this situation one way or another, but she deserved better.

My body cools with numbness, and I slowly lift my hands, staring at her blood dripping from my fingers.

"Who sent you?" Wilder growls the words, yanking my attention away from Gillian's body. He stands over a man, pointing a gun in his face.

The guy grinds his teeth, refusing to answer.

Jerking the gun down, Wilder smacks the man in the forehead with it, causing him to holler. My body freezes, my muscles aching. Wilder kicks the man over and steps his boot right into the bullet wound on his back.

"Which pack do you belong to? Who are you working for?" Wilder stomps his foot harder, making the man scream.

But still, he doesn't answer. He won't. He knows he's a dead man already. Even if Wilder didn't kill him, someone else would. Because he was caught, whoever he works for will automatically assume that he betrayed them.

"Turn around, Kinsey. Don't watch. Cover your ears." Wilder snaps his attention to me, his features sharp and frightening. But I'm not afraid of him. I don't listen to him either. I refuse to.

A part of me yearns to see this asshole get what he deserves. Watching Wilder serve justice on Gillian's behalf helps lessen the hurt and fear roiling through me.

Wilder realizes my mind's set, and instead of arguing, he points a gun at the back of the man's head and pulls the trigger. I jerk at the noise, but I don't turn away, entranced by the blood pooling across the concrete.

Wilder kicks and turns him back over, showing how ravaged his face is from the close contact gunshot. He rifles through his clothes and pulls out the man's wallet along with his keys and phone. He tucks the items into his jacket and strides to me, scooping me into his arms without hesitation.

I don't fight him. All I do is hang my arms around his neck and let him carry me back to the truck. He sets me on the seat only to jog to Gillian, carefully going through her purse until he pulls out a bag of pills.

I dig my fingernails into my palms, counting my racing heartbeats, the thuds so quick that I can't keep up.

Wilder returns to the truck and shuts the door, not waiting before he hits the throttle and peels out, leaving a cloud of smoke in our wake. Silence fills the vehicle as I try to collect myself. If I speak now, my voice will crack. I might begin to sob. I might get hit with a million emotions.

"Hang tight, Kinsey. We're going to get out of here quickly. It looks like you were right, and I'm sorry I didn't believe you. The guy worked for Madam Tamsin, but it wasn't Gillian. It looks like her boss set her up, trying to set us up. We arrived a bit too late, though." Wilder turns down an alley and heads back in the direction of the old shop where he left his sports car. "I'm glad we managed to take care of him though. Word shouldn't get back to Madame Tamsin about us. I didn't give any pertinent information to Gillian's boss either. I think he was trying to find out who we were to blackmail us anyway."

I bob my head, my thoughts scrambled. Of course, Gillian's boss set her up. She was a liability. No one crosses a client and gets away with it, even if it was the man in charge that put her up to it.

"What are we going to do now?" I finally manage to spit the words out. My voice fails me like I suspected it would, cracking and shaking, hoarse even though I wasn't screaming or anything.

"I took her stash of the suppressants along with some other stuff. It should be enough to start us out until we can find another way to get them. I'm going to hunt down her boss and show him exactly what happens when you cross a prince of Gilded Sands. He's not going to get away with this. Neither will Madame Tamsin. She is still one of our targets. We need to weaken her power a bit more to help us out. She has too many connections to the other territories, and I need to break them. She needs to be seen as unreliable and untrustworthy." Wilder rubs his big palm across my leg, smoothing out my trembling the best he can. "But I don't want you to worry about any of that. Let's get you home."

Home. For the first time, I feel like it's the truth. The palace is now my home, and it's time that I truly accept it. This is my life now. I never expected that I would have to trust a pack that wasn't chosen for me, but maybe that's the point. Maybe it's up to me to choose them.

I just hope that things don't grow worse.

I just hope that they stay true to their word and don't change.

But mostly, I hope to survive.

"How's the water, Kinsey?" Wilder stands in the shower with his back to me.

He had filled up the tub while I was rinsing off in the shower, but he managed to keep his gaze in control without looking at me. But I watch him now, staring the whole time while he rinses the blood from his skin, stained from me clinging onto him for dear life.

And he is absolutely sexy. Hot. It was enough to get me to zone out and just appreciate his perfect body as the water streamed over his muscles in rivulets.

"It's getting cold. I think I'm ready to get out." I stand up, splashing in the water.

I catch Wilder watching me in the mirrored wall of his shower, his look of lust sending tingles blossoming through my body. His eyes travel down, following the bubbles dripping from my breasts as the cool air pops them, leaving me bare.

I don't know what gets into me, but I swallow my nerves and cross the small space to the shower, opening the door and stepping inside.

Hot steam fills the air, and I slide around Wilder and into the stream of water, rinsing off. I leave him standing like stone in silence as I move back past him and exit the shower, stealing his towel to wrap around me. There's one hanging for me by the tub, but this is the one I want. It looks twice as large and super fluffy.

He releases a deep purr from his throat, the sound striking me in the clit and turning me on. "Careful, my brat. Keep teasing me like that, and you're going to get yourself in trouble. It's already taken everything in me not to join you in the bubble bath or block you so you couldn't leave the shower." Wilder stares at me, giving in to my flirting and taking advantage of it to drink me in as much as he wants. His hard cock points at me, his desire potent even with the scent of his bodywash and the water.

All I do is smile, his words egging me on, making me want to tease him even more. But I know better than that. As soon as the adrenaline washes away and I have time to think, I know that I will no longer find myself excited. Because the shit show of today was insane. I know it wasn't his fault, but Gillian died. We stole the drugs from her dead body, and I watched as Wilder killed a man. He's dangerous, unpredictable. It makes me hesitate and want to build a wall around myself. What choice do I have? I'm still basically a prisoner here with no hope of claiming these princes as my pack. I'll end up heartbroken in the end and believing in anything otherwise would solidify my naivety.

They can flirt and treat me as if they want me, and I wouldn't leave, given the chance now, but I need to be realistic. What if we're caught? What if the king finds out that they're lying about their sister? What would happen to me then? I need to live life cautiously. The last time that I got my hopes up, they were absolutely annihilated. I almost died because of it. Many others are dead.

Fuck me. Why does my mind have to go and ruin the moment? I just want so badly to rewind my brain and get back in the shower with Wilder. I want to jump into his arms and kiss him, giving in to his affection this time. I want to fuck him until he knots with me, claiming me as his omega. My need grows more intense, but it's just my body and my mind at war with each other. I know better. Once such an act happens, it's over for me. I know how bonding works. No one will ever compare. I'll live the rest of my life unsatisfied and unfulfilled. Unwanted.

I'm already too reliant on these alphas. Reliant on Desmond too. And where does this whole situation leave him? Holly just assumed that because Desmond was a beta that I wouldn't be interested in him, but I don't know. My uncle broke me and changed me. I can no longer think like I had before.

If anything, Desmond would be my safety net. With him, there's a lot less to lose.

"Kinsey, come back here. Let me just hug you for a minute. I can smell your emotions, and it hurts me. I know you're not okay, and I'm not going to demand you pretend to be. What you went through today? It was unacceptable. I take full responsibility, and I'm so sorry." Wilder stands soaking wet outside the shower, staring at me as I bow my head, my eyes burning with tears. I must've zoned out, because I don't even remember drying off and wrapping the towel around myself.

I shake my head, just wishing for a moment alone. I hate him seeing me like this. I don't want his brothers to come rushing to me and treating me as if I'm some fragile woman. I need to process this without everything crushing me. Smothering me.

I need one of those fucking suppressant pills. I almost feel as if I'll die if I don't take one now. Is it a shitty way of escaping? Maybe. But I don't care. They're called suppressant pills for a reason. They'll level out my body and help me put my wall back together now that these men tore it apart and smashed it.

"You don't have to apologize. I knew the possibility of something bad happening. I just—I'm sorry. I'm going to go back to my room. I might check on Holly as well. I want to tell her about the drugs. She should hear it from me. You should update your brothers and let them know. I'll be fine." I stride toward his bedroom door, not waiting for him to respond.

I spot the bag of pills on the table by the door, and I grab it and rush out of the room, knowing that Wilder will stop me if he catches me.

Enzo calls my name from the hallway as if he's been waiting for me to leave Wilder's room, but I don't stop. I run toward the study and where I know I'll find an access door that'll take me to Holly's room.

I slam the door and hope no one chases after me all because I don't want to have to explain myself. I'm not ready to tell them exactly why this fucked up situation got to me even worse than I expected it to. All I want is to just redirect my attention. Away from my attraction toward Wilder. Away from my carnal need to distract myself in the way I fantasize about in this moment, seeing him hard and ready to claim me. How his scent hypnotizes me.

Sex isn't the way to go no matter how much I think about doing it with Wilder. That's how I know I'm acting irrationally. One day and a couple hours of him being caring doesn't make up for how horrible he has treated me up until that point. He can have all the excuses he wants, but I'm not going to let his scent and my deep-seated nature, driven from my order as an omega, control me.

I slap my hand over the keypad, praying that it opens for me. All it does is turn red, none of the guys have programmed it to allow me access yet. I bang my hand on the door, my body shaking, my anxiety getting the best of me.

"Holly? Holly, it's me. I'm back. I thought we could hang out." I hope she can hear the words, and I bang again.

She doesn't respond, and my heart sinks into my stomach.

A familiar scent wafts next to me, and a shadow grows on the wall. I keep my head bowed and my hands in tight fists. Enzo waits for me to look at him, but I can't.

He surprises me by placing his hand on the keypad and opening the thick metal door to Holly's suite. He doesn't say anything and retreats a few feet, not trying to talk or anything.

I puff out a breath and tap my knuckles on the wood, thankful that Enzo doesn't pressure me to talk to him. He simply just opens the panic room door, so I can proceed with my mission.

"Holly? Are you busy?" I ask, my voice choking up as I try to keep myself together.

The door swings inward, and I catch sight of the petite hazel-eyed girl with blond hair several shades lighter than Arsenio's mop of honey strands. Holly cocks her head as we stare at each other and then she steps forward and flings her arms around me, hugging me so tightly that it feels as if she's the only thing keeping me together when I suddenly feel myself crumbling and falling apart.

"Oh my God. Are you okay? Let me get you something to wear. What did Wilder do? I know it was his day with you." The questions tumble from Holly's mouth as she pulls me into her room and shuts the door, locking it to ensure that none of her brothers come in uninvited.

I'm supposed to be her caregiver, and here I am, allowing Holly to guide me to her bed to sit me down. She heads to her dresser and pulls out a couple articles of clothing and helps me dress without question, not bothered by my nudity.

She pulls me to her again and hugs me, comforting me in a way that feels like a family member would. I've gotten many hugs like this from my mom. From my dad. From my cousins. From other members of our pack.

"You don't have to say anything, but just know that I'm here for you. I know I'm young, but I think we can relate, you know. Your history and mine. The fact that I know Wilder is also an overprotective asshole." Holly kneads her hands across my back. "Did he say something stupid? He's so hotheaded, I swear."

I release a long breath, laughter bubbling from my mouth. It feels like a gasp of relief, and I relax and finally let go of the ache and the panic coursing through me.

"He drives me crazy. He confuses me too, but it was not really his fault. We went to pick up some suppressant pills for you and got in the middle of a street war. Someone I knew from before was killed." I keep my eyes shut, focusing on my breathing. "But I'm okay. You're right about your brother being protective. He served justice swiftly and unrelentingly."

"Oh, no. That sounds fucking awful. I'm so sorry. He should've never had you go with him for that sort of thing. I can't believe the others let him. You could've been hurt." Rage fills Holly's voice, and she tenses next to me only to get herself in check.

I peek at her, sensing that she might storm out of here to confront Wilder. As much as I appreciate the sentiment, I don't want her to shout at him for things he already knows. The last thing I need is to put a wedge between them.

Am I protecting Wilder from his sister's wrath? Once again, he's going to owe me, and I'll hold him to it.

I groan and snuggle closer to her, resting my head on the crook of her shoulder. I touch my palm to her cheek and squish our faces together like the million times my mom helped me settle down, especially after my order manifested. She was always good at that sort of thing, and I appreciate the memory now.

"First, I'm supposed to be your caretaker, Holly," I say, rocking the two of us back and forth. "Second, he already knows he made a mistake. He only intended to help you, and at least it wasn't for nothing." Lifting the bag from the bed beside me, I dangle it in front of us. "We got what we needed. Have you heard of suppressant pills?"

Holly eases away from me, turning to meet my gaze. "Suppressant pills? I don't understand."

I guess she wouldn't. She's been sheltered all her life. Even more so now.

"I don't know how much your brothers told you about me and how I got here, but I was hiding who I was by taking these. Something...terrible happened to the pack I was arranged to bond with, and I had to hide who I was or risk getting taken by the Pack Regime. Because I'm not...protected by a pack, a lot of shitty things could've happened to me. We picked these up to help you. You're going to need them. Especially with your upcoming heat. They'll help out and even stop it from happening if you want." I know this is going to bring up a ton of questions for her, but I don't even know where to begin or if

I want to. It's a lot to throw at someone, and Holly has enough problems of her own to deal with.

"I'm sorry that you had to go through all of that. I know you'll tell me when you're ready to. I don't believe what my brother said was reported in the media. I know how the alphas and the authorities are." Holly rests her hand on my knee. "I faced an awful pack. The men my dad had chosen for me were brutal. They didn't want an omega to bond with. They wanted to use me. They wanted to take what they needed and throw me away. They knew I was close to my brothers, and I was a way that they could try to control our kingdom instead of ally with my father. But he wouldn't believe it. He didn't care. He didn't want me here." Holly lowers her voice with the words. "So I ran away. It was Wilder who came up with the plan to fake my death. He collected a lot of my blood himself. He made it look as if one of our enemies killed me and burned me in a fire. They used my blood to make another person seem like me. My hair too. It was awful, but it had to be done." Lifting up her tresses, she shows off an undercut.

I blink a few times, thinking over what she just told me and how vulnerable she must feel. I keep my face expressionless, not wanting to give away the fact that I need to know more about the person they used to feed lies to Holly's dad. Was it someone innocent? Someone who volunteered? Just some poor woman who was in the wrong place at the wrong time?

But I don't want to ask Holly. I would hope that her brothers would protect her from that kind of information. She's still young, only experiencing her manifestation within the last few months. She's still eighteen despite how grown-up she acts. Despite the fact that she is mature and technically an adult.

Fuck the things life does to you to give you maturity. Experience makes you wiser compared to just the number of days you've been alive on this earth. I hate that we both have such experiences.

"I'm so, so sorry you had to experience that. It must've been terrifying." I hug her, letting her bury her face in the crook of my neck this time. Who knew that I would find comfort in another omega in my life? It's strange yet somehow a peace I never knew I would have again. This is the comfort that comes from a pack, and I just wish that it didn't all feel so temporary. Because I had no idea how much I craved this connection. This life.

She nuzzles her nose against me. "It was, but my brothers protected me. The woman who gave her life on my behalf was incredibly sick and they arranged everything to help her back and bring her the mercy she begged for and was denied to her by the Pack Regime. They're incredible, still protecting me even though it could ruin their lives. And I'm not going to lie...I'm happy you're here, Kinsey. You have no idea. Their crazy asses couldn't have gotten more lucky accidentally kidnapping you."

I swallow my shudder, my eyes watering. "I'm happy for it too. Even for Wilder's dickish attitude. I just wish..." Shrugging, I let my voice trail off, not speaking the truth out loud. She has a lot of faith in her pack, which they deserve and earned from her, but for me? Who knows? "I just wish I could forget about some things, you know?" I force my mouth to smile.

"Definitely." Holly squeezes me once more and gets to her feet. "Come on. Why don't we watch a movie or something to help? You can explain what the suppressant pills do. Maybe we can test one? I've always wondered what being a beta would feel like."

My fake smile turns into a genuine grin, and I nod my head. "That sounds like a great idea. Just don't tell your brothers. I want to show them how great they work." And not only that. They'll help me see things more clearly. I'll be able to know whether or not I'm feeling the way I am because of them or because of my pheromones. My hormones. All of my emotions. My true order.

Holly claps her hands, beaming at me. "This is going to be awesome. Serves them right for all the bullshit, huh? They can keep us hidden in this palace, but it doesn't mean we can't have fun."

She's right. For the first time in a long time, I realize that there's more to life than just my order. I need to embrace what I have in the moment, because I never know when it's going to end.

Because in my experience, things that I love and enjoy and crave don't last forever.

If only I could break the cycle now.

Chapter 13

Kinsey

Omega Bonds

I'd be lying if I didn't say I was shocked when I was in Holly's room and none of her brothers came to check on us and still haven't. I remain in Holly's bed with her, sharing the blankets. I've always dreamed about having a slumber party with friends, but my parents never allowed it. Who knew it would be even more fun as an adult? I got to take some time to cook for us, because we didn't want to bother anyone else, and it wasn't necessary to ask the kitchen. I forgot how much I like cooking when I have everything on hand, and I don't have to worry about whether or not I can afford the ingredients.

Holly, on the other hand, needs some cooking lessons unless she plans to bake cookies for every meal. She couldn't survive on her own without burning her place down or eating fast food regularly. Or maybe just cereal. Either way, we had a lot of fun.

"Hey, I'm going to step out for a bit. Maybe we can meet up later? It'll take you a while to get used to the suppressant pills. I know I was dead tired the first couple of days." I sit up beside Holly, nudging her to get her to open her eyes.

She mumbles something with a smile and turns over, burying her face under her pillow.

I chuckle and slide out of bed, stretching my arms over my head. Instead of wandering into the bathroom, I decide to head back to my suite to take another shower. I know that Wilder mentioned that each of his brothers were taking a couple days to watch out for me, and I kind of don't want to remind them of Holly. I'll save that for Wilder's days to infuriate him.

I have to pay him back for his attitude somehow.

I'm too focused on getting back to my suite that I miss the pair of legs blocking my way down the corridor. I trip and screech, hitting my palms on the floor. Fingers latch to the sides of my waist, hoisting me to my feet. A taut chest rests against my back for only a second before Enzo flips me around.

"Shit, baby. I didn't hear the door beep. You okay? Let me check your hands." Enzo adjusts me in his arms, balancing me on his bent knee to free a hand. I tug my wrist back and squirm, sliding to my feet.

"I'm fine. Relax." I hold my palm to his face. "What the hell were you doing on the floor anyway?" I knit my brows together, peering around. "Were you sleeping?"

Flush reddens his face. "Maybe."

I shake my head and step away from him. "Do I even want to know why you were sleeping in the hallway? This place is pretty much a fortress. Especially Holly's room. What do you get out of it? We had the panic door locked and everything."

"Consider me your guard dog. Plus, there was no way I was going to let you sneak out of here without you seeing how devoted to your safety I truly am." Enzo grins at me, his smile widening, his eyes shining.

I laugh and pat his cheek. He captures my hand and presses my fingers harder into his skin, his nostrils flaring as he inhales a deep breath. He frowns and brings my wrist to his nose, inhaling another breath.

I stand still, watching him try to figure out what's up with me. I took a suppressant pill right alongside Holly, and it should obscure my pheromones that might set him off.

I think he realizes it now, because he narrows his eyes and leans in closer, his mouth only inches away from mine.

"You're a total tease. Why would you take one of those pills? Wilder said they were just for Holly." Enzo leans in even closer, pressing his cheek to mine and getting near my ear. "You know you're only punishing yourself, right? You can't mark me otherwise."

I smirk at him, catching on to what he's doing, trying to use his pheromones to excite me. "And you can't scent me to tease me either. The suppressant pills also make an omega less sensitive to..." Pausing, I pull away from him and twirl my finger. "Whatever it is you're trying to do."

He snaps his teeth at me, playfully trying to snatch my hand. I dodge around him and bolt away. A peel of laughter escapes my mouth, and I glance behind me. He hesitates, allowing space to get between us until I reach the bend in the corridor.

Then he makes his move.

I squeal, adrenaline coursing through me as Enzo charges behind me. His long, muscular legs make it easy for him to catch up. Hooking me by the waist, he flips me, hanging me over his shoulder. He passes my room, heading farther down the corridor. I can't see much with the way he holds me, so I pinch his ass.

"Careful, Kinsey. I'll retaliate for that if you don't quit it. I don't think you realize how spankable your ass is right now, especially with it so close to my face. I could bite it, too." Enzo shifts me from his shoulder, catching me in his arms. "I also know why you did it."

"Did what?" I ask, knowing damn well he's talking about taking the suppressant pills. I'll play dumb though. I want to hear it for myself.

He growls under his breath, slowing down. "You're testing me."

I remain expressionless.

Slamming his hand to a keypad on the wall, he opens another door, one that swings out into an enormous entertainment room. I've never seen a theater inside of a home before, but this is a palace, after all. "You think I'm only into you because of how fucking incredible and hypnotic you smell."

"Maybe because you think I'm pretty, too." I smile with the words. "Which I think the same about you."

"Pretty? You think I'm pretty?" Enzo scrunches his nose. "Take that back. I'm far from pretty. Rugged men aren't pretty."

I practically cackle as I run my finger over his jaw. "But that jawline—so beautiful."

"Damn it, baby. I love when you tease me. I'll be a pretty boy for you as long as it makes you smile." Enzo rubs his face harder to my hand, the gesture making my insides hum. I might be numb toward the emotions that come with the scents, but I'm not naive toward the gesture. "I love how it lights up your whole face."

My body warms with his compliment.

"And don't get me started about how sweet you are—I haven't seen anyone outside of me and my brothers treat Holly like that. Especially because you were forced into all this shit." Enzo carries me past an air hockey table and a couple of arcade games. "You're also cunning and smart. Witty. Not many omegas would be able to do what you've done."

I suck in my bottom lip between my teeth, his words igniting something wild inside me. No one's ever said anything like this about me. The attraction between us is so palpable that I shudder a breath, tightening my hands around his neck.

"Mmm...do you want me to go on?" he murmurs, his eyes tracing down my face, his body rippling as I tighten my legs around him, meeting him straight on. "Because I could list everything starting now and still could never finish in our lifetime. You're so perfect, Kinsey."

I fight the doubt rising inside me. A part of me knows that it's dangerous to give into Enzo's flirting. I don't know how realistic it is for me to even think for a second that something could ever come from this. He's royal and his pack is part of the Pack Regime. Wilder confirmed that their father, as their leader and king, will choose the omega that he and his brothers will bond with.

I want so badly to resist to protect myself, but maybe I just need to give in for once. To take something I crave in this moment. Shit happens so quickly in my life. Nothing could ever help me prepare for anything I face. I sure as fuck didn't expect my uncle to murder my parents. I didn't expect him to torture me and the men who were supposed to be my pack by restraining us during my very first heat, driving us all crazy, ensuring that all I could ever feel from the experience was utter agony.

For how he killed each of them, guaranteeing that we would never bond. He'd have done something even worse to me had I not gotten a hold of the hammer he used to pry the anchors free from the wall. I don't think he realized that I had it in me to fight back. But I wasn't going to be some docile, afraid little girl. Because what he did? He took away everything innocent and naïve from me, and I just wish I'd hit him harder, longer, fatally.

I blink a few times, suppressing the memory the best I can. I don't want to ruin this moment. To cut the connection that sizzles between Enzo and me.

So I kiss him. I kiss him as if doing so will be the only reason I'll survive another moment. He devours my sudden affection, spinning me to press my back against the cool wall of...I don't even know where we are. We left the entertainment room, and now the air feels cooler, smells different. But I don't look. I don't care, really.

I just want to explore and taste his tongue, feel the softness of our lips moving together until I can't stand how gentle it is and kiss him deeper, sucking his bottom lip between my teeth to nip him. Our tongues battle it out for control, and he squeezes my ass, lowering me just enough to feel the hardness of his arousal.

And I want more. I crave more.

Enzo was right. There's more to this than our orders, and I'm numb to his scent yet still drawn to him and his lust. I still desire him. I still want the closeness of our bodies together. Feel the heat of him against me.

Enzo breaks away from my mouth, kissing down my neck at the same time he pulls my shirt from my head. I gasp as his lips find my nipple, and he sucks it into his mouth before licking his way to my other breast. I grip onto his midnight hair and squirm, the desire rising inside me as intense as it has been with him before. But this time, I've lost all my reservations. I don't care if this is something that can't last. I'm going to take it anyway.

"Baby, I want to taste you. I need to bury my face in your pussy and find out how wet you are for me." Enzo carries me through the room, and I finally get a chance to peek around at the indoor pool with glittering rocks, a hot tub, and a sloping beach-like entrance.

"I'm drenched. So hot," I murmur.

"I fucking need to know for certain. I can't wait any longer. You're all I ever think about. Crave. I need you to be mine, Kinsey. I don't care about anything else." Enzo nuzzles his face to my throat, nipping my skin, his body and mind battling it out because I took the suppressant pills, preventing him from truly scenting me with his mark, so he does so in other ways, sucking hard enough to make my toes curl.

I moan as Enzo's fingers explore my nipples. He crashes his lips back to mine, kissing me with so much passion I can feel it in my soul. My skin buzzes in anticipation, and I inhale a sharp breath when my back hits the soft cushion of the lounge chair. The thrill of being out in the open, even in this private area of the palace sends my heart thudding.

Climbing on top of me, Enzo rests between my legs and works his way down, stripping the pajamas off as he goes as if the flimsy fabric might be his worst enemy. He glides his tongue down the center of my stomach and kisses around my navel, continuing his mission to find the spot he craves the most. I moan as his lips brush my hip. He traces my omega order mark with his tongue, the sensation building even more warmth between my legs. He undresses me completely, tossing my clothes to the side, leaving me exposed as he devours me with his sapphire eyes. His eyes sparkle with his desire, and he rubs his cock through his pants, showing me the outline of his erection.

I stretch up, grazing my fingers over it, feeling it throb under my touch, but he doesn't let me explore him for long. He scoots lower, placing his big palms on my knees to bend my legs, making room for his broad shoulders.

I arch my back and play with his soft black hair, my muscles tensing as he buries his face between my legs and glides his tongue over my clit, sucking it gently into his mouth, just tasting and savoring my body in a way that no man has done so before. While I'm not a virgin, I don't have much experience outside of taking control of my own pleasure. And the one guy I slept with wasn't very memorable. Because I was only faking it as a beta, and he was a beta, who did absolutely nothing for me. It was more out of curiosity than anything.

I can't think about that anymore.

This will forever be my first real act of pleasure with a man—an alpha—now.

"You taste so fucking good." Enzo slides a finger inside me, rolling his tongue over my body at the same time. "I want to stay right here forever."

Enzo groans, the vibration of his voice sending tingles through my body. He dips his finger in and out, working me up and slickening his hand with my desire. I squirm under the sensation, imagining what it would be like if he would fuck me now, taking what he wanted. But I know what would happen. I wouldn't get pregnant because I'm not in heat, but it doesn't mean he wouldn't knot with me. It would be a bond that would seal whatever is to come. Giving him that kind of power isn't something he would take lightly, at least, if he's being truthful. That's why both omegas and alphas are open to sleeping with betas. We don't get the same kind of attachment. The bond. At least, not with a beta who isn't intended to be part of your pack romantically like Desmond is. Because I know that he is included. Packs tend to be all or nothing when it comes to a woman. If it was just one alpha, then it would only be one bond. But there are so many with his brothers. I wouldn't mind testing the waters with Desmond. I'm attracted to him, after all.

"You're going to come for me now, baby. You ready?" Enzo rubs my inner wall, watching my face as lust weighs my eyelids, my eyelashes obscuring the world.

"Mmmhmm." I gasp at the intense wave of tingles growing through me, his exploration arousing something amazing in my very being.

Enzo licks and sucks and kisses my clit, working his finger in and out of me as he massages a spot inside me that sends my body spasming, pushing the thoughts of his brothers completely away to focus solely on him. I bow forward, grabbing his dark hair harder, trying to ease him away as the sensation grows even more powerful, but he only meets my eyes and whispers for me to let him finish.

My muscles tighten with my orgasm, and I scream and fly back, riding the wave of pleasure that Enzo ignites in me.

"Fuck, baby. You don't know how hard it is to stop. I want you to be mine," Enzo says, adjusting his hard cock in his pants.

I smile and reach for him, wanting him to switch places with me. "It's only fair that you let me taste you too. I can't be the only one getting attention."

"See what I mean about how sweet you are? You damn well know that I don't need extra attention. I'm good with giving you all mine, all the time. I want to give you more. I want you to let me be selfish and deny you." Enzo traces his finger over my pelvis, making me shiver, my body still pulsing.

I shake my head, planting my hands on his chest to push him back, seeing if he'll resist. He only does for a second until I rub my fingers over the length of his shaft pressing to his pants. He groans and gives in. I can tell it takes all his restraint to let me have this sort of control. He's an alpha, after all.

He plays with my hair, tucking it behind my ears to keep it out of my face. I link my fingers to his pants and unfasten them, slowly sliding my hand down to feel exactly what I do to him. He's a lot thicker than I realize, and I wonder if it would hurt to sleep with him.

I push the thought away because I shouldn't have to worry about that right now. I don't need to worry about it at all. I know that my body will prepare itself for me. There is no pain when it comes to the pleasure an alpha gives an omega and only the high of adrenaline from such a rush.

I grab the front of his pants and pull them down further, wanting to strip him to be as naked as I am. I want to memorize his body with my fingers and my mouth. I want to imprint it in my brain to come back to this later when I need something amazing to think about.

He shifts his body, letting me undress him, and I position myself between his legs. He arches up and lets me pull his shirt over his head before he meets me for another kiss, our bodies so close that all I would have to do is ease up a bit more, and he could be inside me. The thought turns me on, and I push him back to resist, gliding my hands down the ridges of his delectable six-pack and to his intimidating erection. I lace my fingers around it and stroke him slowly, starting from his base and working my way up to caress my palm over his tip, feeling the pre-cum dripping. I use it to lubricate my hand, smiling as he closes his eyes and releases a sigh of pleasure. I take my time familiarizing myself with him, listening to his reactions to see what he likes and what he wants more of. I use my other hand to stroke his balls before I finally bend forward to glide my tongue over his tip. His body ripples with his desire, and I peek up at him, watching him stare at me as I part my lips and suck him into my mouth. He plays with my hair, pulling it back and twining it around his hand, guiding me in the way he prefers.

I inhale a breath as I suck him in as far as I can go, and then I add pressure and lick the bottom side of the shaft, twirling my tongue, feeling how his balls tighten with the pleasure radiating from him. I glide my fingers under his balls, massaging the soft skin there without trying to go any farther, but damn, he enjoys it. He moans deep and rumbling, his body flexing. I don't even have to be aware of his scent to know how much he loves this moment. The sweetness of his cock tantalizes me, and I imagine what it would be like to have this forever.

I never thought I would ever be with an alpha, because I thought that my chance to bond died with the men my parents chose for me, but I realize that isn't true now.

"Kinsey, that feels so good." Enzo groans and moans, continuing to hold my head as if he can't stand the thought of giving me complete control. It makes me work harder and faster, bobbing my head while I continue to massage him, just wanting so badly for him to come. I wonder what he tastes like and if it will be different if I do this again while I'm not influenced by the suppressant pill.

He might've been right about me torturing myself, because it drives me crazy not getting the full effect of his pleasure.

"I'm going to come, Kinsey." Enzo tightens his hand in my hair even more, trying to slow me down.

I hum in anticipation, the vibration of my voice sending him over the edge. He grunts as he sits up, clinging to me as if he'll fly away otherwise. Sweetness floods my mouth, and I slowly pull away and swallow, meeting his gaze, his heavy-lidded eyes so sexy in this moment.

He doesn't let me kneel before him for long, hooking his arms under mine to pull me up until I rest naked on top of him. We nuzzle together for a quiet moment, just listening to each other's breathing and our hearts beating. It feels so good to be with Enzo, and he makes it so easy to ignore any doubt that tries to steal my attention.

"Come on, baby. Let me help you get cleaned up. Maybe we can go in the hot tub for a bit. I want your day to be as amazing as you are." Enzo lifts me in his arms, letting me wrap my legs around him and rest my head on his shoulder. I don't think he'll let me walk for the rest of his time with me, his need to dote on me and shower me with his affection stronger than ever now that we've explored our vulnerabilities and our desires.

We head to the shower just off to the side of the pool area, and Enzo sits me down on a bench while he grabs everything we need.

I can't take my eyes off him, watching his muscular body ripple with his movements. His tight ass is absolutely biteable, and he's wrong about me with a spankable ass. Now I'm going to have to try it on him. See if he'll let me get away with it.

But then the adrenaline starts to fade, and I realize how I'm already thinking as if this pack has claimed me. I've found hope in my wishful thinking, despite knowing better than that.

"Kinsey? What's up?" Enzo sits beside me, pulling me into his lap. "You can tell me anything. I miss your smile. Where did it go?"

I laugh at his words, his closeness helping to ease the worry tightening my chest. "I was just thinking. That happens a lot when you put space between us. I just...what are we doing?"

I swallow with my words, resting my head on his pec, feeling his eyes boring into me as if he can read my mind.

"Getting to know each other. We're embracing the fact that fate wants us to be together." Enzo snuggles against me, rubbing his big hand over my side as he lifts me back up, making me face him as he carries me into the steaming stream of hot water.

I try not to frown. "Fate doesn't get a say in this. You know that, right? Your leader—"

Enzo cuts me off with a kiss as if my words pain him, and maybe they do. He eases away, looking deeply into my eyes. "He doesn't control us. I promise you, Kinsey. What am I doing here? I'm here because I want you. You're the most amazing woman I have ever met. I've ever had the chance to know. I want you as my omega. I want to bond with you."

My lip trembles and I can't find my voice.

"Believe me. You've already changed our lives. And now I want to change the future. I *will* change the future. I won't give you up. I want you to be mine." Enzo brushes his lips to mine again. "Will you let me prove it?"

I don't know exactly what to say, so all I do is nod my head and kiss him back. I want what he does, and his words of affirmation help.

It's almost unbelievable.

Surreal.

If only I could shed this veil of doubt trying to suffocate me.

My attraction to Enzo is so clear.

If only we could show the world.

He wants me to be his, but it's more than that. I want him to be mine too.

Chapter 14

Kinsey

Surprise

"Enzo, Kinsey! I've been looking everywhere for you. Get dressed. We need to get Kinsey to Holly's room. King Winston just showed up. He wants to talk about some hostility on the northern region of Gilded Sands." Arsenio stands in the doorway between the pool and the entertainment room. "Hurry!"

Fear shocks me out of my state of pure tranquility, sitting on Enzo's lap as he massages my shoulders while we hang out in the hot tub.

Arsenio grabs a towel from a stack on the wall shelf, and he holds it out as Enzo lifts me from the hot water. My nipples pebble at the change in temperature, and Arsenio gives me a quick once-over, unintentionally peeking at my naked body.

Excitement courses through me at his flash of attention, and I manage to refrain from calling him out for it.

"We should get them out of here. The panic room isn't a secret," Enzo says, frowning.

"Wilder agrees, but we need Dad to see all of us first. We can't risk him asking questions about our whereabouts. After, we can sneak them to the garage and head out." Arsenio looks at me again. "Are you good with that? The suppressant pills work, and no one will know." He rubs his hands over my arms, pushing away the water droplets with his palms. "It'll probably be Desmond without us. The king usually excuses him first."

Enzo growls. "Like fucking hell is he going alone. Dad doesn't—"

"My sons! I knew you two were up to something." A man's voice bellows through the concrete room, sending a shock straight to my chest. Sauntering closer, he adjusts his suit jacket, raising his eyebrows as he unashamedly checks me out, standing naked in just a towel. His nostrils widen with his deep breath. "What a pretty thing she is. Does Wilder know you've been entertaining yourselves with a beta?"

Thank fucking God for the suppressant pills.

Enzo forces his mouth to smile and pulls me in closer, protectively but also as if he wants to prove his father right about entertaining himself with my company.

"Of course. I wouldn't sneak around with how much I enjoy getting on his nerves." Enzo steps back, tugging me with him. "Drives him mad. He won't admit just how gorgeous she is...for a beta." He practically spits out the words.

Chuckling, the king once again closes the space, whacking Enzo on the back. Arsenio stiffens, yet he remains expressionless, his mouth managing to stay soft. How he manages not to react impresses me. Maybe he can give us all a lesson.

"If only you were the eldest. You understand what it takes to get ahead, benefiting from your position and taking advantage of your brother's incessant need to prove his worth. Why don't we push him a bit more? I'd like to see how he handles her in front of me." The king looks at me, his eyes once again flicking down my body. "Why don't you join us for lunch? I'll give you something valuable for around your neck if you test my eldest boy for me."

Oh fuck. What do I do? How do I answer? This is so fucked up. Wilder must've picked up his asshole side from this man.

"Father, please. Wilder is already a bit much. We have to live with him, remember?" Arsenio sighs, rubbing his hand through his dark blond hair.

The king grimaces like a child who was told no to something exciting. He backhands Arsenio's shoulder, the loud slap startling me. He plays it off to be an act of affection with his leering smile, but I recognize the power move. He's picking his battles. "Fine, but I'd still love her to join us for lunch. Consider it a gift for appeasing my sons as they wait for their omega, considering how I have many years of my life left."

Don't scowl. Don't react. Get it together. I chant the words to myself, turning them into my mantra. Offering the king a smirk, I disguise my disgust the best I can. What kind of man refuses to allow his sons to bond until he is ready to step down from the throne? He's so insecure in his position that he sees his children as a threat. I can't even fathom the idea and wouldn't tolerate such treatment if I were a parent. I know that our society has laws, and this man is the authority of his territory, but I would do anything to fight against it. I already do. I've been doing it for years.

"I'd love to, your majesty," I say, realizing he's expecting me to answer. If I were supposed to be an omega, I would wait for my alpha or my pack to speak on my behalf. But I'm acting as a beta. Things are a bit different. Exactly how in this territory where packs take on a royal reign instead of democracy? I guess I better find out.

"Wonderful...I'm sorry, I didn't catch your name." The king looks at me expectantly, clasping his hands together.

I consider making up a name, but nothing comes to mind fast enough. So I stick with what I know. "Kinsey. Kinsey Kane, from the Briar Thorn territory at the edge of Saint Vista, bordering Calico Proper." Saint Vista and Calico Proper are two of the biggest regions in California, and the territory next to the one I was born into is far enough away that he would need to have ties to packs there to discover I don't exist.

King Winston flicks his gaze to Arsenio, clearly showing he considers him of higher rank than Enzo. "I've never been, but perhaps you can introduce my sons to your pack. Gilded Sands strives to make allies in all regions. What brings you to our territory anyway?"

I swallow, keeping my eyes averted to show my respect. "Just visiting. My...aunt bonded with—"

"Dad, come on. That's enough. You can ask her all your questions at lunch. Let us get dressed." Enzo tugs me away another foot. "We'll meet you in the dining hall."

I've never been so relieved for an interruption in my life. I don't know how well King Winston knows the packs in his territory, and I was about to use one I used to know as a child low enough in power that it wouldn't be of any interest to him.

"Very well. I suppose we do have bigger priorities than who you choose to use to...fill your needs." King Winston hangs his arm over Arsenio's shoulder, forcing him to stay by his side.

Glancing over his shoulder, Arsenio shares a quiet look with Enzo. I can't read their silent interaction, nor can I tell what they're feeling based on their scent, but I know it can't be good.

Enzo doesn't move from his spot, clutching my hand until his father and brother leave us, and we can no longer hear their footsteps or murmured voices.

"I'm sorry, baby. He's such a dick. You aren't only something to fill my time. I swear. I want to sucker punch him in the throat for insinuating that in front of you." Enzo spins me to him, lifting me off my feet to bury his face to the crook of my neck. He kisses my throat as he adjusts me, realizing a bit too late that now our bodies touch together, my rising desire damp and warm against his cool skin. And fuck does it turn us both on.

His cock hardens, rising up to rest against my ass. It would be so easy to slip inside me to fuck me. I crave it. Need it. His closeness tests the strength of the suppressant pills.

"It's okay. It doesn't bother me. I know that alphas...and omegas will occasionally fool around with a beta before they commit to a bonding." I keep my voice low, hoping that he doesn't question my response. I don't know how he would react if he knew that I wasn't a virgin. It's not always necessary, but I know that there are some alphas out there that will completely reject the idea of not being an omega's first. But I didn't want that kind of life. I wasn't planning on ever being an omega again. I was going to be a beta until the day I died, even if I had to give up everything just to pay for the suppressant pills.

"I see...you've been involved with someone before." Enzo adjusts me in his arms, making me look at him. But he doesn't scowl. He doesn't drop me or make me feel bad about it. All he does is smile. "How was it?"

I smack him in the back of the head, crinkling my nose. "Enzo."

"Don't worry, baby. I know that whatever beta who thought he had a chance with you probably sucked." He brushes his lips to mine, kissing my pout away. "And it's okay to tell me anything you want. You're mine now, and that's all that matters. Whatever past you have doesn't concern me. All I care about is you in the present and moving forward. I hope that you feel the same."

It's my turn to smirk. "So, what you're telling me is that you have fucked around a lot. Filling your time until you found your omega."

He play-growls. "I don't know what you're talking about. I'm a virgin. My cock has never desired anything more than just you. I've dreamed of you all my life."

This time, I laugh, tipping my head back, letting my voice echo through the concrete room. We both know he's full of shit, but he's right. It doesn't matter. All that matters now is moving forward. Surviving. Figuring out how the fuck we are going to manage any of this now that King Winston knows of my existence.

"God, that laugh is the most melodious sound I've ever heard. I could listen to it all night. You have no idea how fulfilled I feel when you find amusement with me. Because I always want you to be lighthearted and happy. I want you to know that I wasn't joking earlier either. I'll do whatever it takes to claim you, Kinsey. I don't care what my father thinks or what he wants from my life. I'll abandon his territory and the Gilded Sands Pack before I give you up." Enzo's smile fades with his words, his expression sharp and serious and incredibly handsome.

I believe him. I feel it deep in my soul that what he says is what will happen. He'll fight for it. He will fight for me.

"I always thought that I was cursed. That I was unlucky. I had no idea that all those things had to happen to bring me to you and your brothers." I rub my fingers over his cheeks, cupping his face between my palms.

"Except for Wilder." Enzo beams with a smile, his face lighting up once more.

"He just needs a little punishment. A little push. I don't think he's a bad guy anymore. I know what it's like to have a duty to fulfill and not really getting a say in anything." Am I defending Wilder to his brother? Maybe. But I know that Enzo appreciates it. He might be annoyed with his brother, but he does love him. They are a pack, and they do have plans to change everything.

Even me.

"I can't fucking wait. I'll help you. I already know he's going crazy that he couldn't spend more time with you and that you abandoned him to hang out with Holly. All he wanted to do was hold you and show you what he was capable of. But he knows that he has to earn the chance." Enzo lifts me higher, cuddling me and hugging me. "I think he'll be capable. We just have to make it hell on him until then."

I nod my head. "Gladly. I mean, if we can even make it out of this lunch thing. You need to tell me more about your father. About betas here."

Enzo nuzzles his nose to mine, kissing me. "Don't worry, baby. I'll make sure everything goes smoothly. I'll protect you. Always."

I rub my hands down the tight satin dress. It hugs my curves in all the right places and accentuates my cleavage. I didn't expect to have to wear a gown, but I guess that everyone always must dress up in the presence of King Winston. Which is funny, considering that he just saw me in a towel.

My hair hangs over my shoulders, and I push it back, showing off my throat. I know that the guys like it, and I can't help wanting to tease their nature. I've taken a second suppressant pill just to be safe, because the last thing I need is for the king to suddenly realize that I'm an omega in his presence. If that were to happen? I'd be fucking screwed. Enzo would try to murder him, which wouldn't go over too well with the others, considering they have a plan.

If only I wasn't growing impatient. It hasn't been long, but I just want to know exactly what to expect. I need to be prepared for everything. Like today? I hated being thrown off, and now I'm nervous as hell as Enzo escorts me into a grand dining room.

A sparkling chandelier glows overhead, casting fractals of light prisms through the crystals, and rainbows pepper the taupe wallpaper. The warm, dark wooden table expands to accommodate at least fifty people, and I question whether so many people have ever even sat here. The king looks tiny, sitting at the head of the table, especially with Wilder positioned straight-backed in the chair to his right with Arsenio and Desmond to his left.

All four of them look at me, and I try to keep my gaze averted, so I don't risk meeting King Winston's brown eyes. They all must take after their mother with their features.

I can feel the heat of the king's gaze penetrating my skin, prickling the hairs on my arms. His order might not set mine off, but he's undeniably an alpha—one who gives me more attention than I want. I don't know what kind of dirty thoughts go through his head, but I know that he must think something. Enzo said that he's known to sleep around with all the women in his fortress, and he wouldn't put it past him to try to hit on me. And no one denies the king.

So gross. But also, Enzo swore that he would protect me. They will not let their dad do anything to jeopardize my health and safety. Physically and mentally.

"My baby boy. It's nice of you to finally join us. I suspect you decided to have just a bit more fun, am I right?" The king chuckles and whacks Wilder on the shoulder, trying to get under his skin with his words. "At least one of you knows how to relax and have fun."

Wilder remains expressionless, composed and refusing to take the king's bait. I appreciate his ability to remain stoic and unfazed. Because if I were in his place, I'd probably punch him. I'd end up losing my hand or some shit. I don't know what kind of consequences there are for punching a king. Maybe death.

Damn, I have to get these thoughts out of my head. Murder shouldn't be a part of my fantasy. I'm totally fucked up.

"You know it, Dad. I wanted to also pick out the perfect dress for her. You know, practicing." Enzo wags his eyebrows, acting the part of a bachelor alpha, egging his father on unlike his brothers. And he's known for it. He admitted as much, but

I don't need any of the details. He didn't ask any more about mine either. Which is fine.

King Winston claps his hands, chuckling, and a server in a bow-tie struts in from the back arched doorway and crosses the room, carrying a silver tray. Three others join them, and I watch as the three guys and the one woman, all betas, set up a meal on the table. They pour everyone a glass of wine, and one of the men holds out a chair for me, not next to Enzo but a couple of seats away. It's obvious that I am not worthy enough to be dining so close in the presence of royalty.

I feel like crap.

Enzo quickly gets up, pulls out the chair next to him, and walks to me before tugging me along to sit me down beside him, defying whatever expectations the staff thought of me. I swallow and remain stiff and quiet, afraid to even look around. I don't want to see what King Winston thinks about the whole situation, but I hear Wilder grumble under his breath about being disrespectful.

"My eldest son, do I hear jealousy in your voice? You know, you're not bound to be virginal during this time. I'm sure your brother will happily share the beta with you." King Winston leans on his elbows, not bothering with etiquette.

Wilder groans again, grabbing his glass of wine and downing the whole thing.

Enzo lifts his glass and tips it toward his father, offering him a silent cheers. He then proceeds to hand me mine, and we clink ours together as if this is just a normal part of the day.

One glass turns into two, and I zone out, my head spinning. I don't drink alcohol very often, and I haven't been able to afford it over the last year or so, and now I'm regretting busying myself by sipping the red liquid.

"So, you're absolutely sure it was a threat from the Gutter District?" King Winston asks, his face greasy from eating a piece of chicken with his fingers.

"Was either of them someone from Platinum Shores? They have been caught traveling our roads to get in and out. I think they are either trafficking omegas or drugs for Calico Proper. We're not exactly sure. We don't have the evidence to back us up, but I have a couple sources that have offered surveillance as proof. We just need to pay them." Wilder keeps his voice low, though the softness of his tone does nothing for my suddenly racing heart.

"How much? You tell him what happens to them if it turns out to be unreliable? I don't take these sorts of threats lightly." King Winston drops his half-eaten wing on his plate. He picks up his fork and clinks it into his massive pile of steamed vegetables.

I nearly knock my wine glass over as I try to take another sip. It's as if he might've forgotten I was here, because his attention zones in on me, and he doesn't continue right away.

"The usual amount and yes," Wilder says, following his father's gaze to look at me. "Desmond, why don't you take Ms. Kane to have dessert in the garden? I'm sure she would appreciate the view there instead of having to bear through what I'm sure is a boring discussion to her."

Desmond looks at the king. "May I be excused, father? I have nothing useful to add to the conversation. My brothers have everything handled. I'm just to do as I'm told like you've always said."

King Winston opens and closes his mouth, looking like he's ready to argue, but then his face smooths out, and a smile crosses his face. "That sounds lovely. I'm sure you would be interested in the little plaything that Enzo has collected. She's probably a lot of fun and more suitable for you." What a fucking asshole.

If my head would stop spinning and I could rely on my mouth not to say anything that would get me killed, I would respond to him. Enzo must sense how uncomfortable I am, because he stands up, eases my chair back, and takes my hand, walking me all the way around the long table and to where we meet Desmond at another doorway across from where the servers come through from the kitchen.

I wobble on my heels, and Desmond tightens his arm around my waist, securing me to his side. Enzo kisses my temple, and I allow Desmond to guide me from the dining hall and away from the suddenly bellowing voices breaking out behind us. I'm nearly certain the king was only remaining in control because of me, because he doesn't truly know me. He assumes I'm not from this territory and wouldn't want to risk saying too much or doing something that could spread word elsewhere.

"You did amazing, Kinsey," Desmond says, leaning into me. "My father won't question anything."

My tongue feels heavy, and I lick my lips and bob my head, the intoxication controlling me.

"I'm drunk." I don't know why I say it, but it's the only thing that my brain will allow to escape my mouth, probably as a way to protect me from saying something stupid. Though, it's not like declaring that I am intoxicated is smart either.

Chuckling, Desmond spins me around, testing my balance in the process. I teeter over and screech, nearly falling forward. He catches me and lifts me into his arms, cradling me like a blushing bride.

A smile brightens his face, his mellow attitude easy to devour. He doesn't find me a mess. He finds me amusing, and I appreciate him not getting mad. I know some packs would. I'd be considered an embarrassment.

"I bet you are. You know, we only served you two glasses, but you took one of Enzo's. Have you ever had alcohol before, Kinsey?" he asks, nuzzling his nose to mine.

"Yeah...but not like this. Fuck. The world is spinning. Make it stop." I rest my head to his shoulder and close my eyes, praying that I don't get sick.

"I got you. Don't worry. It'll help if you eat something. I saw you didn't touch anything on your plate." Desmond carries me through the palace, keeping me steady without jostling me around. I don't get a good look at where he takes me, because of my blurry vision, and I can't even focus.

The world shifts and the fragrant scent of jasmine and rose permeate the air, awakening my senses. I open my eyes, blinking at the beams of bright sunlight cutting across the pebble walkway leading to a huge gazebo with vines of ivy twining around it. I had only glimpsed the outside of the palace with Wilder when we went to the Gutter District, but now that I have a chance to look around? It's stunning. I wish I could see more of it outside of the secret passageways and the rooms.

Desmond carries me the entire way, greeting another server, already rushing to set up a table of desserts in the shade. A fountain showers water into the air, and the soft splash helps ease the erratic beats of my racing heart.

After finally setting me down, he cups my face and looks me in the eyes. "I'm sorry about the king. This was not supposed to happen. He surprised us."

I dip my chin, rubbing my lips together, my throat dry. "You don't have to apologize. Just help me sit down and get some food in me. I drank too much."

Desmond chuckles. "Anything for you."

Desmond sits down and pulls me into his lap, hugging me from behind, the sensation of his steady heartbeat against my back helping to settle my nerves. He reaches forward and picks up a square of cheesecake, bringing it to my lips.

I take a bite and savor it, my whole body humming, loving the closeness after such a stressful lunch.

Desmond offers me another bite. "Good, huh? I bet—"

The sound of gunfire startles me, and I throw myself forward, my fear controlling me. Desmond lands on top of me protectively, covering me like a shield.

"Stay down. Get under the table. Don't move." Desmond brings a chair and blocks me in, reaching into his suit jacket, pulling out his own weapon.

He aims somewhere to the right, pulling the trigger.

A man screams, and Desmond shoots again.

Silence fills the air.

Chapter 15

Enzo

Attack

I stare at the security feeds on my phone, watching as Desmond shoots a man in the chest and then in the head. I can't believe this fucking shit. Protocol says we need to move to the panic room with Dad, but there's no fucking way we're taking him there. We did not work hard on keeping Holly hidden just to have him realize what we've done, betraying our entire pack in doing so. He'll have our heads. He'll disown us and ensure that we never get power...putting a different alpha in our place. A fucking cousin or ally, someone else just to spite us. He'll maybe even kill us.

"My son, why don't you stay present with us and put the phone away?" Dad says, tapping his knife impatiently on his plate.

I begrudgingly set my phone down, showing it off to my brothers, careful not to let Dad see by blocking it with my wine glass. "Sorry, Dad. I'm trying to get ahead and arrange stuff with our allies to get the information you want."

Dad beams me a smile. If it were Arsenio or Wilder, he would probably yell at them for not keeping him in the loop. But me? I'm Dad's favorite, and we all know it. I'm the only one who can get away with slacking off and talking back. I'm also the only one he ever jokes with about women, and maybe it's because I'm the youngest of his boys. His expectations have been minimal with me.

"There is no need to apologize. I appreciate your hard work, and you're also excused to finish your task. You can inform me of the necessary financial obligations later. It was nice seeing you today, son. You should come to visit me soon. I miss having my favorite boy around all the time. I sometimes wish I could've stopped you from growing up, Enzo." Dad wipes his mouth with his napkin, turning to look at Arsenio and Wilder. "As for you two, we still have some business to settle."

Damn. I feel fucking awful for my brothers. He uses his favoritism toward me as a weapon and a way to manipulate them. We all know it. They have a lot thicker skin than I do, because if I were them, I would probably throw a punch at Dad.

But I don't have time to defend them. They can handle themselves.

I stand up, quickly stroll to the head of the table, and hug my dad, kissing him on the cheek. He smiles and pats me on the back. I turn and quickly stride away before he decides that he wants more of my company.

I have shit to do. Kinsey is probably so fucking scared, and I need to get to her. I need to protect her and get her to safety.

I remain at an even pace until I know I'm out of hearing range and break out into a sprint, stopping at one of our many safes to pull out an extra gun. I'm sure the security team is already sweeping the area, but if these guys got past them and close to Desmond, then something is up. We have a traitor in our midst. Now we can't trust our entire staff and will have to reevaluate everything.

I charge forward and head toward the back exit leading to the garden. Slowing down, I peer through the glass wall with a wide view of our property, spotting Kinsey still cowering in the gazebo.

Without hesitation, I dash from the palace and toward her. Big mistake. I don't see the guy quickly enough and a gunshot rings out at the same time a bullet ricochets off the gleaming wall right near my head. He was waiting for the chance to infiltrate our palace, because no one can go in and out without special access. Half of our security team can't get in unless one of our two leads opens the doors, and all of our staff have very specific instructions on entering. It's to keep us safe but also to guarantee that no one knows about Holly.

"Don't move, Enzo." The deep voice only makes me bristle, recognition setting in. He's from the Platinum Shores Pack. Bruce? Beau? Some B name that I can't recall. We'd been watching his alpha dealing with Tamsin for a while. He'd occasionally do some beta bitch work to receive privileges at the Vixen Lounge.

Shifting, I ignore the douche and aim my gun, firing without assessing the situation. It's enough to get him to duck.

I make my move, tackling the man and punching him in the face. He knees me in the stomach, pushing me off, but I don't let him pin me, grabbing onto him and rolling again. Swinging my arm, I sucker punch him in the throat. And then again in the jaw. Locking my fingers in his hair, I slam his head down hard over and over again until his eyes roll back into his head. A lot of packs underestimate our strength because of our royal status, and we hide behind security, but that's only for show. We spend all our lives training to fight, learning how to use every weapon available, and just studying how to take out enemies. We are ruthless. It's rare, and the only reason why this man isn't dead is because we need answers.

I spot Desmond searching around the property, glancing at his phone. Releasing a whistle, I draw his attention to me and send him a short text to take the bastard I knocked out to a cell, make sure the perimeter is secure, and go check on Holly. Kinsey is my priority, and nothing will get in my way of caring for her.

It looks like Desmond's already taken care of the body of the man he killed, ensuring that our father doesn't see. I hope that this blows over quickly, and he'll never know that we failed to keep our palace safe, especially with him here. It'll leave him suspicious, and he might question everything about us if he finds out why Platinum Shores is really at war with us and that we were the ones to start the feud.

Jogging closer to Kinsey, I quickly whisper her name, letting her know that I'm coming without startling her. She stretches her arms out for me, a small whimper escaping her mouth. Pain radiates deep in my heart at her fear. She's fucking terrified and probably thought the worst. I hate that she had to experience this bullshit at all.

I scoop her up in my arms, hugging her close as she wraps her arms and legs around me, burying her face into the crook of my neck. Warm tears spill from her eyes, soaking the collar of my suit, and all I want to do is kiss them away. I want her to know that she's safe, and I won't let anything happen to her. That I will take care of the bastards who scared her.

"Take a breath, baby. I'm going to get you out of here. It's over. No one's going to hurt you." I stroke my hand down her back, smoothing out her trembles the best that I can.

"That was one of Madame Tamsin's clients. I recognize him from the Vixen Lounge. He was a regular." Kinsey's voice cracks.

Rage ignites inside me, thinking about the douche all over again. Now that I have a moment to process, I wonder how they connected everything back to us. We've been careful. Wilder said that no one caught him when he took Kinsey to the Gutter District.

I'll go crazy obsessing over where the fuck we messed up. Was it during the heist? Something else? One of our allies said too much when we were asking around? Whatever it is, we need to handle it swiftly.

"Fuck, Kinsey. I hate having to ask you this, but can you tell me a bit more? I need to figure out if the threat involves Tamsin with the Platinum Shores Pack or if it's something different. They were our target the night of the heist." I stroll away from the palace and head toward the garage, wanting nothing more than to get her out of here completely.

I know better than to relocate her without first speaking with my brothers but getting space from the place she just experienced trauma might help calm her down. She needs to know that attacks like this are rare, and I'll not stand by and do nothing. She comes first. She's mine regardless of anything. I don't give a damn if my father is here.

"I'll try my best. My head is still spinning. I can barely focus." Shit. I forgot she had been drinking wine. The whole situation sobered me up, but she had two more glasses than I did. Her intoxication won't help any.

I shift my jaw, peering around the area, ensuring no one tries to sneak up on us. "Don't worry about it right now. We're leaving and heading somewhere else while my brothers get the shit settled here. I'm sure they'll call us when the king is gone, and it's safe to return."

"What about Holly? We need to get her. She has to come with us. I don't want to leave otherwise." Her soft pleas help settle down my chaotic thoughts. She's right. We should take

Holly with us, and the fact that she is looking out for my sister solidifies just how amazing she truly is.

I don't slow down, but I do pull out my phone and shoot a text message to Desmond with one hand, telling him to bring Holly to the underground entrance to the garage.

Kinsey remains quiet until I plop her down in the front seat of one of the sedans and then slide behind the wheel. She shifts and throws her arms around me, hugging me and begging for my closeness. Her heart races so vehemently that I can hear it, and I continue to hug her and kiss her tears, letting her calm down before I speak again.

"I have an apartment in the city. I think it's best to take you and Holly there until we can figure the shit out. I'm sure my father will hear about things, and getting our asses out of here will guarantee neither of you are caught up in it." I lean back and meet her watery gaze. "You guys will never be alone. We'll rotate shifts, giving us a chance to clean house of any traitors and make sure no one is a threat. This had to be an inside job for anyone to get on the property, and we will handle it."

Kinsey licks her lips and bobs her head, using the back of her hand to wipe her eyes. I hate that she is going through this. She doesn't deserve this kind of terror.

"Okay." It's all she can manage to say, and I don't prod for anymore. She'll speak her thoughts when she's ready. I'll do what it takes to prove I'm here for her regardless.

I kiss the tip of her nose and then her forehead. "I swear we'll get everything in order. It won't be long until Gilded Sands is under our reign."

Her waning smile hurts more than if she didn't smile at all. "I know."

I hope she believes me. I wish she hadn't taken another suppressant pill, so I could really ensure that she's good. It's harder to read her on her visual cues alone, apart from the fear. She worries about our situation, considering our bond is forbidden in Saint Vista. The only way I can prove I'm in it forever is to act on my promise and see it through.

Silence fills the air as we wait for Desmond, but it's not awkward or unwanted. It calms Kinsey down, allowing me to listen to her heart settling to beat in sync with mine.

It only takes Desmond ten minutes before he appears with Holly. She carries a small bag, and another one hangs on Desmond's shoulder. He already knows the backup plan and where we'd take Holly if we had to. Holly shuffles toward the car and doesn't wait for Desmond to open the door to the backseat. She slides in and frowns at me, peeking over the seat to glance at Kinsey still glossy-eyed and frozen with her nerves.

Desmond circles the car, waiting for me to roll down the window. He leans in and gets close to my ear. "Everything is clear, but Wilder wants some time with the guy. I'll join you as soon as Dad leaves. If he asks about you, we're going to say that you went out with Kinsey."

"Sounds good, brother. I'll send you a couple messages as soon as we arrive at my apartment. Kinsey recognized the guy and might be able to help." I keep my voice low, whispering the words to keep Kinsey and Holly from overhearing. "She's in shock right now, so I don't want to overwhelm her."

Demond nods. "I understand. Now keep them safe, or you'll lose your fucking head. Wilder's promise."

The bastard. How dare he threaten me. He knows that I'm plenty capable of protecting Holly and Kinsey.

Leaning through the open window, Desmond stretches his arm and touches Kinsey's cheek. "I'll see you later, Kinsey. Have Enzo let me know if you need anything. He's going to take good care of you."

Her pouty mouth trembles with her whisper of okay, and I can tell that Desmond wants to just join us in the car right now. But he can't. He needs to help our brothers. And all I want to do is get out of here.

I wait until Desmond disappears back through the tunnel before hitting the opener to the garage. Holly and Kinsey instinctively hunch down, though no one would be able to see them through the dark tinted glass.

I peek in the side of my peripheral vision, spotting Kinsey reaching back and taking Holly's hand. I feel terrible and angry for both of them. Their lives have come crashing down because of alphas, who should be the ones protecting and treating them as the most precious beings in the world. And that's something I want to change. There are far too many brutal pack leaders. They can't see how they're only setting up their lives to fail. They won't have the same loyalty. Others will have enough and rise against them. I've seen it myself. I'm living it now. Look at me and my brothers. Had my father been more kind and caring as the man he should've always been, we wouldn't be in this situation. We wouldn't have to dethrone him. We could've been a family.

I turn on the music, keeping it just loud enough to fill the air. I rest my hand on Kinsey's knee, gently rubbing it until her body starts to relax. The farther we get away from the palace, the more she perks up. She scoots in the seat, sitting more erect, and cleans the shiny stains of her tears.

All I know is I can't wait to draw her a bath, feed her, and cuddle the hell out of her in my bed. I'll fill her with so much of my affection that she'll only be able to think about me and not the other bullshit today. At least, that's my hope. My goal. Today has truly tested me and showed me just how much I want this woman.

I navigate the car into the gated community and straight to my four-story condo with an underground garage. I use the place when I just need to get away from my brothers for a couple of days in the city. While my brothers and I love to live together, sometimes we need a moment apart. We each have our own places throughout our territory, but I have to say, mine is probably the best.

At least for us now.

"Holly, why don't you get yourself settled in your room on the top floor? I'll see about making something for you to eat. I just need a little bit of time with Kinsey, if you don't mind." I shift in my seat to meet my sister's eyes.

Holly thins her mouth. "Sure, but how about I make something for all of us? It's been a while. You could also use a shower, brother. You have blood spatter on your face."

I reach back and ruffle my fingers through her hair, messing up the strands. "You are the best, little sister."

She smiles at me and pushes her door open. "Don't you forget it."

I chuckle and watch her stroll toward the door that leads up, waiting just a couple of seconds before I get out of the vehicle and walk around the hood to get Kinsey from the front seat.

She tries to stand on her own, but I don't let her. I don't want to test the strength of her legs right now. The only thing that flits through my mind over and over is how I need to get her cleaned, fed, and cuddled. I'm a man on a mission, and nothing else will take precedence. Even allowing her to do her own thing can't stop me.

Luckily, she doesn't resist or try to act like she doesn't need me. She accepts my help and hugs me close as I carry her to the master bedroom, which takes up the entire second floor above the kitchen, living, and dining room. At the very top are three guest bedrooms and a rooftop deck that overlooks the city.

Kinsey peers around the room, her muscles relaxing as she finds comfort in a space that probably smells and feels familiar and like me. My scent won't mess with her as much right now because of the suppressant pills, but she'll still recognize me on my belongings.

I don't set her down, carrying her straight to the bathroom, where a garden tub rests on a platform with a view of the park across the street. I place her on the counter and run the water, filling the air with steam.

Kinsey watches as I quickly wash my face in the sink, ensuring that there is no evidence of blood on me before I take her into the tub. She drinks me in as I unbutton my dress shirt and shrug out of my formal clothes. I stand before her completely naked, loving how I can practically feel her gaze tracing over my body, each of my muscles flexing, my desire for her prominent in my hard cock.

She nibbles her lip seductively, her beautiful face softening with her longing, her eyes meeting mine. I step forward and kiss her, unable to resist giving her my affection. I reach around and unzip the back of her gown, needing nothing more than to feel her skin against mine.

Sliding from the counter, Kinsey lets the dress fall to pool around her feet, and I get to my knees and kiss along her stomach until I can tear her panties down with my teeth, not wanting to wait even another second before I do whatever I can to make her feel amazing.

She moans, her knees shaking as I work my way closer to the warmth building at the apex of her legs. Combing her fingers through my black hair, she uses me to balance as I lift her leg onto my shoulder and glide my tongue over her clit, tasting the sweetness of her body. I crave more. So much more. I intend to show her exactly what I want, which is her and my need to claim her as mine on every level.

This is real between us, and it won't change. Giving her my knot to bond with me will cement it. It's the first step in growing a relationship to where we can finally declare our permanent claim of each other during her next heat. I'm so ready to expand our pack and give her the life she deserves...if she wants that sort of thing. I just need to prove that I'm worthy. That I would be an exceptional companion and father. That I wouldn't turn into one of the many alphas that I know have wronged her.

I roll my tongue over her body, slipping my finger in and out of her as I kiss and suck her clit, listening to her moan and feeling her squirm, her back hitting the counter to help keep her standing.

"It feels so good, Enzo," she whispers, her voice breathy with her moans. "I want you. I want you so badly."

My balls tighten with her declaration, and I wonder if she's caught on the wave of adrenaline and lust. I wonder if she's still a bit intoxicated, but it's been a while, and she's no longer wobbling from that.

I don't respond to her right away, continuing working her over until she tugs my hair and moans with her orgasm, her body clenching my hand, her slick so slippery and wet and waiting for me.

God, I want more.

"Baby, you know how badly I want you too. More than anything in this world, and not just sex with you. That's why I'm hesitant to push. I don't want you to regret anything." It hurts to say the words, her features shifting, her body moving away as she spins to turn off the running water. She does it to put space between us instead of worrying about the tub overflowing. She thinks I'm rejecting her. It's not intentional, and it might not even be one of her thoughts, but her body tells me the truth.

I move closer and hug my arms around her, lifting her so she can sit on the counter and meet me at eye level.

I cup her face and stroke my thumbs over her cheeks and down her throat, guiding her head closer to meet me for a kiss. I can't get enough of her. I regret even questioning what she wants. It's obvious that she's not lying or influenced by anything. This is real.

"Kinsey, you're the woman I desire. I want you to be my omega and to keep building on this connection I have with you. My brothers agree, and we plan to give you the world. I want to give you the pack you deserve. If we do this and you accept my knot, you're mine. You're mine and nothing can change that. I want this bond. I want your love and affection. I want your everything. And I want to give you mine." The truth of my words resonates in my soul, and Kinsey searches my gaze, her eyes locking to mine as if she can stare at my very being.

"Enzo...are you sure I'm worth it? I don't have a standing in society. I don't have a pack to bring your territory power. I'm no one. I'm unwanted." She rubs her lips together, her face scrunching with her words as if she hates to even say them out loud.

"It's not a question if you're worth it. It's a question if I am. I'm going to prove it to you every day and every chance I get. That is my promise." I kiss her again, pulling her to me and carrying her to my bed, my mind already set. If she wants me,

I won't deny her any longer. I'm not going to have her think for even a second that I'm rejecting her. This is the moment I've been waiting all my life for, to finally show the woman of my dreams everything I want to give her. Everything I have to offer.

Kinsey nuzzles her face to the crook of my neck, kissing me softly on my throat, taking her time to kiss and touch my body, showing attention to the spots she wants to ensure her scent remains, even if it's suppressed by the fucking pills I suddenly loathe because it stops her from getting what she wants. And I want her to have everything.

"I know this is not exactly romantic, but I just want to know if you've been taught about what happens when we bond." I know only the history she has given me, which includes the fact that she's never been with an alpha.

Tilting her head up, she kisses me again, a smile playing on her lips. "I know the basics. I also know that you will be gentle with me. I trust you with my life, Enzo. My heart, too."

I've never heard such a beautiful thing in my life, and I wish I could hear her say it over and over again.

"I'm falling in love with you, Kinsey. I won't let you down. Ever." I kiss her sweetly, sensually, just taking my time to work my mouth over hers as I run my hands down her body to touch between her legs again.

She moans in response, and I continue to work her over as I prepare to slide between her legs. I don't need words of affirmation or proof that she feels the same. I know it, and I will accept it on her own time and in her own way.

Her breathing quickens as I align my cock to her hot pussy, her body so slippery and wet that I just want to savor every second of this experience. I ease in my tip, listening to her gasp as her body stretches to fit me. I smile and kiss her mouth and groan, the pleasure coursing through every molecule inside me.

I slide my hand under her back to pull her close and use my other one to reach between us to stroke her clit, wanting nothing more than for her to scream in ecstasy.

She moans, her body arching to mine, and begging me to slide in deeper until we meet completely, my balls tapping her ass in a way that drives me wild.

"Speak up. This pleasure belongs to you. I'll not finish until you've had your fill." I hum, my muscles flexing as I thrust faster deeper, listening to her response to guide me.

"You feel—feel—incredible. Keep going." Her sultry, husky voice buries into my skin, awakening a new beast inside me, one that wants to prove my words to be true. Kinsey needs to know that I can take care of her in every way she needs and wants and desires. I'm the alpha she deserves.

I moan and arch my back, repositioning her legs in a way that I can play with her exposed clit easily, watching my body sink into hers in deep, even strokes. I savor how her pussy clutches my cock, the tightness working me up and bringing me closer and closer to my peak. To the moment I've been waiting for. Because alphas only knot with an omega, even if she's not in heat, but as a way to bond and prepare for the life they both need and desire.

It'll just get hotter and more intense, but I can't even imagine that, because this is so fucking incredible. Mind-blowing.

Kinsey stretches her back, her sexy body tensing and clenching mine. Her hard nipples look so delectable that I can't stop myself from bowing forward to glide my tongue over her tits, showing each one attention as she orgasms again.

She grabs me by the back of my neck, pulling me down again as if she needs to feel the weight of my body completely. The scent of her desire wafts in the air, battling against whatever drugs suppress her pheromones, striking me right in the balls in a good way.

"I'm going to come," I say, grunting as her body tightens as my knot locks her in place, bonding us in a way I will never take for granted or forget.

Pleasure and bliss course through me as my body releases my seed, helping prepare my beautiful omega and woman for what's to come. I continue to kiss her and show her affection, rubbing my cheek to hers as I lick down her throat and nip her on the nape of her neck. My balls tighten and spasm with every passing minute, the time it takes lasting for what feels like an incredible eternity that I don't want to stop.

Kinsey digs her fingers into my back, squirming against the pressure, the pleasure emanating from her as she continues to moan and enjoy our bodies together as one.

I finish completely, my nuts relaxing and my body finally releasing Kinsey from its hold. I rock a couple more times, kissing her with enough passion to make her groan and gasp my name.

I smile and nip her bottom lip, lifting her from the bed so she doesn't have to walk. I won't let her do so for the rest of the night as I care for her, starting with a hot bath and then food and cuddles.

I don't even have to leave my room because Holly left the tray at the door, respecting my privacy.

Kinsey's face lights up with an appreciative smile for every one of my gestures, letting me wash her hair and dry her off—kissing me as soon as her head pops through the neckline of my shirt that she cuddles close to her and to the point where I hand feed her dinner and we share the dessert.

I hold her close, spooning her from behind when she turns over to fall asleep.

I've never been so content and happy in my life. If only my fucking phone didn't buzz from the nightstand.

Desmonster: OMW. We have a problem.

I swear under my breath, trying not to move too much because Kinsey's breathing just evens out. I'm glad Desmond is on his way, but now I'm anxious to find out what we are dealing with.

Me: K

I know he hates when I respond like this, but I need to keep my mind clear. If he tells me anything, I might blow up. Kinsey needs me to stay in control in this moment. I'm going to enjoy every last second with her while I can.

Shit is about to get real.

And I will do anything, and I mean absolutely fucking any-thing, to keep my promise to Kinsey. She is my perfect omega.

Chapter 16

Desmond

Brotherly Bond

I t took thirty minutes to convince Arsenio and Wilder not to follow me to Enzo's condo in the city. I can't be certain that there aren't any more eyes on us, and we need to have someone at the palace, but especially Wilder.

Arsenio needed to stay to back him up.

What we found out from the asshole who tried to make a lesson out of us leaves me on edge. Because it was more than Tamsin sending someone to test us. It was one of her wealthiest, most powerful clients, and they're more pissed that we stole Kinsey than they are about the heist. Tamsin arranged a contract for Kinsey with the Platinum Shores Pack, giving them access to an omega without having to trade power or territory for the chance to bond. This is huge and more fucked up than we realized. Their only intent was to breed her.

The idea twists my stomach just thinking about it. We inadvertently saved Kinsey from what I'm sure would've been a horrible life.

I can't think about it. The realization ignites a murderous rage within me.

Stomping the throttle, I race through town, not giving a fuck about those who honk when I cut them off. I swerve and drift around the corner, speeding all the way to the complex. I pull down the driveway, leading into the underground garage, and park my car.

Holly greets me in the stairwell, not giving me a chance to even brace myself before she jumps up and hugs me. "Thank God. I was worried about you. Wilder said I couldn't go home."

I peer past her, trying to see if Kinsey and Enzo wait for me on the landing.

"She's sleeping upstairs. Enzo said to tell you to head up to his suite but prepare yourself. They've...bonded." Smirking, Holly tries to hide her smile, gauging my reaction.

I open and close my mouth, my thoughts whirling. Holy shit. It's hard to control the excitement rising in me. Fear too. A part of me knows that our pack will bond with one omega, and if Enzo took the initiative...what if she doesn't want me? I'm not an alpha. I can't exactly provide everything she needs. I—

"Are you upset? You know Kinsey likes you. Why don't you go up to them? I'm sure she'd be so happy to see you." Holly eases away and smiles at me again, the lightness of her voice helping to ease the concern bunching my muscles. An omega knows, and her reaffirmation kicks my dumbass into action. She's right. I have an undeniable connection to Kinsey.

I chuckle and mess up her pale hair. "Thanks, Holls. You know it's always been a little tough on me, considering my order. If I didn't have those fuckers by my side—"

"Kinsey would still want to be with you. Don't be so hard on yourself. You're a great man and will serve her just as good as our brothers." Holly gives me a shake.

I grin at her and climb the stairs, holding the door open for her to follow me into the living room. She shuffles to her spot on the couch, a blanket piled next to the throw pillow, and she returns to watching TV.

I don't linger long and climb the stairs, cutting down the hallway at the next landing to the double doors at the end.

Holy hell. The scent of sex is strong enough for me to pick up out here. I do have a more sensitive nose than my brothers, but damn. I never smelled anything like this, and it kind of weirds me out. I don't exactly want to smell my brother on anything, especially Kinsey right now, but I push through it and make my way to the room.

I knock my knuckles to the door. "Enzo, it's me."

Taking a step back, I scratch my fingers through my golden-brown hair, rocking on my feet, bracing myself for him to open the door. I'm a bit jealous but not because Kinsey is with

Enzo. I'm jealous because I'm not a fucking alpha. It's never bothered me so much until this moment. A part of me might always be lacking.

Cracking the door open, Enzo meets me with a grin, his whole face lit up unlike anything I've ever seen on him. I give him one look, seeing faint scratch marks on his shoulders, his black hair a mess, and him only wearing boxers. The lucky bastard.

I flare my nostrils, smelling the scent of Kinsey all over him. She made sure of it that everyone would know that they bonded in such a way. And thinking about Kinsey strikes me right in the balls. Fuck, I just want to see her.

Enzo looks like he's about to block my way, but Kinsey's soft voice channels through the air as she calls for him.

I push the door open over his shoulder, catching sight of her cocooned on his bed in the blankets, her cleavage peeking out, but I can't see anything else.

Kinsey sits up, greeting me with a dazzling smile. "Desmond, you're here! I'm so happy you finally made it. What about your brothers?"

What about them? I can't stop the silent question to myself. Because they don't matter right now. All that matters to me is moving closer and ensuring she's okay. She was a mess when Enzo drove off, and the sadness and fear in her emerald eyes imprinted in my head.

"May I come in?" I ask, flicking my attention to Enzo. He has every right to deny me. I don't know how much time it's been, not that I want to know, but he's going to be fucking moody as hell for a while. Obsessed. Overprotective. Possessive.

Enzo dips his chin in silent agreement, moving out of the way. Thank God he still carries some sense.

Wiggling her hands at me, Kinsey sets my heart racing, the new softness of her happiness filling me up in the best way. She stretches more, silently asking me to hurry the fuck up and close the space. I mind myself and stand at the edge of the bed instead of plopping down like I would in any other circumstance.

I take her hand and swing her arm back and forth, forcing my mouth to match hers with my grin. "I see my brother has taken good care of you. I'm so relieved to see you smiling again."

Heat flushes her face, turning her cheeks rosy. "He did. I'm relieved that you're here. I've been worried. What happened with everything? What about that man? He was a regular at the Vixen Lounge. Do you think Madame Tamsin sent him?" The questions spill from her mouth, and I consider leaning forward to interrupt her with a kiss, giving me a moment to think things through. The last thing I want to do is to ruin her special moment with my brother. I don't want to be the reason her smile falters or why she loses it altogether.

"We're taking care of it. You don't have to worry." I squeeze her hand.

"Why don't you relax for a bit and watch some TV while I make you some dessert? I'll send Holly up if you don't want to be alone. I just need a couple of minutes with Desmond."

Enzo strolls to the other side of the bed and leans down, kissing Kinsey softly.

I look away, trying to act like I don't want to kiss her next. But damn. I can't stop thinking about her mouth now. I bet she tastes just as sweet as she smells.

Kinsey looks between us, her nose crinkling. I expect her to argue, and if she did, I know we'd give in and not go, but she says, "Yeah, of course. You don't have to send Holly up right now. I'll just relax for a bit longer and get dressed to join you downstairs. I'd really like to see the rest of the place."

"Anything for you, baby," Enzo says, kissing her once more.

"He's right," I add, hoping my voice doesn't give away my slight jealousy.

Enzo motions for me to follow him, but Kinsey snatches my arm, surprising me. I don't have a chance to catch myself as I fall onto the bed. Enzo sucks in a breath, his alpha nature probably kicking him in the balls. He manages to keep his mouth shut, burning his gaze into us. Kinsey crawls over me, her amazing tits right in my line of sight. A smile crosses my face, and she leans down, brushing her lips to mine.

"Don't think you can come in here and get away with a handshake," she whispers, wrapping her arms around me.

"I just wasn't sure if anything changed. We can talk about it all together later though, if you want." I hug her for a moment, breathing in her hair. I imagine what it would be like to scent her, leaving my mark behind. But it just doesn't work like that for me.

"I'd like that," she says, shifting off me. Flicking her gaze to Enzo, she smiles at him. "I'll be fast."

I push up from the bed and join Enzo in the hallway, looking over my shoulder once more as Kinsey drops the blanket completely, exposing her beautiful naked body to the two of us. And damn. How can I leave that? It takes me patting Enzo's back to get him to even budge from his spot, and Kinsey laughs and waves us away.

Closing the door, I cut off our view and just wait by Enzo for a second as we try to pull ourselves together. I want to support my brother, but I also want to smack him upside the head for moving so quickly. This will complicate things. I don't think I'd ever known of a pack to just spontaneously claim an omega. It has always been arranged, which is in the law of the Pack Regimes across the nation.

"Wilder is going to kick your ass into next week," I murmur, walking beside my brother toward the stairs. "I'll get in the middle though. I'm on your side, man. Kinsey is fucking spectacular."

Enzo waggles his eyebrows, shaking his hands out. "Thanks, brother. It was totally worth it. Like paradise. Knowing what to expect doesn't compare to her actually taking my knot. Kinsey is...it's hard to explain. I know that we're not supposed to make these decisions with our emotions, but she's irresistible. I'm in love with her. She is meant for me. For us."

Living vicariously through my brother will never be enough. I'd curse the fates if they hadn't brought Kinsey to us in the first place. "So you know, I think you're one fucking lucky bastard. My cock is so jealous. I'm jealous. You better not fuck things up. I'll hold you responsible for how things are handled from this point on. If Kinsey for one second thinks that she's made a mistake, it'll be my foot up your fucking ass. Understand?" Should I threaten him? Absolutely. Will he let me down? Never. It just happens to be something that I feel the need to say.

Chuckling, he drapes his arm over my shoulder, giving me a hearty shake. "I wouldn't expect anything less. She only deserves the best of the best. And that includes you. Our girl will sometimes need a quickie, and you're the only one capable."

I swing out and clock him in the shoulder. "I'm not even mad about that. My damn cock will be ready quicker, letting me go round after round."

He chuckles without response, shoving me to move faster. We make our way to the living room, and Holly jumps from her spot on the couch and rushes us, throwing her arms around my brother and me at the same time. Enzo lifts her, spinning her around. They've always been close, probably because they're only a couple of years apart in age instead of the eight years I have on her, and I bet she was rooting for him first instead of Wilder, who has always treated her like his baby sister no matter her age.

"You have no idea how happy I am for you. I absolutely adore Kinsey, and if you guys didn't claim her, I was going to suggest me and her run away and just live as sisters in the wild world out there." Holly tosses her pale hair back, her eyes shining brightly.

"Don't make those kinds of comments, little sis. Wilder would freak the fuck out at the idea. He's already about to blow a coronary." I scrub my fingers across the back of my neck, trying to loosen my corded muscles. "We're in some deep shit right now. You know we're not going to tell you much, but just try to be a bit more obedient. I know how much you hate it. It's just important that he's not a loose cannon. The fact that this asshole emotionally claimed Kinsey without even telling any of us is already going to shake things."

"He's going to be fucking ecstatic. You know he's a dick just because he thinks he has to be. The only thing he's going to be jealous about is the fact that he missed his chance at bonding with her first." Holly's right about that.

My phone buzzes from my pocket, a group message flashing on the screen from Wilder.

Asshole Bro: We're heading your way. I want you to tell Kinsey before we arrive.

I purse my lips, grimacing.

Me: No fucking way.
Asshole Bro: It's an order. I can't handle another moment of her sadness and fear. It almost killed me.
Me: My answer is still no.
Asshole Bro: Enzo, you do it. She needs to know what Tamsin had arranged with the Platinum Shores Pack. It is our duty to prepare her for the worst-case scenario.

Sexy Beast: Prepare her for what exactly?

Asshole Bro: The fact that if we don't get the throne, we might have to face handing her over until we do. Father will not stand by us in this matter.

I swear under my breath and palm my forehead. Enzo reads over my shoulder and spins on his heels, running back upstairs to Kinsey. He left his phone in his room, and Kinsey just got a hold of the messages, responding as Enzo.

I'm going to kill Wilder. He didn't know this would happen, but he should've been man enough to wait to discuss everything with her in person instead of relying on us to take charge of the situation. Despite how we all handle things differently and the fact that Kinsey might be difficult toward him for his attitude, it's still no excuse. He's fronting as our leader and would be the one who takes the throne unless we change our laws.

But if we have this new threat, it will really fuck up our plan. Things have already gone astray.

Asshole Bro: I don't like it as much as you, but we need to be realistic.

Me: You want to know the reality now? Enzo bonded with Kinsey. There is nothing to prepare her for. She's ours. If you disagree, then don't bother coming.

Cool Guy: What? Bonded? Like fucked? She took his knot?

I shake my head, sighing. He knows damn well what it means for an alpha and omega to bond. I think he's more in shock.

Me: Yes, he's claimed her.

I stare at the phone, waiting for a response. But nothing comes. I don't know if either of them knows what to say. They're going to need time to process.

Me: You better get your thoughts together before you arrive. Not only did Kinsey see your text, but now she might question everything. I stand by Enzo. We would like you to stand with us. Kinsey will not feel anything but adoration and love with our protection. If you can't give that to her, then we need to seriously think about the future of our pack.

Am I a dick for throwing this all out there? Maybe. But the last thing I need is for Wilder to come storming in here as if he's still in control. Until Kinsey accepts him, he'll not be in charge of any decisions regarding her. That's just the way it has to be. He has no stake in the matter just yet.

I hope he does the right thing for us and her compared to what he thinks he's obligated to do. I know being in Dad's shadow has fucked with his head, and he's concerned, but he needs to get his act together. Kinsey felt comfortable enough to let him care for her after the incident in the Gutter District. He needs to keep working at it. We can't always intervene with his fuck ups.

A soft hand touches my shoulder. "Hey, Des? Why don't you take this upstairs to Kinsey?" Holly holds out a plate of chocolate chip cookies.

I don't get a chance to take them, though. I hear Kinsey coming down the stairs with Enzo behind her. Her face creases with her anger, and her spicy scent clobbers me, stealing my breath away.

Enzo catches up and spins in front of her, blocking her way. "Baby, come on. Let me—"

She plants her hands to his chest. "I know you want to just cuddle me and give me everything I want, but we need to talk about everything. I know that you guys don't want me to be afraid, but it's the unknown that scares me." Damn. I like the way she stands up for herself in this moment. And she's right. She deserves answers.

She kisses Enzo, getting him to relax. "I know your brothers are on their way, but I can't wait for them. Tell me everything you know."

She flicks her green gaze to mine, though she addresses Enzo. I stare at the two of them in silence, my mind turning to mush. She shouldn't have to deal with any of this. We should've prepared better. Prepared for possibly having to commit treason against the Gilded Sands Pack and the Pack Regime of Saint Vista.

"I don't know the complete details, but you were right about recognizing the man. He was part of the Platinum Shores Pack." Enzo clenches his jaw, his voice deepening to a low rumble.

Kinsey turns her attention to me, pulling Enzo along with her instead of leaving him behind, standing at the stairs. "Do you know more, Desmond?"

I nod my head and motion toward the small dining table in the corner of the living room, the open floor plan giving the condo a more spacious feel.

"One of the Platinum Shore assets had a tracker. They were able to pinpoint our location. One of the security staff was bribed and allowed them in. They went a bit rogue and were supposed to only go after what their alpha had stated, but then the guy saw you." I swallow, trying to remain expressionless. Madame Tamsin usually wouldn't sell an omega and give up that control, but Platinum Shores offered her something she couldn't refuse—a way out of the Gutter District and more power on one of Saint Vista's Pack Regimes.

"Of course. Madame Tamsin's clients don't like when they don't get their way." Kinsey pouts her mouth.

"There's more to it than that. It wasn't that Platinum Shores didn't get their way. They bought you from Tamsin. You were to be theirs permanently." Rage boils through me at the thought.

"No, that can't be right. I was forced into an entertainment contract. Obviously, I never made it. I was going to be a private entertainer for special clients that didn't like to visit the Vixen Lounge." Kinsey shudders with her words, her muscles tense. She slips into the chair and rests her head on her arms, shutting out the world around her.

It kills me having to tell her about what her possible fate could've been. "It's what the man told us."

"God, I'm so stupid." Kinsey's green eyes glass over. "I'm so sorry. I should've known better. I should've told you all."

I close the space to her, engulfing her in a bear hug. "You don't have to apologize, Kinsey. We couldn't have expected you to share that kind of information, and I already told my brother not to pry about anything else and that you would tell us when you were comfortable."

She tips her head back, looking up at me, and I press my lips to her forehead. "Thank you for understanding, but I know that it's important now...I mean, telling you everything."

"The most important thing right now is you, Kinsey." I rub my knuckles to her cheek, pushing her dark hair over her shoulder, exposing her neck. I can't help myself and caress my fingers down her throat, exploring the soft skin.

"Desmond, why don't you take her upstairs to your room and let me catch up with our brothers when they get here?" Enzo's comment surprises me. I thought for sure he'd want to listen to Kinsey spill her heart, but maybe he understands that I might be best in the situation. The scent of her emotions or her order doesn't control me as much as they do him, especially after she gave herself to him completely and accepted his knot.

"Is that okay?" I ask Kinsey, pulling her in for another hug, just wanting to feel the weight of my arms around her and her body against mine. There's something about holding her so close that makes me feel more powerful, stronger.

"Yeah, of course. I'd like that." Kinsey turns to Enzo and Holly. "Just let me know if you need anything, okay? You're welcome to join us, Holly."

Holly shakes her head with a warming smile. "We'll have our own girl time later."

"I'd like that," Kinsey says, smiling at my sister.

I hook my arm around Kinsey, guiding her back toward the stairs. My phone chimes again before we even reach the first landing.

Asshole Bro: Leader of Platinum Shores wants a meeting.
Asshole Bro: Tell Enzo.
Asshole Bro: Video call.
Asshole Bro: Do not include Kinsey.

I slow down and twist, locking my eyes to Enzo. He stares at his own phone screen, glowering at the fact that Wilder assumes he's out of touch.

Sexy Beast: I swear to fucking God if they threaten us, this is war.

That fucker, always messing with my phone contacts.

Asshole Bro: Just keep your mouth shut. I only want you to be present.

I sigh and shove my phone back into my pocket. They can handle all this bullshit. Kinsey needs me now, and I'm not letting anything else get in the way.

"What is it, Desmond?" Kinsey asks, bumping her shoulder to my side. "Is it Wilder?"

Getting my feet to move, I continue to guide her up. "Yeah, but it's all good. My brother can handle him."

Her eyes gloss over with uncertainty. She must sense the fury and fear permeating from Enzo.

"Don't worry, Kinsey. It's going to be fine." If only I wasn't possibly lying...or that she actually believed me.

Chapter 17

Kinsey

The Past

The brilliant full moon shines overhead, lighting the deck aglow. Desmond ignites the firepit and drapes his jacket around me, combating the cold. From the rooftop of Enzo's condo, I drink in the view of the glittering city lights. We overlook a small valley that seems to go on forever. I can't remember the last time I saw something so magical. I had forgotten how beautiful and peaceful a city could look from the outside when the world seems frozen in time.

"Look what I found," Desmond says, shaking a container with what look like marshmallows. "I know you have a sweet tooth."

"You want to roast marshmallows? It's been forever." Who knew something so small could bring me so much excitement?

"With that smile, we're going to roast at least twenty." Desmond chuckles and gets me to switch spots with him, letting me sit on his lap, his warm chest helping keep the cold away.

I grin and take the long wire from him, jabbing it through the marshmallow. I set it on fire, waiting until the outside crackles and smolders, turning black. I blow it out with a laugh, knowing he might judge me for scorching the whole thing.

Desmond pinches the thick wire, carefully plucking my creation from the end. "Arsenio's going to love this. You char them just like him. He swears it's the best way."

I take a bite from his fingers, humming with the sweet, gooey center exploding across my tongue. "I'll fight anyone who argues otherwise."

He peeks at me, his eyebrows raised. "Is that so?"

I shake my fist in his face. "Absolutely."

Poking my sides, Desmond tickles me, and I screech with laughter. I fly from his lap, but he doesn't let me get far, pulling me back to him to press his lips to mine. My giggles fade with my oncoming desire, and I twist to straddle his lap, combing my fingers through his soft golden-brown hair.

There's just something so comforting about Desmond. I feel more in control with him. Every gesture and movement is purposeful. I'm not acting on my lust or pheromones. I'm acting on my pure enjoyment of his company and how he makes me feel as a person.

And not once has he pushed me about my past or demanded answers. This is the moment I've feared facing. He should hear about my history from me and not continue to guess based on old news articles or discover shit from men sent to capture me. He should know exactly what he's getting into with me, especially with Enzo's claim. This could change his expectations and desires, but I need to lay it all out to each of Enzo's brothers, so they can decide for certain if they even want me to be their omega. They wouldn't have had a choice in any other circumstance, but it's not unheard of for only one alpha bonding and the others choosing not to. My parents were like that. Maybe it led to my uncle betraying my dad because of it.

"I can't get enough of you, pretty girl," he murmurs against my mouth, leaning in close, his anticipation hot with his arousal. "I wish I could give you everything you need like my brothers can."

His yearning to be an alpha and disappointment about his true order resonates behind his words, their true meaning opening an ache for him. I'll never grasp what it's like for him, being a beta among alphas, but I can do my best to assure him how his order doesn't define what happens next.

I meet his brown eyes, the amber depths shining in the firelight. "Desmond, you give me something your brothers can't. Unaltered, pure emotions grown from time without influence of pheromones or anything else. I wouldn't change anything about you."

A smile stretches across his mouth with my admission, and he grazes his lips to mine, teasing and testing me, filling me with enough love and desire to send my heart racing.

I've already known my whole life that I would be loved and claimed by a pack, but I never imagined anything like this. The equality despite the orders they manifested into. They're protective of Holly, but they also don't treat her like a resource to gain power. They don't treat Desmond as less than because he's a beta. And they don't fight over who is in control. Even though Wilder can be hotheaded, he never demands anything that'll jeopardize his relationship with his brothers. He's nothing like what I've seen of the king.

"Thank you for saying that. You're so beautiful and caring, Kinsey. I'm so happy you've come into our lives. I want you to know that. I don't give a fuck about your past or any decisions you've made to protect yourself. All I care about is that you're safe and that you know that I'm here. You can tell me anything in your own time. There's nothing you can say that would be a dealbreaker for me. I'm sure Enzo has already said as much, but we want you in our life. We don't care about any arrangements my father could come up with. We're not going to fall in line. I'm not going to accept just a life as someone who can't have the same power as an alpha, because I know that's not true. You've solidified it. We might not be able to knot, but we can still bond." Desmond kisses me again, snuggling me close, savoring my attention as if he's starving for it. And maybe he is. Maybe seeing the way Enzo and I were together awakened something inside him and he wants the same feelings.

"That's all that matters to me. You can fulfill me in your own way. You're just as strong and amazing as your brothers. Your dad is an asshole for thinking anything less than that. I want you. I want everything you have to offer me in hopes that you'll let me take care of you too, Desmond. I don't think I feel this way just because of your brothers either. You're so incredibly sweet and handsome. You're exactly who I need." I rub my palms across his cheeks and down his neck, pulling him closer to me as I slide my tongue into his mouth. The terrors of today fade into a faint memory as I lose myself to his affection. Because he's right. The past can't get me. I need to focus on the here and now and the future. One I'm willing to fight for.

"I feel so lucky, Kinsey. I want you to know that." Desmond doesn't get carried away despite the feeling of his body awakening beneath me. I don't think he will either, not unless I make a move first, but it's more than about the lust and desire between us. I just want to lose myself in the comfort he brings me. How safe I am in his arms. How open and honest I want to be.

And I know he's waiting for answers from me, and I finally feel ready to give them.

So I look into his eyes and prepare to spill my soul to him. Desmond proves he'll ensure that the memories I share don't destroy me. How I know? Instincts. A feeling so palpable that my heart doesn't even race as I think about the day my uncle set my family home on fire and took me away.

"I'm so sorry that happened to you," Desmond murmurs, listening as I work through the memory for him. He doesn't pressure me to relive every detail, stroking my trembling hands.

I lift and drop my shoulders. "There was already resentment because my mom only wanted my dad. My uncle didn't agree with the pack my parents had arranged. He thought that they could do better, and he was entitled to decide, but he didn't have a say because he wasn't my pack's leader, nor was he even bonded with my mom in any way. My parents were monogamous, and my mom just didn't find herself attracted to his brothers. My dad wouldn't push her either. It's hard to explain, considering how close you are to yours." Every pack and household has different dynamics, and the pack that my parents had chosen for me was abnormal. My mom didn't want the same pressure she faced. There was only one alpha, and the others were betas, but they were close. They were kind. They didn't deserve the kind of fate that destroyed them.

I shiver as a thought.

"Were you bonded to them, Kinsey?" Desmond remains expressionless, though no matter how I answer, it won't change anything. Those men died because of me. I almost died too.

"No, my uncle used that against us. He locked us up, tortured us through my first heat, tying me down to suffer alone in front of them." I close my eyes, trying not to get lost in the sudden ache hurting my chest. "It's why I've been taking the suppressant pills. I just...I don't know if I could ever handle going through that again."

Desmond tenses with my revelation, his body hard against mine, his anger turning palpable. But he's not upset with me. He hugs me and kisses me, his cheek shining with a stray tear. I never expected such a reaction, and I kiss the crook of his neck and bury my face against his skin.

He blinks his eyes, his emotions clear on his face. "I'm so sorry, Kinsey. I'm so fucking sorry you ever had to experience that. I can't even imagine the pain and despair. Where is your uncle now?"

I shrug, running my fingers over his cheeks. "I don't know. I don't know, and I don't care. I hope he's dead."

"If he isn't, then he will be." Desmond strokes his hand along my back, smoothing out my trembles.

I don't respond to him. I know if I do, my voice will crack. There is nothing more in the world I want to see than my uncle pays for what he did to me and our pack, apart from bonding with Desmond and his brothers forever. If I had to choose between the two, I would pick them. I would continue to push forward and move on from my past. I would concentrate on helping other omegas with their futures. Because this is proof enough that things need to change. We deserve the right to pick who we belong to and who belongs to us. We shouldn't be left with the aftermath of our parents' decisions.

I swipe my hand across my cheeks, my heart already feeling so much lighter talking to Desmond.

"How about we talk about something else for a bit? I'd love to know more about you and your brothers. What was it like growing up with them?" I reposition myself and grab the wire from him, adding two marshmallows to it. His amber eyes carry a new depth to them as he now helps me carry the weight of my past with me. But I know he gladly does it, and he wouldn't wish it otherwise. He doesn't even have to tell me for me to know that he wishes he could carry it all completely. Because that's what betas do. They share the burden. They keep the packs going and bring stability. If the world could see just how important a beta is, things would be better. The world would be better for it.

Desmond rests his chin on my shoulder, holding the wire for me, setting the marshmallows ablaze until they blacken, and he blows the fire out. "My siblings made it bearable, and we've always been close. Even after we manifested into our orders. It was an adjustment, but only our father treated me differently. I always knew that things could've been worse for me. I'm thankful for the closeness I have to my brothers, even though they sometimes drive me crazy. Did you know that Wilder has a huge fucking problem with scenting everything around him? He's the type that will ensure he will never be ignored."

I laugh. "We'll have to mess with him some more. I find giving him a taste of his own actions to be so satisfying." I already noticed that he managed to sneak touching his brothers just to remind me he's lurking. It doesn't feel like it was intended to be in a creepy way, and more like him being almost hesitant because he knows better than giving in to his true desires. Still, I'm not going to ever let him forget it.

"I will gladly help. I'd be a happy man if it was only you that I could smell all the time." Desmond offers me the burnt marshmallow, and I glide my tongue over his fingers as I take the whole thing in my mouth, watching him watch me, his eyes turning heavy with his lust.

"How much time do you think we have now? I'm assuming he's going to take one of the guest rooms?" I bite my bottom lip with my words.

He chuckles and nods his head. "I know exactly which one. Come on. I think we have just enough time. Let's really fuck with his head the second he enters the condo. Let's make sure he knows that you have staked your claim, and there's nothing he can do now."

My heart flutters at his words. It's not exactly something you tell an omega, but he's right. I have claimed them, and even though I don't know exactly where everything will lead, I know what I want right now.

And I'll do whatever I can to take it.

"They're pulling in the garage now," Enzo says, pushing to his feet. "Brace yourself, baby. Wilder is in one hell of a bad mood. The Platinum Shores Pack really knows how to strike a guy in the balls without even being in the same room."

I rub my lips together, trying to remain expressionless. I wasn't included in the video meeting he and his brothers had with the men who think that I'm suddenly theirs because Madame Tamsin sold me as if I were one of her omegas, but

I know that nothing was accomplished apart from threats and promises to go to war.

"There's one way to ease the pain in his balls…" Am I toeing a line that could get me in trouble? Only in a good way. But I feel bad for Wilder. Who knew I would feel sympathy toward an ass, but he showed me his softer side. And I want to bring it out more in him. He doesn't deserve to spend his life guarded and completely on the verge of always losing his shit because of his fear. Though I know he would never admit it.

"Damn, Kinsey. I think my balls ache now." Desmond surprises me with his teasing, and I tip my head back and laugh, wagging my finger at him. Pushing from my spot, I head toward the door leading up from the garage. I wasn't kidding about wanting to stanch Wilder's horrible mood immediately. We've all just relaxed. Shit might be fucked up, but we can't let it get to us in this moment. Wilder needs to understand that. He's not carrying this burden alone. We do it together.

Enzo whistles and spanks my ass as I pass, heading to the door and preparing myself to attack Wilder in a hug he won't be able to refuse. If he even tries, I know his brothers will hang him upside down and beat the crap back into him.

Sometimes it just takes a little reminder that his place in the pack doesn't have to resemble his father's.

Footsteps and the mumbling of voices hum through the stairwell as Arsenio and Wilder ascend from the basement garage. I watch the door, listening to the beep of them unlocking it. It swings open with force, and Wilder doesn't even have a chance to prepare himself as I jump up, making him catch me in his arms. I bury my face in his throat and softly kiss the spot on his neck that will catch my scent the best. His tense muscles automatically loosen, and he groans and hugs me tighter, adjusting me in his arms in silence, not saying a single word as I just embrace him, letting him know that I'm here regardless of anything.

Because I desperately yearn to make this work. He has it in him to be the man I desire and want, though I know he's afraid outside circumstances will force him to be otherwise. He needs to realize he's the one in control. It'll give him something more to fight for. It'll give him the power he needs.

"Damn, sugar. I'm going to need some of that too," Arsenio murmurs, sandwiching me to Wilder while he hugs me from behind.

I laugh and stretch my neck, puckering my lips and waiting for him to find my mouth for a kiss. In this moment, I know that everything has changed. I'm no longer a question in their lives. They're no longer going to wonder what to do with me, and I no longer have to fear the answers to that. Because this is my subtle way of declaring I want them to claim me like Enzo. I want them to accept me in their pack as their omega.

I want them to fight for me.

I've never wanted anything so badly in my life. The feelings that arise from how protective they are, how strong and capable they are, turns me on at a deep-seated level. This is exactly how it should be for a mate.

"You make it incredibly hard to be mad at my brother," Wilder whispers, finally releasing his hold on me. "I'm sorry that you're going through this because of our mistake."

I meet Wilder's gaze as Arsenio backs up to give us space. He searches my eyes, looking for the pain he expects to find, but I keep my emotions buried. I've already gotten them out. Desmond helped me work through them, so I'm no longer afraid of what will happen. I know these men will do whatever is necessary to protect me. To care for me. They're deserving of everything I have to offer, and I'll prove it.

"You couldn't have known. I don't want you holding onto that, okay? Let's just spend the rest of the night being together as a pack. I think you all need the reminder." I motion to Holly, and she shuffles closer with a smile. "Holly has cooked a meal for us, and Enzo helped with the dessert. I supervised and taste-tested."

Arsenio chuckles. "It's been a while since Holl's had the chance to do something she likes."

Holly opens her arms for her brother. "I forgot how much I missed my independence. There's not much to work with in the panic room, and I hadn't realized how freeing it was not to have to worry about the staff in the palace or getting caught. I know you guys were worried about me being anywhere outside of our home together, but look how amazing this is. I haven't been this happy in a long time."

Enzo opens his arms and squishes Holly and Arsenio against me and Wilder. Desmond joins his other side, pushing us into a group hug. For the first time ever, I hear Wilder laugh. Truly laugh. I never thought a sound could be so musical, sexy, and so full of joy.

"I haven't been this happy ever," Enzo says. "We're going to get this shit done and get the life we want."

"Damn straight." Wilder reaches up and touches my cheek. "No fucking bastard is going to get in our way. Not the Platinum Shores Pack. Not the king. No one."

"Hell yeah. We're going to prove it." Desmond releases a throaty growl with his words. "If they want a war, they'll get a fucking war. We'll burn their territory down. We'll burn ours down too if we have to. Because then, we can rebuild. We can show the Pack Regimes that things are changing."

He's right about that.

I've experienced it myself. The world once broke me, but I just took the pieces and placed them back together, using stronger glue instead of skin and bone.

These men are mine. This pack is mine.

I will do what I have to do to ensure it.

Because I'm not a scared omega. I am more.

Chapter 18

Kinsey

Promises

"Come on, Wilder. It's only going to the store, grabbing a bite to eat, and coming back home. I think we can manage it. We won't be alone." I stand behind Wilder as he sits at a computer in the corner of his room in the condo. Today belongs to him, and he's been wasting it, looking over a bunch of financial statements and whatever else he is responsible for.

"You must take one of the suppressant pills. You also have to have a gun. And I swear if Arsenio doesn't stay within reach of both of you, I'll punch him in his cock a dozen times. He also has to wear the trackers." Wilder leans back in his chair and looks up at me. "Will you seal your promise with a kiss?"

I smirk at his words, knowing that he would give in to my pleas. Holly and I are getting anxious with all their emotions constantly running wild, and sitting on the rooftop deck for a breath of air isn't enough. We don't want to be prisoners here. Enzo has proven time and time again the last couple weeks that this place is safe. We have everything we need to blend in as betas, and this area is mostly inhabited by betas who no longer have packs or those who were kicked out or shamed. Or maybe those who had never had an alpha to begin with. Because it is possible. They're just...not desired by those in power, which is all absolutely part of the alpha order of the Pack Regimes.

I twist my lips to the side and scrunch my nose. "Do I have to? I'd much prefer to just kiss you without you trying to manipulate me."

He returns my smile with his own. "Always calling me out, brat-girl. I just know that I can't be making moves without you giving me signs, and right now, it's hard to read you."

I step away from him and stroll toward his bed, grabbing one of his pillows and tucking it under my arm. I walk around to the small closet next and pull out one of his sweatshirts before shrugging it over my head. Without a word, I saunter from the room and make my way down the hall to where I discovered an unused closet.

I peek over my shoulder, smiling at Wilder as he stands in the doorway to his room and watches me.

Opening the closet, I reveal my nest to him with my stash of their belongings. One of Enzo's pillows, three of Desmond's towels, the blanket Arsenio used a week ago on the couch while we watched TV, and a shirt of Wilder's I found hanging on his chair while he was in the shower yesterday piles on the floor in the small space. I add the pillow I just stole from his bed to my makeshift room of comfort and sit down, curling myself up with it.

I listen to Wilder's shuffling steps, his slow pace driving me crazy. He's been so busy that he hasn't really paid attention to things I do on my own and this is my little way of showing him. I needed a place where I could have all the comforts I need, especially because I know my heat lurks around the corner. I've lost track of exactly when to expect it, but since I don't take the suppressant pills regularly, it'll hit me hard and fast.

"Enzo's going to have to move his ass so you can have a room of your own," Wilder says, kneeling beside me. He squeezes into the closet, his long legs sticking out.

I laugh and shake my head. "Has no one explained to you about omegas and their nesting? I like it here. It feels safe to be alone."

His mouth slackens as he comprehends my words. None of us have really discussed this sort of thing regarding me. He and his brothers have been concerned about Holly. Now it sinks in, Wilder's complexion darkening with his flush skin—but it's not embarrassment. It's raw and sexy, his shift in mood palpable.

"Damn, I'm an idiot," he mutters, rubbing his forehead, smoothing out the lines.

Grinning wider, I bite my lip. "This wasn't exactly part of your plan, but don't worry. We have time. This is just my carnal need flaring."

"Mmm, damn. How could I've been such an ass? I really fucked up with you, and I want you to know I'm doing my best to change." Wilder lies on his side, snuggling close against me. "Do you think you'd ever be willing to give me a chance to truly prove I'm worthy of you?"

I meet his light blue gaze. "Depends. Can you handle me still being your little brat?" Reaching out, I scrub my fingers into his dark chestnut hair and roll on top of him, using his muscular body to propel me to my feet.

He huffs and jerks out his hand, snatching my shirt, but I only pull myself free, leaving it behind. I race toward the stairs, knowing that if I don't hurry up, he's going to catch me, and I know how much he enjoys me making it difficult for him.

"Catch me, and I'll give you that kiss. Maybe more," I call, laughing over my shoulder.

"You better hurry. If I catch you, that bratty ass of yours is mine. I'm going to enjoy seeing my palm print bloom red as I spank you for being such a pain in my balls." Wilder stomps, ensuring his thundering footsteps sends my heart racing.

Damn him. Why do I like the sound of that? Too bad for him. I'm going to use his threat against him just to push him even more.

I freeze at the top of the stairs, widening my eyes. "You're going to what?"

Shit. The expression he gives me makes me feel a bit bad...but not bad enough to break my perfected acting skills.

"Why would you want to do that?" I ask, shifting on my feet, hugging one of my arms over my bare stomach, the only thing covering me being a bra with my pants.

Wilder opens and closes his mouth, rushing the space to me. "Kinsey, I—"

Dodging around him, I swing my open palm and smack him on his ass, shocking the hell out of him. "You've been a naughty fucking alpha, and you're the one who needs a good spanking."

I screech as Wilder lunges, locking his hands around my waist as he lifts me off my feet. I laugh and squirm, stretching in an attempt to spank him again. I manage to whack his ass, making him growl. The world spins around me as Wilder throws me onto his bed, flipping me over and pinning me on my stomach.

His weight sinks into me, and I gasp a breath, inhaling the fragrant scent of the sheets. His mouth brushes my shoulder, and he nudges my dark hair away with his nose. My body hums beneath him, our playfulness smoldering into desire. My attraction to Wilder has grown more intense over the last few weeks since we've been here and he accepted this was it, and a part of me wants to explore him on a level that satisfies my curiosity but also solidifies our bond.

"My little brat-girl, you know exactly what you do to me, don't you?" Wilder murmurs in my ear, the heat of his breath sending goosebumps over my skin.

"I don't know what you're talking about." I arch my back, popping my ass up firmly against him.

His hard-on presses into me, his desire pulsing as he flexes his body. Warmth tingles between my legs just thinking about what he wants to do with me.

"You enjoy teasing me." Wilder glides his tongue over my earlobe, sucking it into his mouth.

"More than anything." I roll my body, grinding against him in a way that quickens his breathing. The scent of his lust permeates the air, hardening my nipples, and his weight suddenly eases off, leaving cool air against my skin.

But I don't remain facing down long.

Sliding his hand under me, Wilder flips me over and snatches my wrists, not letting me grab for him how I want. He uses his knee to spread my legs, positioning himself between them. My chest rises and falls with my panting breath, his closeness awakening something frantic and needy inside me. He's not the only one I'm teasing. My resistance only tortures my own desires.

"You can only tease me for so long before it comes back to bite you, Kinsey." He leans down and nips my bottom lip, stretching it just enough to make me moan. "And not only once." Breaking away from my mouth, he licks down my throat and grazes his teeth over my neck. I bend my head, silently asking for more of his attention, and he sucks hard, leaving a mark before biting me just hard enough to make me gasp again.

Continuing down, Wilder kisses his way to my breasts and uses his teeth to pull my bra away enough to suck my nipple into his mouth. I lock my legs around him, not letting him continue farther. I reach for his shirt and yank it up. Wilder returns to my mouth, kissing me again, and I reach between us and glide my hand down his torso, working my way to his pants until I stroke him through his clothes.

"I'll tease you as much as I want, Wilder. Until you can't handle it." I tighten my hold on him, making it impossible for him to move the way he wants while I explore the length of his cock through his pants.

Growling, he rolls until I land on top of him. I smile and slide lower, rushing to unfasten his pants to slip my hand into them, touching the heat of his skin with mine. I suck my lip between my teeth, watching the lust sharpen his features. He struggles to give me this kind of control, and I know at any second—

Arching up, Wilder grabs my wrist. "You're not going to deny me the pleasure of hearing you moan first. Tasting you. Touching you. I can only take so much of your teasing before I—"

"What are you going to do about it?" I ask, closing the space to brush my lips to his without giving in and kissing him with the passion he craves. "You're all talk."

His eyes narrow as he gives me a once-over. I don't get a chance to react as he pulls me forward, flips me onto my stomach across his lap, pulls down my pants, and spanks me hard on the ass. The stinging sensation surprises me in a good way, and my body clenches as he triggers my adrenaline.

"And you are such a brat." Wilder rubs smooth circles over my heated skin, rubbing away the sting of his palm.

"If you think this is some kind of punishment, continue. I like it." I stretch my neck and smile over my shoulder. "It makes me just want to constantly push your buttons."

He spanks me again. "You're never going to make it easy on me, are you?"

"There's no fun for you in that. That's not your style. I know. I can smell your desire. It's not good enough for me when you are calm and tranquil. But when you are getting pushback... Fuck me." I wiggle on his lap, trying to slide off only to have him comb his fingers into my hair and pull slightly, stretching my neck until he can kiss me on my lips.

"I should punish you for your word choice. You know I would gladly. But once we start, little brat, we won't stop. I'm not one for a quickie, and I know we have things to do." Wilder snags my bottom lip with his teeth again, nipping me just hard enough to make me gasp. Swinging his hand, he smacks my ass only to scoop me up to brush his lips to the hot spot.

"You have things to do. Not me. My only job was to beg you to let me out. Just for that, I'm not letting you get a single thing done until you..." I let my voice trail off, my body humming at the idea of him filling in the blanks and doing as he pleases. I know he won't push for sex, but if he wanted to, I wouldn't resist him.

He growls with his desire and spanks me one more time before tugging my pants off completely. He doesn't undress, only pulling me back upright until I straddle his lap, completely exposed and trembling in anticipation. His eyes burn down my body. His hand follows his line of sight, trailing slowly yet powerfully, massaging into my muscles as he caresses his fingers over my side and then to my hip, working his way between my legs. He holds me in place, watching me as he glides his fingers over my clit just for a second before dipping one inside me. I moan at the sensation, keeping my eyes trained on his as he memorizes me purely with his touch.

"It's taking everything in me not to claim you right now, Kinsey. I know you would let me, except I'm not deserving of you just yet. You might disagree, but that's just how it is for me. But I'll not deny you pleasure. It'll be solely yours." Wilder slides his finger in and out of me, using his thumb to add pressure to my clit, stroking back-and-forth in a way that leaves me squirming and shaking. It feels so good, so intense, and I crave more. I want to touch him too, but he doesn't allow it.

Every time I try, he grabs my wrist with his free hand and tugs me away.

"Your scent is mouthwatering. I can't wait to taste you." Wilder brings his hand to his mouth and sucks his finger, his eyes heavy with lust. "If I go past this, I won't stop. That's a promise. It's far too hard to resist you."

"Then don't." My voice comes out breathy and soft, my whole body buzzing and humming as he works me over again, adding in a second finger and increasing the pressure.

"Kinsey..." He moans and kisses me, silencing my pleas for more as he rubs my clit while sliding his fingers in and out, sending my body spasming with utter bliss. I moan so loudly I'm sure everyone can hear me, so I bury my face in the crook of his neck and bite him softly, sucking his skin between my teeth to leave my own mark on his body. Because he's mine. I don't need a claim to know. I know we'll bond when he's ready.

"Fuck," he breathes, his breath hot on my ear as he slows down. "You are so perfect. So beautiful. Everything I want."

"Then take it. Take me." I suck his throat again, leaving another hickey behind.

"My brat. So demanding. Always pushing." He groans with a smile, rocking his hips enough that I can feel the length of his shaft through his pants. I reach between us and glide my fingers over him, wishing he let me pull his cock free.

I'm so caught up in the moment that it's all I can think about. It's all I imagine for the rest of the day.

"Then give me what I want, Wilder. I can't stand the thought of anything else." I pant as I continue to explore him, kissing him deeply as I slide my tongue into his mouth.

"Yeah, brother. If you don't do it, I will. I can smell her all the way out here." Arsenio's voice hums to the door, unashamedly interrupting our moment.

I smile and catch Wilder's face, his nostrils flaring at the thought. He won't say it, but he gets jealous imagining his brother taking over from here.

"I just want another orgasm. I want to feel good," I say, my voice light with my teasing. "I think Wilder doesn't want me to have one because I'm too bratty. What do you think about that? Arsenio?"

Small taps sound on the door as he groans under his breath, thinking over my question. Wilder narrows his eyes at me and flips me around again to spank my ass.

I squeal and laugh, wiggling and trying to escape his embrace. "Arsenio, help! Your brother wants to deny me."

My heart raps in my chest, my playful invitation for Arsenio to come in hanging in the air. This is Wilder's decision. It is his space, after all.

I bite my lip and grin at him. "I'm just teasing. If you're not okay..."

Wilder spanks my ass again. "Brother, if you come in, you need to help me punish the brat. Do you understand?"

I laugh and crawl away from Wilder as the door swings open and Arsenio strides in as if the hallway is now his enemy. Wilder lets me get to the edge of the bed without saying anything as I hold my arms up, inviting Arsenio to grab me.

"Look at what he's done to my ass," I say, turning slightly to show off the reddening handprints on my butt cheeks.

Arsenio slows down and tilts his head, drinking in the sight of my naked body. I squirm under his desire, but I don't feel vulnerable even though both of them are dressed. I feel sexy and wanted. I feel absolutely beautiful and like the most important woman in the world.

Arsenio curls his fingers into fists and fake glares at Wilder. "Sorry, brother. I think you've handled her enough. My sugar needs a little kiss to make her sexy ass feel better."

I laugh and turn around, shaking my ass in his direction. Wilder growls and grabs me from underneath my arms pulling me to him. He restrains me on top of him only to reposition me, so I can meet his mouth for another kiss.

"I suppose you're right. She does need some gentle affection. I want you to make her moan for me. Because I know that your kind of attention can be just as torturous. I'll keep her in place to teach her a lesson. You're not going to be able to move now, brat. You're going to have to stay utterly still and unable to touch either of us."

I groan at the sensation of Arsenio's hands sliding across my ass cheeks, opening and closing them as he prepares to do whatever Wilder instructs.

"Don't worry, sugar. You're going to enjoy every second of my brand of torture. I promise. Now speak up at any time."

Arsenio positions his body on top of mine just for a second, bringing his mouth to my ear to suck my lobe between his teeth. "And thank you for letting me join," he adds. "I will show my absolute appreciation. You have no idea what this means to me." He whispers the words, keeping them between him and me, breaking his little role-play with Wilder about me being their naughty girl.

I don't speak and instead just moan my agreement, turning back to kiss Wilder again. Arsenio repositions me onto my knees, pulling me back until my elbows rest at Wilder's sides. He massages my ass again, leaning down to kiss the hot skin where Wilder spanked me. I moan in anticipation, the coolness of his lips helping to ease the sting. And then I realize exactly how close I am to his raging cock. I know that he wanted this to be about my pleasure first, but now that his body is so close to mine, I take advantage of the position and grope him with one hand, stroking him enough to make him moan.

"Looks like you're going to torture my brother too," Arsenio says, sliding his finger inside me, testing my body, and discovering how slippery I am.

"He's going to beg me for mercy now. He thought that he could turn you against me to join his side of punishing pleasure, but now he's going to have to endure what it's like to be craved by his bratty little omega." I lean down and rub my cheek to his balls in his pants, just stroking him teasingly without rushing.

Wilder links his fingers through my hair. "Don't you worry, Kinsey. I will remember this for next time."

Next time. I love the sound of that, moaning my excitement at the same time Arsenio kisses my thigh before he glides his tongue between my legs and strokes it over my clit. My whole body buzzes as he tastes me how he wants, murmuring how sweet I really am, while he explores me with his fingers. I prop myself up with my elbows to free my hands and tug at Wilder's pants to pull his cock completely free.

His girth intimidates me, but I know that I can handle anything. I can't wait to feel the pleasure that comes from him. I can't wait to taste his body and what I do for him. This moment is a different kind of bonding experience. This is part of my pack, and I find such satisfaction in knowing how we can bring each other pleasure together. Me giving them what they need and them teaming up to shower me with so much affection that I could survive on it for the rest of my life and perhaps even eternity.

I draw my tongue over Wilder's tip and suck it into my mouth, twirling my tongue and tightening my lips to add pressure. He moans, not even caring that I do this in front of his brother. Arsenio only tightens his hands around my waist and holds me still, using my slick to slip his thumb gently into my ass at the same time he buries his face between my legs, igniting so much pleasure that I lose myself completely to the moment.

Wilder tugs my hair, his fingers resting on my scalp as he guides me up and down, ensuring that I can enjoy the ecstasy that Arsenio ignites through my body without having to think about him.

And I love it.

I love everything about this, and how close I am to both of them. How good they smell. How my body wants more, and how I will be on the edge of a cliff until I get the bond that I need. One I'm willing to wait for. One that will solidify everything even more so.

"How does she taste, brother? Is it as sweet as her scent?" Wilder moans, watching me lick his cock while his brother flicks his tongue between my legs.

Arsenio releases a deep, rumbling noise that shocks my body, sending me over the edge and making me pull away from Wilder as I orgasm, my muscles clenching so tightly that I feel as if they'll never recover.

"Even sweeter. Fuck, look how sexy. She's soaked me. Her scent's going to linger for days." Arsenio gently spanks my ass, massaging my cheeks again.

"Mmm." Wilder stretches and slides a finger between my legs, wanting to find out for himself. I suck his cock back into my mouth, listening to him groan, the two of us burning with our lust and desire. Arsenio bows to wrap his arms around me, wanting to hug me and show me the affection he thinks I deserve.

I don't stop bobbing my head, enjoying how the two of them continue to play with me and kiss me, stroke my nipples and touch every inch of my body in exploration until I feel Wilder's balls tighten under my hand. He comes, the sweetness of his seed making me gasp and tingle.

The three of us pile together on Wilder's bed with me in between them. Wilder rests his chest to my back and strokes his fingers across my shoulder and to my throat. He kisses me softly and nips me, adding a couple of extra marks as he waits for my heart to stop racing.

Arsenio touches my cheek, his hand resting between my legs, just cupping my throbbing body in a way that feels so good and right. Neither of them moves until I catch my breath, and even then, they stay close and just sandwich me between them, ensuring that I stay warm and never have to experience the absence of their bodies before I'm ready.

"You guys are so good to me," I whisper, my voice a bit raspy from my screams of pleasure. "I never want to imagine my life without you. I'm starting to believe in fate."

Arsenio leans in and brushes his lips to mine. "Even so, I would never justify how others treated you in your past as a way for you to have come to us. That was not fate."

He's right about that. I never considered that isn't how I should handle all the terrible things that happened to me, even if it brought me into their arms.

I bob my head and kiss him again, pushing the thoughts away. "I love you. I love both of you. Thank you for saying that. Thank you for accepting me and wanting me. For changing your whole lives for me."

Wilder tightens his arm around my side. "You're the woman of my dreams. Don't give me so much credit. I'm selfishly doing this for myself. Because I can't stand the thought of ever letting you go. I'll be a man worthy of you. It is beyond love for me. You're my sole reason for living now. I want you to know that."

I've never felt so happy. Each day gets better and better. With them, I can finally breathe easily. I feel as if I have found my place in life. My pack. My future.

I will do anything to keep it.

I'm not an omega that will sit back and let things happen anymore. I will stand up. I will stand beside my alphas and my beta.

This is my life, and I'll not lose it.

And I know that Wilder and Arsenio, Enzo and Desmond will guarantee it.

Chapter 19

Kinsey

Real World

“This all feels so normal, doesn't it?” Holly sits across from me in a booth at a small diner a couple blocks away from the condo. Arsenio and Desmond hang out across the room at their own booth, pretending as if Holly and I are on our own, giving us the girl time outside of the condo we wanted.

“It does. I forgot what normalcy felt like. Look at all these betas just going about their day.” I nod my chin toward a table of guys, laughing and smiling at each other.

"Is it weird that I think they are super-hot? I know they're not alphas, but it's like my body doesn't even care." Holly grins at one of them, and the guy winks.

I tense and flick my gaze to her brothers, hoping they didn't see the interaction. They might've let us have a girl time, but if anyone dares show either of us attention, there might be a problem. That's why Wilder and Enzo aren't here. They are not so subtle and aren't afraid to start shit.

Arsenio only smiles at me, missing the interaction between Holly and the beta because he's too busy just sending me all his adoration in invisible streams from across the room. Our connection is so palpable that I'm sure if somebody tried to step between our line of sight, they would hit a wall that would send them crashing to the floor.

I gently kick Holly under the table. "Careful. That could be the suppressant pills. They mess up your judgment a bit in regard to who you find an attraction to. I just want you to keep that in mind. You might like those guys right now, but if you skip a pill, you might end up hating them."

It's all so very complicated, but I try my best to be honest with Holly. I know she craves escape. She yearns for attention that doesn't come from a family bond.

"I guess I'll deal with that if the time ever comes. Distract my brothers." Holly scribbles something on a napkin, grinning at me. "I'll be right back."

Fuck me. A part of me wants to argue with her, knowing that if Wilder finds out that I let her approach these betas, he might lose his shit. Another part of me knows Holly deserves a connection outside of her family and pack. They can't hide her forever. She's going to have to learn how to adapt to the world outside of their royal life if she wants to create something that brings her happiness.

Instead, I decide I can do both. I get up from my seat and saunter across the diner to Arsenio and Desmond.

I peek over my shoulder at Holly strolling past the table of men she finds attractive. She slides the napkin with her number on the edge. Sauntering toward the counter, she sways her hips, and I hold my finger up to her brothers, getting them to stay in place.

"If either of you reacts or try to intimidate the betas, you guys are going to be in trouble. Let Holly have her fun. It has been tough on her to have to go through this. There's nothing wrong with a little flirting. She's giving him her phone number, but we all know that you guys have access. If she wants to talk to them, let her. You can do your background check or whatever bullshit to make sure they're not a threat." I press my palms to the table, giving Arsenio a view of my cleavage.

He stretches up and kisses me, not caring if anybody sees us. "Damn, sugar. If I hadn't seen that cute little heart-shaped mark on your hip, I'd think you were an alpha."

Desmond chuckles and slides his hand over mine, squeezing my fingers. "If she keeps talking like that, I'll gladly bow and kiss her feet."

Heat blossoms across my chest and in my cheeks. I run my fingers through Desmond's caramel brown hair and lean in, giving him a kiss next. I pat his cheek and smile at Arsenio, spinning around to head to the table where Holly now plays with her phone.

I slide into the booth across from her. "You're bold, Holly. Those guys are going to think you're a little alpha with the way you handled that."

She laughs. "I wish. As long as they see me as a beta, it's all that matters." She taps her fingers on the table, staring at her phone, willing it to buzz in her hands.

I flick my attention to the group of guys, leaning over and playing with the napkin Holly wrote on. She doesn't give them a second look, keeping her attention on me. I can't stop smiling at her. I wish I had been as brave over the years. I spent most of the time staring at the fucking ground that I can't even remember exactly what half of the Gutter District looks like. Who knew it would feel so good to be able to sit with my head held high now?

Holly startles as her phone buzzes in her hand. "Oh, my God. It's them. Look."

Diner Guy: Come over here. Let us buy you and your sister lunch.

Her face lights up in a beaming smile.

My stomach twists with nerves. It was one thing for her to give them her number. It's another thing for us to join them, especially with her brothers now watching our every move.

"I don't know what to say. I really want to go over there. Do you think Arsenio and Desmond would be okay if it was just for five minutes? I know you told them something, because they would've flown over here otherwise." Holly looks at me, her eyes pleading as she squeezes her phone.

I don't want to get in the middle between her and her brothers. They're overprotective for a reason and want to ensure she gets the life denied her by their father. But taking these kinds of risks? I don't know.

I rub my lips together. "I think you should ask them. But I also want you to know that I won't join you. I'm sorry. I don't want to even pretend that they have a chance with me."

Holly groans under her breath and quickly types something in her phone.

A moment later, Arsenio stands from his seat and crosses the diner. Desmond follows behind him, keeping a bit of distance as he decides to cut across and head toward the counter where the host waits for customers at the register. I flick my gaze to the guys again, but they no longer look in our direction. They get up and leave, and Holly pouts her bottom lip. I can see the disappointment shining in her eyes.

Now I know for certain it's time we set some definitive rules. She can't live like this. It's not fair. She and her brothers need to come to an agreement on what is acceptable. They wanted me to be her caretaker, and that's what I plan to be. I'm not going to be her warden.

"Are you guys finished eating? Wilder just texted and wants us to meet him." Arsenio holds his hand out to me.

"Meet him where? I think I'd rather just go home. I'm over not being able to do much. I'd rather just watch a movie or some shit at home." Holly crosses her arms over her chest.

Arsenio looks at me. "Is that what you want, sugar? I can tell Wilder no. He knows it's my day with you anyway."

I lift and drop my shoulders. "I'm fine with whatever. Maybe we can stop at the store on the way home and pick up a bunch of candy and popcorn and whatever."

He nods. "Anything for you."

I smile and stretch up on my tiptoes, kissing him softly. Desmond returns to us and nudges Holly with his fist, trying to get her to smile. But she doesn't react. She looks past them at the diner door. I follow her gaze, seeing the four betas outside with another man that wasn't in the diner.

He's an alpha. I thought that this area was heavily dominated by betas and those unattached to packs.

The man looks in our direction, but his gaze doesn't land on me at all. He looks at Holly, and a flirtatious smile crosses her face. Neither of her brothers notices, their attention on me.

After a moment longer, the alpha turns away, his expression remaining even. I don't think he realizes that Holly is an omega, so he doesn't show interest. Whether that's good or bad? I don't quite know yet. It bothers Holly. I can see it in her eyes as her smile falters. It's in her very nature as an unbonded omega to want a pack, but right now, it's impossible. Not until her brothers steal power from the king.

The men hop into a car and don't do anything as we head to the door. Arsenio and Desmond glance at them without much thought. I slide my arm over Holly's shoulders and give her a squeeze. Arsenio strolls on my other side protectively, watching the surroundings. I know he's a bit nervous being out like this, but I don't think we'll have a problem. My blond wig, heavy makeup, and baggy clothing really do make me feel like a different person. I don't recognize myself as I catch my reflection in a car window.

Desmond leads the way to the car and holds open the door for me, letting me sit in the front beside him. Arsenio and Holly take the backseat, and I can't help twisting to look at her, staring at her phone again.

"You guys are a bunch of cock blocks," she says, pulling off the mousy brown wig and showing off her pretty blond hair. "They left because of you. I guess they got scary vibes and then realized that we were together."

I raise my eyebrows, surprised that she even called her brothers out. I tighten my lips as to not smile. I know they didn't intentionally do it, but she is kind of right. I saw the way the other betas in the diner looked at them. Arsenio is clearly an alpha, and they would know it based on his scent. It makes people nervous when they don't have a pack or power.

"Hey now, little sis. All we did was sit there. You can't blame us for that bullshit. If they were intimidated, that's their problem." Desmond taps his fingers on the wheel. "Plus, I think you could do better."

Oh fuck.

I whack Desmond with the back of my hand. "You can't judge them based on that. You might be a beta, but you have the privilege of power because of your birthright as a prince."

He sighs and hangs his head. "Yeah, yeah. Doesn't change my opinion. Holly needs someone powerful and strong to protect her."

"And I'm sure Holly can be the judge of that." I smile at him and touch his cheek. "Omega's clearly know how to pick them when we get the chance. I mean, look at me. My chosen pack is perfect."

A smile stretches across his face, and he turns to me, pulling me closer to him until our lips meet and I can give in to the affection he craves. Arsenio rests his hands on my shoulders from the backseat and squeezes me. I break away from Desmond and swivel to give him a kiss next.

Holly groans. "See? This is what I want. You guys make me so jealous. It isn't fair. I'm not going to have some knights in shining armor accidentally kidnap me and realize that they snagged themselves their forever girl. I have to pursue and take what I want, alpha-style."

I laugh and beam at her. "That's right. And you'll get there. It won't hurt anyone for you to talk to them. Just don't tell Wilder. It won't be long until you'll be free from your father. Isn't that right, Arsenio?"

He covers his ears with his hands. "I'm not hearing any of this. What Wilder doesn't know, won't hurt him, but if he does find out, I'm not going to have my ass handed to me."

"I'll protect you, big brother. I know how to handle a jerk alpha." Holly brightens with a smile, her disappointment shifting with the realization that her brothers aren't automatically denying her the chance to make connections outside of their pack.

"I will stand by your choice, Holly, but we need to be careful. Let me look into them before you get attached to the idea. I want to make sure they are not criminals or something worse." Desmond puts the car in gear. "If you agree to that, then we will humor this."

Humor this? I'm going to have to talk to him later. They need a lesson on how to talk to their sister.

Holly either doesn't care or just ignores his comment and bounces in her seat, clapping her hands. Her excitement fills me with joy, and I can't stop from joining in on her little dance.

The car jolts, and metal crunches metal. My heart sinks into my stomach as someone rear-ends us. What the fuck?

Desmond hops out of the car before I even have a chance to look behind us. My door jerks open, and I gawk at the unfamiliar man, his face scowling in anger. Panic freezes me in place, and it takes me a second to gather my bearings to scream.

Locking his fingers to my hair, the man drags me from my seat at the same time Arsenio hops from the vehicle. Desmond punches another guy on the other side of the car, and I thrash and skid across the ground as the man pulls me with him.

"Let me go!" I scream, clawing at the man's wrists, trying to get him to release me.

Arsenio reaches into the car and pulls out a weapon. He doesn't even get a chance to fire his gun before a man tackles him. Bullets spray, hitting the side door where he was standing.

The shock of it all pushes me to fight harder, and I manage to push myself with my feet, throwing the man holding me off-balance. I swing and punch him in the groin hard enough that he howls in pain and lets me go. Gravel embeds in my palms as I scramble to get away. I'm not a fighter. It's always in my best interest to run, and I need to find shelter. I need to hide.

A whistle cuts through the air. "Kinsey, this way. Hurry." Holly's voice drags me away from the man getting to his feet behind me.

Everything blurs with my unshed tears. My heart threatens to explode from my chest. I can't even get a good look at what's happening to Arsenio and Desmond. If another round of gunfire didn't pop through the air, I would search for them instead. But I know I need to get to Holly. I need to protect her.

"Over here," she says, motioning to the entrance of the diner.

I push my legs to move faster, the sound of pounding footsteps catching up to me. Holly grabs me and yanks me into the diner, only to have a man take her place. He surprises the guy that's chasing me and sucker punches him in the throat.

I screech and nearly slip on the tiles, my clothes dirty and my hair a mess, hanging in my face. Holly helps me up, snatching me away from the fight at the door.

"There's an exit leading out back through the kitchen." Holly pulls me along, not giving me a chance to focus on anything except for staying with her. It should be me protecting and caring for her and not the other way around. But my brain can't think right now. All I want to do is find Arsenio and Desmond and make sure they're okay.

"We'll call Wilder from the car. The Silverstein Pack will get us to safety." Holly's words stir fear in my heart, tightening my chest.

I try to slow down, but she is stronger. Her brothers have been training her to fight all her life.

"I don't understand. What pack?" I lick my lips, trying to catch my breath.

"The hot one. The one that I gave my phone number to." Holly guides me through the kitchen to where a glowing exit sign awaits.

A familiar man stands in the doorway, holding it open for us. He motions for us to hurry, waving his hand. I spot his alpha in his car, idling behind in the back alley. I know better than to get in a car with strangers, but what else am I supposed to do? If I stay here in the diner, the men trying to hurt me might find me. If that happens? I don't even want to think of it. Deep down, I know it's a threat from Platinum Shores or the Gutter District. They must've found us somehow. I wish I knew. We've been extra careful.

"Don't worry, princess. We'll get you to safety." The man opens the back door, and Holly climbs in first, pulling me with her. I practically fall into the backseat, my body refusing to keep up with things. More gunfire pops in the air, and all I can do is say Desmond and Arsenio's names. I'm so scared for them. If something happens...

"My brothers can take care of themselves. Don't worry. The rest of the Silverstein Pack is backing them up. They're not alone." Holly pulls me against her and hugs me close, smoothing out my trembles.

The car barrels forward, screeching the tires and burning rubber, sending a cloud in the air. All I can do is hug Holly and beg my heart to stop racing. I say a silent prayer to the universe to protect my chosen.

If something happens to them because of me, I won't be able to live with myself.

I can't respond to Holly. I can't do anything but stare out the window as the alpha of the Silverstein Pack drives past the parking lot, giving me a glimpse of the fight still going on.

It feels as if I leave my heart behind.

My soul tears to pieces.

Chapter 20

Kinsey

Territory War

Sexy Beast: We are on our way. Hang tight. Why don't you go inside? Holly said you were sitting on the porch.

Me: I'm too scared.

Sexy Beast: Please, baby. They checked out.

Me: I'll think about it. Just hurry.

I set Desmond's phone down, really wishing that I'd have my own now. Enzo had called me immediately on the ride to the Silverstein Pack's house. Apparently, their pack leader and alpha reached out to him personally, informing him that we were safe.

I wish I could've heard the reactions. I wonder what kind of damage we might return to. Because this kind of threat means that the war between Gilded Sands and our attackers is real. We can't just ignore it and hide out anymore. I know that it had to be a Platinum Shores Pack. There is no other explanation.

I sit back, resting on my hands, and stare at the quiet front yard, enclosed with high hedges so that no one on the street can even see me. It's one of the only reasons why I've decided to stay out here. I need to be able to keep an eye out. I just can't trust them, even if they checked out. Even if Holly already acts smitten. Because they obviously know who she is. Their leader called her princess, after all. How? I'm dying to know, but my stubbornness doesn't allow me to suck up my nerves to join them in their living room. They do keep the door open though, and I can hear their soft talking along with the hum of the television, being used as background noise.

If only the scent of something sweet didn't waft through the air and draw my attention.

I recognize Holly's baking immediately. She's done a lot of it lately, and her chocolate chip cookies are unlike anything I've ever had. They have become my comfort food. It's not often omegas get to care for each other like this. It usually only happens with maternal bonds.

"I made you something, Kinsey. It won't be much longer. Do you want me to sit outside with you?" Holly holds a plate, standing in front of the screen door. I spot the alpha behind her a couple of feet away, shadowing her as if he's afraid something might happen. He would be extra careful and on edge, knowing that she is the Gilded Sands' princess. One who should be dead.

Now, I worry. I'm sure Wilder does too. What if they do something crazy because of it?

"No, it's fine. I just need the fresh air. My nerves are shot. I can't stop worrying about Desmond and Arsenio. They won't respond to my text messages. Are you sure they're okay?" I address my question to the man hovering behind Holly. I know it's not customary for a bonded omega to speak openly like this to a strange alpha, but I'm so used to speaking for myself these days. I'm still playing a beta as well. Holly won't blow my cover even though hers is.

The man steps forward, standing so close to Holly that he's practically flush against her. He rests his big hands on the doorframe, filling it with his muscular body. A strange expression crosses her face, and she flushes.

"I assure you, Ms. Kinsey. I received word from my pack. They're doing a bit of cleanup and getting medical attention, then they'll be here. Your alpha's phone was damaged in the fight." The man drops his gaze and looks at Holly standing before him.

I can tell he's trying to check her out, maybe even breath in her scent, but the suppressant pills won't allow him the luxury. It's probably messing with his head.

"Thank you, Mr. Silverstein. I don't know what we would've done had you not helped us." I rub my hands together, turning my attention from him and to Holly. Extending my arm, I take the plate of cookies from her, wanting nothing more than to fill my time with something sugary sweet in hopes that it distracts me until my pack arrives.

"You are very welcome. And call me Beckett. Formal names are not necessary." He offers me a smile and takes a step back. "I will be inside if either of you needs anything. Our home is yours."

Holly glows with her excitement, her attraction to the man quite obvious.

"Are you sure you don't want me to hang out with you?" she asks, bouncing on her feet.

I shake my head. "Why don't you go have fun? It might've been a shitty situation that put us here, but you should definitely take advantage before your brothers arrive."

She grins then disappears, the screen door slamming closed behind her. I eat the cookies in silence, listening to the world around me. I can't see the wrought iron gate dividing the property from the street, but I hear it whine open only a couple of minutes later.

Wilder's familiar car pulls into the wrap-around drive, and he doesn't bother parking it next to the Silverstein's SUV.

Enzo jumps out before Wilder gets a chance to turn off the car, and I hop to my feet and meet him halfway. I jump up and attack his face with my mouth, peppering his handsome features with my lips. My heart picks up in speed again, rattling against him, just wanting him to know how much it prefers to be close. If it could escape my chest just to be with him, it might. The intense thrums prove it.

"God, baby. You don't understand how crazy I feel right now. I was so fucking scared. All I wanted to do was be with you. But you can blame the asshole for it taking so long." Enzo cranes his neck, glaring at Wilder as he strolls up behind him, not rushing to get to me.

I realize it's not because he doesn't want to cuddle me, but he's trying to give Enzo enough space to check me out before he intercepts. I'm sure both of them run hot and high with their emotions, and they might've even fought over everything. I'm sure I'll have to get in the middle of them and Desmond and Arsenio later. Even though it wasn't Desmond or Arsenio's fault, Enzo and Wilder will probably try to blame them. And I'll have to remind them that it could've happened to either of them too. The only fault belongs to the assholes who attacked us. I will not let them blame each other.

"Beckett said you weren't hurt, but I know he was taking you on your word alone. Holly thinks you're uncomfortable here and would rather suffer than have someone else look at you, so tell me the truth. Were you lying to him?" Enzo keeps his voice low, resting his head on my shoulder.

I swallow the knot in my throat, my body choosing now to react even more to my fear. I was able to keep it together if I didn't think about it, but now that Enzo is here, hugging me, all I want to do is break down. I want to cry my eyes out and scream at the sky. This should've never happened. I don't understand why the world is so against me.

What have I done to constantly deserve this threat?

"It's okay, baby. Don't speak if you don't want to. I'll just give you a quick look over if that's okay." Enzo eases me away, and another set of hands wrap around my waist, shifting me.

Wilder cradles me in his arms instead of letting me hug him with my whole body. "It looks like her hands are pretty scraped up. Her knees, too. There's a tear in her pants."

Looks like he's already been examining me and assessing everything.

"I'm so proud of you, Kinsey. You put up one hell of a fight." Enzo grabs my hand and inspects my palms. He gently touches one of my broken nails. "You scratched him pretty good. I bet he will feel that for days."

"I punched him in his balls too," I say, my voice shaking with my words. "I'd have done more but..." I close my eyes, suppressing the memory the best I can. My ears still ring from the gunfire.

"That's my brat-girl." Wilder kisses my temple, his affection helping to ease my whirlwind emotions. "Always go for the weak spots." Grasping my chin, he guides my face until I meet him for a kiss. His warm lips caress mine, sensually, gently, just teasing and tasting my mouth without getting carried away.

Someone clears their throat, drawing Enzo and Wilder's attention toward the door to the house. "Your majesties, welcome to the Silverstein Estate. It is an honor to welcome you into our home."

"Where's Holly?" Wilder asks, his voice gruff.

Enzo smacks him on the back. "What we mean is thank you for protecting Kinsey and Holly. It is our honor to be here."

Beckett chuckles and bows in respect, but Enzo offers his hand to shake. "As a man with sisters, I understand your brother's concern. Come on in. She's baking cookies."

I gawk in fascination, still unsure of the customs in the Gilded Sands territory. In the Gutter District, the authority was more...brutal. It changes as often as a damn pair of dirty underwear, depending on who could overpower which pack and why.

"I see she's already taken over your household. We apologize for that. She's been...sheltered." Enzo strolls ahead, leaving me in Wilder's arms.

He doesn't follow the two of them right away, taking a moment to be with me alone. I stare at him in silence, watching his light blue eyes search mine. It's in moments like these that I wish I could hear his thoughts. It doesn't help that his scent has been muted for me by the suppressant pill I took before our outing. I'm sure it's probably something spicy, potent yet delicious. And it's probably even worse coming into this pack's home.

"I know you like to put on a brave face, but you can be honest with me, Kinsey. What you went through today was terrifying. If I was scared, I know you were freaked the fuck out." Wilder tugs me closer, adjusting me until I can finally wrap my legs around his waist and hook my ankles together, ensuring he can't escape my death grip.

"Was it the Platinum Shores Pack?" I ask, doing my best to keep up my steely façade. It's easier to speak when I have closed myself down.

"We're verifying it now. We got a couple of shots from surveillance cameras on the street. If it was them, then we need to figure out how the hell they tracked you down, and why they waited so long to attack." Wilder scrunches his nose, his face darkening with his frown. "Once we do, we're going to hit them hard and fast even if I have to make something up to my father to get the resources we need."

"Oh." It's the only thing I can think to say.

"Hey, don't think the worst yet. It could've been anyone. We have many enemies, including the pack that wanted my sister. Let us handle it." Wilder kisses me once more, carrying me inside.

I look around for the first time, taking in the grand living room of the Silverstein Estate. Enzo stands rigid near the entrance to the kitchen, one hand scrubbing his neck. I realize he talks on the phone, probably with his brothers. I don't try to launch myself from Wilder's embrace, though. It takes everything in me not to, but I need to trust that they are okay. Wilder and Enzo wouldn't be here otherwise. I bet neither would the alpha of the Silverstein Pack, because his packmates stayed behind.

"Wilder! Thank God!" Holly sneaks around Enzo and jogs in our direction. She doesn't give Wilder a chance to set me down before she flings her arms around the two of us, sandwiching me to her brother.

"I'm sorry, little sis. That should've never happened. I'm just glad that your troublemaking ass happened to disobey me and give a stranger your number. Now they thought you were a beta until their alpha laid eyes on you. Knew who you were immediately. He went to school with me, but we haven't been in touch since. You know how it goes." Wilder keeps his voice low. "Thank the fates that he hates Dad."

Holly doesn't respond. We'll both probably have to face a lecture later, which I'll put a stop to right away. Because Holly needs to be able to have real-life experiences. She needs to be able to know how to make decisions that benefit her and will help her in the long run. Right now, she's used to Wilder deciding everything for her, and she grows anxious about it. I can't imagine her not lashing out soon. Especially with all the threats involving me.

The best way her brothers can help her would be by preparing her for real-life situations such as this.

"Or thank the fates that I'm cute," Holly teases, patting Wilder's cheek from over my shoulder.

He growls at her and steps back. "Watch it. I don't want anyone thinking you're anything other than my little sister."

"Too late for that, big bro." Holly chuckles and strolls away, closing the space to where Beckett stands in silence, watching our quiet interaction.

She sticks her tongue out at her brother, turning her back and standing on her tiptoes to whisper something to Beckett. She is pushing Wilder's buttons, and I can't help smiling about it. He deserves it. We all know he deserves it, especially with his overprotective attitude.

Enzo groans and puts his phone away. "No one could get proper ID from the videos. They all got away, though I would still bet money on it that it was Platinum Shores. They're watching us. They have to be."

"There must be another traitor on our staff. You need to pull up all the logs that give our alternative locations." Wilder finally sets me on my feet, freeing his hands to grab his phone to look at something.

Enzo closes the space to me, wrapping me in his arms, kissing me softly like he's been dying to show me affection since they arrived. I give in to his need, just savoring the sensation of his mouth against mine and how safe his arms feel around me, how comforting it is to have the firmness of his palm pressed against my lower back.

"Fuck. It's not a traitor. Our security got hacked." Wilder fists his hand, looking as if he's dying to punch a wall. But he wouldn't dare. This isn't his home, and he obviously respects the Silverstein Pack enough that he's not dragging us away immediately. But of course, it's not like he can change the fact that Holly was recognized. All he could do is hope that Beckett or the rest of his pack doesn't try to use this against us.

A part of me already knows that they won't. I can see it in his eyes and how he looks at Holly. I won't bring up the fact that they obviously have a connection.

"Hacked? No fucking way. I looked at everything myself." Enzo mutters against my mouth, the vibration enough to send a wave of energy to my core.

"Shit happens. We've been busy, Enzo. Don't blame yourself. They were in and out, and the only reason I can even see it now is that they left us a warning." Wilder surprises me by not lashing out at Enzo. He manages to stay composed and calm even though his words send my heart racing. "I'm just glad that the area is secured. They had to wait for us to leave to know our exact location. Even then, they had to have a little luck. I think they knew someone at the diner. They were paid off. Look at the bright side, they were unsuccessful, and they'll regret ever starting this damn war. We have our own ties to their territory. I'm done with being on the defense. We're going to take more direct measures. Kinsey is not a piece of property. They can't just take her. She never belonged to Tamsin to begin with. The only one who can really assign her is the authority of the Gutter District, which is questionable even then since she's not from there. Tamsin might control the underbelly, but we can persuade them otherwise. And I think they all know that."

His words sink in my mind, filling me up with a dozen more questions. Obviously, as part of the Pack Regimes and the authority of Gilded Sands, Wilder would have that sort of connection to other areas. Especially because he plans to take Gilded Sands from the reign of his father.

"You're right. They're testing us to see if we'll back down." Enzo slides his arm around me, not wanting space between us.

"Which we won't. This will just make things easier for us. They want to fight, then we will do more than defend our girl. We'll take their fucking territory as well." Wilder narrows his light eyes with the words. "I'm sure no one else will put up a fight for it."

Enzo grins and offers his brother his closed fist to bump. "Hell yeah—"

The screech of tires draws our attention to the front of the estate, and I spot a car barreling through the gates.

My heart sinks into my stomach at the sight of Desmond stumbling from the car, clutching his bloody side.

Arsenio tries to catch him before he falls to the ground, but he misses him by inches.

Desmond passes out.

Chapter 21

Arsenio

New Allies

Kinsey screams, her voice ringing through the air as she rushes through the screen door of the Silverstein Estate. Wilder catches her, grabbing her by the waist and keeping her back.

Desmond lays flat on the circular drive, his bloody side staining the concrete.

The lying bastard. He wouldn't let me look at the stab wound in the car, claiming that it was just a scratch. I should've known better. Desmond tends to suck things up a lot more, trying to always prove himself to be powerful. It's always bothered him that he never manifested into the alpha order like the rest of us, though he just can't see that Kinsey wouldn't want him any other way. He will have a relationship with her that none of us ever will, his ability to fulfill needs we might not be able to.

I drop to the ground beside him, dragging up his shirt to inspect the wound. Goddamn it. Another lie. It's not even a knife wound. A bullet grazed him, and it looks like it's been bleeding for a while.

"Let me go! He needs me!" Kinsey shouts, flailing her arms.

"Not until you calm down. You could accidentally hurt him worse." Wilder adjusts her in his arms.

"Kinsey, he's right. Just give us a second." I whistle, pointing to Enzo. "We need a medical kit. Enzo, get your ass over here. He was grazed by a bullet. He's in shock."

"Oh, God," Kinsey says, her voice hitching. Burying her face into Wilder's neck, she suppresses a cry.

Desmond is never going to hear the end of this from me for scaring our girl. His pride got the best of him, and he didn't want to seek medical attention before we made sure Kinsey and Holly were safe. He's probably more in shock than anything. He's one lucky bastard. Had it hit just inches to the right, he'd be dead.

I press my hand over the bleeding wound, stanching it the best I can. He probably thought he was fine enough because he had put pressure on it since his adrenaline numbed his body's response.

"I'm going to beat his ass the moment he feels better," Enzo says, striding closer. He grabs Desmond by his chin and tilts his head in his direction. "Do you hear that, asshole? You're going to get one fucking headache when I knock you unconscious a second time."

Desmond reacts to his touch, groaning and stirring awake. He opens and closes his mouth, but no words come out except for a low mumble of agony.

"Give me some space, assholes. I need to get a good look." Enzo sets a bag beside him, forcing me to remove my hand to look at the wound on Desmond's side.

"How does it look? Is he going to be okay?" Kinsey quietly sits beside Wilder, clutching Desmond's hand.

Enzo pats Desmond on the cheek. "It's just a little flesh wound. I'm sure it hurts like a bitch, but it isn't fatal. I'll get him all cleaned up, give him a couple sutures, some antibiotics, and painkillers, and he'll be good to go."

Kinsey releases a breath, leaning forward and covering Desmond with her body, her boobs pressing right into his head as she hugs him. All I can think about is him being a lucky bastard all around. Kinsey's going to smother him with all her affection until he is a hundred percent better. I shouldn't be jealous of an injury, because fuck that shit, but damn. I could use her tits in my face now. Her kisses and snuggles. All I want to do is pick her up, take her inside, and show her how much I care.

"Arsenio, why don't you let me and Wilder handle this? Take Kinsey inside and get cleaned up. We need to head out immediately." Enzo looks at me as if he can read what's on my mind.

I'm not sure I'll be able to peel Kinsey away from Desmond, but he groans again and whispers something to her that I can't hear.

She eases away from him and nods her head, tears shining in her eyes. He obviously doesn't want her to see him weak like this, and I bet he asked her to get him something.

I rub my hand over the middle of her back, getting her to look at me. She swallows and licks her lips, blinking the tears from her eyes without letting them fall. I scoot over and open my arms for her to melt into. She squeezes me so tightly that I grunt, the breath rushing from my lungs. I get my legs to work and lift her in my arms, wobbling only for a second as I steady her. The Silverstein Pack stands nearby, keeping the space but also paying attention in case we need something. Beckett nods his head to me and moves out of the way, telling me where the nearest bathroom is that I can get cleaned up in. Holly rushes me the moment I step through the doorway inside, and I know that one of my brothers told her to remain there. I give her a quick hug and a kiss on her forehead, and she returns to her spot staring out the window, watching as our brothers work on Desmond.

Kinsey doesn't say anything until I close the bathroom door, setting her on her feet. She quickly runs her hands over me, pulling up my shirt and drinking me in as if she might think I'm hiding a wound like Desmond. Her fingers ignite electricity over my skin, and I snatch her hand and cup it in mine, pressing it to my chest. If she continues this mission to touch every inch of me, I won't be able to focus on anything.

"I'm not hurt. Just a couple of bruises you can see on my face. They were surprise attacks. After I realized what was going on, no one got another punch in. You should see what we did to the fucking bastards." Because I broke someone's arm, knocked out another guy's front teeth, and managed to get in a couple of nicks with my blade.

I don't tell Kinsey though. Only if she asks will I admit to what I'm truly capable of in regard to fighting.

"I still need to be sure for myself." Kinsey reaches up and caresses her fingers gently over the purpling bruise on my jaw. "I can't believe this happened. Those fuckers need to pay."

She says it as if she plans to be the one to punish them, and it fills me with a mixture of emotions. Because while I'd love to see her kick ass, the idea scares me. I don't want her anywhere near those fuckers.

"They will. We're already planning a counterattack. We just have to catch Platinum Shores off guard like they did us." I ease away from her and go to the sink, using my hands to cup the water to rinse the dried blood from my face. I have a split lip that bled down my chin and I look far worse than I feel, which is probably why Kinsey is going crazy over me.

"And how do you guys plan to do that? It's dangerous. There must be another way." Kinsey puckers her bottom lip, her fear making her look extra kissable. I just want to love up on her until she smiles again.

"We're going to go after the weakest packs in their territory and offer them the freedom they've been denied. Once we get enough allies, they won't be able to handle our invasion.

Platinum Shores isn't exactly a desirable territory. People live there because they have to, and they have nowhere else to go. When citizens are unhappy, they're more likely to rebel. And we know that a lot of them are willing to do that. I mean, look at who the Platinum Shores Pack works with? Nobody likes the Gutter District." I want to be as honest with her as possible. I know that Wilder would prefer to hide things to keep her from freaking out, but I know that she needs to know that we have a solid plan. She can handle it. He's always been overprotective.

"And what if it doesn't work?" She remains expressionless, watching me dry my face off.

I sigh, spinning to face her. I back her up against the door, stroking my fingers over her cheek and into her hair, caging her in with my body. "Sugar, it's going to work. And if by some crazy-ass curse that it doesn't, then we'll take it by force. We have the manpower. Our father won't be able to stop us from using what we need."

"He's going to hate me." Kinsey lowers her voice with her words. "He'll blame me if he finds out."

I want to tell her not to worry about him and that what he thinks of her doesn't matter, but I can see that it matters to her. My father is part of our pack. In other circumstances, he'd treat Kinsey as his daughter. As family. She might not get that bonding from him.

It hurts me knowing as much.

It pisses me off more than anything.

I clench my jaw and swallow, trying my best not to scowl at the thought of my bastard dad rejecting the woman of my dreams. "My mother would've cut his balls off if he even tried, you know. I wish you could've met her. She'd have loved you so much."

Kinsey's frown morphs into a soft smile. It's the most beautiful thing I have ever created, her response assuring me that I said the right thing. "Do you think so?"

I nod and greet her smile with my own. "Absolutely. She was a lot like Holly, and I know how much she adores you. I'm pretty sure that if we hadn't seen how perfect you were for us, she'd have either clobbered us in our sleep or asked you to run away with her." I lean in, silently begging for a kiss, wanting to feel her mouth against mine. I don't even care if it'll hurt my split lip. I want the pain as long as it means that I get her affection.

She laughs, her voice lifting my spirits, filling me up in a way I yearn to devour over and over again. I can listen to her laugh forever. "That was my plan. Because I really love your sister, too. I love all of you. You're my pack and my family."

"And you're my mate. My everything. And that's why my father's opinion doesn't matter. He's not our leader. He's not even our father at this point. He's a man in our way, and I'm ready to knock him from our path." I've never felt so ready for something in my life. After what King Winston did to Holly, I'll never forgive him. I'll play my part in this game, but once I win—we win—I will never have a second thought about that man.

She slowly nods her head. "You're right. I shouldn't care about him. He's a vile man. Despicable. The way he treats you guys...I will push him myself. But it won't be just out of your way. I'll push him off a fucking cliff."

Damn. Her threat gets to me in a good way. I know she's capable of great things. She's an omega not made from the choices of her pack. She's an omega built from steel and concrete, from the rubble of her tragic circumstances. She carries an invisible armor that her presence alone shares with me.

"God, Kinsey. I love you. I can't wait for this to all be fucking over so you can have everything you could ever want and desire. Everything you deserve. You will never want for anything. You will never experience this sort of fear again. You'll be protected and treated like the queen you are." I kiss her deeply, letting her feel how my body reacts to hers, my muscles rippling and my body flexing from her closeness. If we weren't in the bathroom of the Silverstein's estate with my brothers waiting, I would claim her right here and now. I want her so badly that I can taste it, the memory of her excitement turning me on even more.

"I love you too. That's a life I crave. A life I know we'll get. I'll be everything you need. That I promise you, Arsenio. I want to help you build an amazing future not only for our pack but also for our people." Kinsey murmurs the words against my lips, the softness of her voice so sexy as she returns my declaration of love with her own.

If only I didn't hear my brothers' voices in the living room. I'd stay in here for the rest of the night if I could, pretending as if the world outside no longer exists, because right now, Kinsey is my world. I want her to be my entire universe.

I don't get a chance to beg her to give me just a moment more of her affection because she nudges me back, lacing her fingers through mine, and pulls me toward the door. Her desire to see Desmond lies in the fact that she is afraid for him. I will not deny her being able to see him for herself just to satiate my needs. I'll hold him down if I have to, so she can kiss every inch of him as her way of making him feel better. Fuck. I don't think I've ever been jealous of him in my life, and to be envious of him getting shot? I'm fucking ridiculous.

"Sugar, wait a second." I slow her down, placing my hand on the door to stop her from flinging it open. "Desmond will lie his ass off about his injuries. Just be a bit careful with him, okay? He's going to want you to smother him with your body, but he needs a bit of time to heal."

"Just tell me what I can do to help him. I want to be his nurse. He needs me." Kinsey doesn't intend to be sexy, but her words strike me right in the nuts. Now I can imagine her in a skimpy nurse costume, tending to my brother.

If he doesn't have those thoughts, I'm going to smack him. Because that's one hell of a way to be nursed back to health.

Maybe I'll help him out and order the tiny number myself. He'll owe me forever.

And maybe Kinsey could wear it for me some other time.

"I'll make sure you have everything you need, sugar. But for now, it'll probably hurt like hell to carry you around. He's going to want to, but you need to remind him that he'll have to wait." I finally release my hand from the door and let her slowly open it.

"I'll make sure he realizes that the wait will be worth it." She smiles at me and tugs me from the bathroom, her mood already so much lighter.

I wish she could keep her smile forever, but the moment her eyes find Desmond leaning heavily on Wilder, looking like he's about to pass out again, her face puckers with concern.

Desmond smiles, forcing his mouth to fight against what he's truly feeling. I don't know if it's because Wilder whispered something to him or what, but he manages to straighten his back some and open his arms for Kinsey. "Thank God you're okay and safe, Kinsey."

"Thank God I'm okay? Thank fucking God you're okay, Desmond. You scared the crap out of me. Come here. I need a kiss. I need to make sure you're truly safe now." Kinsey releases my hand and jogs the rest of the way to Desmond. She doesn't slide her arms around him even though he opens his and instead cups his cheeks and turns his head back and forth, inspecting the bruises on his face. And then she kisses each one of them, nestling her nose to his and sighing against his lips.

A hand touches my shoulder, drawing my attention away from the two of them. Wilder motions for me to join him and Beckett, one of his former schoolmates. Enzo joins the three of us, and Holly stays a couple of feet back, turning her attention toward Beckett's betas.

"You have our full support," Beckett says, offering his hand for me to shake. "We have two spare bedrooms if you would like to stay or have Holly and Kinsey stay here for a while."

The problem with that is we don't have the same security measures. We would have to trust them on faith alone, and sometimes it's not always a good thing. Even though Wilder knows Beckett, people do change over the years.

"That is very kind of you, but we would hate to get you involved in our personal matters. However, we appreciate you standing beside us with the conflicts between our territory and Platinum Shores. We will assess the situation and our options and get back to you if we do end up needing to take you up on your offer." Wilder's words thankfully align with my silent opinion. And he's right about bringing them into our personal conflicts. It could end up worse for their pack.

"I understand, friend. Just let us know what you need. We're here." Beckett reaches into his pocket and pulls out a set of keys. "Take my SUV. No one will recognize it."

"Wait, we're leaving?" Holly might've kept her distance, but I should've known she'd eavesdrop on the conversation. "I don't want to go. What if those guys find us?"

Wilder clenches his jaw. "Holly—"

"Perhaps one of us could escort you as backup until we confirm everything is clear?" Beckett remains expressionless but damn it. I think he has a thing for my sister. I don't think. I know. My first instinct is to swing out and punch him, demanding he keeps his eyes to himself.

But then I see Holly's hazel gaze light up at the idea.

Kinsey raises an eyebrow from beside Desmond, her look screaming that we better not deny Holly the assurance she obviously gets from a pack outside of us.

Damn. Why can't I accept that she's an adult, and something like this could and would eventually happen?

Enzo whacks Beckett on his back. "I think that's a fantastic idea...I mean, if you don't mind. I'm sure you know the area better than we do. It'll give us a chance to pinpoint the Platinum Shores bastards' location."

Saved by the charming asshole.

Wilder flares his nostrils, his frown clear in the fact that he was dead-set on denying Beckett's suggestion, especially because this pulls him deeper into our personal matters.

Holly grins, glancing at Kinsey. "That would make me feel so much better. You all need to focus on Kinsey anyway."

Her comment gets Wilder to lighten up, smoothing his features out.

It looks like the omegas of the Gilded Sands Pack will forever team up to keep us in line. We're in for some fucking trouble.

But whatever keeps Kinsey smiling and Holly laughing.

We'll ensure they get the world and more. Their happiness and safety are what are most important. And it will always be.

Chapter 22

Desmond

Counterattack

“We have a visual on the entire Platinum Shores Pack. They’re crossing into their territory now. It looks like they’re leaving to reconvene. This will give us a moment to breathe and plan our counterattack.” Wilder stands in the doorway of my room, his gaze holding mine. “I want you to stay here with Kinsey. She’s going to take care of you. Enzo and Beckett will be downstairs with Holly. Arsenio and I have to check in with King Winston. We won’t take long.”

I leisurely nod my head and shift on my bed. My side feels a lot better with the pain management Arsenio put in place for me since yesterday’s attack. I was a bit annoyed that my brothers were keeping Kinsey away, using my injury as an excuse because they didn't think I would rest with her in my presence, but I can't really blame them. They were absolutely right.

It's not my fault that Kinsey eases my pain with a simple smile. She makes it easy to forget everything outside of my pounding heart and the wave of desire that emanates from her every time I give her an extra-long look. Every second she's within a foot of me or my brothers. Every moment of her just being here. It makes her irresistible, and I can't deny her body's silent plea for attention. Because as a beta, I can smell the pheromones of both alphas and omegas more intensely, and and she is fucking mouthwatering.

"Keep me in the loop. Are you sure we're good here with Silverstein?" I ask, sitting up and scooting to the edge of the bed, grinding my teeth as to not show the splitting ache radiating from my side.

"Yeah, you're good. Enzo's playing cock-block until we get shit sorted out. I don't know if you caught on, but Holly is fucking smitten. It's annoying the shit out of me. Kinsey smacks me every time I even look at them wrong. She threatened my balls if I even considered getting in the middle." Wilder grumbles with his words, his throaty voice laced with his frustration. He's not used to being pushed around by anyone other than our father, but especially not a woman like Kinsey.

I wish I could've seen it.

I can't stop chuckling now.

"She makes a point, brother. We didn't go through all this shit just to keep her in a bubble for the rest of her life. We agreed that she would get a choice in the matter." I force myself to my feet, grabbing onto the dresser to steady my legs.

"You're all ganging up on me now. What happened to making sure our power was set first? That Holly turned twenty-five, at least. Maybe thirty. She's our little sister and needs the best." Wilder curls and then uncurls his fingers.

"Don't be a misogynistic dick. If that were the case, then Enzo would still have a year before he should've even considered bonding with Kinsey." I grin even wider as he narrows his eyes.

"Fuck off. I just want to make sure Holly is safe. That's what Mom would've wanted." Wilder moves out of my way, stepping into the hallway.

I take advantage of his caution over my injury and smack him upside the head. "We are ensuring she's safe. The bigger our pack is and the more allies we have, the better. Now go get that shit handled with Dad so we don't have to think about him for a while."

Wilder salutes me with one finger and scrubs his fingers through my brown hair instead of retaliating with a punch to the gut like he usually would. "All right, little brother. Don't do anything stupid while I'm gone. Definitely don't let Enzo get a moment alone with Kinsey. We won't see either of them for the rest of the night, and I want to have a family meeting when I return."

"Now that I can agree on. Kinsey is mine today. I might be fucking sore, but I heard she wanted to play nurse. Gotta give our girl what she wants." I laugh and follow behind Wilder, heading toward the first floor where voices hum through the air.

"Desmond, what are you doing up? You're supposed to be resting." Kinsey's sweet voice cuts over the gruffness of my other brothers talking to Beckett. "What do you need? I'll get it for you and take it upstairs."

Wilder growls under his breath. "Damn it."

I can't stop smirking, ignoring his words as he strides past me and motions for Arsenio to follow him to the underground garage. Kinsey rushes to me, blocking my way, so I don't try to join the others. She places her hands on her hips, her scrunched nose as cute as hell. She looks ready to spank me for even being out of bed, and just the thought sends me craving her closeness. "Are you hungry? Thirsty? How is your pain? Come on, you need to go back upstairs. Arsenio says you need a couple of days of rest."

Enzo pats his knee. "Baby, give the man a second to respond. If he's feeling good enough to come downstairs—"

I glower at him, realizing he might be a bit jealous that Kinsey showers me with attention, wanting nothing more than to take care of me. Wilder was right. He's going to try to seduce her when he gets the chance. And now a part of me is jealous of him too.

So fuck that.

I groan and fake pout, wobbling a bit dramatically just to piss off my brother. "Actually, I only came down because of Wilder. Will you help me back upstairs, Kinsey? I could use some help in my room. I can't bend down properly to pick up a couple of things I dropped."

Kinsey smiles at me, keeping her back to Enzo. He scowls, realizing that I can play his games.

"Yes, of course. Let me make you a quick bite to eat, and I can help you with whatever you need." Kinsey stands on her tiptoes and presses her lips to mine.

"I'm so lucky to have you," I say, smiling against her mouth.

"Who knew nearly getting shot in the gut would be something that would make me jealous." Enzo rolls his eyes at me, getting a smack on the arm from Holly.

"Don't play like that." Holly flicks him for good measure. "I'm sure Desmond would have gladly traded places with you to not deal with the pain."

"Seriously. It hurts so bad." I fake a groan again, fucking with Enzo even more.

But then Kinsey's grimace makes me feel bad, because her concern glasses her eyes over.

"I'll be fast." She jogs away, heading into the kitchen.

I don't even get a chance to say something to Enzo before she returns, holding a plate with pasta and veggies, one of Enzo's signature dishes.

"Come on. Let's get you upstairs." Kinsey rests her hand on my upper back, stroking between my shoulders.

Her closeness does ease the ache in my side, the gesture of comfort soothing me on a deep-seated level. I never expected to have someone care about me in such a way that I can feel it in my soul. I wasn't lying about being the luckiest man alive.

I turn and look over my shoulder, grinning like a cocky bastard at Enzo. Holly giggles and smacks him, whispering something I can't hear. Beckett stares in silence, his curiosity clear on his expression with his furrowed brows.

The second we reach the top floor with my room, stolen from Wilder so I don't have to share with Arsenio, I snatch the plate from Kinsey, set it on the dresser, and I spin her toward the closed door to pin her to it. I kiss her with enough passion to make her moan. She gets caught in my wave of lust, her thoughts of tending to me vanishing as I rile her up.

I hook my fingers to the hem of her shirt, tugging it over her head, my need growing more intense by the second. She's the ultimate painkiller for my aches, and I can't get enough of her. I crave more. Feel starved. Deprived even.

"God, Kinsey. I can't get enough of you. Just your closeness eases my pain. The agony comes from your absence." I break from her lips, kissing down her throat. "This is all I need from you. Your body against mine. Your sweet lips. Your—"

Kinsey tugs at my shirt, caught up with her need. The fabric rubs against my bandage, surprising me with a shockwave of pain. I flinch, bowing forward, knocking my head on the door. Shit.

I suck in a couple of deep breaths and wrap my arms around her, hoping that she ignores my dumbass reaction.

Her body stiffens against mine, and I could curse the universe for this fucking injury. There's no way she's going to ignore it now to give me the affection I crave.

"I'm so sorry, Desmond. Let me look at it." Kinsey doesn't give me a chance to deny her, lifting my shirt more carefully to look at the bandage on my side. "I hope I didn't rip out any sutures. Can I make sure it's okay?"

The way she speaks to me, softening her voice and gently caressing her fingers over the tape holding the gauze in place only makes me want to give in to her request. If she will stop worrying after examining me, then I'll be a good patient and allow her the honors.

I nod my head and kiss her temple. "You didn't hurt me. I'm just sore."

She puckers out her bottom lip, but she doesn't look any less beautiful. If anything, her expression picks up my heartbeat, because of how much she cares for me. "I'll be gentle. Do you want me to help change the bandages? You also mentioned needing some things picked up."

I smirk at her, looking around the clean and tidy room. "I might've fibbed about that. I just needed to have a moment alone with you. I've missed you. My brothers have been keeping you busy because they thought that I wouldn't rest otherwise. All I want is this. You."

Her grimace blooms into a beautiful smile, and she releases a melodious laugh, her features lighting up. "You know, Desmond. All you had to do was ask for me. You didn't have to make up an excuse. I love spending time with you. I've missed you too."

Hearing her admission stirs something wild inside me, and I lean in and kiss her again, wishing I could just pick up where we had left off.

She eases away, pressing her back to the door to put an inch of space between us. Playfully patting my chest with her hand, she nudges me to back up. "I want so badly to take care of you. Will you let me? I promise I'll be quick and then we can do whatever you want. Watch TV. Maybe eat in bed. Make a blanket fort. Let me give you a...sponge bath." She bites her lip, looking so incredibly sexy that I am willing to give in to all of her demands.

"Yes." I push her dark hair behind her ear and cover her hand with mine, leading her away from the door and toward the bed.

"Yes?" She stands in front of me, practically herding me with her body until I sit on the edge of the bed. "Yes to what?"

"All of it. But I also have a couple of other ideas." I reach out and hook my fingers to the waistband of her pants, pulling her between my legs. I encircle her waist with my arms, leaning in close to kiss her hip where her order mark identifies her as an omega. "Like...how about you let me eat you in bed? And maybe in the shower. On the desk over there."

Her cheeks blush, her skin warming, and I kiss the skin below her navel. Her fingers comb through my hair. She doesn't resist, just letting me explore her smooth torso.

Goosebumps prickle over her body and I unfasten her pants, wanting nothing more than to strip her completely naked to do as I please. To do whatever she wants.

Because I thought I was a dead man when we were attacked. I thought we had lost Kinsey, and I had failed. It makes me appreciate her more than ever. I don't want a day to go by without her knowing how much she means to me.

"Desmond," she whispers, her voice lined with her desire. "Let me take care of you first."

I hum in disagreement, just wanting to continue, enjoying the sound of her voice as she moans at the slow pace of my fingers caressing the outside of her pants, already feeling the heat between her legs.

She reaches down and grabs my hand in hers while using her other to touch my chin and tilt my head back to look up at her. Her tongue glides over her bottom lip as she shakes her head at me, slowly, sensually swaying her hips as she lowers herself to her knees. I realize it's not her wanting to mess with my bandages. She wants to take care of me in a way that makes my cock throb in anticipation.

Goddamn. How could I deny her?

Her fingers caress my knees as she massages her way up to my thighs until she reaches the waistband of my athletic pants. She holds my eye contact, slowly tugging the elastic away from my body until she frees my cock, and it stands attention, harder than it's ever been in my life. Desire and eagerness course through me. Kinsey gets me to ease my hips up so she can pull my pants all the way down, exposing me to her. Desire weighs her eyelids down, her face so beautiful in this moment with her thick eyelashes casting shadows beneath her emerald eyes. The way she looks at me as if she wants no one else in the world turns me on even more. My muscles flex, and I reach out and comb my fingers through her chocolate hair, playing with the strands. She kisses my thigh, working her way slowly to my cock, her mouth feather-light though it leaves behind tingles in her wake. She laces her fingers around the base, squeezing slightly and stroking me up and down, watching my face as I react to her touch. I moan and twist my fingers in her hair tighter, my body begging me to pull her closer. But I resist. I would gladly suffer this torture to let her have control. I know that's what she craves from me.

"You're killing me, Kinsey. But I'd gladly die right now, knowing that you have chosen me. I wasn't lying about being lucky. I had prepared myself for a loveless life, working beside my brothers." Because I can't give her everything she needs. But I can try my best. It makes me work harder. Strive for more.

"I'm the lucky one too. I honestly expected the same. I never knew that life could be this satisfying. Fulfilling. I had forgotten what it was like to be loved. And the way you love me? It's so perfect. It's just as perfect as the bond I'm growing with your brothers. We will have our own special bond that will be incomparable to anything else." Kinsey strokes her thumb over my balls, igniting pleasure through me. Never breaking eye contact, she eases a bit lower and glides her tongue from the base of my cock all the way to the tip before she flicks her tongue over it. She smiles at me, humming under her breath.

I move my hand from her hair to her shoulder, massaging my fingers into her muscles, unable to keep my hands to myself. I wish I could just touch her and explore her body. I wish I could bring her pleasure now too.

But she doesn't let me. She wants to be the one who takes care of me first.

Twirling her tongue, she teases me before pursing her lips and slowly drawing my cock into her hot mouth, the sensation striking me with a wave of pure ecstasy. I moan and lean back, propping myself up with one hand, watching as she works me over and bobs her head, taking me in as far as she can.

"That feels incredible. You're so sexy. I can't wait to feel how excited you are. You don't know how much you test my restraint right now, Kinsey." I groan and close my eyes, enjoying every second of the pleasure coursing through me.

"You taste amazing. I want you to keep your eyes closed for me, okay?" Kinsey takes me into her mouth again, licking and sucking me a couple of times.

I follow her instructions, keeping my eyes closed, and she uses her hand to push me back on the bed. Fuck me. She's going to climb on top of me to fuck my brains out. I can't wait. And the fact that she demands I keep my eyes shut? It's driving me absolutely wild.

Coolness caresses my cock, shocking my skin, her absence sending an ache through me, but it doesn't last long. Her knees weigh down the edge of the bed at my sides, and she carefully plants her hands to my chest as she straddles me. I moan, a rumble escaping my mouth. Kinsey glides her pussy over my shaft without letting me enter, just grinding against me to show me exactly how wet she is. And damn. I already feel like I'm on the brink of coming. I want so badly to touch her that I blindly reach out, feeling my way over her thigh until I reach the apex of her legs. She guides my hand until I touch her clit, and she gasps with her pleasure, taking control to rub my fingers over her body the way she likes.

"I need to see. Please, Kinsey. Let me see." My voice comes out deep and husky, my desire rolling through me as she remains in control.

"Just a peek," she says, the lightness of her voice igniting even more desire in me. "I just want you to be in the moment completely."

I flutter my eyes open and stare at the absolutely stunning woman straddling me, her pussy soaking wet with her slick, dripping over my balls as she slowly grinds her body up and down my cock while continuing to use my fingers to caress her clit. Her lips part as she pants, and she carefully leans forward, making sure not to touch my side as she brushes her lips to mine, kissing me softly, seductively, just showing me how much she cares for me. I can feel her love as if it's a warm blanket lying on me, weighing me down in the best way possible.

"You are intoxicating. Irresistible. You have no idea how much this means to me. I love you, Kinsey. I just wish I could give you everything you need." I lick my lips with my words, my mind wandering to the fact that I can never be an alpha. I can never have that sort of bond.

She slides her body to the tip of my cock, aligning herself to me. Slowly sitting, she uses her weight for me to push inside her, her soft gasp like music to my ears. "You do give me everything I need, Desmond. More than anything I could ever want, too."

I sit up, cupping her cheeks with my hands, kissing her deeply as she lowers herself completely, her tight body clutching mine as she bounces slowly, just letting me savor every second as she enjoys every inch of me. The ache in my side stings but it's worth it, barely noticeable with the endless pleasure of her tight pussy.

We moan together, our lips turning desperate as our mouths go to war for control. I glide my tongue across hers, moving my hand from her shoulder and around to unhook her bra, needing to feel her bare skin some more. I rub her hard nipples and break away from her mouth, licking down her throat to nip her neck and leave a hickey. She picks up speed, bouncing and gasping, the sensation dragging wave after wave of pleasure, her pussy hot, drenching me with her slick, and pulling me to the edge.

I trace my hand lower, using my other one to dig my fingers into her ass to guide her harder and faster, using my feet to bounce her even more. She screams as her body tightens around mine with her orgasm, the wave of her lust hitting me with the most intoxicating fragrance sets me off.

I grunt as I come inside her, my whole body buzzing and humming, my balls tightening and aching with desire and ecstasy. She crashes her mouth to mine again, slowing her body but not stopping completely as she rides the wave of bliss of her own orgasm.

"I need more. I can't get enough of you," I say, lifting her up with me to set her on the bed.

She pants and bobs her head, letting me turn her onto her stomach. I give her a small spank, her ass so fucking amazing that I can't help myself from touching her, using the slick of her body to tease her ass, and she moans as I slide my finger in.

She squirms and clutches the blanket, her body ready and anticipating me again. I stroke my cock a couple of times as I harden, fully ready to claim her again.

"I want you so badly. You're torturing me now." Kinsey moans with the words, clenching my finger as her body puckers, throbbing for me.

"We can't have that now, can we? I'll give you everything you want, Kinsey." I line my body with hers, sliding my cock into her wet pussy once more, rocking my hips as I continue to play with her ass at the same time, her slipperiness so incredible that I can't get enough. She moans so loudly that I'm sure everyone in the house can hear, and I can't stop the smile from crossing my face. She buries her face in the blankets, wiggling her hips and trying to get me to pick up speed, but I don't give in right away. I take my time, savoring the scents of our lovemaking, how fucking incredible her body feels with mine, and just how perfect our bond is. Because she was right. Our bond will be unlike any other. I can give her the control she needs and the protection she wants. I will give her the world.

I thrust deeper, rocking my body, hitting her just right that she groans and tenses, squeezing her legs to make it even tighter and more pleasurable for my cock. I hold onto her hip and keep a rhythm that leaves her gasping, and she screams again only after a couple of minutes, her body soaking mine as she squirts, her orgasm smelling of sugar and vanilla. And damn, does it make me want to taste her.

"Don't stop," Kinsey says, clutching the blankets, her voice rasping with her pleasure. "I'm going to come again."

I smile and continue with my pace, not changing anything as her screams come faster and louder, her muscles spasming and tightening so hard around my cock that if I didn't know any better, I'd think she was knotting me in place.

The sensation arouses another orgasm, and this time I slide out of her and watch as I squirt across her back, the gesture something I will think about forever.

I grab the blanket and clean her off, slowly turning her over to meet her panting, relaxed face, her green eyes sparkling with her desire. She opens her arms, begging me to cuddle with her, and I lay on top of her, my body full of adrenaline, dissipating the ache of the wound on my side completely.

"I could do this all night," I murmur, kissing her lips. "You make me feel so fucking good. Just your scent, your taste, the heat of your body...I feel better than ever."

She smiles, her satisfaction permeating the air. "I'm up for it. I can't get enough of you, Desmond. This is so perfect."

"It can only get better. Let me draw you a bath. I want to massage every inch of you. You will not fall from this high on my watch." I lift her from the bed, carefully carrying her to the bathroom.

I'm probably going to hurt later, but I don't even care. Seeing her smiling and getting this time alone with her is worth it.

I turn on the tub and fill it with bubble bath, watching Kinsey's beautiful emerald eyes light up as I set her in. I join her, but just sit on the edge, keeping my bandage dry. Kinsey grabs a washcloth and kneels in front of me, cleaning me off first, taking her time to carefully bathe me in a way that makes me feel as if I'm her entire world and there is no one else in this universe besides me.

Getting to her feet, she stands in the water, her body covered in soap, and she slowly turns around and lets me stroke her skin with the washcloth, moaning as I take extra care to rub it across her nipples and between her legs. I use the shower extension to rinse off her body, her skin glistening and prickling with goosebumps. We don't stay in the water long, and I dry her off, taking a moment to comb her hair and kiss her all over again, starting from her mouth and working my way down until I stop at her clit, wanting nothing more than to make her orgasm again.

She moans and doesn't stop me, clutching onto the sink as I finish her once more, just wanting her taste to linger with me for a while longer.

I lift her, taking her back to the bed, yearning to ravish her all over again despite just cleaning off. We only make it halfway across the room before something shatters downstairs.

I frown and listen, hearing Enzo yell out.

Oh fuck.

"Shit, we need to get dressed." Kinsey beats me to the dresser, pulling out a shirt and a pair of boxers. She dresses first before grabbing something for me and helping me pull the shirt over my head. I grab a weapon from the nightstand and head to the door. I crack it open and listen to a fight below. Holly screams. My chest tightens. It's not a scream of pain but one of fear. We're under attack. I know it. Motioning to Kinsey, I get her to join my side. I quietly motion to her to run toward the stairs leading up to the deck on the roof. I need to help my brother and sister, but I need to get Kinsey somewhere safe first.

"We're going to head to the roof. There's an escape hatch that leads down. I want you to run and hide, okay?" I whisper, pushing her to get her cute ass moving.

She doesn't respond with her voice, her body turning automatic with her movements. We hit the roof in a matter of seconds, and I jog around the outside, not seeing a vehicle. Where the fuck did they come from? Who are they? My brother said that they had a visual of the Platinum Shores Pack.

I don't have time to think about it. They could come up here next.

"When we hit the ground, I want you to run left, cut through the yards, and when you reach the end of the block, turn right. You'll find a trail that'll wrap around the community. There's a ditch where you can hide. I need to help Holly and Enzo." I take the ladder first, climbing down before Kinsey to make sure it's safe.

Her eyes widen as she peeks over her shoulder at me. "Desmond, watch out!"

Someone yanks me by my shirt and pulls me from the ladder. I hit the grass with a thud, my side exploding in pain.

A man in a mask stands over me, aiming his weapon. "Don't move. I don't want to shoot you. I'm here for the omega."

He takes off the safety, his hand steady. He's not joking.

"Desmond, listen to him." Kinsey cries with her words, and I flick my attention, spotting a man climbing down the stairs from above her, aiming a second gun. "I don't want you to die."

Scowling, I ignore her pleas. I'm not going to let them take her while I sit here and submit to them because of a damn gun. I'd rather fight.

The man leans forward, closing the space more, growling at me not to move.

I jerk my arm out, trying to grab the gun.

Pain explodes in my skull.

The world turns black.

Chapter 23
Kinsey

Lost

"**S**top! Stop!" I scream, trying to run forward as the man clonks the gun against Desmond's head, knocking him out.

"Shut up, bitch. Be thankful we can't kill him." Two arms encircle me, dragging me back until I hit the hard chest of a beta that smells like body odor and garlic, his breath assaulting me, making my eyes water.

I jerk my head back, hitting the man in the chin. Stomping my bare foot, I try to use my weight to get away from him. He shoves his hands into my back, knocking me forward. His boot connects with my side, winding me. I fall to the grass, struggling to get up. Clawing the ground, I scramble forward, refusing to give up. They just admitted that they couldn't kill Desmond. With that knowledge, I'll keep fighting. I won't let them take me.

"Grab her!" another man yells, his voice shooting fear through my heart.

A hand locks around my ankle, dragging me back. My shirt rolls up and gravel scrapes across my torso. I can't fight from this position. I can't find anything to hold onto either.

"No!" I screech, kicking my free leg but only hitting air.

"Tape her mouth. We're going to draw more attention." My captor drops my leg, releasing me in the circular drive. A car engine hums as a van barrels through the gate, crunching it under the force.

Rolling over, I kick my leg up, smashing my foot between the legs of another beta. The man yowls in pain, cupping his junk. A shadow falls over me, blocking the sun overhead. I smell the alpha before I get a good look into his dark brown eyes, the only feature showing from his full-faced mask.

I open my mouth to scream, but he slaps his hand across my mouth, silencing me with tape. The shock of his smack sends panic through me, clobbering my will to fight. All I can think about is how this is over. My life is ruined.

The alpha grabs my chin, forcing me to look at him. "Come on, sweetheart. Don't get all teary-eyed. You're going to be just fine as long as you stop fighting and be an obedient omega. We're taking you and the other pretty thing somewhere special. Somewhere you'll be coveted and appreciated."

Other pretty thing?

My mind refuses to process what's happening as the man picks me up and hands me to another man in the back of the van. I spot Holly curled on her side with her mouth taped shut and her arms tied together. Tears streak across her cheeks, her body trembling. Rage clenches my very soul, and I thrash, swinging my hand to smack the beta. I do it over and over again, screaming and fighting as hard as I can. Holly whips her attention to me, my fight returning her hope, and she kicks her leg out, striking the beta in the knee.

I brace for him to attack me. I prepare for the oncoming pain.

"Leave them. Hustle," the alpha snaps.

The beta tosses me toward Holly, and I crash into her, bonking my head on her shoulder. The van door slams shut, leaving us in the windowless cargo area.

I push up, rushing to get to my feet. I reach for Holly, but the world jolts, and I lose my balance.

The van screeches as it peels away with us inside.

This might be it.

We're trapped.

Only we can save ourselves now.

"Where do you think they are taking us?" Holly whispers, burying herself into my side. Our captors were too much in a hurry to bind my hands, so I was able to remove the tape covering our mouths and free Holly.

We tried the back doors and the side door, but neither would budge. A metal wall separates us from the driver, and the only way we're going to get out of here is when they open the door.

We have nothing to use as weapons. I don't know how to even prepare for what happens next. I don't think these men are part of the Platinum Shores Pack.

I rub my hand up and down her arm, the gesture comforting the both of us. "I wish I knew. Try not to worry. We're together and we can fight. Your brothers won't stand by and do nothing. They will come after us."

Holly sniffles and rubs her cheek on my shoulder. "It happened so fast. They came out of nowhere. One of the men popped out of the fucking closet. They were waiting for us. I don't even know when they could've gotten in." Holly closes her eyes, inhaling slow breaths. "Do you think it was my dad? Do you think he knows I'm alive?"

I didn't think about that, and now that she mentions it, I can only imagine how pissed he would be and what he would do. I already know the man is a monster.

"I don't know. We were set up by someone. Could be your dad. Could've been the Platinum Shores Pack. I'm sure we'll find out soon. I think the van is slowing." I shift and sit up, pulling Holly to her feet. "We're going to make a run for it, okay? We're not going to just submit to them. They won't kill us. They need us for something."

Holly swallows hard, gripping my arm tighter. "I will distract them. You're the one who needs to get away. My brothers bonded with you. You're everything to them."

I shake my head, clutching the sidewall as the van comes to a complete stop. "So are you. We're family. Neither of us is more important, and we need to fight together. I will not leave you. Now, we need to attack all the soft spots. That's what your brothers said. Go for the groin. Go for their cheeks and eyes, their stomachs, their throats. Do whatever you can."

It's easier said than done. These men are twice our size, and they have weapons. They could use them on us.

"They're going to regret this." Holly's voice strengthens with her comment, her fear turning into anger.

I really hope so because I'm scared. What if they enslave us or something? What if they traffic us to another territory to some awful pack? It's a brutal possibility, and a life I refuse to live. My guys have shown me what I deserve in mates and alphas, and I won't settle for anything less. I won't give in or give up to another.

A car door slams, startling me, and I step protectively in front of Holly, wanting to do whatever I can to help her. I listen to the muffled voices outside, realizing that a woman speaks to our captures. Is it Madame Tamsin? Maybe she managed to get our location from the Platinum Shores Pack and is out for revenge for what happened to her brother. Maybe that's why they took Holly.

I don't get a lot of time to think about it, because the back door clicks as it unlocks. I fist my hands, preparing to charge. I know I'm only going to have seconds.

Holly shuffles her feet behind me, turning toward the side door. Someone clicks the lock on that one too. Fuck me. They must expect that we're going to fight. I don't know which one to focus on.

"Settle down, dears. You're not in any danger. Fighting is pointless, because you're in my compound and there is no way out. So be good girls, and I will be good to you." The feminine voice sounds through the door as someone taps against it. "My name is Madame Samara. I'm your new handler."

Our new handler? She's another alpha like Madame Tamsin.

"What do we do?" Holly whispers, keeping her voice low as she steps closer to me, pressing her chest into the back of my shoulder.

I don't want to admit that I have no fucking clue, but if she's anything like Madame Tamsin, then it's in our best interest to submit and go along with her commands at least for a little bit until we can strategize a plan.

"I'm going to open the door now," Madame Samara says, easing the back door open an inch, letting in bright sunlight that cuts across my face, blinding me for a second.

"Don't fight her," I whisper, swiveling to Holly. "We need to plan better. I doubt she's lying about being in a compound, and if that's the case, there really is no good way out."

The door widens and the cargo space illuminates with sunshine, dimming my vision. I blink my eyes a couple of times as a silhouette comes into view, and Holly slides her fingers through mine and squeezes my hand. I hold her tightly. If we're not going to fight, then I'm going to do everything I can to stay by her side. They will not separate us. That will be a huge mistake, and something I'm willing to risk getting hurt over.

"We won't fight as long as you don't try to separate us. We're family." I pull Holly closer until I can wrap my arm around her, and she secures her arm around me, ensuring that if they disagree that it's not easy for them to pull us apart.

"Now, now, dears. I keep all of my beautiful omegas together unless a client becomes infatuated. And even then, I think you two would be perfect as a pair with your striking contrasts. There are many packs that would love the company of more than one omega. Since you have bonded as sisters, I think that would be all right. As long as you behave." The beautiful alpha stands outside of the van with her hands on her hips. She offers me a smile, showing off her perfectly straight, white teeth, her tall frame and curves fitting for a runway.

"Where are we? Who are these clients you speak of? I have bonded with a pack. I have the mark to prove it." I lift up my shirt and ease down the boxers, showing off the heart-shaped mark on my hip, now pigmented in a tawny color from the hormones Enzo's knot set off in me.

Madam Samara leans in close and presses her fingertip into the mark. "That's not a problem. It will return to normal soon enough. Until then, you will be a server."

"And me?" Holly asks, her voice shaking with her words. We both know that her omega mark will show she's unbonded because she hasn't been claimed.

"We will be servers together," I answer for Madame Samara, refusing to let her even consider separating us. "That was the deal. We don't fight, and you keep us together."

Charging me, Madam Samara shoves her hand to both mine and Holly's chests, pushing us against the van and glowering in our faces. I don't flinch. I will not give her the satisfaction of trying to test me. I knew this was coming, but I'm not going to make things easy.

"Do not speak over me, dear. I'm the alpha here. The Knotty Girls Club is mine. You will respect me as your handler. I'll only treat you the way you deserve, so mind your mouth." She smacks my cheek, purposefully leaving her scent on my skin, the potent musk and white floral fragrance stinging my nose, my body wanting to reject her scenting me because she is not my alpha, nor is she part of my family.

I bite my tongue and lower my gaze to the ground, not replying instead of arguing. Holly trembles beside me, her fear potent in the air, the crisp sent like a salty breeze.

"That's a good girl, dear. You will both be serving our clients. You will also clean up the stage between performances. I'll give you one week to get settled, and then you will earn your keep. I take good care of my omegas, and in return, you have a place to live, anything your heart desires in terms of clothes, jewelry, makeup, and anything else you could need to impress the alphas of Saint Vista. You will get your needs taken care of during your heats, but you won't have to have the commitment. Our alphas don't want that responsibility. Many of them have already bonded with others, and now just seek a bit of...fun." Madame Samara steps back and crosses her arms. "You will discover that you like it here. The alphas are good. And you get what you want and need. Do you understand? We're a family. I ensure my girls have the lives they deserve."

She's out of her goddamn mind. This is a sex club. We have been sold into a sex club. Now, who did it is the question. Because I know that the Platinum Shores Pack had bought me from Madam Tamsin to be a personal entertainer for their pack. This is different. This is similar to the Vixen Lounge. This is one of Madame Tamsin's competitors in the business.

"You can't do this to us. We are not packless." I whisper the words, knowing that they might set off Madam Samara, but I want to make it clear. "The men kidnapped us and brought us here had to be mistaken. You need to turn us in to the authorities of your territory's Pack Regime."

We have a better chance if she does.

"I'm aware of your situation, Ms. Kinsey. My allies were offered a job to return you to your alpha in Platinum Shores, and they took advantage of the situation. That's what Madame Tamsin gets for crossing territory lines. You belong to me now." She turns to Holly. "We had no idea about you, so you're going to be quite special. I can't wait to get to know you, dear. Starting with your name."

Holly thins her lips. "Bianca." It's her mother's name.

I blink a few times, the realization hitting me. Holly was taken because it was convenient.

"You can only blame the Silversteins for not putting a formal claim on you. How they managed to get someone so...exquisite is beyond me." Madame Samara steps closer to Holly again, patting her cheek, leaving her scent behind.

I pray that Holly doesn't argue about the Silversteins, because this might be exactly what we need. We'd have an advantage if she doesn't know. She called Platinum Shores my pack, which changes things. I bet her supposed allies didn't even let her know that they had kidnapped me from the princes of Gilded Sands.

"Now, dears. Follow me. We need to get you to your room and get you situated. Are you hungry? Also, you both will need to shower. Your stench is already getting to me. I can only imagine what it will be like once we are in an enclosed space." Madame Samara holds out her hands to us, not giving us a chance to argue. I don't bother trying to tell her about my true pack, because I don't think it will even matter. She will probably say the same thing she did to Holly. A physical claiming isn't enough.

I gingerly take Madame Samara's hand first, flicking my gaze to Holly until she follows my lead. I hate that I should be strong and take down this alpha before we even step in the building, but my soul screams. I know that the odds are against me, and it's in my very nature to submit when I'm being threatened.

"I only have a couple of rules. I expect you to shower twice a day. Once before you enter the club and once after. You are not allowed to speak to any alpha unless you're spoken to first. You must always clean up after yourself and wipe everything you touch down immediately. When your heats get closer, you will be given a series of different medications to take. It will help prevent pregnancy, possessive alphas from trying to kidnap you, and will also help with other unpleasant symptoms. You'll be given half of a suppressant pill at night, but that's only so you don't bother me. You will have access to your own collection of sex toys to help yourselves out, and it is your job to care for them properly. I will pick your clothes. Some days, you will be required to wear makeup, and other days, I will need your faces fresh. You will be taking photographs for my album and will also receive a mark from me. It's a small tattoo and barely noticeable, but it will ensure your safety from here on out. Because you're my girls now." Madame Samara guides us to a nondescript metal door at the back of a three-story building that looks like it used to be an old library or a bank headquarters or some shit like that. It's much larger than the Vixen Lounge, and there are at least five apartment buildings surrounding the club that I can see.

I can't tell for sure, but I can't see her doing anything otherwise, considering that we aren't exactly in a city. This is a compound. She probably has all her staff in the central location.

"You'll start with my newer omegas, but if you impress me, you girls will eventually get your own apartment. My best ones get to live in luxury. If you have regular clients, you'll get gifts and many other benefits. Sometimes travel. Sometimes a night out on the town. You'll see. The Knotty Girls Club treats their omegas well. There are many who would love to be in your situation." Madame Samara doesn't get a chance to open the door before a man in a suit opens it for her and holds it, greeting her with a bow.

The beta keeps his eyes to the ground and doesn't look at either of us. I glance at Holly again, but she keeps her gaze focused upward, staring at the room before us. It's a kind of lobby with dozens of comfortable-looking couches, tables, a small kitchen, and huge wall mirrors with vanities beneath them. Several racks of clothes line the wall and shoes line the floor below, the high heels looking to go up to at least six inches in height.

Music fills the air, coming in through a hallway. I can't see anything though. A heavy curtain blocks the way.

"This is the main living area. Up the stairs, you'll find all of the new omegas' rooms. Yours is room number three." Madame Samara motions toward a set of stairs next to the hallway, which probably leads into the club. "I'll bring you your outfits in a couple of minutes. Mr. Ron will prepare your meal. Once you're showered and dressed, you can come down and eat here. After that, I will introduce you to the rest of the girls. Do you have any questions?"

Fuck yeah, I have questions. Will I ask them? No. I already know the answer. There's no way she'll give us access to her phone. She'll probably keep watch on us until we don't try to escape. This is going to be fucking torture, but I need to come up with a plan with Holly. I just need another moment alone.

Madam Samara nods her head. "Good. You are excused. Just take the stairs up. Your room will be the third one on the right. Welcome home, dears. I want you to know that you are so wanted. I'm thrilled to have you in my pack. You'll be a marvelous addition to my Knotty Girls."

Madame Samara kisses each of us on our foreheads, clutching our cheeks for a moment. I try to settle my racing heart with a couple of deep breaths, but it only makes things worse as I inhale her dominating scent.

I reach out and take Holly's hand, squeezing her fingers. We watch in silence as the alpha disappears through the curtain, leaving us alone in the living area.

"What do we do?" Holly asks, keeping her voice low.

I look at her, my eyes shining with tears. "For now, we need to be docile. We have to be one of her good Knotty Girls."

Chapter 24

Kinsey

The Knotty Girls Club

It takes everything in me to get out of bed, my eyes burning from the endless tears that wouldn't stop last night. I can't believe an entire day has passed, and while my brain knows it's not that long, my heart feels like it has been an eternity.

Yesterday was uneventful for the most part once we had showered and returned to the living area. Madame Samara walked us through her expectations of being a new entertainer. Luckily, it wasn't as horrible as I had expected. But I know why she does it.

She wants us to want to be here. She will bomb us with love and affection, making us feel like this is somewhere good. She manipulates everything and everyone under her roof. I've seen it happen before. She uses her influence as an alpha to make it seem as if life away from her wouldn't be worth living. She will try to brainwash us into believing that no pack is worthy of our presence unless they pay.

She is like Madame Tamsin, but she hides her hostile attitude well. It doesn't take much to provoke Madame Tamsin. I don't know what Madame Samara's breaking point is, though. I don't want to find out.

She just wants us to be pretty accessories on the clients she favors. We can dance and serve food and drinks, making the wealthy of Saint Vista feel wanted and loved by many to make up for the lack of it in their real lives.

As for her expectations of my body? I know that sort of thing will come soon enough. Once I am broken and brainwashed and unlikely to fight. It's why she mentioned the medication for my heat cycles, which is when I'll yearn to mate. But I won't find out. I'll ensure that it never comes to that for Holly or me. We will get out of here. I have faith in my guys. I have faith in us.

Pushing my thoughts away, I listen to Holly get out of the shower. She didn't sleep at all either. She didn't cry like me, but instead, she held me close and stroked my hair, being strong for me after I was strong for her.

She exits the shower and saunters directly to me, plopping on the bed to pull me into her arms. I laugh as she snuggles her face to my neck and proceeds to kiss my cheek, her comfort helping ease the hard ache clenching my chest.

"It's going to be fine today. My brothers will come for us. I bet they've already gathered the armies and have located us. We just have to be patient." Holly smiles at me and leans away, giving me a little shake. "And when they come, they'll give you so much love that you have to beg for mercy."

Her hope helps fill me up with my own. I need to chant her positive affirmations into the universe and believe this will soon be over. Because the fuckers that took us and sold us to Madame Samara have no idea what they've done. My guys are willing to overthrow their own damn father. They kill without a thought to protect those they love.

That knowledge helps me get out of bed, take a shower, and get dressed.

Holly waits for me to finish, and we head downstairs to the living area, where a dozen voices hum through the air. I've never been around so many omegas at once in my life. Not even at the Vixen Lounge. Madame Tamsin kept them separated from us.

"You're late, dears," Madame Samara calls, her voice ringing from where she sits on a recliner with...whoa. Male omegas? They're not as desirable, but they're rare, and she has two of them, one sitting on each of the chair's arms. "I'll let it slide this once, considering you need a moment to adjust. Tomorrow, I expect you showered and down here by eight sharp. Now hurry and grab your outfits from the rack. Do you remember where your sections are?"

"Yes, Madame Samara," I say, keeping close to Holly. The bitch never told us what time she wanted us to be here. I was never expected to work before the lunch crowd, but I guess I was impersonating a beta.

Holly clears her throat. "I'm sorry. You didn't—"

"We'll be on time tomorrow." I cut Holly off, stopping her from calling Madame Samara out.

"I know, dears." Madame Samara pets the backs of the two omega men. "Now hurry. Missy will help you with your make-up until you learn my expectations to do it yourself."

A woman with dark curly hair wiggles her fingers, sitting in front of the brightly lit vanity station. I recall her from yesterday, but neither of us spoke to each other. I didn't see her come upstairs with the newer omegas. I can only assume she has one of the swanky apartments Madame Samara told us about—the ones she uses to reward those who comply.

Heading toward the clothing racks first, I pick up the small, glittering one-piece, fishnets, and matching stilettos. Holly's isn't much different, and she presses her lips together, hiding her expression. It could be worse, but it could be a hell of a lot better. This is basically lingerie, and there are only four guys I want to see me in something so sexy.

I head to the small partition, blocking the changing area, and I strip out of my pants and T-shirt, taking a moment to gather my confidence to change. I carry the shoes out and watch Holly go behind the partition next. Missy clicks her tongue, motioning for me to sit on the swiveling chair beside her.

Madame Samara watches us in silence for a second before she instructs her men to help her to her feet. The three of them leave the room, heading through the curtain into the central part of the club.

It's only then that I release a deep breath.

"You're nervous, aren't you?" Missy speaks to me for the first time, keeping her voice low as if she doesn't want to get caught but also doesn't want to just sit in silence. "It's actually a lot of fun here. Everyone is friendly and the clients make you feel as if you're the most beautiful woman in the world. It helps you forget that you've been rejected or unclaimed by a pack. My mama didn't know what to do with me when our arrangement fell through." Missy puts an elixir onto a cotton pad and swipes it across my face, surprising the hell out of me.

I startle and squeeze my eyes shut. The cooling sensation of the toner cleansing my skin leaves a tingling trail.

"Kinsey has a pack. She was kidnapped and sold to Madame Samara," Holly says, sliding into the seat beside me.

I jerk away from Missy to look at Holly. "You can't tell everyone that. It'll cause us more trouble."

"Don't worry, Kinsey. Your secret's safe. I'm sure Bianca is just looking out for you. We all know each other's business around here. It sucks that you were put in this position, but your pack was obviously undeserving if they couldn't keep you safe. You're better off." Missy grasps my chin, turning my head back to her.

It takes Holly putting her hands on my shoulders to stop me from lashing out. I know I need to keep my cool, but I hate how she brushes off our kidnapping as if it's our pack's fault and not our kidnappers. That's so fucked up. She is definitely brainwashed.

"Like I said before, you will be taken care of here. Madame Samara ensures that our clients respect us. It's not some scary sex club or anything like that. We're not forced into doing anything we don't want. I have my favorites, too. You should see all the gifts I get. I can't imagine any other life." Missy strokes the makeup brush through a cream foundation and blends it across my face, ensuring my skin looks flawless and even.

I tune her out as she goes on, counting on Holly to drink in everything. I'm sure she'll have questions later, but I'm not even sure I'll have answers. All I want is for the day to be over, so I can return to my room with her for another night of crying.

What am I even thinking?

I need to spend the day figuring out how to contact the guys. If I can find a phone, I can call them. I've memorized Enzo's number. How will I be able to? I will have to put on one hell of a performance, and the thought alone makes me sick to my stomach.

"There. Now be careful what you eat. I don't want you smudging your ruby lipstick." Missy swivels her seat and motions for Holly to take the one on the other side of her.

The two of them don't say much to each other, and Holly just gazes around the room, looking at the other girls as they prepare to head into the club. I skip eating, my stomach too much in knots. I know that we'll have lunch later. The alphas have free range to feed anyone they want. We have to accept drinks too. I just hope I can fake it enough to get close but not too close to some asshole to steal a phone. Or maybe I can sneak behind the bar. Risk looking for Madame Samara's office.

All my ideas seem impossible. Most alphas who come to a club like this don't just leave their phones lying around. They don't make it easy to get caught. I'm sure many of them are supposed outstanding citizens and some even part of the different Pack Regimes across the country. I guess I'll have to be creative.

"You're all done, Bianca," Missy says, calling Holly by the name she gave Madame Samara.

I keep repeating it in my head to ensure that I don't accidentally call her by her real name. I wish I had the luxury of making up one of my own.

Missy turns back to the vanity mirror and touches up her lipstick once more before getting to her feet. Sliding into her stiletto heels, she sashays toward the hallway, disappearing behind the curtain. Only a few of us remain in the living area, and I fidget with the glittering beads decorating the leotard. Holly helps me buckle the sparkly stilettos, and I stand up and give myself a once-over in the full-length mirror.

Holly takes a couple of steps, obviously comfortable in heels, and I touch her hand, getting her to turn back to me.

"I had an idea that I wanted to run by you. There will probably be quite a few alphas wanting our attention, especially because we're only servers and aren't allowed to be their private entertainers yet. I thought that maybe we can steal a phone, but I'm going to need you to make a distraction. Or if you want me to do it, I can." I keep my voice low, hoping Holly can hear the words. No one looks in our direction, not even the beta security guard, and it's the only thing that gives me a bit of hope. I'm sure they think that if we do anything, it would be trying to escape. We'd be more successful to get our pack here. Especially if Madame Samara doesn't know that it was a Gilded Sands prince who claimed me.

"I can distract. It'll be easier for me to flirt, considering I'm unbonded. I know what it will do to you." Holly slides her arms around me and hugs me for a second. "I'm not afraid. You taught me that I can do anything. My order doesn't define me."

I smile to myself, her words helping lift my spirits. I only found out that I could do anything because I had to. I wish it wasn't the same for her, but I'm thankful that I have her in my life.

"Good. Because you're amazing, Holly. Now let's get this shit over with. Let's get home." Home. Saying the word out loud gives me the strength I need to stroll through the curtain and face the club.

I avert my gaze to the floor, ignoring the omegas dancing on stage, performing erotic stunts on poles for entertainment. There aren't many alphas in here yet, but it looks as if Madame Samara serves brunch. A bartender makes bloody marys and mimosas. One of her omegas saunters from the kitchen, holding a tray with different breakfast foods, taking them to her.

She sits next to two unfamiliar alphas, just peering around the club. There is a pack in a velvet booth on the other side of the room, and a single alpha sitting at the bar. There are definitely far more omegas than alphas in the moment, and it's probably why they've arrived early.

These must be the regulars and have first dibs on who they want to entertain them. And unfortunately, because there are so few alphas around, my plan to steal a phone might have to wait. Because everybody here already has a companion. I'm meant to serve only.

I remain by Holly's side, strolling across the club in our skimpy outfits. Our gazes train to the ground, and we manage to make it to the bar without attention from anyone.

"New girls, you work for me until told otherwise. I want you to get your cute asses on the floor and offer everyone a drink. This is the early morning special. It's included in the entrance fee." The bartender motions to a stack of trays behind the bar. "If they'd prefer something else, let me know. These are our regulars and our best-paying clients. Make sure you get nice and close, so they tip." I knew it.

I nod my head. "Yes, sir."

The bartender sets a tray down and fills it with champagne glasses. "Don't call me sir. My name's Quinten."

It's only now that I realize he's not a beta, but he doesn't act like the usual alphas. He must owe something to Madame Samara. I can't see why he'd be a bartender for an omega club otherwise.

I bob my head again, grabbing the tray of mimosas. Holly watches how I carry it, and mimics me, balancing it on her palm. She's probably never served anyone in her life, but thankfully she manages to make do even in her tall heels.

"Head to the elite booth first. They'll want to finish up soon to have a little performance from Missy and Becca." Quinten motions to the velvet booth with a pack. "The leader likes to be called Daddy, but you're free to call the others anything you find suitable. Don't call them asshole, though. I know you'll want to."

I remain expressionless toward his comment. I wonder how much he knows, because he's treating us nicer than I expect from an alpha who works for Madame Samara. She did mention that they treat their omegas well here, but I don't trust that. Good people don't buy kidnapped omegas. They don't love bomb them and try to brainwash them.

"Thanks for the tip," Holly says. She speaks with a sugary tone, her smile matching her bright face.

"Anytime, Bianca. We want you to be happy here." The bartender flicks his bar towel at us. "Now shake your cute asses all the way there. Let's get some money. Get me a good tip and I'll buy you each something you want."

What? I don't really get a chance to think about his comment, because the alpha at the booth whistles and waves his hand in our direction.

I straighten my shoulders and hold my head up, but I keep my gaze trained on the floor, my fake eyelashes veiling my vision. It's better this way. I don't have to look at the guy directly, stopping my heart from pounding in overdrive.

As if Holly has been preparing for this role her entire life, she sways her hips as she saunters forward. She blocks my way when she greets the pack, leaning slightly forward to show off her cleavage as she sets her tray on the table.

"Hey, Daddy," she says, addressing the leader of the pack. "I have the perfect drink for you. Would you like a bloody Mary? A mimosa? Perhaps something...sweeter like me?" She giggles with her question.

I'm stunned by her boldness. The sweet girl just took on one hell of a role, and I don't think I've ever been this impressed by how an omega handles an alpha.

"What pretty Knotty Girls. You two are new here, aren't you?" The alpha, Daddy, stands up from the booth to give us each a long once-over. "Madame Samara has outdone herself. How could a pack ever deny omegas so exquisite?"

"Only idiots." This comes from another man at the table. He's another alpha, but clearly not the leader.

"Isn't that right, handsome?" Holly giggles again, the lightness of her voice making her seem even younger.

"Wouldn't I love to just rub it into someone's face right about now?" Daddy smirks with his words, holding his hand out to me. "Come here, Knotty Girl. You're shy, aren't you? You don't need to be nervous. I'll take care of you. You'll never need the bond of a pack with me around. And if those fuckers ever realize what they gave up, they'll be jealous. If only

I could see their faces. Do you know who denied your family the honor?"

I slowly step closer to him, setting my tray next to Holly's. His comment gives me an idea, and I say a silent prayer to the universe that he doesn't smack me or some shit for even suggesting this.

"I do, Daddy. It would be something else to see such a sight. I have the bastard's phone number memorized if you want to mess with him." Goosebumps prickle over my skin, my whole body tensing for this to go either extremely terrible or perfect.

Daddy tips his head back and roars a laugh. "Oh, you naughty thing. If that's not the funniest request I've ever had. But I don't know."

"Look who's the idiot now," the other alpha mutters, resting his hands on the table. "You're all talk, Brett. This pretty omega looks like she'd fucking blow you for the small act, and you just tease her."

Growling, Daddy swings his fist and clocks the man in the shoulder. He reaches into his suit jacket and pulls out a phone, holding it out to me. I see he's the type who accepts all challenges.

"You know Madame Samara won't let her get on her knees for me yet, but maybe you can sweet talk her into it sometime, you naughty thing." The man waves his phone at me. When I go to take it, he laces his fingers around my wrist and pulls me closer, spinning me until I sit on his lap, feeling the hardness of his desire beneath me.

I try not to react and force myself to laugh, sounding a lot more maniacal compared to Holly.

She slides into the booth next to us and giggles, bumping her shoulder to the man. "Now, you're making me jealous, Daddy. Me and my sister come as a pair. We've done everything together all our lives."

She is way too good at manipulating these alphas. I can learn from her, now that I see her in the real world and out of the protective shadow of her brothers.

Daddy stretches his arm over my shoulder only to reach for Holly, stroking his knuckles against her cheek. "Well, hell. I guess there's going to be a lot of things to look forward to. I'm going to have to talk to Madame Samara about your contracts."

Holly beams a smile. "Now, now, Daddy. We just got here. We have to see what kind of alpha you really are."

A dark look crosses his features, and he splits his lips in a wicked smile. "You bad girl, teasing me like that. Come on, naughty thing. Let's show your sister what kind of things I'm willing to do for my omegas. Call the men who rejected you. I want to have a word with them."

My hand shakes as I dial Enzo's number, praying he answers. I don't know what to do otherwise. It's not like I can leave him a message. I just hope he manages to stay in control long enough for me to tell him where we are and who we are with. But I can't be obvious about it. If I'm obvious about it, Madame Samara will figure me out. The alpha might too.

The phone rings, and the man snatches it away for me and puts it on speakerphone. I was hoping that he would do a video call, but he might be full of shit about willing to do whatever. It's easier to be just a voice on the line.

"Who the fuck is this?" Enzo growls with the words.

Daddy howls a deep laugh, smacking his hand on the table. "That's a lot of attitude for a man who rejected such a beautiful omega. I'm just calling on her behalf to tell you that you're a fucking idiot. You're the scum of the earth, and I'm going to enjoy the hell out of..." He looks at me, waiting for me to say my name.

"Kinsey," I say, a little louder than necessary. I just need Enzo to hear me.

He doesn't respond right away, and Daddy leans in closer to me, his fragrance growing more potent, like musk and sandalwood.

"This Knotty Girl, Kinsey, is gonna make me one happy man. Maybe I'll give you a little hint of all the things I plan to do to her. I can already smell her desire for me." He's full of shit, because the last thing I feel is horny. All I feel is freaked the fuck out that Enzo's not going to figure out where we are unless I say something.

I clear my throat. "You're right, Daddy. Omegas at the Knotty Girl Club know exactly how we want to be treated."

Again, Enzo doesn't respond.

Daddy groans deep in his throat. "Looks like the bastard can't even find his voice to speak. Give me a kiss, sweet girl. I'll—"

"Don't you fucking touch her! I'll kill you! Kinsey belongs to the Gilded Sands Pack. If you even touch her, I'll take your fucking hands." Enzo roars the words, his anger like a lash against my very being.

Daddy stiffens beneath me, a deep growl reverberating through his throat. He shoves his hand to my back, knocking me off him. I hit my knees on the ground, my body blooming with pain. Holly jumps to her feet and grabs my hands, pulling me up. Daddy knocks the table forward with a holler, chucking his phone against one of the mirrored walls, shattering it.

I brace for him to come after me.

I brace for him to lift me off my feet and strangle me to death. I never expected such a reaction, but whatever Enzo said triggers him into being a monster.

"Brett, get out of my club. We don't tolerate violence here." Madame Samara materializes in front of me and Holly.

He points his finger at her. "But—"

"I said get out!" Madame Samara pulls a gun from a holster, pointing it at the alpha. "You're banned for a month. Now, leave. All of you."

Everyone in the club gets to their feet and exits the building without arguing.

Madame Samara looks at me, her head tilted. "Did I just hear that you're bonded with the Gilded Sands Pack? I was told it was Platinum Shores."

I tighten my jaw and nod my head. "Yes. Those bastards kidnapped me from Gilded Sands for Platinum Shores not from them."

A smirk crosses her face, her eyes shining with a glint of something wicked. "Interesting. Go up to your room. Both of you."

I open my mouth to argue, but she steps forward and points toward the door.

She nudges my shoulder. "I said go."

Chapter 25

Kinsey

Visitor

"Kinsey, there's someone here to see you." Madame Samara stands in the doorway of the club. "Bianca, I want you to head back to the club. You're not of the Gilded Sands Pack's concern. The Silversteins have nothing that they can offer me, so you will continue to be one of my Knotty Girls."

Holly opens and closes her mouth, preparing to argue. I reach out and rest my hand on her knee. There's no way her brothers would ever leave her behind. She needs to just wait to see what happens.

"I told you," I say, getting to my feet. "The pack that brought me here played you."

Madame Samara scowls at me, stepping into the room and making me freeze in place from fear. "Mind your mouth. So you know, the Gilded Sands Pack had no idea that they were bonded to you. It makes this rather interesting. Now, come along. Let's not keep our guest waiting." Madame Samara grabs my hand and drags me forward. She looks over her shoulder at Holly. "Get back to work."

What the actual fuck? Who's here to see me? What does she mean that the Gilded Sands Pack didn't know about my bonding with them?

Holly purses her lips and exits the room, peeking at me from over her shoulder. Madame Samara stands beside me in the hallway, staring at the side of my face. But I don't look at her. I can't stop thinking about what the hell is going on.

"Kinsey, did you hear me?" Madame Samara touches my chin, forcing me to look at her. I meet her brown eyes and blink a couple times, trying to get myself together. "I wanted to apologize for not asking more specific questions and just assuming anything about your pack. Had I known you were bonded with the Gilded Sands Pack, I would've reached out to the king sooner. He will reward me far more than any client here could."

My muscles tense at her comment. King Winston? She contacted, King Winston? Oh fuck. This isn't good. He thought I was a beta, and now he'll realize that I was only posing as one. What if he gets angry, thinking that I was purposefully messing with his sons and kingdom? He could have my head or some shit. I don't even know what to do. I wish I had a moment to talk to my guys. Even Holly. I don't know how to fix any of this.

"He's here?" I ask instead of accepting her apology. Because it's not really one. She is using this to her advantage. She doesn't feel bad about anything except the fact that she could've had more sooner than now. She could've arranged things differently. Now she might have a new enemy in the Platinum Shores Pack, because she thought she was getting me from them.

"Of course, he is. I alerted him immediately of the error of my ally. He was rather concerned and came immediately. And now I must ask you to tell him that I treated you with the utmost care. This kind of alliance can make a huge difference for my club. If you're a good girl, I'll make sure that your...friend...is well taken care of." Things are clicking together for her. She told people we were sisters, but it's obvious we're not. But now that she mentions Holly, panic tightens my chest. If the king is here—

An alarm blares, cutting off my thoughts. I jerk away from Madame Samara and cover my ears protectively. The noise deafens me, and I spin around, expecting someone to attack. Madame Samara abandons me, rushing toward the stairs. She doesn't say anything as she descends, disappearing.

I hesitate for only a second before getting my shit together and running after her. But I don't plan to chase her. I need to find Holly. Whatever is going on might be our chance to leave.

We have to get out of here, especially if her father is nearby. I can't risk him finding out that she's alive. I promised my guys that I would care for her, and even if we're not together right now, I won't let them down. Holly is as important to them as she is to me. We are family. We are a pack.

I kick off my heels, lifting one up and clutching it to use as a weapon. I don't know why the alarms go off but usually it means that there is some sort of fight. Alphas like Madame Samara have many enemies. This shit probably involves me, but I don't want to find out.

I reach the living area and press my back to the wall, trying to stay hidden in the stairwell as the girls flood in from the main club. I spot Holly next to Missy, and I look around for security. Only the beta remains here, Madame Samara nowhere in sight.

It gives me the bravado to show myself. He's only one man, and he's not even an alpha. I have a fighting chance if he confronts me, especially if Holly's by my side.

I wave my hand. "Holly! Holly, we have to go!"

Holly's eyes widen as she turns to me, realizing that I said her real name out loud. It's too late for me to play it off otherwise, so I rush to close the distance to her. The beta hollers my name, telling me to go back to my room. I ignore him and meet Holly, the other girls just standing around, looking confused and scared by everything.

"Your dad is here. We have to leave. I don't know what's going on, but this is our only chance." I lock my fingers through Holly's and tug her.

I spot the beta moving in my peripheral vision, and I swing my arm out with my stiletto, smacking him across the head. He growls and stumbles, damn lucky that I missed hitting him with the point of the heel. It's enough to get him to slow down, though, and that's all we need. The backdoor is now unguarded.

"Run!" I scream, dragging Holly with me until she picks up her pace. She kicks off her heels, and together we shove open the backdoor, the world engulfing us in bright light, the sunshine blurring my vision.

I run, swinging my arm in front of me until I can see properly, my eyes adjusting to the light. I cling onto Holly's hand, ensuring she stays next to me. I spot a couple of guys running from other buildings, and I ignore them, not letting them slow me down. I'm not afraid of them shooting me or anything. But they will chase me. I can already sense it.

"If they catch us, fight like hell. Do whatever you can. Hit them in all the soft spots, remember." My voice cracks as I say the words, my heart pounding in my ears. I'm more scared than I've ever been in my life, yet the fear isn't even for myself. It's for Holly. I didn't expect I'd ever feel like this for another omega, but Holly is my family now. I won't let her brothers down. We're both a priority to them, but I know how to handle myself outside a palace. I know how to deal with the shit of this life. I'm terrified to even think about what will happen to Holly if her father finds her. What will happen to Wilder, Desmond, Arsenio, and Enzo if he finds out. Everything will be ruined. Everything they've worked for will be destroyed. All because they fell in love with me.

I don't want to be the cause of their destruction. How could I ever live with myself?

It's the thought that gives me the strength to push forward, staring down the first man who gets in our way. I don't slow. I don't falter. I run as fast as I can with Holly, and we stretch our arms out, putting space between us. We use the sheer force of our fear and our bodies to knock the guy onto his back. Holly kicks him in the balls, and I grab her, forcing her to run. This isn't about getting these guys to stop. This is about getting out. She could seriously hurt someone if she wants to, but we don't have time.

"All exits will be blocked. I think we need to find somewhere we can climb the fucking wall." I lick my lips, my mouth dry from my heavy breathing and exhaustion.

"Look." Holly points down one of the small drives, leading to a parking lot on the perimeter right next to the wall. A couple of cars sit parked against it, and one of them just might be high enough for us to climb over with each other's help.

Hope rises in me.

"Hurry!" We can do this. I know we can do this. I pull Holly, and we run, our bare feet slapping against the ground.

"Stop them!" a man yells from somewhere behind us.

"They won't get far." Another man's voice booms through the air. "They're surrounded."

I can't stop myself from looking over my shoulder. It's then that I realize they're not talking about us. They don't even see us. The second my eyes lock onto the back of Wilder's head as he aims a gun at another man, I can't stop from screaming out his name. Relief floods through me. They're here. I can't believe they're here.

Wilder spins, aiming his gun at the two men. Opening and closing my mouth, I watch as they train their weapons on him. They come to a standoff, neither of them shooting.

"Come on, Kinsey. We have to go. They'll find us." Holly drags me, not letting me risk my life to run in Wilder's direction, despite him being so close. And she's right. What am I going to do? Stand in the middle of a gunfight and hope for the best? No. I need to trust that Wilder knows what he's doing.

I need to take care of me and Holly first. It's what he'd want.

Ignoring the ache in my chest, I run beside Holly in the direction of the compound wall. If we can just get out, we can find somewhere to hide. Many betas would help us find our packs, and for once, I'm glad to not be impersonating a beta.

We reach the small lot of parked cars, and I climb onto the trunk and help Holly up. From here, we get a better view of the world around us. Wilder remains frozen, aiming his gun. I shield my eyes from the sun, peering around. I know his brothers won't be far.

But where are they?

Shit.

A loud pop rings through the air, startling me. I whip my attention back to Wilder, expecting to see either him or the guys surrounding him shot. I release a breath, my heart threatening to spill free. It didn't come from any of them.

"Fuck, let me help you up first." I climb onto the sedan's roof with Holly, managing to see just over the block wall.

I startle at the sound of another gunshot, and pieces of concrete sprinkle through the air. What the actual fuck? Someone just shot at me. Holly grabs me and pulls me down as another pop deafens me. I don't understand. Why are they shooting at me?

"We need to go somewhere else. Maybe we can hide until your brothers find us." Adrenaline courses through me, keeping me from losing my shit. My body numbs, the sensation of jumping from the roof of the car not even fazing my bare feet. I help Holly from the roof, and we take shelter as another bullet hits the ground and ricochets beside us.

A man sticks his head up from the other side of the wall, standing on something, peering into the compound. I don't recognize him. I don't know what the hell is going on, but now I'm more terrified than ever.

A whistle sounds through the air, and the man turns his attention away from us. Blood and brain matter explode from a wound on his head, and he falls back and disappears.

"Kinsey, Holly. Shit. Are you hurt?" Desmond's voice shatters the steel wall protecting me. He rushes from between two apartments, keeping his gun aimed at the ground. "We need to take cover. This is an utter shit show."

"Who was that guy?" My voice squeaks with my words, my body trembling as my adrenaline wears thin. It's as if my body knows that as long as Desmond's close, I'm safe.

How true that is? I don't know. I'm as safe as I can be.

"A security personnel for the Platinum Shores Pack. We had a run-in with them. We thought it was them who took you." Desmond places his arm over my shoulders and then his other one over Holly's, getting us to jog with him toward where he came from, the two buildings acting as a protective barrier.

"They hired somebody, but they double-crossed them and sold us to Madame Samara." My voice shakes with the words. "We were to be entertainers for the Knotty Girls Club. She had no idea that you had bonded with me. She—"

"Desmond, get down!" Enzo shouts, his voice striking me in the chest.

Desmond drags me and Holly to the ground, shielding us with his body against one of the walls. Another round of bullets blasts through the air, the sudden battle freaking me the fuck out. I bet Madam Samara regrets ever making this deal. I bet she regrets ever buying us in the first place.

If only I didn't feel as if we won't ever make it out of here alive.

"I'll cover you. Get them inside." Enzo jumps from the second-story balcony of the apartment building landing in a crouch a few feet away.

I don't get time to process anything before Desmond yanks me up, pulling me and Holly along the wall and back toward the main building.

"I want you to go inside and take shelter. Madame Samara won't kill you. We need to call a truce with her and take care of the Platinum Shores Pack. This will all blow over fairly quickly. We just need you to stay safe. We will not leave here without you." Desmond hauls open the door to the main building and the living area, where dozens of scents smack me in the face.

I open my mouth to argue with him, but there really is no point. He's right about us staying here. I'm no match against gunfire. I don't know how to even use a weapon. He would also be far too distracted if I stayed beside him. His focus would be solely on me.

"We're on the second floor. Room three. We'll lock ourselves in." I quickly kiss Desmond, wishing he could hold me for a moment longer. He nudges me to Holly and offers me his knife. I take it without question and pull Holly with me toward the stairs.

We don't make it far. A beta materializes on the landing and charges us. We don't have anywhere to run, so I grab Holly, and we dash toward the curtain leading to the main section of the club. There has to be another way out. I don't want this guy putting his hands on either of us.

"Stay the fuck back! I don't want to hurt you," I say, pointing the blade as he tries to charge us.

A couple of the girls cry from the club area, and Holly sucks in a deep breath as warm air engulfs us, the heat of the colorful lights, dozens of people crowding in, and all their fragrances permeating around us.

"Holly?" A familiar voice draws our attention from behind us. "Oh, dear God. My baby girl Holly. I don't understand. You're...dead."

My body cools as I listen to King Winston speak his mind out loud. It's enough to give the beta a chance to grab onto both me and Holly. He digs his nails into my shoulder, and I wince in pain. Holly whimpers, her fear getting the best of her.

A deep grumble reverberates through the air. "Get your disgusting hands off my daughter." King Winston pulls a weapon from his belt and aims the gun at the beta. "Do it now."

His protectiveness shocks me, and I shrug out of the man's hold, taking advantage of his sudden fear of the king.

"Your majesty, please forgive my brother for his audacity. He had no idea..." Madame Samara lets her voice fade off for a second. "*I* had no idea that the princess was here. I called you because of Kinsey. The princess told me her name was Bianca. She was with a different pack when she was picked up."

King Winston flares his nostrils, his eyes roving over me, his expression sharpening for a split second. I expect him to react, his anger exploding to take out everyone in the room, but he manages to compose himself. The rage in his eyes dissipates, and his hazel irises sheen over.

He holsters his gun and opens his arms. "My God. I don't believe it. Come here, daughter. You have some explaining to do, but none of it matters right now. I am in shock. I can't believe you're alive. I thought I lost you forever. You have no idea how happy I am."

Holly stands frozen as the king closes the space and engulfs her in a hug, lifting her and spinning her around. He cups her cheeks with his hands and kisses her forehead, smothering her with his affection.

Still, she doesn't move.

"You must've been so scared. Where have you been all this time? With her?" He eases away and narrows his eyes at me. "An imposter. Who sent you to mess with my kingdom?"

I don't have time to react before King Winston charges me, lacing his fingers around my neck. He shoves me against the bar, hitting my back on it. I cry out in pain. He's far too strong to fight off, and I'm afraid he's going to murder me right here. The blade falls from my fingers, clattering on the floor.

"Tell me. Now!" He roars with the words, the vein bulging in his neck.

He triggers my fear so badly that all I can do is hang limply as he holds me up by my throat, my body refusing to cooperate. I can't breathe, his grip tightening. If he doesn't let me go soon, I'll pass out. I could die.

"Dad, stop," Holly says, trying to grab him by the shoulder.

He swings his arm and knocks her back, sending her sprawling across the floor. Nobody intervenes. Madame Samara just stands there with her arms folded across her chest. Her pack members stand nearby in silence. The omegas in the club watch in shock and horror. I bet they haven't seen an alpha treat an omega like this before. Because I know that Madame Samara has brainwashed them with kindness. She would never allow an alpha to hurt one of her precious possessions.

But I don't belong to her.

I open and close my mouth, trying to gasp in a breath that doesn't come. He's not even going to give me the luxury of pleading for my life. I can't even beg for mercy or explain. He's too caught up in his wild emotions. The feral, spicy scent of peppers and something more potent like amber and musk steals my senses. It doesn't help my survival instincts.

"Tell me!" he shouts, spitting in my face with his anger. He's so lost in his wave of rage that I don't even think he realizes that I can't tell him anything.

The world dims as shadows crowd my vision. I never expected to die like this. I never really expected to die at all. I expected to be a servant to one of the Pack Regimes. To be used and abused and mistreated for the rest of my life if I couldn't maintain my beta persona. But then that all changed when I met the princes of Gilded Sands.

But their father will destroy any chance I have.

I just wish I could see them one more time.

I wish I could apologize for the destruction that followed me.

"Dad! I said, stop!" Holly holds a knife to the king's neck, nicking his throat with the blade enough to get him to release me.

I drop to the ground and hit my knees hard on the floor. Gasping, I inhale breath after burning breath, my body wanting to curl in on itself. I just want to lose myself to the darkness. I'm too afraid of what happens next.

I can't believe Holly threatened her own father with a knife on my behalf.

"Kinsey is my friend. She is our family. She was not sent by anyone. If you would just calm down and let us speak, we could tell you as much." Holly's hand trembles and she finally lowers the knife, taking a step back. She grips the weapon, her eyes darting from me to her father.

"What did you say?" King Winston asks, his hands clenching into fists, his voice deep with his simmering anger.

"She said Kinsey is ours. We have bonded. We have claimed her as ours. Now, step away. If you have a problem, you need to face me." Enzo stands in the hallway leading toward the living area.

Wilder, Arsenio, and Desmond appear behind him, their faces all bloody and beaten, bruised and in need of attention from me. My whole body hurts at the sight of their injuries, but my heart fills up with so much joy that they're here. That they've come for us.

Wilder steps past Enzo and strides directly to me, lifting me off the ground and into his arms. He grabs Holly's hand next and pulls her with him, putting space between us and the king.

Turning his attention to Madame Samara, he says, "We have handled your enemy for taking what doesn't belong to you. We will consider these omegas as payment for our services."

What? A dozen questions flit through my mind.

Wilder swivels to his father next. "Now is not the place to discuss family matters. Please join us at our palace tonight, and we will tell you everything. But right now, we need to get out of here. We have only temporarily put a stop to the impending war headed toward our territory."

Wilder doesn't wait for King Winston to respond. He heads toward his brothers, not giving anyone a second look. The power he radiates gets to me in a good way, and I bury my face into his throat and inhale a deep breath of his calming scent, my heart finally settling.

"Slow breaths, Kinsey. You're safe now. We got you." Wilder strokes his hand across my back, just holding me as Arsenio drapes his arm across Holly's shoulders, keeping her within his protective shadow.

I lick my lips, my mouth dry from my screaming. From the pain inflicted on me by the king. "What about your dad?" I can't help asking. I know this isn't over.

"We will handle him. We're taking you home," Arsenio responds, talking for Wilder. "Just let us take care of you."

I bob my head and rest my cheek against Wilder. "I'd like that. I've missed you all so much."

Enzo kisses the top of my head. "You have no idea how much we've missed you. We've made it clear that you are ours. And it's time that the world knows."

Tears prickle my eyes, but they're made of pure joy. Full of hope and faith. Full of excitement for my future. I had no idea I'd find a pack with the Gilded Sand princes. I had no idea I'd have a family ever again.

They belong to me. They're all mine.

Forever.

Chapter 26

Kinsey

Claimed Forever

"The king thinks it's best to wait until tomorrow for a pack meeting. He wants time to process everything and give you all a chance to cool off." Desmond stands in the doorway to Wilder's suite, glancing at the five of us sitting huddled together in the sitting area.

"Fucking great. He wants time to plan something." Wilder rubs his scruffy face with his palms.

"I'll contact our allies and have them on standby. That's all we can really do tonight." Arsenio tugs his phone from his pocket and taps the screen.

"Which means you need to get some rest, little sister. Do you want me to walk you to your room? We can watch a movie." Enzo stretches his arms over his head.

Holly purses her lips, frowning. "I know you're worried about me, but I'm fine. You have bigger priorities." Flicking her gaze to mine, she gives me a small pout. She doesn't have to voice her concerns about me out loud, but I know she fears more for me than herself. "I have someone I need to call anyway."

I get to my feet and pull Holly up, hugging her tightly. We remain in our spot, just embracing each other while her brothers watch in silence. Tears burn my eyes. Everything hits me at once, and I sniffle.

"Thank you for saving my life today. You have no idea how much it means to me." I ease away, blinking my eyes.

Holly swipes her own cheeks. "That's what family is for." Turning to her brothers, she smiles with her watery eyes. "You better take the best care of her. I'll kick your asses otherwise."

Wilder chuckles for the first time tonight, his voice melodious and velvety, igniting warmth inside me. "It'll be my sole mission from this point on. Now stay out of trouble. We're going to talk about your new friends some other time." And by friends, he means the Silverstein Pack. We all know that Holly is interested in them. It was obvious that they felt the same.

She reaches forward and scrubs her fingers through his hair, messing up the dark strands. "Yeah, yeah. It's like you'll never see me as an adult."

Wilder groans. "Just call us if you need anything. Love you, Holly."

She beams a smile and heads toward the wardrobe, choosing to take the passageway to the panic room, where her bedroom remains. We watch her leave and listen to the access door click closed. Desmond watches from his phone, ensuring she reaches her suite, though I highly doubt anyone will be getting into the palace anytime soon.

"Enzo, why don't you make our girl something to eat while I get her all cleaned up? Arsenio will help me make sure all her scratches are taken care of. Desmond, I want you to run through security once more. Maybe pick out a movie for us all to watch." Wilder gets to his feet and engulfs me in a hug, kissing me softly. "Is there anything in particular you're in the mood for?"

I ease away from his mouth, a smile playing on my lips. I know what they're all thinking. I can smell their desire in the air, their need growing stronger by the second now that we're alone with each other.

"I'm in the mood for some cuddles. From all of you. Can we just lay down for a bit? I feel fine. I don't think I could eat anything right now. I just...I really fucking missed you." I lace my arms around Wilder's neck, my whole body buzzing at his closeness.

Arsenio comes up behind me, the warmth of his chest against my back stirring something amazing inside me. He lifts my hair and kisses my throat. "We missed you too. You have no idea how fucking scared we were. We thought we lost you."

I turn around to face him, cupping his face and kissing him next. "Never. Let me prove it. I'm here. This is real. You're my pack." My heart picks up speed with my words, the idea all-consuming as it demands I give in to my nature as an omega. I want so badly to solidify my physical bond with all of them. I need it. I crave it. I feel as if I'll die if I don't claim them all as mine now and in this second. Because who knows what tomorrow will bring. Who knows what shit show life will throw at me.

"I want everyone to know you are ours. Irrevocably. Always. You're our omega. Our perfect match. There will be no denying it after tonight. That I promise you." Wilder nips my shoulder, sliding his arms around my waist, pulling my shirt over my head.

I smile and bite my lip, turning slowly as I meet his sparkling blue eyes. Enzo touches my hand, silently begging for my attention. I kiss him next and reach out blindly to caress my fingers over Desmond's arm as he waits in anticipation.

"Tell us what you want from us, baby. I'm ready to bow at your feet and give into every single one of your wants and desires. Even if it doesn't include me right now. I know we haven't talked about this yet. But we are a pack. We all plan to fulfill your needs in every way you could ever want." Enzo sucks my lip between his teeth, kissing me deeper as his hands explore my bare side.

"If you want to be alone with any of us first, just say so. I'm good either way. I know you have enough love for all of us. We just want you to be happy and comfortable." Desmond kisses me on the temple, his hands joining his brothers' to explore my warm skin.

They sandwich me between their muscular bodies, the four of them caging me in protectively, ensuring that nothing in the world can get to me now. There's nothing in the world that could mess up this moment. I never really thought about how I would build a relationship with my chosen ones, because they had already been chosen for me, but this? I can't wait to build things ourselves.

"I don't want any of you to leave if that's okay." I reach up and stroke Desmond's cheek with my fingers before drawing my hand lower to play with the front of his shirt. "You're my pack. I want to bond with all of you. I want to show you just how much you mean to me. I crave to drown in your affection. To know what it's like to survive on your love alone."

Wilder groans deep in his throat, the noise vibrating across my skin as he lifts me and carries me to the bed, tossing me on it as if he can't wait for even a second longer. A light, breathless laugh escapes my mouth, and I rub my legs together, resting on my elbows as I stare at the four of them closing in around me on Wilder's bed. We would usually have a shared room for something like this, because from what I know, packs don't usually bond and work together unless I'm in heat, but we aren't like anyone else. We are all equal here.

I glide my tongue teasingly between my lips. "Don't you even think about joining me until you lose your clothes." My heart thrashes with my words, my body buzzing as I drink in their reactions.

"Damn, baby. Command more from me." Enzo tugs his shirt over his head before his brothers and unfastens his belt, kicking out of his pants without an ounce of shame or hesitation. He flexes his arms, showing off his bulging muscles and how spectacular his body is, rippling and ready for me.

I giggle as he kneels on the end of the bed, stroking his hand over his cock, his anticipation zapping me with a wave of pleasure. "Since you were first, I want you to kiss me...everywhere."

Arsenio releases a breath and yanks his shirt over his head, undressing faster than Desmond and Wilder as they join in, stripping to show me how excited they are for this moment.

"Help me out, brother. Get those pants off her." Enzo kisses my mouth first, slowly caressing his tongue to mine as Arsenio's hands latch around my waist to ease me up.

Wilder pulls my pants down, exposing my thong to all of them, and I squirm as Wilder slides his hand across the warmth building between my legs as he snatches my panties out of the way to rub his finger over my clit. Enzo works his way lower to suck one of my nipples into his mouth. Desmond kisses me next, and Arsenio plays with my other nipple, the four of them touching me everywhere with their warm hands, just exploring my body until I can barely take it. I reach out and lace my fingers around Arsenio's cock, rubbing my fingers up and down the shaft. Desmond whispers how happy he is to be with us, and I murmur how much I want to taste him.

Enzo continues down, kissing my torso as Wilder rips off my panties completely with his strength, stretching my leg enough to get his brother to reposition himself between them. Shifting up, Wilder plays with my boobs as he strokes himself, and Desmond caresses my bottom lip with his fingers, getting me to suck his middle one into my mouth before he pulls me up just a bit to where he can prop me on the pillows and guide his cock between my lips, giving me what I've asked for.

I continue to stroke Arsenio blindly, feeling the slipperiness of his pre-cum on my hand. Enzo massages his finger across my clit as he spreads me open wider and kisses me between my legs, sucking and licking my body, sending a wave of pleasure through me, my body so hot and ready for more. I moan so loudly, the vibration of my voice causing Desmond to moan with me. Wilder guides my other hand to his body, and he helps me stroke him, the four of them giving me all their attention while also letting me give them what they crave.

I am a vessel for their pleasure, but they're my conduit for bliss. I feel so beautiful and loved in this moment, taking time to give each of them attention at once. My body and mind are pulled in four different directions but don't separate me. Instead, it binds us all together.

My body clenches, and I squeeze Enzo's head between my thighs as an orgasm rises through me, the intensity making me gasp and arch my back. Desmond slides out of my mouth, letting me scream in pleasure, taking the time to watch my expression.

"She's nice and ready for you, brother. It's time you bond with our girl." Enzo repositions my legs, stretching them up and exposing my body to the four of them. I open my eyes and drink in the looks of the lust crossing their faces. Wilder takes Enzo's spot and touches my clit, stroking me in a way that leaves me breathless. He teases my body with his fingers, rubbing me just right for a moment before he lifts my hips and holds me half curled to align our bodies.

"I'll prove to you every single day that I'm worthy of your love, Kinsey. I'll fight against the entire world for the future of our dreams to make it a reality." Wilder teases me with his tip, his promise sending a wave of love rushing through me.

I stretch up and hold my arms out, just wanting him to hug me for a moment, to kiss me and shower me with the love and affection I crave from this moment. "You've already proved yourself. I love you, Wilder. I'm ready for this. I'm ready to be your mate forever. I want your mark and knot."

Enzo, Desmond, and Arsenio show me silent attention by touching me and warming me with their closeness. They've been waiting all of their lives to claim an omega, and this moment will only give us more power and strength as we solidify our promises with a bond that can never be broken. Because when I give my body, Wilder is mine forever. And the support his brothers give us only makes things that much more incredible. Because they have spent their whole lives preparing to rule the kingdom together. They've been preparing to share an omega, and I have never been so thankful that it's me. Our bond is far stronger than anyone can ever comprehend because it is built on more than just packs wanting power. It's built on love and respect. It's built on hope and faith and the idea of creating our own perfect family.

Our bond will change everything. I'm certain of it. I've never been more sure of anything in my life.

Wilder slides deeper inside me, his raspy moan turning me on in a way that makes me dig my fingers into his shoulders, his girth stretching me wider, the pleasure intense in the best way. His eyes lock on mine, and I feel the world fade away as he rocks his hips, igniting passion through my entire body.

He starts slow, just savoring me, watching my reaction and inhaling deep breaths of my scent, letting these things guide him to know exactly what I want and need. He kisses me, rubbing his thumb across my cheek, combing my hair and thrusting harder but keeping his rhythm at the perfect pace that leaves me screaming against his mouth in ecstasy. He breaks from my lips and sucks my throat, leaving a hickey that will linger for days. His brothers help keep me in place, ensuring that I feel every inch of Wilder. Enzo shifts behind me, letting me use his chest as a backrest, and Desmond and Arsenio lift my legs until I lay on top of him, the sensation of his hard cock beneath me driving me wild.

My body is so ready, my slick dripping over him, and I gasp, knowing that he will use it to bring me even more pleasure, because my body was made for this. I'm built for pleasure, and my alphas know how to return the ecstasy.

"I want you, Kinsey. Let me claim that sweet ass. Wilder will make sure it feels so good." Enzo murmurs the words, kissing my throat as he squeezes my ass cheeks, my body sandwiched between him and his brother. "Isn't that right, Wilder? Once our girl takes your knot, she's going to see fucking Heaven."

Wilder moans at the thought, rubbing his fingers over my clit, his body rippling in anticipation. I can smell his lust, the sweetness getting to me in a good way, and I know it's coming. I know he'll finally claim me as I take his knot, my body wanting his seed and a future together. With this moment, a promise of forever follows, his mark claiming me as his for my upcoming heat.

I feel the pressure a moment before my body sings with my orgasm, and Wilder bows down to kiss me, his mouth crashing against mine as his knot locks us in place, ensuring an orgasm that will last seemingly forever. His lips muffle my moans, and Enzo kisses my throat, shifting my body just enough to tease my ass with his tip.

I squirm, my whole body buzzing, the spasms so intense that I just ride the wave, never wanting it to end. "More, Enzo. Give me more," I say, gasping my words, wanting to feel as much pleasure as possible.

I inhale as he slides in deeper, slow and carefully, listening to my body and waiting for me to accept him, the pressure turning into pleasure as I feel Wilder more intensely. Enzo rocks his body into me, the two of them penetrating me in a way that makes me see stars.

Arsenio slides his fingers through mine and kisses the top of my hand while Desmond continues to stroke himself, turned on by the way his brothers claim me. I meet his gaze, his breathing heavy with his lust, and I lose myself to the pleasure until the pressure of Wilder releases me, his knot loosening, and he kisses me once more.

"My perfect omega. Will you accept Arsenio now?" Wilder eases away from me, watching as Enzo connects with my body a couple more times as he comes, the tightness and wetness of my slick getting to him far more quickly.

I moan and grab for Arsenio, and he rolls me on top of him, wanting my body on his, my boobs pressed to his chest. His lips meet mine, tasting and teasing me with his tongue. He grabs my ass and squeezes, sliding my slippery body over the length of his shaft and uses his cock to rub against my clit, getting me off before sliding inside. I moan and bite his throat, leaving a mark of my own on his skin. He grunts and pushes into me, his body sending another wave of pleasure through me.

I take control, pushing my hands to his chest, riding him and bouncing on my knees, wanting to watch his face. Arsenio groans in pleasure, his hands guiding my movements as he helps me by clutching onto my hips. Desmond kneels beside us, grabbing my chin to guide my face to his to kiss me. Enzo does the same, kissing me next, and Wilder strokes my nipples, ensuring that the pleasure doesn't end. They all show me so much attention that I never want this moment to stop. I imagine just how amazing things are going to be, especially when we grow our pack. This is about love and pleasure and power and hope. It's about us together.

"You are so fucking sexy, Kinsey. I'll never get enough of you. I promise you the world, and I won't let you down. You're mine. My heart belongs to you. My mind and body too. My very soul is yours." Arsenio pants with his words, his muscles rippling as I stroke my fingers across his nipples and work my way up to rub my hands over his neck and cheeks, making sure that he smells my scent forever. There will be no doubt that he is mine.

"I love you. My soul belongs to all of you. I promise I'll be everything you need and want. I will keep you guys together with this bond. You're all mine. Mine." I roll my body, feeling the pressure of Arsenio as he prepares to knot with me, his muscles rippling and flexing, his handsome face sharpening as his forehead scrunches, and he pulls me down, wanting to feel my body against his. Another orgasm grabs hold of me, stealing my breath, and Desmond silently moves behind us, kneeling between mine and Arsenio's legs, teasing me with his finger to add pressure to my ass, knowing that it'll bring me even more bliss. I moan and scream as my body clenches, the adrenaline leaving me nearly high on their love, and I beg for Desmond to enter me too. I want to know what it's like to be loved and enjoyed by all of them at once in this moment.

Spreading my ass cheeks, Desmond uses my wetness to slide into me, the pleasure of Arsenio's knot sending goosebumps and tingles across my body in wave after wave through our long-lasting orgasm, triggered by his knot and seed filling me. My throat goes dry with my moans, and I lose myself to the moment, savoring every touch, every kiss, the heat of their bodies around me, and the safety and protection, the possessiveness of them coming together as a pack to claim me as theirs.

Heavy breathing fills the air to join in with melodious music of our pleasure, our moans in sync and the wave of ecstasy potent in the fragrance wafting from all of us.

Desmond finishes just before Arsenio, and the two of them press their weight against me, making me feel so utterly and completely safe. My body continues to hum as the four of them cuddle me, taking turns to kiss me and whisper their affection into my ears. My body begins to settle, but they don't let me crash. They give me all of their attention as we move into the bathroom, and Wilder starts his shower, filling the room with steam as they take turns bathing me and cleansing our bodies, our hearts beating wildly and our needs still strong.

I've never felt this way in my life. I only thought my world would be full of loneliness and disregard. I thought I would always live a life as an unwanted. But now? I know I'll live a life of unwavering loyalty. Strong bonds and endless love.

It's all I could ever dream of.

My past will never define my future. It's the here and now that'll show the world just how strong I am. How adored. Loved.

And I will ensure that my pack always feels the same.

Chapter 27

Wilder

Confrontation

I just can't wait around for King Winston to decide what the fuck he's going to do. He said he wanted a pack meeting yesterday, but then he canceled. And then he canceled again today.

I know he's doing it to fuck with me, and I'm not going to allow it any longer.

"Are you sure you don't want all of us to go?" Arsenio asks, standing at the entrance to the garage.

I shake my head. "No, I'm going to do it alone. I'll confront him and force him to come here for the damn meeting. I need to make sure he's not planning anything. It'll be too obvious if we all go. Just stay here and keep watch. Monitor all the security feeds."

Do I really want to go alone? No. I can't trust myself that I won't try to knock King Winston's teeth out. I need to be on the offense instead of the defense. At least then, I know what I'm getting into compared to trying to stop any sort of attack. It's not often that pack members go against each other, but it's also unheard of for alphas to pick their own omega instead of their leader. King Winston isn't our leader any longer. I can't even call him my father right now.

I open the car door and slide behind the wheel. Kinsey's voice echoes out, and I spot her dashing down the drive toward us. Enzo follows behind her, and she races ahead, her eyes wide and her radiant brown hair blowing behind her.

I step out of the car and cock my head, my brows furrowing. "What's the matter? What happened?"

Kinsey launches into the air. I catch her, engulfing her in a hug. She buries her face in my throat, kissing me and breathing in my scent.

Enzo drags his knuckles across my head. "Nothing is the matter. Well, except maybe for the fact that Kinsey is about to spank your ass for trying to sneak out without telling her."

I groan and hug her tighter. "My brother was supposed to keep you busy. I wasn't going to be long."

"Doesn't matter. I expect you to always give me a fucking kiss goodbye." Kinsey clutches my face, brushing her lips to mine. "Do you understand?"

I chuckle and nod, smiling against her mouth, kissing her again. "You make it hard to leave. Now start acting like a brat, so I can get out of here and hurry back to you. Catching my father off guard will push things in our favor. This isn't a fight or a war. I just need to confront him and make him face me. He's purposely putting things off to fuck with our heads, and I want him to know that I won't tolerate it."

Kinsey releases a breath, her mouth tightening. "Don't be surprised if you come back to me rolling around in your bed. I have my eye on that new pillow of yours."

I tip my head back with a laugh, hugging her tighter, my whole soul and mind wondering how I could've ever resisted her in the first place. Setting her on her feet, I spin her around and spank her ass, getting her to walk back to Enzo.

"It better just be you. Maybe take a toy from my brother's collection. If I smell any of them on my stuff, you're going to be in real trouble, my brat-girl."

"*My* collection? That's all Kinsey's." Enzo grins and snatches her away from me, knowing that if I get even another moment, I might not go. He kisses her neck. "Isn't that right, baby? I've been collecting things all my adult life just for her pleasure."

Her face flushes, her scent growing stronger. "I wouldn't know. We haven't had the chance to play."

Goddamn it. Just the thought tightens my balls.

"Hmm... We can start right now. You won't think about my brother for a second, so you won't even miss him." Enzo wags his eyebrows at me.

I flare my nostrils. "Consider it a warm up, Enzo. The second I get back, her pussy is mine."

"Then you better hurry." Kinsey extends her arms out to me and hugs me from Enzo's arms.

He spins her away, running with her back to the grand entrance of the palace, not bothering to hide her from the staff any longer. I sigh, staring after them. Now that I got another kiss from Kinsey, I really fucking don't want to confront the king.

Arsenio pats my back, drawing my attention away from Kinsey and Enzo. "Are you sure you don't want me to go with you?"

"No, but I'm going alone anyway. Keep watch, okay? I'll call you when I get there, so you can hear the whole thing for yourself." I pat Arsenio's cheek, knowing how much it annoys him. Payback for him fucking with my shit.

His features sharpen, and he nods. "I'll be ready to intervene if necessary."

"Let's hope not." I turn away from Arsenio, get back into my car, and turn on the engine.

He watches me back out from the garage, and I stomp the throttle, squealing as I skid a couple feet across the smooth drive and turn around to head toward our gates. I open them before I get there so I can drive straight through, and I wave to the security guard.

I speed the entire way to my father's fortress, the structure old yet well taken care of, the property has been in our family for nearly two centuries. It's odd to see something as such outside the city, but the king wants people to remember our powerful lineage and how we have kept control over this territory for as long as it has existed.

Slowing down, I head toward the back gate where the staff enters. My father probably won't be monitoring any of it, trusting his cousin and the head of his security to watch everything on his behalf. While we're the foundation of our pack, we do have more than just our immediate family as part of our line.

But I don't really consider anyone outside of my brothers and sisters as part of our pack. I don't trust anyone who blindly follows my father's rule.

The gate swings inward upon my arrival, and I shake Castiel's hand through my open window. If he knows about what happened, he doesn't say anything. He doesn't look suspicious or nervous either. I'm nearly certain my father has kept it all to himself. We probably are an embarrassment to him, and he needs to figure out how to handle it first.

Which is why I'm here.

I drive down the winding road toward the towering stone fortress twice as large as our palace. A long rectangular fountain shoots streams of water into the air, and hundreds of rose bushes line the paths, the floral fragrance overwhelming me, reminding me of my mother. Roses were her favorite, and she had vases of them everywhere. It's one of the few scents that make me sad, and I roll up my window to help get it from my mind. Because if my mother knew what my father had planned for Holly, she would have murdered him in his sleep.

They had a complicated relationship, not unlike many other alpha and omegas, because their bond was arranged. They had to cultivate their union and work hard on finding a common ground. I do believe that my father loved my mother, which is why he was quick to try to betroth Holly immediately after her manifestation into the omega order because she reminded him too much of the woman that had been his world.

Damn. This is why I hate coming here. All the memories of my childhood come flooding back. The cold change in my father after my mother passed away. How it had always been me and my siblings as he chose to focus on power.

But now his reign must end. Gilded Sands needs rulers who care about its people. About their own.

I park my car under the grand covering with a glittering chandelier sparkling rainbow speckles of light across the circular drive. An unfamiliar beta in a uniform opens the door, standing in silence as I head toward the arched entrance lined with metal and glass, and old fixtures and stone flooring that hasn't ever been changed. Cool air swallows me as I enter the fortress where I grew up, the majestic entrance like a museum. A huge mural decorates the wall in front of me, our family crest matching the one on the flags in our territory, the swords and crown with a rose declaring our power.

"Prince Wilder, what an unexpected surprise," a feminine voice says, the head of our household staff materializing from the hallway. Aunt Melina wipes her hands on her apron and offers me a smile, holding her arms open. "Come give your auntie a hug."

I force my mouth to smile, wishing that I hadn't run into my mother's sister. She was a complete contrast of her, which I think is the only reason why King Winston didn't try to send her away to do something else in our territory. She's been living here since the day my parents bonded, and after my mother's passing, she helped us growing up.

"Have you seen King Winston?" I ask, giving my aunt a hug.

She frowns and takes a step back, giving me a once-over. Betas tend to have a stronger sense of smell, and she would recognize that I have claimed an omega as my own.

"He's been in his study for days, having asked for privacy. I've been leaving meals at the door. Is everything okay? I know it's none of my business, but what have you been doing?" Aunt Melina tightens her lips, crossing her arms over her chest. "There were rumors from your cousin that there were a couple attacks."

I stare at her for a long moment, knowing better than to divulge any sort of information. I don't know where her loyalty lies, and now is not the time for me to find out. "I'm sorry, Aunt Melina. I'm in a bit of a hurry. I must see my father immediately."

I don't wait for her to try to ask any more questions and dart past her, striding toward the royal study, up a spiral staircase, and at the top of one of the towers with a view of Gilded Sands and beyond that, the rest of Saint Vista.

When I reach the top, the heavy door remains closed, though light filters in through the crack beneath. I don't knock, pushing it open, finding my father sitting at his desk with his head bowed. I stare at him in silence and wait for him to look up at me, but he doesn't. I don't think I've ever seen him look so defeated. So depressed.

"You're avoiding me," I say, keeping my voice even in tone. I step into the study and close the door behind me. "I would like to get this over with. What do you plan to do, father? I know I've disappointed you."

Tipping his head up, King Winston meets my gaze. "Did you know? Did you know Holly was alive?"

I straighten my shoulders, remaining expressionless. I had expected him to immediately yell about bonding with an omega. Now I realize how wrong and self-centered I was to assume that it was my actions with the woman of my dreams that would piss him off. I was a fool to assume it was because I let him down. It's because of Holly. And right now? He looks like he's grieving. He never even so much as frowned after we had faked her death. He showed no emotions. But maybe that was all a ruse, because he shows them now.

"No. I had no idea." I've lied all this time that it's easy to do so again to his face. There's no point in telling the truth. I'm already going to be facing consequences for my betrayal.

"I can't believe it, you know. All this time, I had been questioning my choices. I had thought I had failed as the leader of our pack and as a father. I had been consumed with my poor decision. And now? It's as if the universe has given me another chance. It's as if your mother is looking down on me, demanding me to make up for choosing someone unbearable for Holly. I had no idea she despised my choice so much that she faked ending her life because of it. I...oh, son. I'm so happy she's alive, but I can't face her. I can't look her in the eyes. She was willing to lay down her life to protect that omega. And to discover that you, my son, and your brothers, have bonded with her? Someone is setting us up, and we need to figure out who. I'm just afraid that you're already too lost to your alpha tendencies and your bond to Kinsey to see things clearly." King Winston rests his elbows on the desk, his face a series of wrinkles with his frown.

I let his words sink in, my mind whirling. I never thought in a million years that my father would regret anything in his life. I don't know whether or not I should truly believe him. But he looks so sincere. He sounds it too.

"Dad, I don't know what to tell you. Kinsey isn't working for anyone. She was a happy accident to come into our life. She was in hiding and passing as a beta. It was our doing, bringing her into our lives. We had confiscated some contraband from a dealer outside of our territory crossing through. She happened to be part of that. A victim." I feel as if I'm just drawing straws, hoping to see everything he wants to believe.

"Where did she come from? Son, you know that we have an agreement. You're not to take an omega. I can see how fond you are of this one, but you need to be smart. If you fancy her so much, then it's fine if you want to keep her around. She can be your dirty little secret. I have my own as well. But there must be another one day when I retire from my position." King Winston rubs his shoulder, rolling his neck in a circle, his muscles bulging with the movement.

Anger rolls through me, trying to consume my sensible rationale. I need to swallow my pride and my need to shout that there will be no one else and take this as a win for now. Because it gives us time. It helps keep the peace between the king and us.

"I understand, father. Thank you for showing me mercy despite my poor judgment. I'm just so...infatuated with this woman. She is perfect." My heart picks up speed as I declare my feelings for Kinsey out loud.

My father thins his lips. "She is rather beautiful, my son. I could see why you wanted to bond. I just don't want you to get heartbroken. We have a kingdom to run, and we need to keep our appearances. If this gets out, then we could have a possible war at hand. Especially if she comes from another territory."

"You don't have to worry. Kinsey is packless. Her chosen have died. That is how she ended up with the dealer. She was caught after running from the authority, and they took advantage of her." I cross my arms, strolling closer. "Now, why don't you join us for dinner? My brothers are anxious to speak with you. And I think you should be open with Holly. She is hurt. She is scared of you. If you truly regret your decision, just tell her. We can mend things."

King Winston closes his eyes with a sigh. "I suppose you're right. We must get answers over her whereabouts. We need to know who helped her. Samara had mentioned another pack. If they had betrayed us—"

"Father," I say, cutting him off, knowing where his thoughts are headed. "If you confront Holly and start threatening the pack who did help her fake her death, you might as well not see her at all. She was obviously desperate. And as far as I can tell, she was passing as a beta. It is very possible they didn't know. That is how she ended up at the club. She had arrived before Kinsey." Fuck. I hope he believes me. This is getting far more complicated. I don't know exactly what Madame Samara told him. It was obvious that she had called him because of Kinsey and not Holly. King Winston was there to investigate, considering that nobody knew she was bonded to us. Samara had been told otherwise.

King Winston narrows his eyes, his face reddening. I regret interrupting him, but he's quick to act and be suspicious instead of thinking things through. He stands from his desk, the scent of his anger assaulting my nose, the spice of chili tensing my body.

"How dare you interrupt me and tell me what I should do." Fisting his hand, King Winston swings his arm.

I stand still, bracing against the force of his punch, letting him hit me instead of dodging out of the way. It's not the first time we've gotten into a fight like this, and I know better than to fight immediately.

He steps back, his chest heaving.

I rub my cheek. "I'm sorry, father. I'm only being honest. We face a delicate situation with Holly. You said it yourself. She was willing to die instead of going through with bonding with a pack she hated because of your poor decision. Please, let's just hear her out first."

I tighten my hands into fists, preparing to fight back this time. His anger sharpens his features for only a moment longer before he puffs out of breath and turns his back on me, rubbing his hands to his neck and through his cropped hair.

"You're testing me, son. I wouldn't expect anything less from you. And you're right. I'm letting my emotions get the best of me. Thank you for speaking your mind." Turning back around, King Winston opens his arms to me.

I grind my teeth and step forward, letting him embrace me for the first time in years. I don't think I even remember the last time he hugged me.

"I've been trained by the best," I mutter the words, my body screaming to get space between us. Because if I don't, I might shove him. Just because he might feel remorse over his actions, doesn't mean shit yet. It's what happens next that will direct my decision in the situation. "Now, let's go to my palace. The others are waiting."

King Winston releases me and dips his chin in agreement. "Okay, my son. You're right about us needing to deal with this now. I'm just ready to have my family back together again. I'm ready to move on from this and prepare for a better future."

"Good. That's all we really want." I reach into my pocket and glance at my phone, making sure that Arsenio heard everything.

"Give me an hour. I'll meet you there. I promise. I won't let you down this time." King Winston straightens his shirt, his appearance unkempt and disheveled.

I force my head to nod, though I don't want to leave without him. I don't want him to have another moment to think things through, but I don't have a choice. If I argue, it'll just make things worse. "I know, father. Holly will see. We would love to formally introduce you to Kinsey as well."

"I'd like that. I'll see you later, son." King Winston motions for me to leave.

If only I believed him.

If only things could be that easy, and we could move on from all of this.

If only I could believe that any future under his reign could be better. But things are going to change.

He will see.

Chapter 28

Enzo

Interrogation

"Wilder just pulled up. King Winston isn't far behind." Arsenio stands in the doorway to my suite, his suit pristine and up to King Winston's standards. Our dad wouldn't expect anything less. "Are you all ready for this? We need to expect an interrogation. Do you have your story straight, Holly?"

After hearing the conversation between Wilder and Dad, we've been prepping Holly and Kinsey, ensuring that their stories are perfect. We can't risk a flaw to make our father question the truth.

"I don't want to see him." Holly crosses her arms over her chest and leans back on the loveseat, curling her feet up. "He's going to push me too much. I'm afraid I'll mess up."

Kinsey drapes her arm over Holly's shoulders and hugs her. "You're not going to mess up. You're going to make him regret his entire existence. He realizes he can't fuck with you. I saw the look in his eyes when you stood against him at the club. He knows you're not the docile omega he can just sell."

"If only I felt strong." Holly rests her head against Kinsey's, the two of them making it hard for me to get them to get up to follow me. I don't want to make them do anything they don't want to, but I know this has to be done. We must confront our father in a way that makes him realize that he can't push us around like he used to.

"It's going to be fine, little sis. Our story is impeccable. We have the proof we need to show that Tony was a traitor, and that way, no one else gets involved." I've never been so thankful for one of our trusted staff to betray us. Because now we can deflect attention away from us and put it on him. Somebody had to be close enough to Holly to help fake her death that wasn't us. This is the best plan.

"Your brother is right, Holly. We just need to stick to our story. We met at the club. It was all a coincidence." Kinsey rubs her hands together and pushes to her feet, offering her hand to Holly. "I recognized you from the photos in your brothers' rooms. We bonded over the fact that we had both been in shitty situations. And don't forget to tell your father how much you missed him and how thankful you are for him rescuing you when he did."

My chest puffs with pride at Kinsey's comment. She knows exactly how to handle assholes like my dad, and I know she'll help my sister through this. I wish she didn't know how, but I'm thankful for it.

Holly crinkles her nose. "I hate this."

Kinsey turns and hugs her. "Me too. But we're going to get through this. I promise. Your brothers will take care of us."

"Damn straight," Desmond says, adjusting his suit jacket as he shows up behind Arsenio outside my suite. "Let's go downstairs. King Winston is at the gate."

He offers his hand to Holly, getting her to follow him. I stride to Kinsey, lifting her into my arms. I would carry her around all the time if I could, so I take advantage of it while I can. I know that Arsenio wants to do the same. Our girl's feet will never touch the floor if we can do anything about it.

"Take a deep breath with me," Kinsey murmurs, meeting my gaze. "Your muscles are tight. You're driving my senses wild. I just want to help you relax."

I rub my lips together and nod my head. "There's only one way to do that, and we don't have time."

Her cheeks flush, tinting rosy in color. "Enzo..." The sweet marshmallow scent of her lust strikes me in the balls, turning me on. My cock hardens, and I drop her a couple of inches, so she can feel exactly what she does to me.

"Or maybe we do." My voice deepens with my desire, my words purring from my mouth. I capture her lips and kiss her, gliding my tongue over hers until she moans and digs her fingers into my shoulders, fully ready to let me take her here and now. It would be so easy. I'm not even sure anybody would stop us.

Kinsey eases her mouth from mine and rubs her fingers up and down my neck, playing with my hair. "Maybe you can figure out how to rush your father and get him the fuck out of here. All of the stress is getting to you. It's getting to everyone."

I growl, thinking about my father and how his presence already ruins my mood. "You're right. I can't wait to get the shit over with, so I can bring you back here, get between your legs, and hear you scream my name, baby. Get you to talk dirty to me. Finally get to test out your toys."

Because damn. I know she's ready for my kind of fun. I want nothing more than to spend all night teasing and pleasuring her the way I want.

Arsenio smacks me between the shoulders hard enough to get me to focus. "It'll piss off King Winston if we keep him waiting. He's coming in right now, so get your mind out of the bedroom. We all need to have clear heads."

I scowl at him, despite knowing he's right. I just...I'm so fucking tired of always having to be on guard and ready to battle for this kingdom. Being royalty and in power should be easy when it comes to our pack. We shouldn't have to worry about our father and instead worry about any outside threats.

"Run ahead, big brother. You know he tolerates me more. I just need to have an extra minute." I roll my shoulders and kiss

Kinsey again. Just feeling her so close gives me the strength I need to focus.

I adjust her in my arms, moving her to my back, so she can cling to me and leave my arms free. Arsenio strolls in front of us, choosing the stairs over the elevator. Desmond and Holly finish our line, ensuring that I don't turn around to run back to the room. I need to stop being a chickenshit. I don't know why I'm so anxious about all of this. We can handle our dad. He is one fucking man. And I'm a goddamn good alpha and prince. I know my shit around here, and I can fight. He can't intimidate me like he used to. I'm not a little boy for him to beat into place.

"My sons!" Dad's voice bellows through the grand entrance of the palace, his presence demanding attention as always. "My beautiful daughter. I'm so sorry it took me so long to come and visit. Some territory matters have come up, stopping me from getting to you."

He's full of shit, and we all know it. He knows we know it. Yet, here he is, trying to make stupid ass excuses instead of just admitting that he is either plotting against us or too fearful to face us. Too ashamed to face us.

Holly doesn't respond to him, clinging onto Desmond, using him as a shield. It's enough to keep King Winston from charging her in confrontation. Because we all know that this isn't a reunion. This is an interrogation.

"Why don't we head to the living area? The kitchen staff has made some hors d'oeuvres before dinner. Perhaps you would like some wine?" Arsenio greets our father with a bow, offering him an arm to half-hug him at the same time as guiding him toward the grand sitting room we rarely ever use, choosing to remain in our own suites and out of the staff's way.

"That sounds wonderful." King Winston claps his hands together, startling Kinsey.

She shudders against my back, squeezing me tighter. She remains silent as if she fears even a simple breath could bring his attention to her. Rage simmers inside me. It pisses me off just knowing that the woman of my dreams fears my father.

We follow everyone in silence, Wilder leading the way with King Winston. I can't stand the quiet, so I pull out my phone and turn on the surround sound, playing the classic rock my father favors. The melodious ballad along with the guitar rift hums through the air, soft enough to let us hear each other but enough to get my father to grin at me from over his shoulder.

"You're way too good at sucking up," Arsenio murmurs, slowing down to stand beside me, waiting for King Winston to pick a seat.

The bastard picks the middle of the couch, patting the seat beside him as he glances at Holly. It's a power move, forcing her to be within his reach. Wilder flicks his gaze to mine and then to the plush chair, silently motioning me to sit away from them with Kinsey.

I shift Kinsey from my back and into my arms, plopping down with her on my lap. Arsenio vanishes down the hall leading toward the kitchen, and Wilder curls and uncurls his fingers as he sits on the other side of King Winston.

"How familiar this is," King Winston says, swiveling in his seat to stare at Holly. "My beautiful family back together. What a dream I pray to never wake up from."

Or a nightmare I wish could be over.

I fake a dumbass smile, reaching out to offer my fist to Dad. "Now, if only we had booze."

"Yeah, to numb the fucking awkwardness," Kinsey whispers, her voice a breath near my ear.

"On it, asshole." Arsenio appears with a bottle of wine and a tray of glasses, ensuring the staff doesn't enter.

I stand up, stealing the bottle, forcing Kinsey to hold onto me for dear life. I fucking love feeling her legs and arms tighten around me, and my mind wanders to thinking about how easy it would be to hike her dress up to fuck her. I pour enough glasses for everyone and down one in one swallow, pouring a second.

Fucking fuck. We need to get this shit over with. King Winston purposefully prolongs the silent torture by holding his glass up.

"Let's make a toast to new beginnings," he says, smiling at Holly, his jaw clenched.

I mutter the words, downing my second glass. Kinsey sips hers slowly, her eyes glued to King Winston as he sets his glass on the coffee table. Holly clutches the stem of her wine glass, and if she were any stronger, she might break it.

Something shifts on Holly's face, and she scoots to the arm of the couch, putting space between her and our dad. She opens and closes her mouth, her anger radiating from her with the scent of paprika and something hotter. King Winston flares his nostrils, picking up on her anger.

Fuck me. This was a huge mistake.

I slide Kinsey onto the chair and stand up, rubbing my hands together. "Dad, Holly's still trying to process everything that happened. Why don't you give her some space? She's been through a lot."

King Winston whips his attention to me, his rage growing by the second. I expect him to yell. I expect him to throw punches.

He surprises the hell out of all of us by drooping his shoulders and shaking his head, his scowl smoothing out. "I know, and I'm sorry. It's unfair for me to expect to pick up where we left off after everything."

I swear everyone holds their breath.

"I've made some grave mistakes as your father and pack leader, Holly. I can't blame you for acting out of desperation. I had no idea you were so unhappy with the thought of bonding with the Righteous Waters Pack." King Winston reaches out and touches Holly's knee. "I had no idea—"

"No idea? You had no fucking idea? I told you! I begged you to change your mind and choose someone else." Holly heaves a breath, her body shaking. "They didn't want an omega to bond with. They wanted to use me to get to our pack. They wanted to destroy our kingdom."

King Winston doesn't respond. He doesn't look at Holly or acknowledge what she says. He's a fucking coward. She deserves more than his steely facade.

"So I planned my death. I wanted you to feel the pain that I did. I wanted all of you to think about what happened to me for the rest of your lives." Holly narrows her eyes at our dad. And fuck. She's convincing. I can almost feel her wrath as if it is directed at me. I know she's doing it to clear our names, so that we don't get held responsible for helping her, but it makes me feel like crap.

"You couldn't have done this on your own, daughter." King Winston remains calm, his face only showing remorse. But I can tell he's acting. This is an interrogation, after all, but Holly is taking control of it so he can't trick her or make her mess up. And I'm fucking proud of her for it.

"Of course, I couldn't have. I had nothing. You took away everything from me. The only thing I had left was my order, and I used it to my advantage. I convinced one of the staff members to help me. He took me to his alpha, and she helped me pass as a beta...until she realized her brother was growing too fond of me. Betas can't have an omega, even if I was passing as one. So he betrayed me. He betrayed us." Holly turns her glare to King Winston, meeting his eyes. "I shouldn't have expected anything more."

"Who was the alpha?" King Winston reaches out and grasps Holly's chin, making her stiffen.

"It doesn't matter. All that matters is that I'm out of that awful club. That we could have the new beginning that you want." Holly's mouth trembles, her eyes watering.

My chest tightens, seeing the sadness flicker across my sister's face. Kinsey laces her fingers through mine as if she knows that I need her to help support the rest of our pack.

King Winston growls, his muscles flexing as he surprises us by jerking out his hand and lacing it around Holly's throat. "Tell me who the alpha was!"

Holly swings her hand and smacks King Winston across the face hard enough to send his head turning sideways. I launch across the coffee table, crashing into my dad at the same time that Arsenio pulls Holly out of his line of wrath. I pin King Winston down on the couch, fisting my hand and preparing to punch him.

"Everyone, calm the fuck down. We're all in shock right now." Wilder grabs my shoulder, getting me to release our dad. "Come on, brother. Let him go."

I glower, refusing to back down.

"You're leaving, Father. You'll give us all some space, and you'll let Holly tell you her side in her own time. I'm sure there's a reason she isn't quick to talk. She has been through a lot, and I won't allow you to push her when she's in such a fragile state." Wilder holds his hand out to our dad, waiting until he finally relaxes and waits for me to get off, so my brother can help him to his feet.

I don't know how Wilder does it. All I can think about is clobbering our dad for trying to use force to get answers from Holly. I can see that Arsenio and Desmond are holding back as well. If Kinsey wasn't now clinging onto Desmond, he would be by my side, proving that just because his order manifested as a beta doesn't mean that he can't be as powerful as an alpha. Especially when we're together. We're a pack. This man standing before us isn't our father or our king. He's a fucking coward. His reign will end.

King Winston adjusts his suit jacket and dusts his hands on his pants. "You're right, son." Turning, he looks at Holly with Arsenio. "My dear daughter, you have my sincerest apology. My anger wasn't intended to be directed at you. I'm just so upset about the time we lost and the grief we've been put through."

Arsenio squeezes Holly, stopping her from responding.

"I'll walk you out, Father." Wilder touches between our dad's shoulder blades, guiding him toward the foyer and grand entrance leading out.

We watch him go. My whole body stiffens as the realization sets in. This isn't over. We'll still have to answer for everything.

We need to act first.

We need to act now.

Reaching into my jacket, I unholster my gun. I will end this today. I'll get justice for how Holly was treated. I will fight and ensure that the king can't ruin our future with Kinsey.

Gilded Sands is ours.

I'm going to take it.

I've run out of patience. The king's reign ends here.

Chapter 29
Kinsey

Biggest Monster

My heart stops at the sight of Enzo striding toward the foyer, clutching his gun in his hand. My stomach twists. I can smell his powerful fury from my spot beside Desmond. His father's reaction toward Holly sets him off, and he loses himself to the monster he needs to be to protect us.

But I fear that his father might still be a bigger monster.

"Arsenio, stop him!" I call, trying to break away from Desmond. "Enzo, please. Come back here."

He looks at me over his shoulder and shakes his head. "This has to be done."

Except I know what happens if he kills his father before they take over the territory. His father must bow down to one of them as the next heir, or it will leave everyone open for a hostile takeover.

Arsenio charges after him, latching his hands to his shoulders and yanking him back. The gun goes off, the pop deafening. I cover my ears, standing in shock. The bullet hits the wall and ricochets, fissuring one of the framed pictures. I rush forward, my mind whirling. I reach Arsenio and Enzo, getting between them and giving them each a once-over, ensuring that neither of them was hit by the stray bullet.

Enzo growls and tries to take advantage of the distraction, but this time I grab onto him, letting him drag me a foot before he realizes I'm not letting him go.

"Enzo, stop. I mean it!" My voice booms through the room, my need to get him to see things clearly tensing my body. "If you kill him, this will all be over. You know what will happen."

"Our chances are better. I don't care if it leaves us open to a war. We need to take out our enemies immediately. I'll not put you in the line of danger. I would not risk him coming up with a way to retaliate. You saw how he reacted when he didn't get his way. He's unhinged. He has no business being a king." Enzo laces his fingers around my wrist, stroking his thumb until I can't hold on to his shirt.

My fingers loosen, and he holds my hand, pulling me close until my body rests flush against his. His blue eyes darken with the hot spice of his anger mixed with something sweeter. His desire breaks through, my closeness easing his wild aggression.

"And he won't be. But it needs to follow tradition. We will already be shaking up enough as it is, brother." Arsenio stands behind Enzo, grabbing his gun and turning the safety back on. He doesn't give it back, choosing to tuck it away instead as if he doesn't trust Enzo not to go after their father as soon as he has a chance.

"I know, but what if it all falls apart? I can't risk losing Kinsey. The way he acted with Holly? Fucking despicable. He needs to pay for that. He needs to face the consequences of his actions. He's not leadership material. I don't know what the fuck got to his head, but we can't continue on like this." Enzo shifts on his feet, eyeing the grand corridor that leads directly to the front door of the palace.

Arsenio blocks him, anticipating him to dodge past him. The two of them standoff, their muscles flexing, their eyes never breaking from their staring contest. This is one hell of an alpha challenge, and it makes my whole body hum. This is not the time for me to be turned on, but seeing them so worked up? Smelling their scents and knowing that they're going wild because of me? It gets to me in a good way. I feel as if I'm the most important woman in the world. And to them? I know I am.

"Let him go, Enzo. The king got in his car and is pulling away." Desmond grasps Holly by her elbow. "He needs to run or some shit. Go to the gym, Enzo. I need you to cool off. But don't you fucking try to leave this palace to go after him."

I grab Enzo by the front of the shirt and pull him to me, standing on my tiptoes to kiss his jaw. "I'll go with you. I need to run off this adrenaline or something. I can't stop shaking."

My comment does the trick, getting him to break away from his challenge to Arsenio. His features soften, and he tilts his chin down, kissing me sensually, awakening more desire inside me.

"Please, take care of me. We both need to settle down." I rub my hand across his neck and down his chest, his all-consuming presence making it easy to push away the world around us.

I hear the others leave as Wilder arrives, but he doesn't say anything to either of us. He lets me give his brother my utmost attention.

Enzo lifts me up, carrying me toward a secret passageway that'll take us to his wing of the palace. My heart picks up pace as my body relaxes, knowing that the others will have things in control by the time I get Enzo to settle down. I know how much he needs my attention. To know I have faith in him and that I believe we'll get through this regardless. And it's not only his father's actions that get to him. He feels as if he's lost someone. His father isn't the man he thought he was, and it just keeps getting worse and worse for him. I understand. I thought the same when my uncle broke up my family and killed my parents. When he betrayed me.

But I don't want to think about that now. All I want to focus on is Enzo and how good his arms feel around me as he lowers me just a bit to feel the length of his hard-on pressing against his pants, ready and throbbing for my body.

Cool air engulfs us as we kiss the entire way to his suite, his ability to focus on me and manage to get us to his room without any problem impressive. I still can't stop thinking about how protective he was. How he went after his own father on Holly's behalf. How he stood up for me. How he wants to ensure our future and our well-being as a pack.

Enzo tangles his fingers through my hair and bends my neck slightly, kissing my throat as he opens his door and kicks it shut, the room warmer than the corridor. I roll my body against his, just wanting to feel the pressure of his muscles through my panties, and he squeezes my ass as he sets me on his bed, not even hesitating before he gets on his knees and hikes up my dress, getting between my legs. The billowing fabric covers his head, not giving me a view, and I squirm in anticipation as I lose myself in the sensation of his mouth kissing up my thigh as he uses his fingers to slide my panties down. I moan, bending my knees to spread my body wider for him as he draws his tongue across my pelvis, working his way down to the seam at the apex of my legs. I clutch the blankets and tip my head back, savoring the pleasure he creates in me.

The sensation builds and builds as I come to my peak, only to have Enzo ease away, denying me my orgasm. I groan and yank at the skirt of my dress, using my knees to stop him from pulling away.

"More," I breathe, my voice raspy. "Feels so good. I'm not done."

"You taste amazing, but I want you to resist. I'm not ready for you to scream my name yet. Let me play with you a bit longer, baby. I love seeing your knees shake. Feeling your thighs tighten around my head. The wait will be worth it." Enzo rubs his big hands on my knees, pulling my dress up as I lift my hips, allowing him to pull it over my head, leaving me panting and squirming under his lustful gaze.

He licks his lips and holds his finger up to me, getting me to remain in my spot as he shuffles toward the display case of toys along the wall, toys he's been collecting all of his adult life for his perfect omega. Me.

Excitement zings over my body, and I wiggle and scoot up farther on the bed, unhooking my bra to leave me completely exposed for him. He picks a couple things off the shelf, and when he turns and looks at me, his muscles ripple as he drinks me in, his excitement pressing hard against his pants.

A smirk crosses his handsome face, and he takes a moment to arrange things on the end of the bed. The wait tortures me, and I pant, reaching to touch between my legs to help relieve the anticipation.

Shrugging out of his suit jacket, he takes his time to unbutton his shirt, dropping it to the floor along with my dress. He unfastens his belt and pulls it free, snapping it teasingly.

"Turn that ass over, and let me get a good look at you, baby. I want to see how wet you are for me." Enzo adjusts his cock in his pants, stroking it through the fabric.

I shake my head with a smile, continuing to explore my body with my fingers, arching my back and ignoring him.

He play-growls, grabs my legs, brings me to the edge of the bed, and flips me over. He spanks my ass with his palm before snapping his belt over my sensitive skin, making me moan as it triggers my adrenaline. His cool fingers touch my stinging skin, and he turns me back over, only to grab my hand to pull it away.

"You will not take that honor away from me, baby. I want you to hold still and let me learn what you love most." Enzo slides his pants down, showing off his hard, muscular body.

I lean forward and reach for him, locking my fingers around his girth to stroke him a couple times before he pins me back down with one hand, reaching for a small vibrator that he turns on to tease my skin.

I moan so loudly at the sensation of the toy humming against my clit. I've never tried anything apart from my hand. My body shutters with pleasure, my eyes rolling back.

He can't even deny me another orgasm. My body clenches and my muscles spasm so quickly that I gasp and shut my legs, the sensation all-consuming. Bliss sparks through every cell in my body. Every molecule. It penetrates deep into my soul.

"Damn, baby. You like that, don't you?" Enzo grumbles, the gruffness of his voice sexy. I want to listen to him all day. "Let's see if I can get you to squirt now. I want you to soak me."

I rub my thighs together, keeping my legs closed, the motion so intense that I take a few deep breaths, watching him pick another toy, one that curves into a U-shape. I tremble in antic-ipation as he teases my center, sliding in the thicker part of the vibrator while turning it on. My muscles tighten as he adjusts the toy, the other side of the U fitting perfectly over my clit, the sucking sensation stealing my breath away. My soul feels as if it's about to escape my body, and I squirm and clutch the blankets, reaching for Enzo until he hovers over me, the heat of him warming me as he crashes his lips to mine, smothering my moans with his mouth as I hit my climax again.

My teeth chatter, goosebumps prickling over my skin, my entire body crashing on a wave of pure ecstasy. I can't speak. I can't do anything except scream my bliss, my body exploding in a way it's never done before.

"Enzo," I gasp, reaching for him. "I can't take anymore. I need you. I need your knot. Let me satisfy you now."

He practically purrs, easing the toy from me before feeling my wetness. "Not yet, baby. I want another one of your orgasms. It's mine."

Holy shit. My eyes roll to the back of my head as he places a small vibrator on my clit, my body holding it in place. Using a remote, he grins with his excitement, increasing the speed.

"Enzo, fuck! I can't take it. I need you. Fuck me! Fuck me like I want." I shout my words, breaking my hand free from his hold on me.

"Goddamn, I can't deny you." Enzo removes the vibrator and slides his hands under my ass, pulling me to the edge of the bed where he stands.

Aligning our bodies, he thrusts into me, rocking his hips as he holds my legs spread open, his hips making me ache in a good way. Adjusting my leg, he reaches for the vibrator's remote, turning it on to pulse over my clit. Energy courses through me, my screams of pleasure ringing through the air.

He grunts with each deep thrust, his knot locking in place, binding us together in the way my very being craves.

Bowing forward, Enzo rests his elbows on each side of my head, kissing me deeply, passionately, devouring my moans with his mouth as if they're all he needs to survive on for the rest of time. My orgasm crashes over me in an electric wave, my body trembling as spasms roll through me, curling my fingers and toes. I clutch onto Enzo, scratching my nails over his shoulders as I break from his mouth to suck his throat, nipping and scenting him, wanting my mark to brand his skin so the world can never deny that he's my alpha.

"I can't wait to knock you up, Kinsey. The thought turns me on so fucking much. You're my girl. My mate. My entire universe. Just knowing what it'll be like when your body is ready for my seed makes me the happiest man." Enzo grasps my chin, guiding my mouth to his. Our tongues fight for control, and I give in, letting him shower me with all his love and affection.

"I want that so much, Enzo. To build a pack with you. To know just how safe and powerful we'll be with you and your brothers," I murmur against his mouth, locking my legs around his waist, savoring the satisfaction we get from each other, our orgasms stealing away our thoughts and words, until nothing else remains but our love and pleasure. The two of us together.

Enzo shudders as his knot loosens, but he doesn't stop making love to me, kissing me until I relax and pull him down to press his weight on me like a comforting blanket of his adoration and affection.

"You make it incredibly hard to leave this bed." He rolls off me only to pull me on top, so I hug him with my whole body.

His heartbeat thrums in sync with mine, and I close my eyes, just listening to the melody of our hearts as one.

Enzo strokes his hand on my back, massaging my muscles as he pulls the blankets around us. "I want to stay here with you forever."

I smile and slide over, nestling into his side. Drawing circles on his chest, I memorize the muscular planes with my fingers. "We can stay here as long as you want. I'm not going any-where."

"Good," he murmurs, kissing my temple. "That's all I ever want from this life. You and me. Love and pleasure. A life of content and fulfillment."

"Our pack, together forever." I hum, the thought awakening a flood of warmth in my core.

He smiles. "The perfect life."

"More than perfect." With Enzo, Wilder, Desmond, and Arsenio, I know I'll get the life of my dreams. We'll have an incredible future. The world will be ours.

Chapter 30

Kinsey

Warning

*B*astard Brother: *Come downstairs. We're not serving you in bed again, you bastard. We need time with our girl, too.*

"Your brothers don't want to serve us breakfast in bed," I say, faking a pout.

Enzo stretches his arms over his head, his muscles rippling with his movements. He snatches the phone from my hand and tosses it toward the end of the bed. Rolling on top of me, he grins as he kisses me, his hand reaching between us to tease between my legs. His desire is as insatiable as mine. It'll only grow stronger and stronger in the coming weeks. Because I had been taking suppressants for so long, it's possible that my heat will come early and last longer. It's one of the side effects I never really considered since I had planned to suppress my order forever. But now? I smile and bite my lip, moaning as he explores my body.

Enzo's phone buzzes from the edge of the bed, the low sound continuing as if Wilder sends text message after text message.

"We should at least respond and tell him if he wants me, he can come and join us," I say, grazing my teeth on his shoulder.

He chuckles and shimmies lower, kissing my breasts and working his way down my torso as he blindly reaches for his phone. "Tell them they don't have to serve me. I'm about to eat the only breakfast I'll ever need."

Setting the phone on my hip, Enzo kisses my thigh. I giggle and moan, snatching the phone as I squirm, squeezing his head between my legs, stopping him from burying his face. He play-growls at me, locking his fingers to my hip, trying to pin me. I tip my head back and laugh, squealing with excitement, his determination as ferocious as his sexual appetite.

Bastard Brother: Enzo, you fuckhead.

Desmonster: Take whatever time you need. Don't listen to the impatient asshole.

Arshole: Keep stealing my time, and I'll fuck with your shit.

Bastard Brother: Shit. Come down.

Bastard Brother: Enzo!

The phone buzzes in my hand, another text message popping up. My heart sinks into my stomach.

King Douche: Good morning, my sons. I've decided you will host our pack meeting at your palace. See you within the hour.

I sit upright and lock my fingers into Enzo's midnight hair, my sudden fear slowing him down and stealing his attention away from his mission.

"The king is on his way." I show him the phone, my desire fizzling out completely. We haven't seen him since Wilder kicked him out. Enzo hasn't communicated with him at all either, his anger rising every time he thinks of him.

"Fucking hell. A pack meeting? He's full of shit." Enzo throws his phone, clattering it against the wall.

Reaching for him, I guide him closer, wrapping my arms around him. "Take a breath. Your brothers will handle him."

His handsome face sharpens in a series of lines, his anger flaring. "I need to face him. My brothers need me. We need to stand strong together."

A bang on the door rattles the wood, startling me. Enzo whips his attention toward the door, flaring his nostrils.

"Brother, I'm coming in," Wilder says, his voice a rumble through the air. "Did you look at your fucking phone?" The door swings open, and Wilder strides into the room. He peers around, his gaze capturing mine as I hold Enzo.

"We're fucking getting up now." Enzo eases away from me and slides off the bed, not bothering to cover up his naked body. "King Winston can fuck off if he thinks we're dropping everything for him."

Not that it matters. Wilder keeps his light blue eyes locked on me, drinking in my exposed body, the scent of my desire mingling with his and Enzo's.

"Sounds like he chucked the phone before seeing the second message." Desmond appears in the doorway, carrying a tray of food. The scent of syrup and fruit teases me, setting my stomach off. "Platinum Shores sent him a warning. The king wants to know how we plan to handle them."

Enzo swears under his breath, hopping into his pants. He runs his fingers through his black hair, combing down the strands. "Fuck."

"Relax. We have this handled." Arsenio strolls into the room with Holly by his side. "He just wants to test us. It's not something we won't pass."

Setting the tray of food on the table, Desmond motions toward me. Enzo cuts me off, holding a shirt out for me to slide on. He holds up a pair of my yoga pants next, and I brace against him as he helps me pull them up. Desmond sets a couple of plates on the table, choosing to bring breakfast to us after all. Holly remains quiet as she takes a seat, mindlessly taking a bite of her pancakes.

Wilder motions for me to come sit with him, and he cuts off a triangle of the pancake and gives me a bite before taking one for himself. The guys practically shovel their breakfast down while I take slow bites.

The edges of my vision shadow, and I blink a few times. Tingles blossom over my fingers and I rest my back to Wilder.

I grip the table, shaking my head. "I feel—"

Desmond falls out of his chair, startling us, and Holly leans forward on the table, pressing her cheek to the wood. Arsenio gets to his feet and braces his hand on the table.

Wilder swears under his breath. "Shit. We've been drugged."

The world turns black, my whole body turning numb. I don't know how much time passes, but a few voices stir me awake. A crash echoes through the room, and Wilder hollers in pain.

My mouth opens and closes, but no words come out. I blink my eyes, my vision blurry, but I see a tall man standing over Wilder, pointing a gun to his head.

"That is unnecessary. He will not attack. Isn't that right, son?" King Winston's voice draws my attention away from the tall man, but I can't move. I can't see where it comes from. "Consider the two omegas as restitution for your trouble. Take them and leave. I'll handle my pack from here."

Panic seizes my chest, but I still can't move. I'm too disoriented, and my vision keeps coming and going along with my consciousness.

"You're a generous man, your majesty. It was a pleasure meeting with you." Hands grab under me, lifting me from the floor.

My heart breaks, my whole body screaming with anguish as the world moves around me.

I can't believe this is happening now. We should've seen this coming, but my guys never expected it to happen under our roof. The king set us up. He drugged us. And now…he's tearing my life apart.

He's destroying everything.

"I hope you will consider my other offer." King Winston comes into view, his silhouette a dark blur against the light behind him filtering in through the window.

"I've already considered it." The gruff voice stirs even more fear inside me. I flutter my eyelashes as I watch the strange man aim a gun. "The answer is no."

He pulls the trigger, the loud pop ringing in my ears.

King Winston falls to his knees.

The man carries me away.

To be continued…

Books by Ginna Moran

SAINT VISTA PACK REGIMES OMEGAVERSE WORLD

The Knotty Girls Club

The Knotty Princes Club

BONDS OF STEELE SHARED WORLD

Knotty Lessons

THE WOLFPACKS OF SHADOW MOON ISLAND:

Wild Wolves

Savage Wolves

Feral Wolves

THE VAMPIRE HEIRS WORLD

La Vega Vampire Showstoppers
Vampire Nights
Bloody Nights
Renegade Nights

The Divine Vampire Heirs
Blood Match
Blood Rebel
Blood Debt
Blood Feud
Blood Loss
Blood Vows
Blood Holiday

The Royale Vampire Heirs Series:
Rebel Vampires
Rebel Dhampir
Rebel Match
Rebel Heir
Rebel Fight

Academy of Vampire Heirs Series:
Dhampirs 101
Blood Sources 102
Coven Bonds 103
Personal Donors 104
Blood Wars 105

SERIES IN THE MATES OF MAGAELORUM WORLD

The Pack Mates of Lunar Crest:
The She-Wolf Games
The Wolf-Mate Trials
The Omega Hunt
The Witch Chase

Fated Mate of the Dragon Clans
Caged by Her Dragons
Freed by Her Dragons
Saved by Her Dragons

SEVEN SINNERS WORLD

The Seven Sinners of Hell's Kingdom:
Her Personal Demons
Her Deadly Angels
Her Darkest Devils
Her Sinful Saints
Her Twisted Sinners

STANDALONES

Fame (Society of Secrets) - Contemporary Shared World
Rise from the Flames

About Ginna Moran

GINNA MORAN IS the *USA Today* Bestselling author of over seventy novels including the popular The Pack Mates of Lunar Crest and The Seven Sinners of Hell's Kingdom reverse harem novels.

She always carried a fascination for all things paranormal and wrote her first unpublished manuscript at age eighteen. Her love of the supernatural grew stronger through her adult life, and she now spends her days with different creatures of the night. Whether it's vampires, werewolves, dragons, fae, angels, demons, or mermaids, Ginna loves creating and living in worlds from her dreams.

Aside from Ginna's professional life, she enjoys binge-watching TV, crafting and design, playing pretend with her daughter, and cuddling with her dog. Some of her favorite things include chocolate, mermaids, anything that glitters, learning new things, cheesy jokes, and organizing her bookshelf.

www.ingramcontent.com/pod-product-compliance
Lightning Source LLC
Chambersburg PA
CBHW060942190726
48286CB00005B/1383